AVENGED

Franny Doyle has always known that her father Patrick has been no good. Still, she adores her dad and knows that he would lay down his life for her – after all she is his number one girl and he has taught her everything she knows. But when something terrible happens to Patrick, Franny realises that he has some very dangerous enemies. Delving into Patrick's past, Franny becomes involved in a high-stakes game. She's not afraid, Patrick has taught her to be a fighter and she's determined to make him proud, even if it means paying the ultimate price – her own life.

AVENGED

AVENGED

by

Jacqui Rose

Magna Large Print Books
Long Preston, North Yorkshire,
BD23 4ND, England.

British Library Cataloguing in Publication Data.

Rose, Jacqui
    Avenged.

    A catalogue record of this book is
    available from the British Library

    ISBN   978-0-7505-4160-2

First published in Great Britain by Harper 2014
An imprint of HarperCollins*Publishers*

Copyright © Jacqui Rose 2014

Cover illustration © Rekta Garton by arrangement with
Arcangel Images

Jacqui Rose asserts the moral right to be identified as the author of
this work

Published in Large Print 2015 by arrangement with
HarperCollins Publishers

Magna Large Print is an imprint of Library Magna Books Ltd.

Printed and bound in Great Britain by
T.J. (International) Ltd., Cornwall, PL28 8RW

Acknowledgements

A huge thank you to Lydia, my editor at Avon/HarperCollins for all her hard work and vision in helping me to turn this book into what I wanted it to be. Of course a huge thank-you also goes to the rest of the team at Avon. And to Judith Murdoch, my agent, I want to say a big thank-you because the way you have helped me, believed in me during this phase of my writing career will never be forgotten. To my friends and family and my glorious, full of life, full of love and full of adventure children, none of this would mean anything if I didn't have you. And lastly for me it is so important to thank you, the readers, for your support and loyalty, feedback good and bad! Because as the saying goes, without you, none of this would be possible.

This book is dedicated to survivors everywhere.

Eye for eye, tooth for tooth, hand for hand, foot for foot, burn for burn, wound for wound, stripe for stripe.

Exodus 21

PROLOGUE

SOHO – 2013

There it was again. The sound coming out of the darkness. Somebody was in the kitchen. Slowly getting out of bed and trying not to make any noise, Patrick Doyle crept over to his walnut dresser.

With his eyes adjusting to the night, Patrick carefully opened the top drawer. Putting his hand to the back of it he quickly found what he was looking for; his Colt .380 Mustang.

With the gun already loaded, Patrick cocked back the trigger and readied himself. Taking a deep breath and feeling the adrenalin rushing round his body, he headed out of his bedroom, onto the top landing.

He stood with his back against the wall, listening to the muffled sounds coming from behind the kitchen door. He counted down in his head, steadying his breathing; steadying his hand, ready to aim.

Three. Two. One... Patrick kicked open the door, slamming his full six-foot-three body sidewards into the kitchen. He yelled out into the darkness, bellowing instructions to the shadowed figure standing by the table.

'Stay still! Stay the fuck still if you don't want me to blow you clear away!'

'Patrick, it's me!'

A deep sigh was heard and the light switched on. Patrick's face was full of anxiety as he threw down the gun on the table. 'Holy Fuck!... Jesus Christ!... Have you lost your mind? I could have killed ye. Don't ever do that again. Why didn't you tell me you were coming?... Franny?... Franny? Are you okay? Have you been crying?'

Franny Doyle looked at Patrick and burst into tears. She felt so stupid. She was thirty-four years old and instead of planning her future with Jack, the man she was supposed to marry next year, she was running home to Patrick; something she'd vowed she'd never do.

Wiping away the tears from her piercing green eyes, Franny snivelled, feeling more foolish than ever.

'It's all gone wrong, Patrick. I should never have got engaged; it hasn't been right for a long time. I know you never liked him, but I thought it'd get better over time; then when I found him in one of the clubs almost sucking the face off some woman, we had such a row and...'

Not giving Franny the chance to finish, Patrick's eyes flashed with anger. 'Tell me he didn't lay his hands on you, because I swear to God I'll kill him. The no-good piece of...'

It was Franny's turn now to interrupt. Pushing her long chestnut hair out of her face, she implored Patrick. '*Please*, can we do this tomorrow? I'm tired and I just want to get some sleep.'

'No, we can't, not till I know if he put his hands on you.'

Franny shook her head sadly. 'No, Patrick, it's

not like that; anyway, you taught me how to look after myself. So, nothing was broken – only my heart.'

Patrick slumped down on the tall-back kitchen chair, all his pumped-up adrenalin leaving him. 'Oh Franny, I'm sorry, do you want to talk about it?'

'No, not now. Maybe tomorrow, but there isn't really much to say. It's over and I'm not going back. Would you mind if I stayed here while I figure out what to do?'

Patrick's face lit up. 'Mind? I'd love it. The place has never been the same without you. Get yourself into bed and I'll bring you a cup of hot chocolate.'

Franny smiled, saying nothing as she stood up and kissed Patrick on the top of his head before walking out of the kitchen.

Five minutes later, Patrick Doyle stood with a steaming cup of hot chocolate in the doorway of Franny's bedroom. She was fast asleep and, even though there were so many questions he wanted to ask her, he wasn't going to wake her; instead, he walked into his own room, taking a sip of the drink and wincing as the hot liquid scalded his tongue.

As Patrick put the gun away into the back of the drawer again, he froze as his hand rested on a small silver chain and cross. Grasping it tightly in his hand, Patrick squeezed his eyes closed, stopping the stem of tears as he whispered the words. 'Mary! Mary! Why couldn't you be here with me, Mary?'

1

IRELAND – 1979

'To be sure, Patrick Doyle, if you don't came out from behind that tree right now, I won't be going to the church dance with ye.' Mary O'Flanagan stood with her hands on her hips pursing her lips in frustration.

Without coming out from his hiding place, Patrick shouted; his voice warm. 'And who will you be going with instead, Mary?'

'There's many a boy who would take me, Paddy. I might go with one of the Barker boys from the next village.'

'You'll do nothing of the sort; I won't allow it.'

Haughtily, Mary answered. ''Tis nothing you can do if I want to go with someone else, especially if I'm not your girl.'

Sixteen-year-old Patrick Doyle stepped out from behind the tree. His raven hair flopped over his blue eyes and his handsome face was veiled with mischief. He grinned. ''Tis plenty I can do, and besides, who told you that you weren't my girl?'

Mary blushed, looking younger than her fifteen years. 'So I am your girl? 'Tis news to me.'

Patrick grabbed her by the waist, spinning her round.

'You've always been my girl and you always will be.' Patrick paused, then gave Mary a cheeky wink before adding, 'Do I get a kiss back then?'

Mary screwed up her face. 'You get nothing of the sort. I keep telling ye, you'll have to wait until we're married.'

Patrick scratched his head and smiled, his eyes twinkling. 'And do we have to wait until we're married to hold hands?'

Mary stood for a moment contemplating this thought. 'There's nothing sinful about that.'

Patrick smiled, taking her hand in his. He held it gently, and they walked down the potted road in silence as the Kerry rain began to fall.

A car horn beeped behind them before a familiar voice yelled out from the driver's window. It was Father Ryan, the local priest. 'Mary O'Flanagan! What do you mean by this public display of affection! Do you not know fornication is a sin?'

Mary hid her smirk. 'I'm sorry, Father, I didn't know the bible said it was wrong to hold hands. I can't recall that passage; is it in the New Testament?'

Father Ryan's eyes narrowed. 'I hope you're not being cheeky.'

Mary's pretty face feigned innocence. 'No, Father, of course not; just showing my interest.'

'Well that's as may be, but it's not to be done. Do you hear me? Especially with a Doyle.'

Patrick spoke up. 'I am *here*, Father.'

Father Ryan stared at Patrick. The boy always made him feel uncomfortable, and he certainly didn't want a God-fearing girl like Mary to have anything to do with him. He was definitely going to have a word with her parents. Ignoring Patrick, Father Ryan addressed Mary again. 'Now get home, your mother will be worried and you'll be late for choir practice tonight.'

Mary nudged Patrick gently. 'She will indeed, Father, but maybe she wouldn't worry so much if I got home quicker. Perhaps you could give me a lift and save her the worry?'

Matthew Ryan sighed. It was true, it would be a godly thing to do – lessening the worry of one of his parishioners by getting her daughter home before dark – but it was also true that his car had just been valeted, and the last thing he wanted was to have Mary and Patrick messing up his back seat with their wet clothes.

Before Father Ryan had made up his mind, he looked in the driver's mirror. His heart began to race. From over the horizon, he saw a familiar car, the sight of which filled his whole being with dread.

'Quick! Get in! Get in!' Father Ryan's voice was urgent and, almost before Mary and Patrick had a chance to do as he asked, he set off down the road at full speed.

His car raced over the bumps, sending them all flying up in the air as the small green Lada hurtled down the un-tarmacked road. But Father Ryan's driving was no match for the car behind.

The other driver drew alongside the Lada, signalling the priest to pull over. Father Ryan spoke with urgency to Mary and Patrick, who were both looking shaken.

'Now, not a word; none of your lip.' He glared at the two teenagers who nodded their heads in unison.

Pulling up by the side of a large hedgerow,

Father Ryan wound down his window again, letting in the blistering rain.

Everyone stayed silent as a tall figure clad in an expensive trench coat and a floppy hat walked round the back of the car, tapping the roof.

A craggy face appeared. 'In a rush? You want to be careful driving like that, you could do someone damage.' Donal O'Sheyenne, the man the whole of County Kerry feared, roared with laughter as he watched Father Ryan's face blanch.

Turning his attention to Patrick, who was sitting motionless in the back of the car, O'Sheyenne sneered, wiping off the drips of rain running down his face.

'Well, well, if it isn't Paddy Doyle. I've been looking for you, and now here you are in what I like to call God's chariot.'

Patrick didn't say anything. He felt Mary's hand squeeze his as she trembled, though he wasn't sure if it was through fear or cold.

'I want you to come with me, Paddy I've got something to show you.' Patrick's head shot up at O'Sheyenne's suggestion. He scrambled for an excuse.

'I can't... I have to get home; my da will be waiting.'

O'Sheyenne snorted. 'The only thing waiting for you at home, Doyle, is a drunken fool.'

A flash of pain shot through Patrick's eyes, much to the amusement of O'Sheyenne.

'Leave the boy alone.' Father Ryan spoke up but immediately regretted it as his hat was knocked off his head by a sharp prod from Donal.

'I think you're dear forgetting yourself, *Father*.

21

Never ... *never*, try to tell me what to do.'

O'Sheyenne walked to the back passenger door, flinging it wide open. He leant in and spoke to Patrick. 'Get out! You and me are going to go on a little drive.'

Knowing he didn't have a choice, Patrick Doyle slowly got out, watching as Father Ryan quickly sped away.

2

Awkwardly, Patrick climbed into the back of O'Sheyenne's car. As he did so he immediately lurched backwards, scrambling in desperation to get out of the seat – but he was shoved back in by O'Sheyenne.

'It's a fine thing when a man doesn't introduce himself. Patrick, meet Connor Brogan. You remember him, don't you?'

Patrick's heart pounded as he glanced to the side. There next to him was the beaten and blood-drenched body of Connor Brogan, a local man from the village, barely recognisable in his naked swollen form.

Wanting to turn away but trapped by the mesmerising horror of it all, Patrick noticed Connor's hands were tied and a coarse gag cut deeply into the sides of the man's mouth.

O'Sheyenne leant over Patrick, grabbing hold of the unconscious man's hair to lift his head up and slapping him hard in his face.

'Will you not say hello, Connor? Have you lost your manners as well as your balls?'

Patrick began to tremble. His voice was weak. 'Mr O'Sheyenne, please, I'd like to go home.'

Donal chuckled. 'So you shall, Dorothy, but not before we attend to some business. I could do with a fine young lad like you working for me ... what do you say?'

Patrick looked down, shaking his head. 'Thank you for asking and ... I ... I appreciate it and all, but I'd rather not.'

O'Sheyenne raised up Patrick's chin with his finger, staring into his eyes. 'When I say, *I could do with a fine young man,* what I mean to say, Patrick, is you'll be working for me whether you like it or not. We wouldn't want you to end up like Connor here, would we?'

Inside the Brogans' house, Patrick stood trembling as Donal dragged Connor under his arms and, without much effort, pulled him up onto one of the wooden chairs.

Connor's head immediately slumped forward as Donal walked back to the far end of the room before he took a run up to strike Connor hard in the stomach with the chain he held in his hand.

Seeing that there was no reaction or even a flinch, Donal dropped the heavy chain back into his bag. He wiped his brow, taking the sweat which ran down the bridge of his nose onto his sleeve. It didn't take a doctor to tell him Connor would be lucky if he made it through the night.

Putting back on the shirt he hadn't wanted to get dirty, Donal winked at Connor's wife who was sitting wide eyed and frozen with fear in the corner of the cosy tiled kitchen.

'I must say, Mrs Brogan; you've certainly got a nice place here... What's that you say?... No, I still can't hear ye.' Donal stood with his hands on his hips, bursting out into raucous laughter. 'Oh, don't look like that. I'm only playing. I ask you, what's a man got if he hasn't got his sense of humour?'

Donal roughly pulled away Mrs Brogan's gag. She immediately began to scream.

'God forgive you, Donal O'Sheyenne. You'll be sorry for this; don't think you can get away with it. I'll make sure they lock you away. If anything happens to...' The hard slap across her face stopped her saying any more.

Donal grinned at Patrick, who was standing terrified in the corner.

'So, what have you got to say now, Paddy; still not keen on working for me?'

Turning his attention to the crying baby in the corner, Donal bent over to look at the child. 'Now then, what's the craic, young man? You'll wake the dead with that yelling.' Picking up the infant he was met by Mrs Brogan letting out a tirade of panic and terror.

'Take your hands off him!... You hear me, O'Sheyenne! You leave him be. Or ... or...'

Almost throwing the baby into Patrick's arms, Donal swivelled round to face the woman. His face thunderous. 'Or what? What are you going to do?'

Tears flowed down her face. 'Just leave him... *Please.*'

24

'Leave him? I think I'll be taking him, don't you?'

Hysterical now, Mrs Brogan cried out, causing the baby to scream louder. 'No... No you can't! He's my baby, O'Sheyenne.'

O'Sheyenne smirked. 'Whose baby?'

'Mine ... he's mine.'

O'Sheyenne pulled up a chair next to Mrs Brogan as he lit a cigar. 'That might have been the case at one time, but the thing is, Mrs Brogan, you didn't keep up the repayments; even after the first warning I gave you, and now look where we are.'

Clancy Brogan's eyes flashed with angry desperation. 'We paid you everything you asked us to. We gave you *everything* we had, O'Sheyenne; when we picked him up from the convent you told us it would only be three payments. *Three.* You lied to us.'

O'Sheyenne nodded. 'So I did, Mrs Brogan. So I did.'

Talking through her tears, Clancy continued. 'How did you expect us to keep paying you every week? We're just an ordinary couple; you know that, O'Sheyenne. We could hardly put food on the table over the winter, let alone keep up with your demands.'

Looking bored, O'Sheyenne studied his nails. 'Me heart bleeds for you, so it does. But the way I see it is; how much do you want this child?'

'You know we want him. No-one could love him more than we do.'

'Then you should've thought of that before you threatened to go to the Gardaí.'

'We wouldn't have done it; it was ... it was just my husband's way of trying to make you stop... Wasn't it enough for you we gave the baby a good home?'

'There was many a couple who wanted him, Mrs Brogan; who would've paid a higher price, but as Connor was a childhood friend of mine me sentimental side got the better of me; I put you at the top of the list. And look at the thanks I get.'

'I'll find the money. I will, just...'

Mrs Brogan's voice trailed off as Donal O'Sheyenne put one hand over her mouth, placing the other on her leg. He pushed up her paisley blue dress; his fingers moving along her thigh, twisting inwards; pressing into her pale flesh.

Glancing at Patrick, he gestured with his head. 'Go on, get out of here.'

Patrick didn't move. Although he was terrified, he wanted to stay and help Mrs Brogan, though he wasn't quite sure how.

'I said, go!'

Patrick still didn't move – that was, until he heard the warm voice of Mrs Brogan, talking to him softly through her tears. 'Off you go, son. You need to get out of here.'

'But...'

There was a deathly fear in her voice, but Clancy Brogan gave Patrick a small smile. 'I'll be fine... This is no place for ye.'

With tears in his eyes, Patrick put the baby back in the cot. A moment later he began to run.

Donal grinned, feeling Mrs Brogan's legs trying to close together. He jammed his knee between

26

them, pinching her inner thigh. 'Don't play hard to get. I can feel you want it.'

Panic-stricken, Mrs Brogan screamed. 'Get off me, you bastard!... Get off me!'

Donal ignored her cries; keeping her legs open he rammed his fingers up into her crotch, enjoying the touch and smell of her as she screamed with newfound terror.

Ten minutes later, Donal zipped up his trousers. 'Can I trust you not to say anything, Mrs Brogan?'

Mrs Brogan stared at him in contempt. She whispered hoarsely. 'You can do nothing of the sort, O'Sheyenne. I'll *not* be silenced by fear.'

Donal nodded his head. 'That's what I thought and that's why you give me no option.' Bizarrely, Donal's eyes filled with tears. 'Now would you just look at that, Mrs Brogan? Tears.'

Kneeling down, Donal faced her. He glanced sidelong at the lifeless body of Connor.

'To be sure, your husband was a good man and it'd be a lie to say I won't miss him, but I can't have people talk me business. A man could get into trouble for that. You do understand, don't ye?' Donal paused deep in thought, before smiling manically.

His eye lids narrowed, eclipsing and casting a dark shadow into his green eyes. 'It's a shame you won't keep your mouth shut but no matter – there are other things that silence a person apart from fear.'

With a sudden movement, Donal leapt forward, grabbing Mrs Brogan by her throat. With no time to react, she was instantly overpowered by Donal's strength as his hands gripped tightly round her neck. Frantically her hands scratched at his, desperate for some relief from Donal's tightening grip.

With her eyes bulging, Donal, not once taking his stare away from hers, watched Mrs Brogan's eyes turn from white to bright crimson.

Feeling the life drain away, Donal released his grip and unceremoniously let go of her body, allowing it to drop to the tiled floor.

Putting on his hat, he walked over to the cot. He wrapped his wet coat round the baby before carrying it out into the storm-filled night.

3

The battering rain that soaked into Patrick Doyle's brown coat as he ran along the uneven road made no difference to him. Neither did the charges of lightning that illuminated and struck the tops of the swaying sycamore trees; all he wanted was to get as far away from the Brogans' house as possible.

Wrapping his oversized raincoat around his lean body in the hope of stopping the baying wind chilling his already cold bones, Patrick took a quick glance behind him. The road was empty; the village just outside Sneem in County Kerry where he lived had a population of just under a thousand and public transport was nearly nonexistent, so he knew the chance of anyone coming along was slim.

Glancing over his shoulder again, Patrick saw the distant glare of car lights coming over the horizon and the shape of the familiar Mercedes. The sight filled him with terror. It was O'Sheyenne.

Frantically, he picked up his speed; his heart racing faster and faster as the rain, pocketed by the Kerry wind, swirled in the air, battering his face.

Patrick knew he couldn't outrun the car and get to the side lane in time; petrified, he threw himself into the hedgerows, feeling the gorse cutting at his skin.

The car hurtled past; O'Sheyenne hadn't seen him as he raced along the road, sending up a spray of water. After waiting another five minutes, Patrick began to run. He was nearly at the church now and it was almost as if what he'd seen back there in the Brogans' house hadn't been real.

Desperately trying to distract himself from the images of the Brogans in his head, Patrick thought about his dad, Tommy Doyle; the man he'd once looked up to. The man he'd once been able to trust. But since his mother's death from an accident ten years ago, his father had drowned himself in whiskey and self-neglect.

His father was a hulk of man who had at one time been hailed a hero as one of Ireland's finest champion boxers, but now his days were spent drinking, and his nights bare-knuckle fighting to earn the money which barely put food on the table but always put the drink in his belly.

Even though Patrick had only been six when

his mother had died, he missed her so much. Even now he didn't truly know how she'd died. He'd been told she'd fallen down the stairs and broken her neck, but there were various stories and rumours around the village as to how it'd really happened. He'd heard she'd been drunk. He'd heard she'd been sleep-walking. But, worst of all, he'd heard his father had had something to do with it.

With the church coming into view, Patrick shook himself from his thoughts, falling into the heavy wooden doors and flinging them open to be greeted by a sea of heads turning towards him.

'Patrick Doyle, what's the meaning of this? Do you not know what it is to be in the house of God? If you're not here to attend choir practice then kindly leave.'

Patrick, giving a weak smile to Mary, stood trembling, suddenly painfully aware of his own appearance. His black hair hung soaked and matted over his forehead. His sodden second-hand clothes clung to his body and bubbles of rain water squirted out in tiny streams from the hole in his shoes. He was desperate to tell Father Ryan what had happened after the priest had driven off. He needed to tell him about the Brogans, but he was unable to find the words.

'Well? Are you staying or leaving?' The harsh tone of Father Ryan's voice echoed round the church.

With Patrick not forthcoming, Father Ryan grabbed him by his arm, pulling him to the back of the church.

'I'm speaking to you, Doyle. What have you to

say for yourself? What's going on?'

Patrick stammered, 'I ... I ... er...'

Father Ryan slammed down the prayer book on the back of the wooden pew, making the young children in the choir pews jump with fright. 'Speak up, boy; I haven't got time for this.'

Patrick paled. 'It's O'Sheyenne.'

Hearing the name, Father Ryan shoved Patrick even further away from everybody's hearing. He lowered his voice to a whisper. 'What's happened?'

'After you left, Mr O'Sheyenne ... Mr...'

Much to the frustration of Father Ryan, Patrick stopped, fear preventing him from saying anything else.

'For God's sake, boy, tell me.' Matthew Ryan paused, then caught sight of something on Patrick's coat. With trepidation, the priest spoke. 'What's that?'

Patrick looked down in horror at the bloodstain on his coat. It must have come from Connor when he was next to him in the car. But before he was able to answer the priest, the doors of the church were thrown open.

Standing, swaying in shock, was one of the villagers.

'Quick! I've just passed the Brogans' house. Their door was open... I think they're both dead.'

As the cutting Irish wind whipped round his face, it seemed to Patrick Doyle that the whole of the village, led by a tight-faced Father Ryan, had decided to find out what was going on; an unholy candlelight procession of curious onlookers

31

followed him down the road towards the Brogans' tiny cottage.

The lane down to the cottage was slippery and Patrick could feel his feet moving faster and faster as he hurtled along the road. Images of the Brogans and O'Sheyenne flashed in his head, combining together in a confusing mix of panic.

He ran whilst the rain continued to splinter down, causing him to lose his balance. He scrambled up, feeling, yet not reacting to, the sting of his hands as they grazed and bled from the hard stony ground. He was first to arrive at the Brogans' house; even though he'd seen the horror of it all only an hour or so before, looking at the bloody scene again made Patrick freeze at the door then turn to be sick.

He could see Connor's blood splattered all over the walls, the lifeless bodies of the couple in the middle of the room and, in the corner, the empty cot.

'Saints and the holy mother preserve us! Who could have done such a thing?' A villager spoke as he stood shoulder to shoulder with Patrick at the door. A throng of people came up behind, pushing eagerly forward in an attempt to get a look at the horror which lay within.

'Did anyone see anything?'

The room fell silent as dozens of onlookers, squeezing themselves into the kitchen, formed a circle around the room, staring at the slaughtered couple.

'I saw someone earlier coming out of here.' A man Patrick recognised from the local bakery spoke up.

'*Who? Who?*' The cry sounded around the room.

'I couldn't make out his face. I was a distance away and it was dark, but the person I saw coming out of here was tall ... strong looking, to be sure.'

The villagers looked puzzled, reflecting on the baker's words, before another voice shouted out from the back.

'That sounds like Tommy Doyle!'

In a cacophony of gasps, prayers and cries, the villagers began to shout out. '*He's capable of something like this*', '*I always knew he was trouble*', '*The man's a monster*', '*It must be him.*'

Alarmed, Patrick turned to face the crowd. 'No, it wasn't my da!'

'Then he'll be able to tell the Gardaí that... Call them! Call the Gardaí! Tommy Doyle should pay for this.' The shout was bellowed out by a man from the back of the room. As the crowd joined in again, shouting their agreement, Patrick's blood ran cold.

'No! Please! Wait! Me da didn't do it. I swear it wasn't him.'

The man from the back continued to talk. 'We all know what he's like when he has a drink inside him. Raging for a fight. 'Tis still a mystery what happened to your mother.'

Patrick's face reddened. His anger and hurt shone through. 'Leave my ma out of it; this has nothing to do with my da, I tell ye!'

Someone else called out. ''Tis no mystery; we all know what really happened to poor Evelyn.'

Patrick cried, 'Stop!... Stop! You don't understand. He didn't do it.'

The first man shouted out again, 'Where is he anyway? We need to find him. Everyone, go! Do not stop until you find Thomas Doyle.'

Patrick swirled around to look at Father Ryan. 'No, wait. Father, tell them. Tell them me da couldn't have done this ... he couldn't have, because ... because... I know who did!'

'Really? We'd all like to hear this. Tell us, Patrick; we're fascinated.'

Slowly, Patrick turned round to look at the person who'd just spoken, watching as the crowd parted. There, in front of him, was Donal O'Sheyenne.

Patrick spoke, quietly at first, then he became gradually louder. 'It was him... It was him! Father, it was him!' Patrick pointed furiously at Donal.

Father Ryan opened his mouth to speak but it was Donal who got there first. He stared at Patrick, dancing amusement in his eyes. 'Are you sure about that? From what I just heard it was your da.'

'He *never* had anything to do with it. You know that.'

Donal gave Patrick a wry smile, menacing in the candlelight. 'There's no point trying to defend him, Patrick. The sins of your da's actions are probably dripping from his hands as we speak, wouldn't you say so, Father Ryan?'

Father Ryan gave Donal a hostile stare but turned away quickly as Patrick began to address him.

'Father Ryan, you've *got* to believe me.'

Matthew Ryan shifted uncomfortably. 'Enough,

34

boy! Let me think.'

Patrick was distraught. 'It's true! You've got to believe me.' He looked round at the sea of people; his eyes pleading with them as he saw the condemnation on their faces.

'I saw Mr O'Sheyenne earlier. I swear. He had Connor in the car. He'd beaten him up then and afterwards he came back here to finish the job.'

Donal smirked. 'I've no idea what you're talking about.'

'It's true!'

O'Sheyenne shook his head. 'Then why didn't you say anything then, hey boy? Why would you not say anything to anyone when you saw me with this poor wretch in the back of my car? Why didn't you tell Father Ryan earlier or even call the Gardaí?'

To no-one in particular, Patrick cried, 'I tried. I did. I was going to, but I couldn't because...'

Donal interrupted. 'Because it's not true. This is a mighty big accusation, Patrick, and seeing I was with Father Ryan most of the night, it's also an untrue one. Not even a good man like meself can be in two places at once.'

Patrick shouted. 'You're lying! You're lying.'

'Shall we put it to the test, Paddy?' Donal turned to speak to Father Ryan. 'I was with you all night. Isn't that right, Father?'

Stammering slightly, Father Ryan fidgeted with the hooks on his cassock as he felt the gathered crowds stare.

'Yes ... yes. That's right. Er... Mr O'Sheyenne had come to see me earlier and was waiting for me to finish choir practice. He was sitting at the

35

back of the church the whole time.'

Patrick shook his head furiously. 'No! No! That's impossible; you know it is!'

'Stop, boy!' Father Ryan snapped at Patrick. 'I don't want to hear any more.'

Red-faced and holding back the tears, Patrick gawked at the priest. His voice rasping. *'Please, please, you know I'm telling the truth—'*

'Don't make this harder for yourself. Get yourself home now.' Father Ryan stared into Patrick's face. The man was inches away, allowing him to see the crease of tiredness around the priest's mouth and eyes.

Through a haze of tears, Patrick stumbled out of the cottage; desperate to find his father to try to warn him.

He couldn't make sense of what was happening, but most of all, he couldn't understand why Father Ryan had lied.

Once Patrick and the other villagers had left the Brogans', Father Ryan grabbed hold of Donal's arm, who looked down at the grip with amusement.

'Can I help you, Father?'

Father Ryan hissed through his teeth. 'Look at the carnage you've caused. Hold your head down in shame.'

'My head, Matthew? I'd say you'd need to hold yours.'

The priest's face was a picture of rage. 'It's not me that has blood on my hands.'

'I'd say that was a matter of opinion, wouldn't you?'

Father Ryan pointed at the slaughtered couple.

'*This. This* has nothing to do with me.'

Donal tapped Father Ryan on his back and grinned; bursting out into laughter. 'Why, Father, you crack me up, so you do. It must be wonderful to purge yourself of your sins.'

'A massacre wasn't what we agreed.'

'I don't think you're in a position to agree anything.'

Father Ryan's face flushed. 'I have no option but to go to the Gardaí, O'Sheyenne.'

Donal grabbed Father Ryan round his throat, squeezing it hard. Barely able to breathe, the priest wheezed, 'I can't be part of this.'

'I'd say you already are. All I need you to do is go along with it being Tommy Doyle until I tell you otherwise and figure something else out. Do I make myself clear?'

Father Ryan gave a tiny terrified nod. Satisfied he'd made his point, O'Sheyenne let go of the priest's neck, watching whilst he gasped and struggled for breath.

'Now I'll bid you goodnight, Father, and I'll leave you with a little word of advice: if you're ever thinking of going to the Gardaí again, take another look at the poor Brogans. We certainly wouldn't want such a godly man as yourself ending up like that now, would we?'

37

4

Mary O'Flanagan sat on her bed in the darkness and shivered. She was soaking wet and there was no way she was going to be able to get herself warm. There'd been a power cut. Nothing unusual there; it was a regular occurrence in the village, but tonight the difference was that she was alone.

There was no way she'd be able to start the parlour fire without her da. Besides, the logs in the yard were probably soaking wet, which meant she'd have to get the wood from the shed in the back field on her own; and one thing Mary O'Flanagan hated was the dark.

Her parents had gone out; taking it upon themselves to join the search party for Patrick's father. She wasn't quite sure what good they'd do. Her own father was a tiny, timid man and if he *were* to come across the formidable Tommy Doyle hiding out, she was certain he'd bag himself. Not unkindly, Mary laughed out loud at the image in her head.

Thinking about Tommy Doyle made Mary wonder about Patrick. She hoped he was all right. She hadn't been able to talk to him but he'd looked as handsome as he ever did when he'd stood soaking wet in the church that evening.

She and Patrick had been friends as far back as she could remember; much to her parents' dismay. And a few months ago he'd made her swear she'd marry him once he'd made his fortune.

'Patrick Doyle, I'm a good Catholic girl and good Catholic girls don't swear. Perhaps if you came to church more often you'd know that.'

'Don't be acting the maggot with me, Mary O'Flanagan. The Dublin chancers would blush to hear the mouth on ye.'

She'd pushed him gently. 'Feck off, Paddy!'

'Ah, you see. How can I make ye me wife, Mary, if you've a tongue which would eat the head off a viper?'

'I never said I'd be your wife, Patrick Doyle, and you're no more likely to make your fortune than poor Bridget Henley with those rotten apples she sells.'

'Well, that's a fine thing to say to a man, Mary O'Flanagan!'

She'd scoffed, but the kindness had shone through her eyes. 'A man, Paddy? You're nothing more than a boy.'

'I'm sixteen, Mary, and I can hold me own.'

She'd fallen silent before saying, 'And if I were to marry you, Patrick. What would we name our first child?'

Patrick had pondered on the question. 'I take it, it'll be a boy.'

Indignantly, she'd replied. 'It'll be no such thing. It'll be a girl and I shall call her Franny.'

Patrick had burst out laughing. 'Franny? And what sort of name is that?'

'Francesca. Franny for short. And for your information, it's a good Catholic name, Patrick Doyle – but that's something you'll know nothing about either.'

'Well, I won't allow it! Franny. Have you ever heard the like?'

She'd pulled a face but she'd had a twinkle in her eye. 'And have you ever heard what a pig you are, Patrick Doyle? And, to be sure, I certainly won't be marrying you now.'

'Then I'll just have to marry old Bridget Henley.'

'You'll do no such thing ... and to think I had a present for ye. I shan't give it ye now.'

Patrick's face had lit up. 'For me? You remembered me birthday?'

She'd spoken haughtily. 'I did indeed. Not that you deserve anything, not now you're going to marry Bridget Henley.'

'Oh Mary, you know you're the only girl for me. And I reckon if I kissed poor Bridget her false teeth might fall out.'

She'd grinned at the thought and then taken a tiny box out of her coat pocket and handed it to Patrick.

He'd opened the box with delight on his face. In it was a silver chain with a tiny cross on it.

'Do you like it?' she'd asked eagerly. 'I saved up all year.'

His eyes had glistened with tears. 'I love it, Mary. Like I love you. I should give you something.' Patrick had looked around, then seeing an early bloom of gorse, the bright yellow pea-flower which in the spring months seemed to light up the landscape of Kerry, ran to pick some.

She'd shouted. 'Patrick, you'll tear your hands on the prickles–'

'Then tear them I will. I have to give my girl a blossom.'

40

After five minutes of Mary giggling and Patrick struggling with the stems of sharp tiny spikes, he'd conceded defeat and returned with just a dozen yellow gorse petals.

'When we're married, Mary, I'll fill our house with flowers, but for now here's a petal for every month of the year. Every month that I love you.'

She'd taken the petals and smiled sweetly. 'Well, to be sure, it's true to say in me life I've never wanted a *whole* bunch of flowers. Why would I want that when the real beauty is in the petals?'

Patrick had winked at her, grateful for her kind nature.

'You know what they say around here, Mary? *When gorse is out of blossom, kissing's out of fashion;* so it looks like we're in luck.'

They'd laughed as they always did, pushing and shoving each other in jest, then Patrick had caught hold of her and leant in for a kiss.

Sitting on the bed, Mary jolted herself out of her memories; not wanting them to go any further because she certainly didn't want to have to confess them to Father Ryan on Sunday.

On the day Patrick had kissed her, she'd cycled all the way to the church at Kenmere – almost twenty miles away – to make her confession. Even though the hard seat on her bike had rubbed and caused painful blisters on her inner thighs, it'd still been better than having to confess to Father Ryan.

She *certainly* wasn't keen on making the long trip again and she *certainly* wasn't going to make a confession here, at St Peter's, so the easiest thing was to have no more thoughts of Patrick, *especially* in the direction they were beginning to head.

About to take a deep sigh, Mary suddenly held her breath. She heard the creak of the wooden stairs. There it was again. It wasn't her parents; they always yelled a cheery hello as they entered through the side door. The creak sounded again, only this time louder.

Mary's mouth began to dry as her heart pounded. Almost immediately her eyes filled with tears as her whole body began to shake, terror gripping her.

As the howl of the wind swirled through the trees, and the rain struck against the arched window, Mary heard footsteps coming along the landing. Petrified, she opened her mouth to cry out. Then she heard her name.

'Mary? Mary?'

Cautiously, Mary got up; tentatively crossing to the other side of the room.

'Mary?' The voice, just outside, was gentle and hushed.

'Patrick? Patrick? Is that you?' She reached for her bedroom door, opening it quickly, but she suddenly let out a scream. A large hand pressed against her face and a small beam of torchlight hit her eyes.

'Mary, for the love of God, I'm not going to hurt you. I promise. Just don't scream.'

The hand was lowered from her mouth and Mary stood staring into the face of Tommy Doyle. She stepped backwards, reaching out for the wall behind her.

'What ... what are you doing here?' Mary tried not to show her fear but she could hear it in her voice. 'You do know the Gardaí are out looking for ye?'

'Ah Jaysus, Mary. Don't look so frightened. I never meant to give you a fright. Patrick would have me guts if he thought I'd scared ye.'

Seeing her fear, Tommy spoke again. 'I never did it love. I swear.'

'Then why don't you tell them that?'

Tommy shook his head. 'When I heard they were looking for me, I knew I'd never stand a chance. Who's going to believe me? I know what they all think of the likes of me.' There was a long pause as Tommy stared pleadingly at Mary. Tears brimmed in his eyes. His voice was soft as he spoke. 'Connor was my friend; there's no way I would hurt him, or Clancy for that matter. For all her nagging ways she was a good woman.'

Even though Mary could smell the alcohol on Tommy as he spoke, she began to feel more at ease. She smiled. 'I know, Mr Doyle. She was a lovely woman; fierce kind to me.'

'Call me Tommy.'

Mary bristled, yet again feeling uncomfortable. It didn't feel right to call an adult by his first name. Then, as if he could read her mind, he spoke.

'To be sure, if you prefer to call me Mr Doyle, I'm grand with that as well.'

In the distance, above the sound of the storm, voices and barking dogs were heard. Tommy turned in panic to Mary. His face was strained, his voice full of urgency.

'You've got to help me.'

Mary turned her head towards the sound of the

voices. They were coming closer and they were sure to be here in a few minutes. 'I can't... I...'

'*Please*, Mary, I can't think of anyone else. They won't be suspicious of you.'

'What about Patrick? He'd help you. I know he would.'

'I can't risk going back home; they'll be bound to be waiting there and I'm not going to jail for something I didn't do.' Tommy's eyes were wild with fear. 'Please, you've got to help me!'

Just then, a voice came from downstairs. 'Mary! We're back. If I didn't know better, I'd say this storm was the wrath of God. I've been a God-fearing man all me life and I've never...'

The voice became inaudible as a crack of thunder broke above the small house. Mary looked at Tommy.

'That's me da, Mr Doyle. Even if I wanted to help ye; it's too late now. I'm sorry.'

'Mary! Didn't you hear me calling you from downstairs?'

'No, Da.'

'Well I was. We've come to check on you, to make sure you're all right. You can't be too careful with a man like that on the loose.'

Mary stood at the top of the stairs as she watched her da walking up the wooden stairs, followed by other villagers. Then, a moment later, trailing behind dressed in black, Mary saw the ominous figure of Father Ryan.

Father Ryan, her da, her mother, the Brogans, Tommy and his late wife, Evelyn ... even Donal O'Sheyenne, who her father was too frightened to have anything to do with. All of them went right back to childhood. All school mates, playground pals; every single one of them.

They'd shared their childhood, their youth and eventually their adulthood together, yet the power and disdain Father Ryan held over his contemporaries, in particular her da, made her seethe with anger. Though it didn't do her any good: each week it was inevitable she'd feel obliged to confess these dark thoughts she had about Father Ryan *to* Father Ryan, who she was certain smirked with pleasure as he handed her more Hail Marys than she'd known him give anyone else.

Addressing what her dad had just said, Mary spoke quietly. 'You don't know if it's him, Da. Mr Doyle has always seemed a nice man.'

Mary's father was standing opposite her, dripping pools of rain water on the highly polished mahogany floor. He smiled at his daughter.

'Ah, you're a good girl, Mary, blessed with innocence so you are; seeing no wrong in people. I know you're sweet on his boy, Mary, but Thomas Doyle is *not* a nice man. Even when we were children he was no different, always getting into scrapes. Isn't that right, Father Ryan?'

Father Ryan scowled, irritated at the chatter. 'Now is not the time to talk the hind legs off a donkey, Fergus O'Flanagan. Plus I think it's time we had a talk about allowing Mary to be sweet on the Doyle boy.'

Fergus hung his head. 'Yes, Father. Sorry, Father.'

'Aye, well that's as may be, but sorry without action won't see you through the gates of heaven, Fergus, nor keep Mary on a virtuous road. Come

45

and see me tomorrow and we can discuss it.'

Mary glared at Father Ryan, not just because of his unwelcome interference in her life but because of the way he spoke to her da. She'd always hated it and he'd always done it – belittling him in front of everyone. It angered Mary all the more knowing that they'd gone to school together.

'Mary, we've come to check the rooms to make sure he hasn't come here.' Fergus spoke, trying to assert himself once more.

Standing poised in front of her bedroom door, Mary spoke haughtily, gently pushing away the torch her dad held near her face. 'I've been here all night, Da. I think I'd know if your man had broken into me bedroom.'

Fergus looked vacant then nodded. 'Aye, I suppose you're right.'

Remembering O'Sheyenne's words, and wanting to look thorough, Father Ryan interjected. 'Well, we can't be too careful. A man like that needs to be brought to justice.'

'A man like what, Father?' asked Mary.

'Leave it, Mary.' Fergus spoke quietly, hating any form of confrontation.

For a moment Mary hesitated, seeing the plea in her dad's eyes, but there was one thing Mary O'Flanagan had always been and that was fiery.

'I'm sorry, Da, but no. I won't leave it. You've already tried and convicted him, so he's no chance, has he? All of ye decided he's guilty. Shame on you all.' She directed her anger towards the other villagers standing on the landing and to Father Ryan whose unease at the situation made him bellow.

46

'Fergus O'Flanagan, I said control your daughter!'

Mary watched as her dad opened his mouth to say something to Father Ryan. She willed him on. Finally he was going to stand up for himself, finally... But a moment later, and much to Mary's dismay, Fergus closed his mouth, turning to her in anguish, very much aware of his own weakness.

'Mary, Father Ryan is right. You've no place to speak like that. Now let me check your room. The others can check elsewhere in the house.'

Ashamed of himself, Fergus pushed past his daughter and stepped into the neat tiny bedroom. He looked around then froze. Standing in the far corner was Tommy Doyle.

Fergus turned to yell for help but Mary grabbed him, whispering, 'Please, Da. Don't say anything.'

Fergus's eyes were filled with horror. What was going on? 'Come away quickly, Mary. Go and get the others.'

'No, Da. He came to me for help.'

'Mary, you don't understand, he's...'

Mary snapped, interrupting her father. 'Of course I understand. I'm not an eejit... Tommy didn't do it.'

'Then he can explain that to the Gardaí. It's nothing to do with us.'

'Please, Da. He only wants the chance to talk to Patrick.'

'No, Mary.'

Tommy stepped forward out of the corner of the room. He spoke directly to Fergus.

47

'You've known me since we were bairns *and* me poor dead wife, Evelyn too, and not once in all that time did you ever know me to lay a finger on her or any one of my friends. Drunk or not. I like a fight, so I do, and you know that's what I do to make me money, but I wouldn't hurt a hair on those I cared for.'

'There's always a first time, Tommy, and of course there's the...' Fergus stopped, knowing he'd said too much, but it wasn't hard for Tommy Doyle to guess what Fergus had been about to say.

'The rumours? Is that what you were going to say?'

Fergus blushed but held Tommy's gaze. 'Aye, Tommy, that's what I was going to say. The rumours never stop about how Evelyn died; folk round here think you had something to do with it, and now this.'

Tommy shook his head. 'I never had anything to do with Evelyn's death, Fergus. If the Gardaí accept that, why can't you?' And as for Connor and Clancy, God forgive you for thinking that.'

'You were seen by their house.'

'I wasn't near there tonight, but even if I was, what are you saying: that a man can't walk in his own village without being accused of murder?'

Fergus said nothing. It was true: for all the man's brute strength and quick temper, he'd never seen Tommy Doyle *actually* raise his hand to anyone he knew and when Evelyn had been alive he hadn't once heard her complain about his ways.

'I ... I don't know, Tommy.'

'Please, Fergus. I wouldn't ask if I wasn't desperate. All I'm asking is to pretend you haven't seen me, so I can go and speak to me boy. Just give me that.'

Fergus shook his head as he quickly backed out of the room. 'No, I'm sorry, I can't.'

'Well?' Father Ryan stared with contempt at Fergus, which didn't go unnoticed by him.

Fergus turned to look at the others, then back at Father Ryan. 'Sorry?'

'Fergus, are you completely stupid?'

Fergus O'Flanagan looked at the other villagers, watching their tittering laughter and feeling the humiliation he so often felt. He turned, cutting a hard long stare at Father Ryan before saying, 'Well, it's like me daughter says. She would've noticed if your man had broken into her room.'

5

Father Ryan sat in the near dark, a solitary candle burning in the corner. It flickered, caught by the wind which crept under the ill-fitting wooden door. The ticking of the grandfather clock echoed loudly in the room, competing with the sound of the rain.

The gilded bible Father Ryan had received on the day of his ordination lay open on his lap at Corinthians. His intention had been to seek solace in the words but he was too tired, plus it was almost impossible to see the tiny print in the candlelight. He sighed. There was no telling when the electricity would come back on, but there was no point in getting annoyed.

Some of the locals and Gardaí were continuing to search but he'd needed to call it a night. Yawning, Father Ryan reflected on the events of the evening. It'd been a difficult night and there was still no sign of Tommy Doyle. Which he supposed might be a good thing. He wasn't sure what O'Sheyenne was going to do but, whatever it was, there were bound to be more repercussions.

'Father?'

The unexpected voice cut through the dark, startling Father Ryan to his feet. 'Saints preserve us. Have you never heard of knocking, Helen?'

'I'm sorry, Father.'

'Well, what is it?'

Father Ryan's housekeeper, Helen Flanagan, stood in the room, her round face glowing with ruddy excitement as she embroiled herself in an air of gossip and melodrama. Her voice was loud and chirpy.

'What a terrible night, Father; my blood's running cold to think we have a murderer in our midst. I was talking to him only last week when I was buying a quarter of tobacco for Fergus; to think it could've been me lying dead and not poor Mrs Brogan.'

Exasperated and sorely irritated by Helen's love of the dramatic, Father Ryan spoke impatiently. 'And why would Thomas do that, why would he decide to kill you?'

Helen glanced around, whispering as if there was someone other than herself and Father Ryan in the room. 'Why does a mad man do anything, Father?'

'For goodness sake, Helen; Thomas Doyle is not a mad man, he's a drunken scoundrel. Not everything is as it seems.'

Helen Flanagan was clearly having none of it. 'That's as may be, Father, but I won't sleep well tonight knowing he's at large, thinking we could be murdered in our beds at any time. Look what he did to my poor cousin, Evelyn; threw her clean down the stairs, so he did.'

Father Ryan's face clouded over. 'We don't know that's what happened to her, Helen; rumour and gossip are dangerous things.'

Ignoring what the priest was saying, Helen leant further in to speak. 'Now tell me, Father, is it true that Tommy Doyle chopped off the Brogans' heads and hung them from the rafters like hocks of ham? Mrs Rafferty told me she saw it with her own eyes.'

That was it. It was all too much for Father Ryan. He raised his voice, shocking Helen enough to cause her to throw herself down in the armchair; holding her chest in a dramatic fashion.

'Enough of this nonsense! I expect this kind of talk from Mrs Rafferty, but you of all people should know better.'

Helen Flanagan lowered her eyes, feeling slightly ashamed of herself. Then, remembering the reason she'd *actually* come, a smile spread across her face. 'To be certain, Father, you probably haven't eaten, so I thought I'd bring you some of me homemade scones. If truth be told, I actually made them for Mrs Brogan but she'll no longer need them where she's gone. I said to Fergus...'

Father Ryan held up his hand, unable to hear any more of Helen's idle chatter. 'Thank you, Helen, I'm sure I'll enjoy them with a cup of tea. Just leave them on the table.'

Busying herself, Helen got up. 'I'll put the kettle on then, I fancy a brew myself.'

'No!' Father Ryan shouted, rather too quickly, as he pulled a face. He could almost taste her insipid tea and its ever-present thick skin of milk. Quite how anybody could turn what was supposed to be a relaxing, refreshing beverage into what could only be described as a depressingly lukewarm, tasteless drink each and every time, he didn't know.

Helen looked at him in shocked silence. Quickly Father Ryan tried to appease her. 'What I meant to say is: no thank you, Helen, I'm rather tired and I think we should all get some rest.'

With Helen gone, Father Ryan sat down again, but it was no good – he wasn't going to get any sleep now. There were too many things to think about. He sighed and stood up. Putting on his long black cloak over his cassock, Father Ryan headed back into the night.

'Me da? Are you sure?' Patrick looked puzzled.

'What do you take me for, Paddy? Of course I'm sure.' Mary O'Flanagan shook her head, exasperated. 'Come *on*, we haven't much time.'

'I don't know.'

'Well I do. *Come on!*'

Patrick Doyle hesitated, concern etched all over

his handsome face. 'I...'

'Don't you trust me? Is that it?'

He looked hurt at the suggestion. 'Don't say that, Mary. You're my girl, but I need to go and speak to Father Ryan and tell him what I know.'

Mary's voice softened. 'Look, just come and see him. He needs to talk to you. I know it wasn't him; I just know it.'

'That means a lot to me, Mary... I know who did it.'

Mary's eyes were wide open. 'How?'

Patrick didn't answer. He stared at Mary; he was so grateful to see her. He'd been running about the Kerry countryside looking desperately for his dad; terrified for him and wanting to speak to him to tell him about O'Sheyenne. His dad must have had word they were looking for him, and he'd be hiding. Patrick had watched in despair as he'd heard the sounds of the other villagers searching for his father, hungry, like a pack of wolves hunting for their prey.

After hours of futile searching he'd come home, wiping away the tears he'd never show anyone, and in the abandonment of hope and filled with desperation, he'd done what he'd never done before: he'd prayed. Prayed his dad would come home. Prayed it was all just a rotten dream; so that when someone had knocked at the door, hard and relentless, he'd run to it, assuming his prayers had been answered. But instead of his dad it was Mary O'Flanagan who'd been standing shivering on his doorstep; wet right through, telling him she knew where his father was.

And now, as he stood by the front door, it

struck him that his prayers *had* been answered in a way – in the form of Mary. *His* Mary. She'd come to tell him where his dad was, reassuring him everything would be all right.

The gentle touch on Patrick's arm interrupted his thoughts. 'Hey, Paddy... It'll be okay.'

He nodded. 'Mary, can I tell you something? But you have to promise you won't tell a soul...'

'Yes; I promise. Go on.'

'When you and Father Ryan left...'

He stopped, suddenly realising it might be dangerous for Mary to know what really happened with Donal O'Sheyenne and what he'd seen and heard. He shook his head. 'It doesn't matter; it can wait. Come on.'

'No, go on, Patrick; what were you going to say?'

'Not now.'

There was a slight hurt in Mary's voice. 'I thought we didn't have any secrets from each other?'

'We don't, and that's why I'm going to tell you later.'

'Honestly?'

Patrick nodded. 'Honestly.'

Following Mary out into the rain-filled night, Patrick felt a sense of foreboding.

The woods that led to the back field were dark and treacherous and, for the fourth time in the space of less than five minutes, Patrick cursed loudly as he tripped over the unseen bracken which hooked and trailed round his legs, sending him headlong into the wet earth.

54

'I'm glad to see you find this funny, Mary O'Flanagan.'

'Do you see me laughing, Paddy?'

'No, but I can hear ye.'

Mary sniggered to herself. Although she was worried about Patrick, she still couldn't help enjoying this time she was spending with him. She was sixteen and even though her parents would go mad, she'd made up her mind she was going to say yes to Patrick the next time he asked her to marry him.

They wouldn't get married straight away, she'd wait for him to make his fortune, as he always said he would. Perhaps they'd even go on a honeymoon, then afterwards get a little cottage in the same street as her mum and dad. And after that? Well, they'd make babies. Lots of them.

At the last thought, Mary found herself blushing. She wasn't sure why. There was nothing sinful about love; that much she did know, and although Patrick and his father didn't go to church, they were still good people. She wasn't certain Father Ryan would agree with her but then she wasn't always certain *she* agreed with Father Ryan.

Suddenly realising where they were, Mary called out. 'We're nearly there, Paddy. Can you see the shed?'

Before Patrick could answer, he heard a noise. 'What was that?'

'I didn't hear anything. Come on.'

Patrick reached out, grabbing Mary by the arm to stop her going any further. 'Quiet. There's someone there... Look!'

As Patrick spoke he crouched on the ground, pulling Mary down with him. He watched as a figure he couldn't make out hurried past. Mary began to speak but Patrick quickly silenced her, gently placing his hand over her mouth.

'Wait here.'

'Not alone, Patrick! Not in the dark! Let me come with ye.'

'No, Mary. Just stay there, I'll be back in no time... I promise.'

With Mary's pleas sounding in the distance, Patrick ran back through the woods. He needed to know what was going on if he was going to be able to prove it was O'Sheyenne and not his father who'd killed the Brogans. It was strange for anyone to come into these woods; there was no reason to – unless of course you were trying not to be seen. They led nowhere apart from to the two houses on the other side of the village. One of these lay empty and the other was owned by the Brogans.

It certainly wasn't the quickest route round to them; in fact, it took almost double the time, and on a night like this, along a treacherous path, perhaps even longer. So what anyone was doing here at this time of night, Patrick didn't know, but he was certainly going to find out. He was sure it'd have something to do with O'Sheyenne.

Whoever it was certainly seemed to be in a hurry. Patrick found he needed to run to keep up; but all the time he made sure he stayed far enough behind not to be seen.

Darting across the craggy, mud-soaked land, he spotted a break in the woods and crouched behind a tree. He couldn't see the person now but they couldn't have gone that far.

Leaning his head further round, Patrick suddenly froze as he felt his arm being grabbed. He turned round; a lamp was held up to his face.

'Patrick Doyle, what are you doing here?' It was Father Ryan. His voice cold and harsh.

'I ... I...'

'Well, boy?'

'Er ... nothing ... nothing, Father.'

Father Ryan cut his eye at Patrick, exclaiming, 'Nothing! How can you be doing nothing late at night in the woods? And why are you looking like that?'

Patrick looked round. His voice quiet but urgent. 'I have to talk to you... It really *was* O'Sheyenne who killed the Brogans; I saw it with my own eyes. I'm going to try to prove it. He killed them because they were threatening to go to the Gardaí.'

Father Ryan looked uneasy. Hesitantly, he asked the next question. 'Do you know what about?'

Patrick nodded, looking fearful. 'He's selling babies. The Brogans owed him money for their child and they couldn't pay, so I think they were going to tell the authorities about it.'

Father Ryan clenched his jaw, gripping Patrick even harder as his face darkened. 'Have you told anyone else about this?'

'No ... no.'

'Are you sure?'

Patrick began to feel frightened. 'I swear I haven't.'

Relaxing slightly, Father Ryan spoke mainly to

himself as he started to march Patrick out of the woods.

'Good ... good; keep it that way.'

Patrick tried to pull away. 'Father, *please*, wait, I have to go back for...'

Father Ryan snapped. 'For what?'

Patrick looked back into the woods. He couldn't possibly tell Father Ryan about his, dad hiding in the shed, or the fact Mary was waiting for him. 'Nothing ... it doesn't matter.'

With that, Patrick let himself be dragged away, looking over his shoulder as he went.

One thing Mary O'Flanagan had struggled with all her life was listening to what people told her, which was why she found herself following not far behind Patrick when he'd told her to stay where she was. But now, as she crouched in the dense wet bracken in the pitch black, unable to see where he had gone and not understanding why he was taking so long, she wished she'd stayed put.

After another few minutes of crouching in the dark, Mary attempted to stand up, but as she did, she found herself being pushed back down into the muddy undergrowth as a hand covered her mouth, a silent scream freezing on her lips.

6

The light broke over the village as the rain continued to fall, and an urgent banging was heard down the main street as Fergus O'Flanagan pounded on the door of the rectory.

'Father! Father!'

It took a few minutes for the wooden door to be opened and a tired-faced Father Ryan to appear in his dark blue robe, looking annoyed.

'What in the name of heaven is all the racket for, Fergus?'

Fergus's face was drawn and pale. 'It's Mary. Something's happened to her. It's terrible, Father.'

'What?... What are you talking about, man? What's happened?'

'Mary. Our Mary. She's been ... she's been attacked.' Fergus's eyes were wide open with fear as he spoke the next words. '*Tampered* with.'

Father Ryan looked concerned. 'Where is she?'

'At home with Helen.'

'What has she said?'

'Nothing, Father; she barely spoke when she got in. It took an hour or more for her just to tell us she'd been attacked.'

The priest nodded. 'Have you called the doctor?'

'No, Father. We didn't like to until we'd come to see you.'

Father Ryan continued to nod his head

solemnly. 'Aye, Fergus, you've done the right thing. And the Gardaí?'

'Not yet; Helen wouldn't hear of it.'

'Well, let me get dressed and I'll come as quick as I can... And Fergus, don't say anything to anybody else.'

The O'Flanagans' household held a tension reserved only for the most unspeakable of circumstances. Helen O'Flanagan was sitting with her head in her hands in the wooden rocking chair by the parlour fire. Hearing the door, she stood up, collapsing almost directly at the sight of Father Ryan and her husband. Her sobs filled the room and they were only interrupted by the wailing that came through the floorboards from upstairs.

Still on her knees, Helen reached up and took hold of Father Ryan's hands. Her usual happy chatter was muted, replaced by a terrified anxiety. 'Thank you for coming, Father. She ... she...'

Father Ryan raised his eyebrows as Helen burst into tears again. 'Where is she?' he asked.

Helen nervously fiddled with the hem of her blouse. She sniffed loudly. 'Upstairs in her room. I haven't spoken to her; I thought it was best to wait.'

Father Ryan touched his face. 'Sensible. You've done the right thing. These situations have to be dealt with sensitively. Now, I don't suppose you could make me a cup of tea, could you? And Helen, not too much milk.'

Helen dutifully jumped into action, getting up from the floor and momentarily putting her anguish to one side. She wiped away her tears.

'Of course, Father; forgive me. I'll make you one straight away.'

Father Ryan gave a tight smile, wiping the palm of his hand on his black cassock as he looked at the O'Flanagans. He was pleased they'd come to him instead of calling the doctor or the Gardaí. It made things easier. He was in charge of the parish, responsible for the emotional and spiritual wellbeing of his flock, as well as for saving their souls from sin and temptation. Therefore it was up to him to decide what was going to happen.

'Right, I'll go and talk to her. I'd appreciate it if I wasn't disturbed.'

Helen looked concerned. Her eyes darted from Father Ryan to her husband. Her apprehension at questioning the priest was apparent. 'Er ... don't ... don't you think it would be best if I came in? Perhaps she'd find it easier to talk if I was there.'

Annoyed at being doubted, Father Ryan scowled momentarily, but his face softened along with his voice. 'Nonsense, Helen. Mary will speak to me and if she needs to confess anything, she'll do it without your presence. I can't see how it will help you fussing around her. Now, I'd really like my tea before I go up. I really am parched.'

Turning briskly, Father Ryan walked out of the parlour and found his way up the wooden stairs.

Tommy Doyle stretched awake, feeling a bolt of pain shoot through his back. He groaned audibly, remembering where he was and why he was there. He hadn't meant to sleep but he must have dozed off in the early hours and now, although the rain was still beating down, bringing gloom to the skies, he could tell by the light that it was late morning.

Tommy stood up shivering, feeling the damp of his clothes chilling his flesh. Looking around the shed, he knew he needed to get out of where he was. Perhaps make his way across to Castlecove. He had friends there and it'd be easier to get to the mainland if he had a place to hide out for a while.

Reaching into his pocket for his packet of tobacco, Tommy frowned, hearing something. It was the sound of dogs barking. And the more he listened, the more he realised they were coming nearer. Soon they'd be here.

Grabbing his coat, Tommy dashed out of the shed. He ran, slipping on the wet grass as he went. The dogs were getting closer. The only way out was to go down by Lincoln's farm and along by the river.

Beginning to run across the open field, he heard his name being called.

'Tommy Doyle, stay where you are!'

There was no way he was going to stop. Picking up his pace, Tommy headed for the far side of the field.

'Tommy Doyle!'

He raced across the field, trying to keep his balance on the slippery earth. Out of breath, he got to the fence and began to climb, but only a moment later an agonising pain struck him, sending shooting pains through his body. He fell back to the ground with the growling of the dogs tearing into his leg being drowned out by his screams.

'Get them off me! For feck's sake get them off me!'

As blood poured from his torn flesh, Tommy heard the sound of men running towards him and giving orders to the dogs to let go. But the absence of the dogs' teeth ripping into him didn't free Tommy of the excruciating pain. He held onto his leg, rolling round in the mud crying out. His voice weak and barely audible. 'Help me!... Help.'

'There's no help where you'll be going, Doyle.'

The men began hauling him up off the ground just as Tommy Doyle blacked out.

7

Father Ryan stood in the middle of Mary O'Flanagan's room with a cold cup of tea in his hand. It'd never been hot. It was brought up lukewarm and now there wasn't even a chance of taking a sip as the thick layer of skin from the milk floated unappetisingly on the surface.

It crossed Father Ryan's mind that Helen's housekeeping skills were just as dire as her tea-making and her cooking; perhaps after all this business had been sorted out, it would be time to give the woman her marching orders. He'd only ever hired her as a gesture of goodwill, but that had certainly gone on for far too long.

A big snivel brought Father Ryan back to the present. He looked at Mary who was sitting on the bed shaking, eyes red and swollen from crying.

'Now then, Mary, I want to know *everything*. Everything you can tell me. *Everything* you can remember.'

Mary huddled further down under her overly starched bed sheets, unable to look directly at the priest. Ashamed. Hurt and confused, she curled up in the foetal position, inconsolable and wanting to speak to her mother, wondering why she hadn't come up.

The cold air from the covers being turned back gave Mary a fright, prompting her to sit up. Suddenly aware that the lower part of her body had been exposed by her nightdress riding up, she quickly tugged down the flannelette garment over her knees.

Hugging herself, she stared at Father Ryan, uncomfortable with his hostile gaze and speech.

'What sinful acts have you been party to, Mary O'Flanagan?'

Terrified, Mary edged back into the hard metal bed frame as Father Ryan sat down next to her.

'None, Father.'

'I'll ask you again. What sins of the flesh have you partaken in?'

'None. I swear. On the holy bible, I swear.'

'Then you need to tell me what happened, otherwise I have no alternative but to think you played some part in this.'

Mary paused and gazed down at her hands. She could see the mud from the woods still under her fingernails, and under her middle fingernail was a slight trace of dried blood.

'Well?' Father Ryan's voice interrupted her thoughts. She looked at his face and saw no kindness.

'I can't remember, Father.'

'Rubbish. Have you forgotten that I am a servant of God, and, that being so, your lies are direct lies to our good Lord?'

Mary buried her head in her hands as tears dripped through her fingers. 'I swear I can't remember ... please, please can you get my ma?'

'Your mother wisely wants me to sort this out before she talks to you. She's worried that perhaps in some way you ... how shall I put this, Mary?... You invited this.'

Mary shook her head furiously. 'No! No! It wasn't like that.'

'Then, if it wasn't, tell me what it *was* like; otherwise, as I said before, I can only assume the worst.'

With no choice and taking a deep breath, Mary tried to overcome her shame. 'I was in the woods.'

Father Ryan looked shocked. 'The woods!'

'Yes, I was with Patrick, but he saw someone. Patrick told me to stay where I was but I got frightened and followed him. And then, when I was waiting there, I...'

'Go on.'

'I got up, thinking I should go back because I couldn't see Patrick any more and, as I did, I felt someone grab me and push me back down from behind. They put their hand over my mouth and...' Mary stopped and threw herself back onto the bed, racked with sobs and self-hatred.

Father Ryan's voice was steady. 'Mary, continue.'

'I can't. I'm ashamed, Father.'

'Of what?'

'Of where he touched me. Of what he did.'

'And where did he touch you?'

Mary blushed, her pale face turning scarlet as the memories and the pain rushed through her body. She wished her mother had come to sit with her. Then it suddenly dawned on her why she hadn't. Her mother was ashamed. And Mary didn't blame her.

'Mary?' Father Ryan's voice cut through the silence.

'I'm sorry, Father. He ... he touched me all over, and then he put his thing inside me. It hurt. I cried out but no-one came.'

Father Ryan exuded venom as he sat next to Mary. 'And why didn't you try to stop it, Mary? Or perhaps you liked it?'

Fervently, Mary shook her head. 'No, Father. No!'

More to himself than to Mary, Father Ryan spoke. 'And you *never* saw his face.' It was a statement rather than a question but Mary answered anyway.

'No. Nothing. I didn't see anything. It was so dark, and I know this sounds silly, Father, but I closed my eyes. I didn't want to see. I just didn't.'

For a few moments Father Ryan sat in silence mulling over his thoughts. He gazed up at the ceiling, catching sight of a tiny spider making its way across the length of the old wooden beam. With a renewed intensity, he chose his words carefully.

'Mary. Can you recall what time this was?'

'No, Father.'

'And you say you never saw the person's face who did this to you?'

'No, Father.'

Again, Father Ryan fell into a brooding silence. The minutes passed and twice Mary found herself peering at the priest, checking to see he hadn't fallen asleep. Eventually he spoke.

'I myself saw Patrick in the woods last night; hiding and skulking as if he were running away from something. And when I asked him what he was doing, he couldn't tell me. I thought it most strange at the time, but now it's beginning to make sense.'

Mary looked puzzled. 'What do you mean?'

Father Ryan sighed loudly, irritated by the baffled expression on Mary's face. 'What I'm saying is that Patrick Doyle, cunning as he is, made you think you were there on your own. He *wanted* you to believe that.'

'But why, Father? I'm not following you.'

'Is there anything between those ears of yours, Mary?' Father Ryan snapped, berating Mary as he often did. 'This is how you ended up in such a sorry state.'

Mary bowed her head, biting back the tears, making Father Ryan soften slightly.

'I think it was Patrick. I think Patrick was the one who attacked you.'

Mary scrambled off the bed and began to scream. Loud and vociferous. Her piercing cry reverberated through the house, bringing Mr and Mrs O'Flanagan flying up the stairs; bundling

67

themselves through Mary's bedroom door with terror on their faces.

'Get out!... Get out!' Father Ryan bellowed at them. He stood up, pointing to the door without bothering to turn his head to look at Helen or Fergus, who both quickly and timidly backed away, out of the room.

With the same thunderous tone, Father Ryan boomed at Mary, 'Mary O'Flanagan, cease that noise. This is a time for being calm and rational, child.'

Mary held onto the end of the bed, hyperventilating as the realisation of what the priest was saying sunk in. 'I can't... I can't...'

With speed under his feet, Father Ryan dashed across to where Mary stood and with a raise of his hand he slapped her hard across her cheek, welting a red mark. Immediately her hysterics dropped into a deep painful sob.

Smoothing down his cassock as he sat down, he murmured to himself. 'I'm sorry to have to do that, but nobody needs to hear such noise and it certainly won't help things... That's better. Now Mary, let's try again.'

Through her sobs, Mary gasped. 'It's impossible, Father. Patrick wouldn't do anything like that. He wouldn't. He loves me.'

'Nonsense, child.'

'He does! He does! Look what he gave me.' Mary went to her chest of drawers and brought out a tissue. She unwrapped it carefully to reveal the twelve dried and pressed yellow petals Patrick had given her. Mary spoke triumphantly. 'See.'

Father Ryan's face twisted into scorn at the

sight of a handful of shrivelled petals. He could hardly believe his eyes.

'What in the name of God are you showing me, Mary O'Flanagan?'

'A petal for his love for every month of the year.'

'Ye God's Satan has addled your mind,' Father Ryan hollered. 'He no more loves you than Lucifer loves the cross.' Father Ryan paused, composing himself. 'I don't like to shout, but this is a serious matter and difficult for all of us; truths need to be told, so you have to stop thinking he loved you.'

'I swear he does. We were even going to get married.'

'Mary, you have a lot to learn. We're all just flesh and blood, and what keeps us from sin and temptation is our following in Christ our saviour.'

'No, you're wrong. There's no way Patrick would do this, you don't know him like I do.' In her torment, Mary couldn't contain herself; she blurted out the words, for once unafraid of the priest. 'And how would you know, anyway? What do you know about love? You've never loved anyone in your life.'

Father Ryan became rigid, blinking a couple of times and then, to Mary's surprise, he smiled sadly. 'That's where you're wrong, Mary. I know very well how it feels to be in love. How it is to think about a person the very moment you wake up and the very last thing at night. To be afraid of the life you had before them and the life you'd have without them. For the rays of the sun to feel warmer when they're next to you.'

Mary looked amazed. 'Who was she, Father?'

'Someone I used to know a long time ago.'

'And why didn't you marry her?'

There was a forlornness in the way Father Ryan answered. 'Our paths went different ways; we didn't want the same things.'

'What was her name?'

'I've said too much already.'

Mary thought for a moment. 'Then surely you must be able to see that Patrick loves me.'

Father Ryan's face tightened again. He sighed. 'You're not thinking straight. It's not love, Mary; it's lust.'

Mary put down her head before blushing, something that didn't go unnoticed by Father Ryan. 'What is it, child?'

Mary spoke very slowly, biting on her lip. 'He did... He did kiss me once.'

'Mary O'Flanagan, I warned you about this. I thought you were God-fearing.'

'I am, Father. I am.'

'Then why didn't I know about this before? Why didn't I hear it at your confession?'

Mary shrugged her shoulders, too fearful to admit she'd cycled to the next village to make her confession.

'This proves it, Mary. First you don't see the person's face. Then I see Patrick lurking suspiciously in the woods unable to tell me why and then...' Matthew Ryan stopped, closing his eyes and shaking his head.

'And then what, Father?'

'And then that *kiss*. Don't you see, there seems to be no question; Patrick Doyle raped you.'

Mary's hands shot over her mouth, partly to

stop another scream and partly to stop herself from vomiting.

It didn't make sense, what Father Ryan was saying. It just didn't. Patrick was decent. He was gentle. Not rough. Not cruel like the person who'd violated her in such a brutal way. No, it was impossible. She wouldn't believe it. She wouldn't.

The only thing Father Ryan was right about was the fact that she *hadn't* seen whoever it was. She hadn't even *heard* them come up behind her. And it'd been Patrick who'd insisted she stay there alone, even though she'd wanted to go with him. So maybe...

Mary's body jolted upright. No, she wasn't going to think like that. Patrick could never have done anything like this.

Using a gentle tone, a tone rarely heard by Mary, Father Ryan broke her thoughts.

'To be sure, it's hard to think or understand how someone we trusted could do this to us, but think clearly. Let shame not cloud your judgement. It starts with you rebuffing Patrick's advances over and over again, and, by doing so, the sins of the flesh take over his mind. Then, when you're in the woods, he sees an opportunity. And like the devil himself, he creeps up on you; taking your innocence in the way he did.'

Father Ryan held Mary's gaze.

'But–'

'No, Mary. Patrick Shamus Doyle is not a God-fearing person.'

'But–'

'No. Do not make any more excuses. It's as clear as the presence of Christ within me... I'm

71

sorry, Mary, I really am.'

Confused and looking like a timid child, tears rolled down over the red mark on Mary's cheek. 'Where is he, Father?'

'Don't you worry about that; you'll never have to see him again. I'll make sure of that. Patrick Doyle will pay for what he has done to you. Mark my words, Mary. Mark my words.'

Father Ryan got up. He went to leave but stopped, turning back to Mary. His tone inquisitive. 'One thing puzzles me though; why were you two in the woods last night in the first place?'

Mary opened her mouth to say something, but she hesitated. Putting her hands behind her back, she crossed her fingers, then answered gently. 'No reason, Father ... no reason at all.'

The banging on the front door startled Patrick. He quickly pulled on his trousers, running down the stairs in the hope it was his father. Opening the door, only semi-dressed, Patrick's face dropped. It was the Gardaí. His thoughts raced; panic making him speak quickly.

'What's happened?... Is my da all right?... Where is he?'

The tallest Garda, dressed in full uniform, looked at Patrick with an air of contempt; tiny eyes staring from under a mass of brown eyebrows.

'Patrick Doyle? You need to come with us.'

'Is he all right?... Nothing's happened to him, has it?'

Uninvited, the Garda stepped into the small hallway. 'Get dressed.'

'*Please* ... just tell me what's happened.' Patrick

was full of fear; anxious for his father.

A sneer appeared on the Garda's face. 'Oh, I think you know very well.'

'No, I don't. I'm worried about him.'

The Garda took hold of Patrick's arm so hard. it made him wince. 'You're in serious trouble; I'd say at this moment your da is the least of your worries.'

8

Through a hazy gaze of pain and medication, Tommy Doyle stared at the gnarled face of Donal O'Sheyenne leaning over him in his hospital bed.

O'Sheyenne nodded to the Gardaí. 'Come back in ten minutes.'

With the Gardaí gone, O'Sheyenne turned his attention to Tommy, pulling the hospital covers to expose the injuries.

'That looks nasty.' With a grin, Donal squeezed his fingers hard into the bandaged legs. Tommy let out a scream.

'I swear. I don't know anything... I don't...'

'Save your breath, Tommy; I'm not here for a confession. I've got a proposition for you; it'll be worth your while.'

'And why would I want anything from you?'

'Because from where I'm standing I'd say you need all the help you can get. And it's not like we haven't had dealings before.'

'I don't need your help, O'Sheyenne. I'm not

73

interested in anything you have to say. So why don't you crawl back to the hole you came from?'

O'Sheyenne chuckled. 'That's fighting talk for a man accused of a double murder.'

Tommy stared at Donal. 'I never did it; you'll see, I'll prove it.'

'They already think it's you, Doyle, and what with the question mark still over Evelyn's death ... well, if they were to find a piece of bloody rope in your house, the same rope used to tie up poor Connor, to be sure, that would seal your fate, wouldn't you say?'

Puzzlement spread across Tommy's face. 'They won't.'

'Well really, that all depends, because it's quite conceivable that in the next hour our local Gardaí will get a call telling them exactly where to find it in your pantry. But as you say, you don't need my help; so I'll bid you good day.'

O'Sheyenne started away to the shouts of Tommy Doyle.

'You'll not set me up, O'Sheyenne; you'll not!'

Donal turned round and grinned. 'Oh, but I already have... Unless of course you'll reconsider my proposition?'

Tommy growled, 'I don't even know what it is.'

O'Sheyenne walked back to the hospital bed, straightening the covers in feigned concern. 'I wouldn't worry about that; simply put, Doyle; you've got no choice.'

Five minutes later the two officers, who were more accustomed to dealing with vandalised crops and drunken villagers, came back into the ward.

O'Sheyenne smiled at them.

'I think we have the wrong man, gentlemen,' His voice was authoritative. 'I think the blame lies not with Thomas Doyle as we first thought but with his son, Patrick Doyle.'

'Is this true, Doyle?' One of the Gardaí spoke up.

Tommy nodded solemnly. 'Aye, I'm afraid it is. I saw him with my own eyes coming out of the house, and so did Mr O'Sheyenne here; we were together.'

'Then why didn't you tell us this before, Doyle? Why run when the men came for you?'

'I panicked when I heard they were coming after me. You know as well as I do that rumours still mill about the circumstances of me late wife's death. I was afraid no-one would believe me... It's a good job Mr O'Sheyenne here was with me ... and Father Ryan of course.'

Donal nodded. 'It's a grave business, so it is... Tell them the other thing, Thomas, I'm sure they'll be wanting to hear it.'

Tommy paused, glancing at O'Sheyenne before looking at the Gardaí directly. 'Patrick hid something in the house. You'll find it behind the porridge box in the pantry ... it's a rope. A bloody rope.'

9

Father Ryan sat at his dark wooden desk in St Joseph's Orphanage and Home for Unmarried Mothers. It stood on top of a hill called the Five Acre Trees, though no local knew why it was named so; the hill was neither five acres nor had it ever held any trees for as far back as anyone could remember.

The building of St Joseph's was forbidding. Tall, dark and gothic. The unwelcoming black wrought metal gates were held together by a large heavy chain and allowed no unauthorised visitor in and no resident out. But it was here that Father Ryan liked to sit and think – undisturbed and without interruption. Today, however, was the exception to the rule. Instead of getting the peace and time to reflect as he'd hoped *and* needed, Father Ryan was facing Donal O'Sheyenne who stood stonily opposite him.

Father Ryan hadn't been sleeping well with what seemed like relentless pressure, and prayer had brought him little comfort, as it seldom did these days, and certainly no answers to his ever-increasing problems.

Sighing, he turned his attention back to Donal and to what he was saying.

'So you see, Matthew, it's all worked out well after all.'

Father Ryan's voice was emotionless. 'Not for

the Brogans, or for the boy.'

'He knew too much and rather than use the chance to work for me he began to sound off. These things have to be done.'

'Thomas Doyle is a rogue indeed to be part of your wickedness.'

'If I recall, it wasn't so long ago you needed him for your own ... how should I put it ... inconvenience.'

The priest craned forward, pointing his finger at Donal. 'How dare you! That wasn't the same at all.'

'You don't want me to talk about your secret, Matthew? I'm sure a lot of people in the village would be most interested in what the real Father Ryan is like.'

Like a man possessed, Father Ryan stood up from behind his desk and rushed over to where Donal stood; hissing out his words. 'Don't push me. You might think I haven't got what it takes to take on a man like you, but be careful, O'-Sheyenne. One day. Mark my words... Tread very, *very* carefully.'

Donal looked down at Father Ryan's clenched hands and grabbed them. He pulled the priest's scrunched-up fists to his own face to mockingly punch himself with them, then exploded into peals of belly laughter.

'Oh for the love of God! To be sure, Matthew, you've got a good craic in ye, so you have! I could swear those words were those of a fighting man. A threat no less. To me! Me! Donal O'Sheyenne.'

It was all too much for Father Ryan. He leapt again at Donal, pushing O'Sheyenne's six-foot-four frame backwards to snatch hold of the lapels on his trench coat.

'You'll pay for this, O'Sheyenne! I swear; you'll pay.'

Donal O'Sheyenne had been surprised many times and *by* many things in his life, but it occurred to him that, at that moment, Father Ryan attacking with such vigour and bravado was perhaps the biggest surprise he'd ever encountered, which was why it took him a moment to react.

However, instead of dishing out a ferocious beating – as he'd usually lay on any man who dared to challenge him – Donal O'Sheyenne found himself staggering around the room in blind hysterics, having to wipe away the streaming tears of laughter running down his face.

'Stop! Stop! No more! By Christ, you'll have me passing out. Look at me, man, I can hardly breathe for laughter!'

Incensed by the further mockery, Father Ryan – losing control altogether – ran up to Donal, who by now had collapsed with delighted amusement into a large brown leather chair.

About to bring down his fist with the full force of his anger and humiliation, Father Ryan froze as the door suddenly opened and a shrill voice sounded.

'Tea, Father!... What in heaven's name!' A nun stood open-mouthed in the doorway of the study carrying a pot of tea, a plate of biscuits and a look of horror on her face.

Father Ryan blushed and dropped his fist. 'Saints in heaven; have you ever heard of knocking, Sister?'

The nun said nothing, still startled by the sight which had greeted her.

Composing himself and wiping away the tears, Donal got up from the leather chair. He winked; charm snaking its way into his smile.

'Why, Sister Margaret, don't look so startled. Father Ryan was only showing me how the other day an ungodly scoundrel attacked a poor innocent man in the street.'

The nun's face drew both relief and concern from Donal's explanation. 'Why that's terrible. I hope the man was all right and a good Samaritan was able to intervene?'

Donal grinned. 'There was such a Samaritan, Sister. In fact, you're in the same room as him. It was Father Ryan who selflessly, and with no thought of his own safety, procured the man from a terrible fate.'

The nun's face lit up in pride. 'Is this true, Father? Did you really save a man from such a sinner? Were you hurt?'

Not letting Father Ryan reply, Donal spoke with mischief in his voice. 'Now, Sister, no more questions. We know how modest Father Ryan is.'

'But...'

Donal interrupted the nun. 'Enough, Sister. Do they not say flattery is a sin? "The Lord shall cut off all flattering lips, and the tongue that speaketh proud things." Psalm twelve, verse three.'

The nun giggled as she looked at Donal. 'Father O'Sheyenne! You really...'

'Sister Margaret, you know as well as anyone I left the church a long time ago. I am, unlike Father Ryan here, just an ordinary soul.'

79

'To me, Father, a man of God is what you'll always be. It was a sorry day when you decided to leave the priesthood; though the good Lord will never leave your side. Is there nothing that will tempt you to come back to our fold?'

Irked at this conversation, Father Ryan interrupted. 'Sister! That is quite enough! You can pour the tea and leave us, and I would be grateful if this discussion *wasn't* broadcast to the whole of St Joseph's.'

Donal smirked; amused at the discomfort of Father Ryan as he tried to pretend all was well.

'There's no need to be too hard on Sister Margaret, she was only interested to hear what a good Samaritan you were, as I was when I was sitting in the chair.'

Watching the nun finish pouring the tea, Donal addressed her. 'Thank you, Sister, you can leave us now.' The nun nodded, pushing the plate of biscuits into Donal's hands. As she turned to walk away, he stopped her.

'And, Sister?'

'Yes, Father O'Sheyenne?'

'You're looking lovely today.' Donal chuckled as Sister Margaret, blushing in pure delight, scurried out of the room.

Once the door was shut, Donal turned back to Father Ryan.

'Now where were we? Oh, I know. You were attacking me.'

Father Ryan, who by now had regained his composure, glared as Donal continued talking. 'I've got a married couple downstairs who've come for the Brogans' baby.'

'Have you no shame? Connor and Clancy are barely cold and you're already getting rid of their baby.'

'As you rightly point out, they're no longer with us, so I can't imagine they'll make great parents.'

'Are you even human?' Father Ryan shouted, his face red.

'I provide a service, and that doesn't come free; they know what they're getting themselves into.'

'I doubt that. These people are desperate for a child; they'll do anything to make it happen; even make a deal with the devil and I will no longer be a part of it; you will cease to use St Joseph's as your market place.'

Donal's voice was laden with mocking contempt. 'Now you know that's not possible, Matthew.'

Father Ryan placed his hand on his stomach. He was feeling unwell; it was more than he could cope with, and he was certain he was getting an ulcer. The whole situation was too much. It'd gone on long enough.

'It's over.'

Donal chuckled. 'Pardon? Me poor ears aren't hearing you correctly. I could have sworn you just said, *It's over.*'

'That I did, Donal O'Sheyenne. This all has to come to an end and here is the end. We had a deal.'

Donal nodded his head. 'We did indeed and it's worked out all round. You've got everything you wanted and so have I, so why make the walls come tumbling down, why bring trouble on yourself!'

81

Father Ryan stiffened. His voice was almost pleading.

'I did *all* you asked of me a long time ago. I've paid my dues over and over. I live with the shame of my sins, and I ask God for forgiveness and for him to allow me through the gates of heaven, and now what I ask of *you*, Donal O'Sheyenne, is to set me free from this ... this deal of *Shylock*.'

Donal sniffed, popping a whole biscuit into his mouth. He didn't usually go in for melodrama but it amused him how worked-up and dramatic Matthew Ryan was being. *Shylock*. The man who wanted a pound of flesh for every money owed. But Father Ryan was wrong to compare him to Shylock because he wanted more. Much more, and therefore he wasn't going to let the priest walk away from this.

'I think we both know that's not possible, Matthew. You're up in it as much as me.'

'It's wrong. I always knew it was, but...'

Interrupting, Donal smiled nastily. 'But you turned a blind eye to it back then because *you* needed something from me. And you got it. And now you owe me. Besides, what difference does it make? Childless couples get a new baby and I get what's owed.'

'How is it owed to you? They aren't your children. They're children of God and that being so no money should pass hands in the process.'

Donal sneered. 'Let's get something straight. They're hardly children of God. They're the bastard offspring of whores and drunks. The unwanted of the poor, the needy and simpletons. If they didn't go to the homes we arrange, they'd end

82

up in the industrial schools. So everybody wins.'

'What about the Brogans? Connor and his poor wife, did they win, Donal? They were good people and you killed them. Striking them down like stray dogs.'

Donal chuckled. 'That's what I always liked about you, Matthew. The way you put things. I remember your sermons were always passionate; full of the flames of hell, warning the sinners of their wrongdoings. I can see that hasn't left you.'

Father Ryan leant forward, trying to keep his temper under control. 'Is there nothing resembling decency in you? How you ever became a priest...'

Donal looked at Father Ryan flatly. 'I became a priest for the same reason you did, Matthew. For power. And I left for the same reason. I just wanted more of it.'

'Shame on you, O'Sheyenne.'

Donal took out a cigarette, holding Father Ryan's gaze as he lit it. 'The Brogans knew the rules. A charge for the baby and payment each week thereafter. If a payment can't be met, then the baby has to be returned. They didn't keep up with their payments.'

'So why couldn't you have just brought the baby back to St Joseph's?'

'To be sure, Matthew, no-one wanted things to end up like they did. Messy business all round. I liked Connor, I told that to his wife when we became ... *better acquainted*. They'd had the choice of returning the baby, but Connor didn't want to do that. *He* wanted to talk. Now have you ever heard of such a thing? Talk me business. I tell

83

you, has the world gone mad?'

Donal stopped to chuckle. He shrugged his shoulders. 'So what was I supposed to do? Ruin everything I'd worked for? They left me no choice.'

Father Ryan's face turned red. ''Tis not a man that stands before me. 'Tis Lucifer himself.'

Donal's eyes cut a stare. 'Is it, Matthew? Are you sure it's not Lucifer who you see in the mirror? Is it not you who has gone along with accusing Patrick Doyle for the killing of Connor Brogan and his wife? 'Tis nothing priestly about accusing an innocent young man.'

'The boy is *not* innocent,' Father Ryan answered. 'What he did to Mary can't go unpunished.'

'Maybe not, but as we both know Patrick is innocent on all other counts. You are more guilty than he.'

Father Ryan turned his back on Donal. He watched the rain beat against the paper-thin window as his mind took him to the events of the other evening.

The killings of the Brogans – Donal had given him no option *but* to lie about it. What else could he have done? And it wasn't as if Patrick was entirely innocent; sins of the flesh must be punished in the severest of ways, so perhaps he could live with the fact Patrick would be held responsible for the Brogans' killing. God would be his judge and he would make his peace with God.

And besides, even if he valued his own life so little as to let it be known that Donal O'Sheyenne was responsible for the murders, it wouldn't make a difference. No-one would want to listen. Only a fool would cross Donal O'Sheyenne; they'd be certain to meet the same grisly fate as the Brogans, whose only sin was to want a baby in their childless marriage, which he had helped to arrange. And then of course there was the other matter. The other matter he didn't like to think about. The one which had him in O'Sheyenne's grip.

No, there was nothing he could do about O'Sheyenne right now. He hoped there'd come a day when the man would be held accountable for each and every sin, but today was *not* that day.

Turning back round to face Donal, Father Ryan spoke, feeling more settled. 'Fine, Donal. You win, do what you must with the baby. But, as God is my witness, this will be the last.'

Donal winked. 'Matthew, we go through this every time. It'd be quicker all round if you didn't put us through this each time.'

'How dare you!'

Donal O'Sheyenne said nothing; getting up to walk for the door. Stopping suddenly he turned to look at Father Ryan. When he spoke, his voice was cold.

'"Be watchful. Your adversary the devil prowls around like a roaring lion, seeking someone to devour."' Then as if as an afterthought, he laughed, adding, 'Peter five, verse eight.'

Donal O'Sheyenne smiled at the couple as they stood cooing over the Brogans' baby. It was true, he was a handsome young fella, which was always good when it came to finding prospective parents. The price he charged for the child reflected that. It was much more difficult to get rid of the ugly ones and often they would be confined to a life in

85

orphanages and industrial schools.

'What happened to his real mother, Mr O'Sheyenne?' The prospective father spoke to Donal.

O'Sheyenne walked to the window. It always fascinated him as to why would-be-parents asked this question. He wasn't sure if it was simply out of curiosity or if they wanted to ease their consciences by being able to say to each other that they did the right thing in buying somebody else's child. Like a lot of the babies, the 'Brogans' baby' had been born to a sixteen-year-old girl, whose *boyfriend* had promised to marry her if she slept with him. Of course, like so many of the other girls in St Joseph's, she'd been unceremoniously dumped the next month, heartbroken and pregnant.

Her parents had been mortified with shame and had quickly packed her off to St Joseph's where she'd had the baby. The girl had wanted to keep him, but her parents had said that that was unthinkable, just as it was unthinkable for her to go back home. So the baby had been taken away and she'd been carted off to one of the Magdalene laundries run by the nuns, where she'd been ever since.

'Did she die?'

Donal turned back to the prospective parent. 'Excuse me?'

'Did the child's mother die? It's just, he's such an adorable baby, I couldn't imagine anyone wanting to give him up.'

With a wry smile, Donal answered. 'That's one way of putting it... Now, if you're happy with

86

him, we can go over the terms and conditions again.'

The couple nodded, beaming smiles. 'Oh yes, we'd love to have him. We think he'd fit right in.'

O'Sheyenne sat down behind his desk, playing with the paperknife. 'Good. Well, as I say, there's a one-off payment which you need to pay now, followed by two other payments a couple of months later. But you do appreciate if you don't honour the payments I'll have no choice but to bring him back to the orphanage and put him up for adoption again.'

'Oh, we'd never not pay, Mr O'Sheyenne. We want a baby so much.'

'I just don't want any misunderstandings, I has something similar quite recently...'

Encouraged by his wife, the man got out his chequebook and quickly squiggled the agreed amount on the cheque. He tore it off and pushed it across the desk to Donal.

'We'd like him. We're happy with all your terms.'

O'Sheyenne looked at the cheque then stretched out his hand to the man and winked.

'Congratulations; you're now the proud parents of this beautiful baby boy.'

10

Mary O'Flanagan covered her ears. She didn't want to hear anything else the Gardaí had to say. In fact she didn't want to look at them either; if she'd had it her way, she wouldn't be here at all. Though in actual fact, *here* was only the back room of the tiny hall running alongside the village bakery.

The back room of the hall doubled as everything. For plays, for cake sales, for council and church meetings, even a few times for evening mass when a large sycamore tree had fallen on the church and destroyed part of the roof. And now it seemed the room-doubled as a Garda station.

Mary glanced across to her mother who was looking stern, her expression full of shame and blame. It'd been at her insistence that Mary had come here. The Gardaí had already spoken to her, but now they wanted to ask her what seemed to be the same questions all over again.

Her father, Fergus, hadn't insisted, though only because he wasn't speaking to her. He hadn't spoken to her since *that* night, so he hadn't been able to insist on anything at all. The only thing he *had* done was cry. Cry and turn his head away when she walked into the same room as him.

She knew it was a sin to have sex before marriage.

She'd known about the sins of the flesh since

she was little, but she also knew her parents blamed her for what had happened and now, she was to blame Patrick, because that's what Father Ryan had told her.

She'd asked to see him, but they hadn't let her. Perhaps if she'd been allowed to speak to him, he'd have been able to tell her this was all a terrible mistake and explain what had really happened.

But now she was so confused about everything, she couldn't think straight. They kept on telling her over and over again how it was Patrick who'd done this to her, and now they were saying he had also killed the Brogans. None of it seemed to make sense.

She'd tried to tell her mother – who overnight had changed from the happy chatty person she loved into someone cold and harsh – that she really wasn't sure it was Patrick. But her mother had gone to get Father Ryan who'd once more explained she was being foolish to think otherwise, and that there was no doubt that it had been Patrick who had done this to her. And even though she didn't want to believe it, everyone had insisted there was no other explanation. So what other choice did she have than to believe it herself?

Ever since that night her love for the boy she was going to marry had turned into shame, hurt and pain. And as she sat in the back room, covering her ears, with judging and accusatory eyes turned on her, Mary O'Flanagan knew that, from this day onwards, she never wanted to hear the name of Patrick Doyle again.

Patrick wiped his eyes carefully. They were sore

89

from crying.

No-one had really told him what was going on and since *that* night, his whole life had been turned upside down. He'd been taken to the back room of the hall by the Gardaí, who had asked him about Mary and the Brogans. Later, they'd interrogated him about Mary again and when he'd asked to go home, they'd refused him, instead taking him in a car to some place he didn't know, to ask yet more questions about her.

No-one would tell him anything. And now he was locked up in a room, in a building, in a place he wasn't familiar with, listening to the sounds and screams of people he couldn't see. And although he was the grand age of sixteen, he was frightened.

Patrick heard a jangling of keys. The door opened and he was greeted by the sight of two priests robed in black from head to toe, with large wooden crosses and rosary beads hanging down to their beltlines.

The taller priest, whose head was shaved, displaying a large prominent scar, addressed Patrick 'Doyle, you're going to be moved to the west dormitory along with the other boys whose case is still being investigated by the Gardaí. You'll obey all the rules or face punishment. Do I make myself clear?'

Patrick's eyes widened with panic and for a moment he couldn't say a thing. When he was able to speak, his words came tumbling out.

'I never touched the Brogans! I didn't! I didn't! I swear, Father, it was nothing to do with me. You've got to believe me! You've got to.'

The sudden pain on the back of Patrick's head was almost unbearable as the smaller priest brought down the wooden paddle he kept on a long piece of string around his waist.

Patrick screamed out, cupping his arms around his head as his tears and blood fell to the floor.

'Enough of your impudence, boy. Here at Our Lady's you only speak when asked a direct question. Do you understand?'

Patrick nodded and as he did so he felt the pain of the paddle strike him again, though this time his arms – already holding his head – shielded him slightly.

'You were asked a question, Doyle. Nodding is for donkeys.'

Patrick wiped the tears away from his face. 'Sorry, Father. Yes, Father.'

Satisfied that Patrick was beginning to understand the rules of Our Lady's Industrial Reform School, both priests turned, walking out of the sparse room.

Quickly and empty-handed, Patrick followed. He touched the silver chain and cross round his neck which Mary had given him. He'd never taken it off since the time she had presented it to him on his birthday. That had been his happiest day and all he could do now was to hold onto the memories of it

Patrick had brought nothing with him and was still dressed in the same clothes he'd been wearing when the Gardai had come to his house. He was confused and scared. He needed to talk to someone; ask them to take him home, *ask* them to believe him. But who? There was no-one.

As he continued to think about the nightmare he found himself in, the fear rose up again and Patrick found himself having to breathe heavily in an attempt to stop himself from screaming.

'Doyle! Hurry up!' The priest's shouting startled him.

Jogging to keep up with the priests who strode along the long dark corridors with purpose and pace, for the first time Patrick was able to take in his surroundings. And what he saw, he didn't like.

The industrial school he'd been brought to was for the neglected, abandoned and unwanted, as well as for juvenile offending boys, and it was larger than any other building Patrick had ever seen. In fact, the largest building *he'd* seen was the community hall back in the village.

It was overwhelming. The maze of corridors weaved along, forking off into other identical corridors, which were lined with black bolted doors and steel-barred windows. There were locks and chains almost everywhere he looked. Paintings of priests looking fearsome and merciless hung from the dull mint green walls and oversized crosses were strewn everywhere.

Once outside in the large courtyard, the cold and rain hit Patrick, whipping into his face as he was marched across the parade ground. He saw a crowd of milling boys huddled together, trying to defend themselves from the Irish weather.

The boys varied in sizes and age but were all dressed in the same grey hessian trousers and shirts; misery was engrained in their dirty, strained faces. As he hurried to what he'd find

92

out later was the punishment wing, the other thing he noticed were the haircuts. They were short and crudely cut, with not one of the boys having their hair longer than half a centimetre in length. Absent-mindedly, Patrick touched his own thick head of hair. A sense of foreboding rushing into him.

'Hey, Culchie! What's the craic with those manky clothes you're wearing? Fallen out of the donation box, have we?' The call was from a boy who stood at the far side of the parade ground. His expression challenged Patrick. 'New boy. Oi! I'm talking to you!'

As Patrick turned, to look at the boy, the rest of the gang he was standing with began to laugh; pointing and staring at Patrick as if he were a clown in the circus.

Patrick's natural fighting instincts suddenly took over and without thinking, he responded. 'For sure, the only manky thing I see is your fecking face.' The moment Patrick had spoken, he regretted it. The two priests, who he had forgotten for a moment, swirled round. Their faces full of fury.

The punch to the side of Patrick's head floored him. He could feel the icy ground underneath as his hands scraped in the wet gravel in an attempt to get back on his feet. He was aware of the cat-calling from the boys and the seemingly distant, angry voices of the priests; admonishing him. A moment later, Patrick Doyle blacked out.

'To be sure, he thinks he's Sleeping Beauty.'
Patrick's eyes slowly opened and for one glorious

93

moment he thought he was back at his house, curled up in his own bed. But as the ice-cold cup of water hit Patrick, along with the sound of laughter, the stark reality of his surroundings came flooding back.

'He's awake! He's awake, Father Marley!' Patrick heard one of the boys shouting out in delight.

'Quiet, boy! Unless of course you want me to beat out the excitement of the devil in you!'

As Patrick lay on the bottom of the metal bunk bed, the priest's portly face came into view, looming and peering over, silently studying him.

A minute later, satisfied with the examination, the priest mused, 'You look fine, boy. I hope you're not a child who uses ill-health to justify slothliness. It is, as you know, a deadly sin ... or perhaps you don't. I was informed you come from a family of heathens. Those who have turned their back on Christ our saviour.' Then to himself, the priest said, 'Very sad. Very sad.'

After a moment of reflection by the priest had passed, he continued speaking to Patrick.

'Perhaps if this hadn't been the case and your father had been God-fearing you wouldn't have ended up here. Now get up, boy. There's a lot to do. For a start, your hair needs cutting. We can't live amongst vanity. Another deadly sin – almost as treacherous as the sins of the flesh; though you will, I know, understand a lot about *that* one.'

Patrick stared at the priest, puzzled by what he'd just said.

'Another thing which shan't be tolerated is touching yourself. That, boy, will *not* be stood for. A punishment fit for the sin will be deployed. Do you understand, Doyle?'

Patrick's face turned scarlet. 'Yes, Father!' The priest nodded, and with that he walked away, leaving Patrick surrounded by the curious stares of the other boys.

The inquisitive glances were broken by a bellowing, angry voice from the back of the dorm. The boys stepped aside, parting the way for the aggressor to appear.

'So this is the lad who thought he was good to taunt me. Let's see how hard you are now.'

Patrick recognised him as the boy from the parade ground. He stood facing Patrick, sinewy in frame but clearly able to handle himself.

Patrick got up from the bed, immediately feeling a shooting pain in the place he'd been punched by the priest, but he didn't let it show. He couldn't. He mightn't have ever been outside his own village before, and was admittedly ignorant in many ways of the world, but one thing Patrick Doyle *did* know was that to show weakness was to show you were inviting trouble.

Patrick glanced at the other boys; up close for the first time. They were all dressed in the same dull clothing with the same dull look in their eyes. How long they'd been here, Patrick didn't know, but it was clear it was every boy for himself.

There was no question of backing down from the challenger. It was obvious to Patrick the boy was looking for a fight whether he wanted one or not. Sighing with resignation and hoping it wouldn't come to blows, Patrick squared up.

'If I remember rightly, I was minding me own.

95

It was *you* who called me first. I'm not looking for a tear, but mind, I'll not walk away from one either. It's down to you.'

The boy looked at Patrick, weighing him up in his disdain. He turned his sneer into a contemptuous smile and as Patrick continued to stand his ground, he noticed there was a look of uncertainty in the boy's green eyes.

'Well, 'tis lucky for you I'm in a good mood, new boy, otherwise you may well have felt a bunch of knuckles down your throat.'

Patrick didn't say anything. He could tell the boy was going to leave it, and that suited him. He didn't need trouble, not with the boys and *certainly* not with the priests. All he wanted to do was get out of the place and go back home. The only thing he hadn't worked out was how the hell he was going to do that.

As the boy turned to go, he barked a warning to Patrick. 'But let me make it clear to you, new boy. It's me that runs this dormitory and I'll not have any country rat coming in to try to take over. They call me Killer, and to be sure, I'm not called it for nothing. You'd do well to remember that.'

Patrick stayed silent. He stared, watching Killer – who couldn't have been any older than he was – walk across to his area of the dorm.

Patrick was about to sit back down but, for no apparent reason, Killer struck out at another boy who'd been minding his own business lying on his bed. The kick was hard and cruel, carrying the weight of Killer's heavy boots and hatred behind it. From across the dorm, Patrick listened

96

as Killer taunted the younger boy.

'You grubby bleedin' nigger, get out of me fecking sight. I can't stand the sight of ye and the smell of ye is making me sick to my stomach.'

The boy scurried off his bunk bed, much to the amusement of Killer and his gang. Killer grabbed the boy by his shirt.

'Knock into me, will you? What were you trying to do, nigger boy? Looking for a fight?'

The boy's face was full of fear and his eyes darted about the room as Killer held him tightly. Patrick could see tears of terror rolling down his cheeks.

To the delight of the other boys, who cheered and bellowed and stamped their feet in encouragement, Killer's fist smashed into the boy's face, splitting open his lip.

The boy, his mouth covered in blood, began to talk, desperate to stop the unprovoked attack. He blubbed an apology to Killer, who stood with amusement on his face at the boy's obvious terror. The boy trembled as he spoke.

'Sorry, Killer... Sorry! I never meant to.'

'You never meant to what? Be a nigger?'

The roars of laughter sounded around the dormitory and, egged on by the boys' jeering, Killer slapped the small black boy around his face.

'Leave him alone!' It was Patrick who spoke. He walked up behind Killer, his fists clenched with anger.

'I *said* leave him alone.'

Killer grabbed the boy around his neck, putting him in a headlock before turning round to look at the person who dared challenge him. He sneered.

'I told you. I run this dorm; 'tis none of your business what I do to the nigger, but mark my words, you'll be next.'

Undaunted by Killer's threat, Patrick shouted. 'Me name's Patrick. Patrick Doyle, and I'll tell you again; *leave him alone.*'

Killer looked around at the other boys who were all entertained by the confrontation. 'And what are you going to do about it, new boy?'

'I won't have to do anything if you let him go. Pick on someone your own size, you bloody bollocks. Now leave him alone; otherwise 'tis you who'll get it.'

Killer didn't move. He grinned nastily and gripped the boy even harder so he squealed.

Patrick looked at the boy ensnared in the grip of this six-foot lanky boy. He saw the tears and the fear etched into his face.

'Let him go, you bastard!' Picking up a bible that lay on the small locker next to where he now stood, Patrick aimed and threw it with all his might, hitting Killer directly in the face.

The corner of the hardback bible caught Killer on his lip, squirting blood across and down his body. He yelled out, partly in surprise and partly in pain, cupping his hands over his mouth before unleashing his anger. His face was bright red and his eyes bulged as he screamed at Patrick

'Come here! Come back here!'

Killer dropped his grip on the boy, enabling the terrified child to wriggle free and scrabble to the safety of his bed. He then lunged at Patrick, taking a swing at his head. He missed; instead grabbing hold of Patrick's top and causing it to rip.

Patrick allowed his natural gift for fighting and his survival instincts to take over. He turned and head-butted Killer, splitting open the boy's forehead and causing a river of deep red blood to gush out.

Enraged, Killer swung at Patrick through searing pain to the soundtrack of cheering boys. His fist connected with Patrick's nose with rifle-like precision.

The pain took under a second to hit him, but instead of it hampering his efforts it drove Patrick on. His eyes widened and his fists beat as he jumped on Killer, battering him in a blind rage.

The two boys' blood and sweat combined together. Grappling arms, kicks and bites were all poured into the mix as they rolled on the floor, both determined to be the victor.

On the ground now, Patrick felt his sides being booted by the circle of other boys. He knew he had to get up if he were to stand a chance. With one huge effort and summoning the last of his strength, Patrick ground his elbow into Killer's face, damaging his already broken nose.

With Killer swathed in agony, it allowed Patrick to get up from the concrete floor. He leant over him and began to finish off the fight. He gave a final kick to his opponent, making it clear he was the winner.

Panting and exhausted, blood running into his mouth, Patrick now pointed at the other boys. He stood firm in front of the petrified young black boy as he spoke.

'This is to all of you. So listen carefully at what I'm saying. You leave him alone, do ye hear me?

Any of you come near him again. *Anyone.* I'll kill you, make no mistake.'

Patrick held the gazes of the other lads before turning round to look at the boy. He winked and got a grateful smile in return. The boy looked shyly at Patrick. He spoke quietly with a slight lisp. 'My name's Cabhan, but everyone calls me Cab.'

Patrick winced in pain as he wiped the running blood from his face. Putting out his hand he said, 'Well, Cab, it's good to meet you. My name's Patrick.'

The boy grinned, relief and gratitude coming out in the form of tears. 'Not as good as it is to meet you, Patrick. For sure, I'll never forget what you've done. Not for the rest of me life.'

11

It was the sixth night when Patrick was woken by Father Marley.

'Doyle? Doyle?'

Sleepily, Patrick answered. 'Yes, Father?'

'Come with me ... and be quiet and be sure not to wake anybody.'

Getting up out of his bed, Patrick followed the priest without question.

Father Marley led Patrick along the cold deserted corridors in the frayed cotton pyjamas they'd given him when he'd arrived.

At the end of one of the hallways was an

austere-looking brown door. Not usually afraid of many things, Patrick felt a chill of fear pass through him. Although he knew it was pointless, he began to back away.

Father Marley caught him by his arm, whispering, 'Hurry up, boy.'

The priest went through the door first, closely trailed by Patrick, who followed him down the shadowy stairwell. At the bottom Patrick was hit by a strong smell of cheap bleach. Again the priest hissed at Patrick.

'Come on. There's no time for loitering.'

Even though Patrick was wearing only his thin pair of pyjamas he was hot and he could feel the droplets of sweat running down his back as Father Marley took him into one of the basement rooms.

In the far corner stood five men. He recognised one of them. It was the priest with the prominent scar he'd spoken to on the first day. The others, Patrick hadn't seen before.

Silently, Father Marley walked towards Patrick He said nothing, only nodded to the other men who quickly came forward, grabbing both of Patrick's arms.

Instantly, Patrick began to wrestle with them but he was overwhelmed by their strength and number. As he was pushed down over a table Patrick felt his pyjama bottoms being yanked down.

An excruciating pain shocked through Patrick's body as one after another of the men took it in turns to sodomise him; tearing him apart with every thrust. As Patrick's screams of agony and terror were disregarded his soul was filled with vengeance which would never leave him, until the day he died.

12

Although she didn't know it, Mary O'Flanagan was doing only marginally better than Patrick. It'd been several weeks since the night in the woods, but it still haunted her and was as vivid and vicious in her mind as it had been the day it happened.

Often in the night, her thoughts drifted to Patrick and, although she wouldn't allow herself to dwell on him, she missed their friendship.

She'd heard they'd taken him to an industrial school in another county. But that's all she knew. She didn't know much even about what was going to happen to her; no-one would talk to her and she certainly wasn't going to ask questions.

She'd only found out about Patrick in passing when Father Ryan had stopped her after evening mass last week, enquiring if Patrick had told her anything that he had said was a secret. He hadn't, and even if he had, she wouldn't have spoken to Father Ryan about it.

She knew she'd never been clever – in fact the other children at school had made fun of her, calling her *muddled Mary* – but she did know there was more to why Father Ryan was asking her questions than just a pastoral interest. She didn't know quite how she knew, and she certainly couldn't attempt to explain it, but whenever she saw him now, she avoided him even more now than she'd done before.

Sighing, Mary went downstairs but stopped short of entering the parlour as she listened to her dad's raised voice.

'I don't want to lay my eyes on her. Each time I see her I think of the shame she's brought to my house. I want her gone. Gone!' Fergus O'Flanagan was shouting in anger, yet his true feelings were ones of desperation and sadness for his daughter. He just didn't know how to show it, nor did he know what he was going to do, so instead he resorted to the easiest of the emotions: anger.

'Fergus, try to calm down.'

'How can I calm down, Helen, when we have nothing less than Bathsheba in our midst?'

'Don't exaggerate, Fergus,' Helen Flanagan snapped at her husband. 'You sound like Father Ryan.'

The smashing of a glass prompted Mary to open the door. She was greeted by the sight of her harassed-looking parents along with something else, which sent a chill down her body. Cold fear ran through her.

'Ma, what's going on?' Her voice trembled. Even as she asked the question, Mary knew exactly what was going on, but hoped she'd be reassured by a different answer.

Helen O'Flanagan stood tight-lipped as she faced her daughter. 'These are the nuns from St Joseph's. They've come to take you, Mary. It's for the best.'

Mary screamed. She held herself, tears of

103

anguish down her face. She ran to her mother, grabbing hold and tugging on the flowered dress she was wearing.

'Please! Please! Ma, don't send me away! I'll behave; I'll do anything you ask me to. Anything.'

'It's gone past that, Mary. You should've have thought of your behaviour before you started to hang round with Patrick Doyle.'

Mary turned to her father. 'Daddy, please help me.' Fergus turned his back and shook his head, not wanting to acknowledge his daughter's terror.

Seeing her dad's reaction, Mary howled at the top of her voice as she continued to pull at her mother's clothing.

One of the nuns stood up and crossed over to where Mary was trembling in hysteria. The nun raised her hand, slapping Mary hard across her face; her voice spiked as she spoke, with anger flashing in her eyes.

'Mary O'Flanagan, you will refrain from that noise. You have brought shame on your family and you have no place in the community in your present state.'

'I didn't do anything! It wasn't my fault! I swear, Sister. I swear.'

The nun looked at Mary sharply. 'You shall address me by my full title... *Sister Margaret*. Do you understand?

Mary didn't say anything, only sniffed and wiped her nose as she bowed her head, too afraid to look at the nun who stood scowling at her.

Ignoring her daughter's distress, Mary's mother spoke up. 'Mary, no matter what you say about it not being your fault, you'd already invited the affections and attentions of that Doyle boy. You certainly aren't blameless in the whole affair. If you'd listened to Father Ryan telling you to stay away, this would *never* have happened.'

Mary's head shot up. She was about to say something but in the corner of her eye she saw the menacing figure of Father Ryan entering the room.

As he walked in, Mary noticed her mother's demeanour change into a quiet respectfulness as she fussed about the priest.

'Oh Father, it's so good to see you, take a seat. Take a seat. I hope you can talk some sense into Mary.'

Father Ryan's face was pinched but after a moment he smiled kindly, taking Helen's hands in his. 'I know this is difficult for us all, but you must try to be strong. It's not sense she needs, Helen; it's rules. Rules that the sins of the flesh shall not be allowed.'

It was all too much for Mary she began to sob loudly and then began to wail, touching her stomach and crying. It was only last week she'd found out that she was carrying a baby. The thought of being pregnant had never really crossed her mind.

'Calm down, child. Calm down!... Mary! I'm talking to you. Do you hear me?'

She spoke between her tears. 'Sorry, Father ... sorry.'

'You shall go to St Joseph's where you'll have the baby. After that, you shall be able to come home, if of course your parents will allow it.'

'What ... what about the baby, Father?'

Father Ryan was livid. It wasn't right for her to

worry about a child conceived in such a manner. 'What happens to the baby is no concern of yours, Mary.'

'But...'

'Mary O'Flanagan, I can see Sister Margaret has her work cut out with you. Hopefully by the time your baby's born you will have learnt your lesson.'

Mary's eyes were wide open. 'Won't I be able to come home before that, Father?'

'That will be impossible. Quite impossible.'

'No! It *is* possible.' All eyes turned to see Fergus standing by the door, clenching his hands together in anguish.

Father Ryan's eyes narrowed, not quite believing what he was hearing. 'Pardon?'

Asserting himself, Fergus cleared his throat. 'I said, my daughter *can* come home in between.'

Sister Margaret supported Father Ryan in his contempt at Fergus's suggestion. She spat out her words. 'That will *not* be appropriate. We cannot allow Mary to walk around the village in her condition. What message does it give out?'

For many years, probably as far back as he could remember, Fergus O'Flanagan had never stood up for himself, especially against Father Ryan. He'd been pushed around all his life and he'd no doubt that he'd continue to be pushed around, but today, as he hovered in the doorway facing the hostile, incandescent stares of all but Mary, Fergus O'Flanagan knew it was time to put his foot down. As much as he struggled to come to terms with what had happened to his beloved daughter – he was doubtful if he'd ever be able to speak to her properly again – he wasn't going to abandon her completely.

To the mortification of his wife and to the pride of his daughter, Fergus O'Flanagan stood tall, addressing the room.

'My daughter *shall* come home. Once a month. Father Ryan, I'll make sure she's kept away from the village but I will not turn my back on her. This is not up for discussion *or* negotiation.' And with his words ringing in everyone's ears, Fergus left the room without saying goodbye or looking at his daughter.

13

Just as everyone in the village thought they'd seen the last of the spring rains they started up again, and much to Father Ryan's annoyance the church roof began to leak once more.

With a groan of a man defeated, Father Ryan sat on the front pew of the eighteenth-century church, staring up towards the altar and listening to the drips of water raining into the metal bucket.

His mind wandered to Patrick Doyle. The business of what to do with him was taking too long. He was hoping it'd all have gone away by now. It'd been playing on his mind and he was sure this was the reason he couldn't find any salvation in prayer.

'Father.' The voice was rough and Father Ryan

jumped. The moment he saw who it was, he scowled.

'What on earth are you doing here, Thomas Doyle?'

'I was wondering if you'd heard how Patrick was doing?'

Father Ryan drew his body in tightly. 'I'm surprised you haven't written, yourself.'

Tommy sat down next to Father Ryan, causing the priest to shuffle along the pew to widen the distance between them.

'I don't think that's wise under the circumstance, do you?'

Father Ryan didn't speak for a moment; instead he nodded, contemplating Tommy's words.

'Well, Father?'

'Well what?'

'Have you heard how the lad's doing?'

Father Ryan looked at Tommy. He could smell alcohol and he could see his eyes were bloodshot. 'I have, and as far as I can gather from the priests all is well with the boy.'

'Well that's grand. Just grand.'

Father Ryan stood up to leave. He had things to do. Making his way down the aisle, he turned, annoyed to see Tommy still sitting firmly in his seat. The last thing he wanted was to leave a drunken man in the house of God. He spoke curtly.

'Now, will that be all, Thomas?'

It was a minute before Thomas Doyle stood up to face Father Ryan. His face bemused. His eyes cold and dark.

'No, it isn't, now you come to mention it. Actually it isn't.' Tommy stopped to grin, before saying, 'I'd like to make a confession... Forgive me, Father, for I have sinned.'

Father Ryan paced the floor of his living room. He'd sent his housekeeper, Helen, home. He needed to think and having her fussing around with badly made cups of tea was not conducive to contemplation.

He'd gone over and over it. Tried to ignore it. Put it out of his mind, but he couldn't, no matter how hard he'd prayed. So now there was only one thing for it. Only one person who could help him.

Putting on his coat, Father Ryan, not for the first time, hurried out into the pouring rain.

Donal O'Sheyenne sat in his conservatory smoking a Cuban cigar. It was something he liked to do. Something he always did. Every night at nine o'clock he'd stop everything to indulge in a habit he'd started the first time he'd killed a man; at around the age of fifteen.

Whatever else was happening, it had to wait whilst he smoked and savoured every last puff, and that included Father Matthew Ryan, who was now sitting opposite him looking very jumpy.

Leaning back, Donal smiled to himself. Matthew knew well enough not to interrupt him when he was enjoying his cigar. It always amused him, but today especially. It was clear Matthew had something on his mind. And the man was desperate to discuss it.

'Why, Matthew, you look like a man with something on yer mind.'

Father Ryan opened his mouth to speak but Donal held his hand up to silence the priest. 'Now, now, you can see for yourself I haven't finished me smoke. You wouldn't want to disturb a man in the height of pleasure. Why don't you do some of that praying you like to do so often? Purge some of those sins.'

Matthew Ryan stood up and scowled at the same time as Donal roared with laughter.

Under normal circumstances Father Ryan would've spoken to Donal, but he'd seen for himself what happened to the men who thought it was worth interrupting.

'Oh for the love of God. Go on. Go on. To be sure, Matthew, I can't enjoy my smoke with your face as long as Hag's Glen. Come on. I'm listening.'

Without hesitation, Father Ryan spoke. His words rushing out. 'I need your help. I've thought about it. I've prayed about it and I keep coming up with the same answer; but I need your help.'

It took only a heartbeat for Donal O'Sheyenne to break out into machine-gun laughter, incensing Matthew Ryan even further. 'I'm sorry, Matthew; I thought you said for a moment that *you needed my help.*'

'I know you find this amusing, Donal.'

Donal's face dropped. His voice was as cold as his stare.

'Amusing?... Amusing? I call it a fucking cheek. I'll give you this, you've got some front on ye.' Donal walked across to where Father Ryan stood uneasily and picked up one of the guns lying on the expensive yet garish marble coffee table. He

110

pointed it at Father Ryan.

'Where is your God now, Matthew?'

Father Ryan put his hands up; he dropped to his knees, trembling and kissing the cross which hung around his neck His voice shook as he spoke.

'Donal ... please... There's no need for this ... please... *Our...*'

'For the love of God, I'm only joking. Has everyone lost their humour? Get up, Matthew. Get up. Why, for the love of all that is holy, you're shaking like a leaf. Now of course I'll help you. That's what friends are for. We are friends aren't we, Matthew? Holy brothers, no less.'

14

Donal O'Sheyenne sat in the visitors' room of Our Lady's opposite Patrick Doyle.

'So how is it going, Patrick? You've lost some weight, so you have. There's nothing more than skin and bones.'

Patrick was staring at Donal. He'd no idea why he was here. When Father Marley had called him to say there was a visitor – his first since he'd arrived here a few months ago – he'd assumed it was his dad. The joy he'd felt at finally being able to speak to his father, to finally find out what was going on, had almost made him disobey and forget the rules of running along the corridor. But when he'd walked into the room and seen the tall, threatening figure of Donal O'Sheyenne, his heart had dropped and he'd almost screamed out in frustration.

'For sure you don't look pleased to see me, Patrick. Why, I've come all this way and I at least expected a smile.'

Patrick said nothing. His head was spinning. Life at the industrial school was getting more tortuous and the only thing keeping him sane was his friendship with Cab. An unlikely one, but it worked. He kept Cab safe from the bully boys of the school, and Cab nursed his mind and sometimes his body after the almost nightly trips to the basement.

'Come on, Patrick, if you don't say anything, I'll turn me tail around and go back home.' As if to prove his point, Donal got up. Patrick's hand shot out, grabbing hold of Donal's arm. His voice was strained and tears pricked his eyes.

'No... No. I'm sorry. I just wasn't expecting you.'

Donal winked, sitting down. 'Now that's better. A smile never hurt anyone did it?'

'I was expecting me da.'

'Your da? They really haven't told you anything, have they?'

Patrick nodded fervently. 'How is he?'

'Drunk.'

A flash of hurt came to Patrick's eyes, but he didn't react. The fight was beginning to drain from him and although Donal O'Sheyenne was certainly not someone he would've chosen to sit with for any length of time, desperation did strange things to people.

112

'I suppose you're wondering why I'm here?'

Patrick began to nod but stopped, having been indoctrinated by the priests that nodding was bad and that the consequences of such mannerisms would be a severe beating.

'Yes, Mr O'Sheyenne, I was,' he answered listlessly.

'Tell me something, Patrick. How are you enjoying yourself here? I hope the priests are treating you well?'

Patrick stared at Donal for a minute before he looked up towards the priests standing on guard in the far corner of the room. He caught Father Marley's cold gaze and quickly turned away.

He spoke in a hoarse whisper. 'They are, Mr O'Sheyenne.'

Donal gave a decisive nod. 'Good. Glad to hear it. Now then, I have a proposition for you.'

Patrick was taken aback. This man had made him watch as he'd slain Connor Brogan, and now here he was talking to him as if they were father and son.

As if reading his mind, Donal said, 'I can see you're wondering what this is about, especially as I know the last time we saw each other, there was … how shall I put it? Let's just call it a misunderstanding. Things were said, fingers pointed, but I'm sure you're not going to hold that against me once you hear what I've got to say.'

Donal stopped grinning at Patrick and leant closer; his eyes twinkling in delight.

'I tell you what, Paddy boy; I'm partial to a good guessing game so I am. I'll give you three goes. You need to guess why I'm here. Fail to

113

guess, then I'll stand up and walk away and you will not see me or the outside world for a very long time... So go on, guess.'

Patrick looked on in horror. No part of him thought Donal was joking. But he had no idea. How could he? How could he know why a man like Donal O'Sheyenne had come to see him instead of his dad?

'I ... I don't know.'

'That's one guess.'

Patrick's face was full of fear. 'No! No! I was only saying I don't know. That wasn't a guess.'

Donal studied his nails. 'I make the rules, Patrick, not you. And *I* say, that was a guess. So now you've got two more goes. Use them carefully.'

Patrick's eyes darted around, unformed thoughts rushing through his mind. 'Is it about Mary? Has something happened to Mary?'

Donal's head flicked back as he roared with amusement.

'You know nothing, do you? But no, that's not why I'm here. Now then, this is me favourite part, Patrick; when there's only one guess left and there's a man staring down the barrel of a gun. It always amuses me to see the fear in their eyes as I pull back the trigger. Then bang. Kiss goodnight.' Donal stopped again; he looked round then whispered. 'You see, Paddy boy, I have no doubt what sort of time you're having here. I had the misfortune of knowing Father Marley a long time ago, and I know what kind of ... tastes he has. So make this guess good, Paddy. Make it good.'

It was too much for Patrick. He broke down, his hands covering his face as the tears ran through his fingers. His body shook, racked with the fear and pain of the last few months. His voice was weak and his vulnerability was in every word. 'Help me ... help me. Get me out of here.'

'Pardon?'

Patrick drew up his hunched body, staring at Donal. 'Get me out of here.'

A wide grin spread across Donal O'Sheyenne's face. He laughed hard, joining Patrick in his tears.

'Why, Patrick Doyle, for there must be a God looking over ye. You guessed it. Right on your last chance, you got it. That's exactly why I'm here, Paddy boy. To get you out of here. Tonight.'

Stunned disbelief hit Patrick's face. 'But why?'

'Let's just say the Lord works in mysterious ways.'

Half Patrick's thoughts were on what Donal was saying, but the other half was on the fact that O'Sheyenne himself was a cold-blooded killer, and as such there was a new kind of fear beginning to grow in him at the thought of having anything to do with this man. But then, how bad could it be? Surely even Donal couldn't be worse than another night in the industrial school and Father Marley.

Patrick spoke in a hush. 'And you're really going to help me?'

Donal nodded. He sniffed, slightly bored now. 'That I am. That I am. Now, I'm not a man to repeat meself, so you need to listen very carefully to what I'm about to say.'

Cabhan Morton sat on the bottom of the grey

115

metal bunk beds, watching his friend brimming with excitement. He hadn't quite grasped the full gist of what Patrick was trying to say, but he did understand that the sinking feeling he had in the pit of his stomach was directly related to what Patrick was telling him.

'So it's great, Cab. Great. Of all the people. Him. Donal fecking O'Sheyenne. I can't quite believe it. And once I'm over that wall, Cab, then Our Lady's and that fecking bastard, Marley, will be only a memory to me. Isn't it great, Cab?'

Cab gripped hold of the thin sheets on his bed. His throat prickled as he fought back the tears. He looked up at Patrick, staring into his blue eyes. Staring into the face of the only friend he'd ever had in his life.

As he continued to stare at Patrick, Cab croaked out the desperate words, 'Take me with you, Paddy. Don't leave me here.'

It was only in that moment that Patrick Doyle realised he hadn't stopped to think how Cab was feeling. He looked at his friend's face, his black velvet skin, and he saw the crushing hurt in his eyes. 'Cab... I'm sorry. I should've thought how you'd feel.'

Cab's brown eyes were bright; slight hope returning. 'So take me with you then.'

Patrick sat on the bed next to Cab. His voice was low as he glanced around the dormitory.

'I can't, Cab. I'm sorry. Jaysus. I'm so sorry.'

'But why? I won't be any trouble. I swear.'

The guilt hit Patrick. The thought of leaving Cab to the mercy of the boys along with the mercy of the priests was too much for him. His

116

pain for his friend turned to anger.

'By Christ, Cab. Don't look at me like that. I've looked after you when no-one else bothered. Why can't that be enough? Can't you just be happy for me?'

The tears rolled down Cab's face. 'But I *am*. I *am* happy for you. The idea you'll be able to get away from Father Marley makes me want to laugh out loud, so it does. To see his face when he realises you've gone. But, Paddy, I can't be here without you. I just can't... I'll die without you.'

Patrick grabbed Cab by his shoulders, squeezing them tightly. 'Listen to me. You'll be fine. Do you hear me? You'll be fine. I'll never forget how you've looked after me. I owe you, Cab. I won't forget ye. I swear. I'll write to ye when I've sorted meself out and when it's time for you to leave this godforsaken place, you come to me.'

Cab's head dropped down. 'You know I'll never get out of here, Patrick. I can't do it any more. Especially without you.'

Patrick shouted; he didn't want to hear it, especially as he knew Cab was speaking the truth. He raised his voice.

'Enough, Cab! Enough! Is it me heart you're trying to tear out?'

'What's going on over there?' Father Marley entered the dorm just as Patrick raised his voice. 'Well, Doyle?'

Patrick locked eyes with Father Marley but, instead of the usual fear, Patrick's eyes held a challenge.

'Nothing.'

The strike across Patrick's face was hard and

cruel but he didn't flinch. He ground his teeth, savouring the moment. Savouring the pain. Things were going to be different now. By midnight, he would be gone.

Father Marley raged. 'Haven't you learnt your lesson yet, Doyle? How many strikes in the name of the Lord will you need to break the spirit of the devil?'

Defiantly, Patrick answered. 'I don't know, Father. You tell me. Perhaps there's nothing you can do when the devil lives inside ye. Maybe the devil knows evil when he see it.'

For a moment, Patrick thought Father Marley was going to hit him again but the priest turned away, walking into the middle of the room to address the whole of the dorm.

'Right, lights out, boys. I shall be patrolling the halls tonight and I do not want to hear *any* talking, otherwise the appropriate punishment will be employed. Do I make myself clear, boys?'

A unison of 'Yes, Father' echoed round the dorm before the lights went out and every boy fell silent.

As his eyes became accustomed to the darkness, Patrick could make out the ceiling of the room. He knew exactly what he had to do. Donal had warned him not to fall to sleep but there was no way that that was going to happen. This was his chance; probably his only chance to get out of the hell which had been his home for the last few months.

Waiting in the black of the night, Patrick could hear the suppressed but heart-rending tears of Cab. He hated himself for the pain his friend was in, but there was nothing he could do. It was about saving himself now. Putting his hands over his ears to block out the sound, Patrick Doyle turned over and began the countdown to freedom.

The chapel bell struck eleven forty-five and Patrick sat bolt upright. The moonlight was streaming through the window of the dorm and he could see the moon high in the sky. It was time.

Taking a deep breath to slow down his pounding heart, Patrick slipped off the bed. As he moved away, he felt his leg being pulled.

'Patrick, can't I–'

'Don't say it, Cab. Listen, I'll write.'

Patrick could see the white of Cab's eyes in the darkness. He turned away quickly, not wanting to witness his friend's turmoil, but Cab's strained voice made him turn back once more.

'Paddy; good luck ... and thank you. Thank you for being my friend.'

Patrick said nothing. With Cab's voice echoing in his ears, he hurried out of the dorm.

Outside in the corridor, he pressed his body against the wall, wanting to stay in the shadows. The plan was to meet Donal at the garden gate, and all he had to do was get there.

Creeping past the other dorms, Patrick refused to allow in the thought of what would happen to him if he were caught. The idea of the brutal punishments which would be administered drove him on.

Through the labyrinth of corridors adorned with religious trappings, sinister in the shadowy night, Patrick made his way towards the grand hall which would take him out into the garden. Then to the gate of freedom.

Coming round the corner, Patrick froze. He could hear the distant voices of some of the priests. Not just that, they were getting closer.

The grand hall was only metres ahead but Patrick knew all too well how the large dark mahogany doors creaked and whined as they opened. But if he stayed where he was, here in the shadow of the moon, there was no question of him not being seen.

The voices became louder. He had to make a decision quickly. Either chance them turning off towards the chapel or chance them coming down the corridor and him being caught.

Making up his mind, Patrick looked both ways. He darted along the remaining part of the corridor, flinging himself on the door and pushing it wide open as it creaked, seemingly louder than Patrick had remembered.

There was no doubt that the priests had heard the doors. Glancing over his shoulder, Patrick's stomach turned as he saw the looming figures of three priests. They were right behind him and there was no way he could make it out of the grand hall window without being seen.

Quickly he threw himself under one of the long dining-room tables, sliding himself under the purple drapes of the tablecloths. His body shaking with fear.

A minute later, the lights were flicked on.

'Hello?' Patrick recognised the voice of Father Marley and he felt sick.

'Is anyone in here? Show yourself now!'

To Patrick Doyle, every breath he took sounded as if he were shouting. Afraid that the fear gripping his body would overwhelm him and make him cry out, he placed his hand over his mouth, closing his eyes in a desperate bid to calm himself.

He listened to the footsteps of Father Marley walking round the grand hall, his shoes squeaking on the highly polished floor.

A moment later he saw the black leather of Father Marley's shoes stopping next to the table he was crouching beneath. His breathing shortened as he heard one of the other priests talking.

'It's more likely they ran out of the hall than ran in.'

'You're probably right. Come, I'll make that tea I promised for you.'

Even after the lights in the hall had been switched off by the priests, Patrick stayed frozen with fear. Terrified that if he moved Father Marley would appear like an apparition.

It was the bell of the chapel striking midnight which jogged Patrick into action. He scrambled out from underneath the table, remembering the words of Donal O'Sheyenne, who'd warned him that if Patrick wasn't there on time, he would go without him.

The window of the great hall didn't take much force to break. The wooden chair shattered it, cutting through it as easily as a knife through water.

Patrick pulled himself up, using one of the wooden chairs to step on. Grabbing the sides of the window frame, he ignored the sharp glass cutting into his palms as he jumped down, landing hard on the pebbles below. His only focus was on getting to the garden gate.

He ran across the grass, tripping over himself in his speed. He could see the gate in front of him. This was it. As he approached he saw the gate open and the tail, dark-clad figure of Donal O'Sheyenne standing in the entrance holding a set of keys for the gate.

'For a minute I thought you weren't coming. I was about to go and leave ye.'

Patrick's forehead dripped with sweat and for the first time he felt the sting of his damaged hands. Donal grinned.

'Ready to get to freedom, Paddy?'

Patrick nodded, catching his breath as he followed Donal into the deserted lane which ran by the side of the industrial school. Getting to the car, Patrick turned to take a last glance at the vast, sprawling building where he'd suffered un-imaginable torture.

Turning away, he looked at Donal waiting by the car.

'Come on, get in, Paddy. We've got a long trip ahead of us.'

Patrick held his hand out. 'Wait. Can you wait?'

Donal's face had a look of puzzlement. 'What?'

'Just wait ... wait. And if you can't, just go.' Without further explanation, Patrick bolted back through the gate, hurtling across the grass as quick as he'd come. He saw the broken window of the grand hall and, dragging the bench underneath it for extra height, Patrick scrambled back into the hall.

Patrick's heart raced as he ran back along the

corridors, back through the labyrinth, but this time he didn't feel afraid, only determined.

Bursting back into the dorm, Patrick charged towards the bunk bed in the corner.

'Well, come on then if you're coming!'

'You…You came back for me?' Cabhan Morton sat up in his bed, tears glistening in his eyes. 'I knew you would. I knew it. I knew you wouldn't have left me. I'll never let you down, Paddy. I'll give me life for you. Just you wait and see.'

Patrick grinned. 'Do you mind if we save the speeches till we're out of here, then you can pour your words on me whilst I think of how much an eejit I was to come back for ye.'

Cab smiled back, knowing Patrick was kidding. He dashed out of bed, following his friend under the curious eyes of some of the other boys who'd woken up.

Alongside Patrick, Cab looked tiny. His diminutive frame was thin and undernourished from years of being in the industrial school; he'd been given up at three by a mother who didn't want him.

'Are you sure we won't get caught?'

Patrick shook his head kindly as they made their way along the corridor. 'We will if you keep talking. Come on.'

Patrick picked up his speed. He didn't know why but he was brimming with confidence, the fear of being caught slipping away as they ran into the grand hall. They were nearly there now.

He glanced at Cab. He knew he couldn't have lived with himself if he'd left him here. Each day his friend seemed to be disappearing right in front of him as the brutality of the place slowly killed him.

Getting to the broken window, Patrick whispered. 'I'll get up first, then I'll pull you up.'

Cab nodded, looking smaller than ever as the fear gripped his body. Patrick pulled himself up, this time grimacing at the pain as the glass dug into the already deep bloody wounds on his hands.

'Right, give me your hand, Cab.'

Cab stretched up but screamed as he felt his body being pulled back. It took Patrick a moment to understand what was happening. There behind Cab was Father Marley, gripping onto him.

The priest's voice was cold and angry. 'Come here, boy!'

Cab was terrified. He stared up at Patrick who was desperately trying to pull him up.

'Help me, Patrick! Help me!'

'Did you really think you can escape, boy!'

Patrick bellowed at the priest as he watched him trying to pull Cab down. 'Let him go. Let him go!'

With one last huge effort, and just as the far doors of the great hall opened and four priests ran towards them, Patrick pulled Cab up, managing to release him from the grip of Father Marley.

Patrick was aware the priests were only seconds behind him. He heard their shouts and orders, yelling for him to stop, but he didn't turn round, knowing that once he was out of the window, the likelihood of them catching him was slim.

Slamming down on the grass, he picked up Cab, dragging him up by his arm.

124

'Keep going! Keep going!' Patrick glanced to the side and saw tears running down Cab's face as they darted across the grass. He also saw the kitchen door fling open and a stream of priests hurtling out to catch them up.

For Patrick now, it wasn't about saving himself any more; it was about saving Cab. With that thought in his mind Patrick drew on every bit of strength he had to reach the garden gate, praying Donal would still be there.

Through the gate they ran, and a few feet away was Donal's waiting car.

Patrick swung open the door, literally pushing Cab in head-first.

'Drive, Donal, drive!'

'Why, Paddy boy, I thought you'd never ask.'

As the red lights of Donal's car faded into the distance, Father Ryan stepped out of the darkness from the nearby woods. He stood and watched, a self-satisfied look on his face. He shook his head, pondering. The path of the Lord was an odd one and often a tricky one but, for the first time in a long time, he felt a sense of grace. A sense of peace at what he'd done. Yes, Father Matthew Ryan was indeed certain there'd be a place in heaven for him after all.

15

Patrick Doyle sat in stunned silence as he watched the lights of Kerry rush past. He glanced down at Cab, who was fast asleep across his lap. It was the first time he'd known his friend to sleep so soundly. Peaceful and safe. Unlike the feeling he had in his heart as he listened to Donal's tale of Mary.

'Pregnant? *How?*'

Donal's high-pitched laughing startled Cab slightly from his sleep but he was soothed by the reassuring hand of Patrick's on his head.

'Now, that's a joke if I ever heard one, Paddy. And you say it with such conviction. I like a man with humour. You and me are going to get on just great.'

Patrick held Donal's stare as he peered at him in the rear-view mirror of the car. 'By Christ, Paddy boy, you're serious about Mary, aren't you? They all said...' Donal's voice trailed off.

'I want to go and see her.'

Donal shook his head. 'Now you know that's not possible. You've got a ferry to catch. It's bad enough that you bring the nig-nog along with ye, let alone do a detour.'

'Don't call him that,' Patrick barked. 'His name's Cabhan.'

Donal smiled, taking in the flash of anger in Patrick's eyes.

'I like you, Paddy. You've got fire in your belly and you've got the balls to go along with it; but as for going to see Mary, that won't be happening.'

'I said, take me there. I need to see her.'

Donal's voice became threatening. 'And *I* said, that won't be happening. We've got a long drive to the port and they'll be looking for you.'

The quiet, menacing whisper into Donal O'Sheyenne's ear surprised him almost as much as the sharp piece of glass from the broken window, held against his throat.

'I want you to drive me to Mary. I'm not afraid of you, Donal. Not any more. Once upon a time just your name alone would've frightened me, but after a few months inside that place, it's surprising how much a person can change. The kind of fear you experience there has nothing on you. *Nothing.* So I'll say it once more, only this time you're going to do as I say. *Take me to Mary.*'

Donal O'Sheyenne pulled on the handbrake; screeching the tyres to a grinding halt. Carefully he moved his head to the side, aware of the glass still pressed against his skin.

'Paddy?'

'What?'

A loud roar exploded from Donal's mouth. Bursting laughter which shook the car from side to side, rocking the motor vehicle as tears rolled down his face. He banged his chest trying to catch his breath but struggled. The sight of Cab sitting up in the back sight made him laugh harder, sending near hysteria through Donal's veins. Patrick and Cab watched, fascinated by the man's manic hysterics.

Wiping away his tears, eventually Donal calmed down enough to speak.

'Fine. Fine. I'll take you. Just for that craic alone, I'll take ye.' Then Donal's face dropped. He grabbed hold of a distracted Patrick, pulling him over the front seat and disarming him of the shard of glass from his hand to press it into Patrick's cheek.

'But if you ever pull a stunt like that again, I'll slash you and your nigger friend here from head to toe. Understand?'

Patrick's eyes were wide open. He nodded quickly.

'Yes ... yes.'

Putting the car into gear Donal patted Patrick on the back.

'Oh by Christ, Paddy boy. You and me, we're going to get on just fine, so we are... Come on then, let's get you to this girl of yours.'

Mary O'Flanagan lay in her bed. Once more refusing to think of Patrick. Once more refusing to acknowledge that she had doubts it'd been Patrick who'd attacked her in the woods that night. But as she lay in the poky room that she shared with four other girls at St Joseph's, she hated what her life had become, and the only way for her to deal with it was to hate the one person she'd really loved – Patrick.

Since she'd been at St Joseph's she'd only been home a couple of times; not because she wasn't allowed to, but because she couldn't bear to see the look on her da's face as he gazed in horror at her growing belly. The disgust and contempt she'd seen in his eyes had sent her running back to St Joseph's. Running back to the cruel vicious nuns, because anything was better than seeing the pain in her father's eyes.

Mary sighed, placing her hand on her distended belly. She was almost due. The months had passed so quickly but, instead of hating the growing life inside her, she'd begun to love it. Each kick, each turn of the baby warmed her heart.

But what chilled it was the fact that time wasn't on her side. Within six weeks or so she'd have her baby and then, as decided by Father Ryan and her parents, and without her say-so, she was supposed to give her or him up and get on with her life as if nothing had happened. But as Mary lay listening to the sound of the rain, the tears trickled down her cheeks; she knew she wouldn't be able to do what was expected of her.

'Mary? Mary?' The voice came from the shadows of the room. Mary sat up, terrified the nuns had been right after all and the devil had come to take her soul.

'Mary! It's me, Patrick!'

Mary gasped, slamming both hands over her mouth, a mixture of fear, delight, anger and surprise rushing through her body.

Patrick stepped further into the room, the moonlight lighting him up. His face shone at the sight of Mary and he ran to her as Donal O'Sheyenne stood back watching the pair together. He spoke to Patrick quietly.

'Paddy, you've got five minutes. Nobody will think it's odd me being here but we don't want to

129

hang around.' He stopped then tipped his hat to Mary. 'Howya, Mary. Almost ready to drop I see.'

Donal walked out of the room, leaving a stunned Mary to stare at Patrick. Not wanting to wake the other girls, she hissed through gritted teeth: 'What are you doing here? I thought you were in the industrial school; locked up where you belong.'

'I was, Mary, but I had to get out of there... I had to come and see you.'

'Have you no shame, Patrick Doyle? Would you come and taunt me after doing this? Weren't you satisfied with what you did to the Brogans? You had to hurt me as well... If you don't get out, I'm going to scream. Do ye hear me?'

Patrick shook his head; he knelt down by Mary's feet.

'Mary. Please. I never knew. Nobody's told me anything about what's been going on. I only found out about what had happened to you tonight.'

Mary's voice went higher as her face went red with anger.

'Don't lie to me. The whole of Kerry knows what you've done. You're evil, that's what you are. The Brogans and then me. *Me*, Patrick. *Me*... I thought you were my friend; I thought you loved me. We were going to get married.'

Patrick kept shaking his head. 'Mary please. Connor and Clancy Brogan wasn't anything to do with me. It was O'Sheyenne. I saw it with me own eyes.'

Mary looked at Patrick with scorn. 'Yet here you are hanging about with him.'

'Mary, *please*. You've got it all wrong.'

'Have I? Don't pretend. You were seen. You were *seen* by your da running away from the Brogans' house. All the time pretending it was someone else. How could you? Did you really think you'd get away with it? Did ye?'

'Mary...'

'Don't think I'm not going to call the nuns. Don't think I'm not going to scream.'

'Please, Mary! You've got it wrong! Me da must've got it wrong. I didn't hurt anybody.'

But Mary was on a roll and had no intention of listening to anything he had to say.

'And this, Paddy? *This.*' Mary pointed at her stomach. 'Did you think so little of me to not only take the lives of innocent people but to ruin my life as well? All those dreams we had. All those plans.'

He spoke gently. 'Me Mary? I loved ye. It wasn't me. I wanted to marry you. I *still* want to marry you ... whoever it was who did this to ye, I'll hunt them down. I'll kill them for doing this.'

Mary's body shook with her sobs. 'Why are you doing this to me? Why are you lying to me?'

Patrick started to cry with Mary. 'I wouldn't do this. Not hurt ye. *Please,* you've got to believe me.'

For a moment Mary thought of the Patrick she used to know. The Patrick who'd made her laugh. The Patrick who'd cared about her when it felt like no-one else did. But then her hurt and pain, along with her lost dreams, turned once more to anger.

She raised her voice. 'Get out! Get out! I never want to see you again!' The other girls began to

131

stir in their beds, making Patrick look round fearfully.

'Please, Mary. Quiet! Someone will hear ye.' Patrick rocked on his knees. He put his head in his hands. None of it made sense. None of it.

Alerted by Mary's cries, Donal walked back into the room.

'Paddy boy, we have to go... Paddy. Now!'

'How can I leave her like this? I need to find out who did this to her. I need to show her it wasn't me.'

'There's no more time; we have to leave. You can think about all this when you're well away from here.'

Patrick turned to look at Mary, his eyes pleading with her. 'Come with me, Mary. Come with me. I'm going to England.'

'I'd rather be dead than go anywhere with ye. I hate you! I hate you, Patrick Doyle!'

Tears pricked Patrick's eyes. He grabbed hold of her hands. 'Once I'm gone, I won't be able to come back. I won't even be able to write to ye. They'll be looking for me, but I swear I haven't done anything. I swear. Just come, Mary.'

Donal pulled Patrick by his arm. 'You've had enough time, Paddy. Don't be a fool – unless of course you want to go back to the industrial school.'

Patrick knew Donal was right; he began to walk away but not without imploring Mary: 'Mary, listen to me. Come to England and you can have the baby. They won't let you keep it here. You know that. Come with me and I'll help ye. We'll be in England before sunrise. We're going to get the ferry tonight. Please, Mary, I love ye.'

There was a flicker of something in Mary's eyes and, just for a moment, Patrick thought she was going to change her mind; but instead she opened her mouth and began to scream.

Outside in the car, Patrick took one last look at St Joseph's. In his heart he knew this would be the last time he'd see Mary. Absent-mindedly he touched the chain and cross round his neck as he often did for comfort. But there was nothing comforting about it any more. He didn't want to be reminded of her; it hurt too much. Sadly and slowly, and for the first time since she'd given it to him, Patrick took off the chain, placing it in his pocket and vowing to himself he'd never wear it again.

16

Mary O'Flanagan was miserable. She'd been miserable since *that night*, but her misery had deepened since she'd seen Patrick. In fact it had rooted itself in her very soul and now she found she couldn't go through more than ten minutes without thinking of him.

It'd been a month since she'd seen him and, as was to be expected, his escape from the industrial school had been the conversation of the village and St Joseph's since then. Sister Margaret had questioned her, her parents had questioned her, and once again she'd been left with the feeling it

133

was somehow her fault. And as Mary sat watching her father chop wood and try to ignore the fact that she even existed, part of her wished, for all he was and for all he'd done, that she'd gone with Patrick when she'd had the chance.

The more she thought about it, the more she realised the chance she'd thrown away and the further she sank into the grips of deep misery. Going to England with Patrick had been the only opportunity she had been given to keep her baby.

'Da?' Silence.

'Da?' Silence. It was the same each and every time she spoke to her father. To get him to say anything she had to speak to him several times before eventually she'd get some sort of noise from him: a grunt; a moan; a sigh. But that was it. Never anything else. Having no success with getting any conversation out of her father, Mary headed out into the field and up towards the woods.

It was raining but it felt good to be outside. Mary could see the woods in front of her but she decided not to go any further; she hadn't been in them since *that night* and she doubted she ever would.

In the daylight they looked harmless – swaying trees arching over dense grass and bracken – yet for Mary they held so much fear as well as sadness.

She'd begun to blame herself; angry she'd made the decision to go into the woods *that night*. If she'd listened to what Father Ryan had told her about being a God-fearing girl, none of this would have happened.

She breathed deeply, feeling a pain in her chest.

Each time she thought of Patrick, the pain would come and she'd have to sit down.

Hearing a sudden noise, Mary's head shot up. From behind the largest of trees she saw the figure of a man, though who it was she couldn't make out. Her heart began to race and she started to back away. About to turn and run in fright, she stopped as she recognised him, her tension draining away. She smiled. 'Howya, Mr Doyle.'

Thomas Doyle stumbled out of the woods, looking blurry-eyed. He held a bottle of whiskey in his hand. Taking a swig, he slurred his words. 'I'm fine, Mary; it's good to see ye.' He took a step forward towards her.

Biting her lip, she spoke quietly. 'I don't suppose you've heard from Patrick, have ye?'

Tommy snorted, his voice loud and raucous. 'I won't be hearing from him; none of us will... Good luck to him!' He raised the bottle in the air, gazing up to the sky.

Not wanting to but unable to help herself, Mary started to cry. Tommy reached out his hand, wiping away her tears.

'Now, what's all this for?'

'I miss him, Mr Doyle, but I hate him at the same time.'

Tommy nodded his head, pulling Mary in for a tight hug.

'You'll get over him, Mary. Come here.'

Feeling uneasy, Mary tried to push Tommy away but he squeezed her harder.

'Mr Doyle, *please* ... you're hurting me.'

'It'll be fine, Mary. Keep still.'

'Mr Doyle! Let go!'

Tommy's hands began to wander over Mary's body. He grunted as he nuzzled his face into her neck. 'Don't struggle, Mary. Shhh ... don't struggle.'

Mary felt Tommy's hands beginning to lift up her dress. She fought harder; twisting and twirling to get out of the unwanted embrace. As she did so, Tommy growled. 'What's the matter? Stop being a silly girl.'

Mary was sobbing. 'I don't want this, get off me ... please, please get off me!'

'You didn't complain so much the last time.'

'What?'

A grin spread over Tommy's face. 'You didn't struggle so much last time.'

Mary's face drained pale white. Horror and terror at Tommy's words as the realisation of what he was saying hit her.

Tommy touched Mary on her stomach. A cruel edge to his tone. 'How is the baby, Mary? It would be nice if it's a boy, especially now Patrick's not around.'

She shook her head, putting her hand across her mouth.

'It was you!... It was you! No... No... No.'

Tommy winked. 'Yes, yes, yes.'

'But everyone told me it was Patrick... Father Ryan said... He said to me, it was Patrick.'

Tommy laughed. 'He may well have told you that, but he knows differently. I confessed me sins to him just before Patrick ran away from the industrial school.'

She screamed, turning to run. Faster and faster through the fields, along the tiny lanes of the village and up towards the rectory.

She felt a terrible pain cut down her side and for a moment she had to stop to catch her breath. She could see the rectory just in front of her and she ran, banging on the door with both fists, screaming Father Ryan's name.

The door was opened by Father Ryan's housekeeper, Helen O'Flanagan. Her mother.

Helen stood there looking bewildered at the sight of her daughter, hysterical and shouting inaudible words.

'For the love of God what is it, Mary? You're making a show of yourself... Are you all right? What's happened?'

'Where is he, Ma? Where is Father Ryan?'

Helen didn't know what to say; she'd never seen her daughter in such a state.

'He's in church, Mary, but over my dead body will a daughter of mine walk the streets in such a state. Calm yourself. Now! Tell me what's happened ... *please.*'

Mary's eyes flashed, her anger rose and without hesitation she turned and ran towards the church, ignoring her mother's calls to come back.

The rain began to fall as Mary approached the church. Her dress clung to her, soaked by the downpour. Flinging the church door open she saw Father Ryan kneeling down to pray. She yelled from the back, startling the priest and causing him to jump up and hold his chest.

'Saints and mothers, what in the name...'

Mary's breath was staggered. 'You knew!... You knew it wasn't Patrick. All this time you led me to believe it was him.'

Father Ryan looked around nervously. His voice was low and harsh. 'I don't know what you're talking about.'

The anger rushed through Mary into her words; she began to shake. Her whole body encompassed with fury.

'Don't lie to me! Don't lie! I trusted you but all along you knew it wasn't Patrick. You knew it was Thomas Doyle.'

Father Ryan had at least the decency to look ashamed, but it didn't last long before his guilt turned into a rage. He walked up to Mary, grabbing her and shaking her.

'How dare you talk to me like that, Mary O'Flanagan? It was you who encouraged them; I told you to be careful but you wouldn't listen. You thought it was a game egging men on with your ... your lustful behaviour. Dancing and flouncing around. You are as much to blame as Tommy is.'

This time the sting on the cheek wasn't Mary's, it was Father Ryan's as Mary slapped him hard; years of pent-up hurt and humiliation dished out by the priest went into the slap. She stared at Father Ryan as he held his cheek, feeling beside herself as the tears ran down her face.

'I had the chance to go with him. I had the chance of starting a new life, but because of you – *you* – I turned him down. And you know something else; he didn't care. He didn't care the baby wasn't his, he would've taken care of me, but I told him I hated him. And now I'll never see him again because of *you!*'

Father Ryan held onto Mary's wrist. He twisted it round and she yelped. His eyes bulged in fury.

'If it wasn't for me, Patrick would be still in the industrial school. It was me who got him out of there. Once I knew the truth, I made sure the mistake was rectified. You should be thanking me.'

Mary shook free of the priest's grip. Bemusement filled her voice. 'Thanking you? It was you who put him in there in the first place. But you were covering for Thomas Doyle. Why? And Patrick told me it was O'Sheyenne who killed the Brogans. Is that true?'

The priest flinched under Mary's gaze. Her questions were making him feel uncomfortable.

A sudden pain ran through Mary's body. She bent forward holding onto the pew.

'You need to go home, Mary. Get Fergus to go and get the doctor.'

Through the crippling pain, Mary shook her head, beads of sweat dripping down her face.

'No! So you can come and take my baby? No! You're not taking it. I'll wait for Patrick, tell him I'm sorry.'

Father Ryan shook his head. 'Patrick's long gone, Mary, you and I both know that. You should've gone with him when you had the chance. And now it's too late.'

'It's not too late for my baby. You'll never get your hands on it. *Never.*'

'You've got no choice, Mary. The decision's been made. Stop making this harder for yourself. Once you have the baby, you can get on with your life; put this all behind you. Pretend it didn't happen.'

Mary stared at Father Ryan, seeing the priest

for what he really was. She turned and ran out of the church towards her home. As she ran down the lane, she could see her parents ahead of her, tight-lipped with looks of concern etched on their faces.

It was her mother who spoke. 'Mary O'Flanagan, I hope for your sake you haven't brought any more shame onto this family. What's going on?'

Mary, desperate for her mother's affections, threw herself on her. 'It was never Patrick,' she cried, her words rushing out in relief and desperation. 'It wasn't him. I knew it. I knew it. I spoke to Father Ryan and he knew it, too.'

Helen looked at her daughter, not quite understanding what was going on. 'You're talking gibberish, Mary.'

Wide eyed, Mary pulled back and looked at her mother. 'It wasn't Patrick. The night in the woods – he had nothing to do with it.'

Helen, hearing the words, grabbed her daughter, shaking her as she whispered in her ear. 'Don't you dare talk about the sins of that night. Whoever it was or wasn't does not take away the shame of what happened. What you did. The quicker you get rid of that ... that thing inside you, the better.'

Mary stared at her mother. 'I want to keep it.'

Helen was enraged and she was relieved to see Father Ryan hurrying down the lane towards them. He'd know what to do and say, unlike her husband, who stood, his head hanging low.

'Father, *please*. Do something.' Helen's words were directed to Father Ryan, a helplessness in them which the priest recognised and under-

140

stood. 'This is neither the time nor the place. You need to get her home, Helen; she's had a shock.'

Mary shook her head, hysteria and the enormity of the situation taking over. 'No! No! I'm not going home. I'm going to go to Patrick. He'll have me. I'm going to keep the baby. It's my baby!' The last words were screamed out and the few onlookers walking past began to stare.

Father Ryan shook with rage. 'Get home, Mary O'Flanagan! There is no place for you in the community and certainly no place for that bastard child of yours. The moment it is born, it will be gone from our lives and you, Mary, will stay at St Joseph's until I see fit.'

Mary's eyes glanced at her mother, then at her father, both of whom were both nodding in approval at what Father Ryan was saying.

'You can't! You can't!'

Hating public shows of defiance, Father Ryan spat his words. 'I think you'll find I can. This whole situation has been too much for you, Mary. The nuns will be able to give you the support and teaching you need; in a year's time I am sure you'll be well enough to come back home.' Father Ryan then took hold of Mary's arm, marching her down the street towards her parents' cottage.

As Father Ryan turned to admonish Fergus O'Flanagan, Mary took the opportunity to pull away. With a quick flick of her wrist, she easily escaped his grip, running down the lane and cutting through the fields.

She didn't know where she was going as the rain hit her face and the billowing wind blew up the leaves and bracken. All she could think of was

Patrick. Patrick. The tears streamed down her face as she stumbled along. She'd told him she hated him and the pain she'd seen in his eyes haunted her.

A sharp pain in her stomach brought her to a stop as she bent over, panting and trying to get her breath. Where was she going? There was nowhere to go. She looked around frantically, seeing the tiny village in the distance, knowing they'd be out looking for her. Taking her back to St Joseph's to lock her up as if she were a criminal.

All she wanted to do was keep her baby. And she would. She would. There was no way anyone was going to take it away from her. She hated what had happened. She hated Thomas Doyle but she didn't hate her baby. *Her baby*. And there was no way she was going to allow Father Ryan to take it away.

Mary tilted her head to one side, blinking into the rain as she looked up into the grey sky, not quite remembering how she'd got to the river. The rain, which at first had felt so cool, no longer chilled her. The wind, which had billowed and cut through her thin dress, no longer held the cold. And as Mary O'Flanagan jumped into the icy water below, she felt only a warmth and relief that she was going to keep her baby after all.

17

The boys playing down the stream near the old bridge had decided it was time to go home. The rain which they thought and hoped would pass battered down, soaking their woollen jumpers and causing their skin to itch.

The taller boy, deciding he wanted one last throw to try to beat the skimming stone record of the village, crouched down, preparing himself for a twelve-bounce bob. Bringing back his arm, with one eye closed, focusing in on the prize of being able to tell the other boys he'd beat their record, he suddenly screamed, frantically pointing to the water.

Without thinking of his own safety, the boy, no older than fourteen, waded in, calling to his friends to go and get Doctor Murphy and Father Ryan.

The river was rough but it was late autumn, which meant the water wasn't too deep and it was just about possible for the boy to keep his balance as he dragged the pregnant woman from the water. He held onto a branch, gripping it hard to help him to pull her out.

The water weighed her down and he was afraid he wouldn't have the strength to carry her out onto the bank, so he was grateful to see an army of people running towards him, led by Doctor Murphy and followed by Father Ryan.

'That's Mary O'Flanagan!' A voice shouted from the back of the crowd as Doctor Murphy knelt down by Mary's still body. Her face was blue and the icy waters had paled her skin, lending it a marbled effect.

'She's not breathing!' Doctor Murphy spoke to no-one in particular as he pressed his head against her chest. He looked up at the milling crowd, speaking warmly to Fergus. 'I'm sorry. I'm so sorry. She's gone.'

Almost unable to take in what was happening, Fergus staggered through his words. 'What ... what about the baby?'

Father Ryan, who was standing a foot away, turned and snapped, 'What about it, Fergus? "He who takes their own life shall be damned." Perhaps this is for the best. God's will.'

The punch which landed on Father Ryan's chin surprised every onlooker, who secretly wished they'd done it themselves.

Fergus stood over Father Ryan who scrambled in the wet grass, floored by the blow. Wiping the tears away, Fergus trembled with rage and hurt as he fell to his knees, cradling Mary's head in his arms.

'This is *my* daughter. My daughter, not yours, mine. I let her down. We all did. All of us, *Matthew*. All in God's name. And the only *will* here was ours, *Matthew*. Ours. We pushed her to this.'

Turning his attentions away from Father Ryan, Fergus spoke to Doctor Murphy. 'I want you to save the baby.'

Doctor Murphy, saddened by the whole affair, spoke gently. 'We won't be able to get her to hospital on time. It's too late. By the time we get her there, the baby will have died. I'm sorry, Fergus, I truly am.'

'Then do it here.'

Doctor Murphy looked around the crowd, letting Fergus's words sink in. 'Here?'

'You heard me.'

The doctor's face was full of shock. 'I can't, Fergus ... it wouldn't be right.'

It was Fergus O'Flanagan's cue to explode. Pent-up emotion came pouring out as the guilt of what he'd been a part of was realised. His voice rose above the sound of the rain and the bustling river.

'Right? Right! You talk about right, yet is it right I'm holding my dead daughter in my arms? There's a chance to save her baby and I am asking ye, begging ye, to help.' Fergus paused a moment, then added, his voice turning cold.

'If you won't do it, I will.'

Nobody there that day had any doubt that Fergus was serious as he took a long blade out of his pocket which he'd been using to work in the log shed earlier that day.

Doctor Murphy held onto his arm. 'Fine, Fergus, I'll do it.'

The horror on Father Ryan's voice translated into his voice. 'You, shall do no such thing, Murphy; this is the devil's work.'

Doctor Murphy stared coolly at Father Ryan. 'No, Matthew, this is not the devil's work, this is me doing what I do and helping to save a life. Now if you'll be kind enough to step aside, we haven't got much time.'

As Doctor Murphy took out his surgical instruments from his bag, most of the onlookers turned away, but Fergus stayed watching, seeing it as penance for the misery he'd brought to Mary.

He watched as Doctor Murphy lifted Mary's dress, pressing her stomach expertly and with delicate precision as he cut from her navel to her pubic bone, opening the skin in a wave of red blood and tissue. The blood ran down Mary's body, mixing with the rain to form a pool of crimson round her.

Doctor Murphy plunged both hands inside Mary, making Fergus retch. Then quickly and expertly, and with one last hard pull, Doctor Murphy, looking triumphant, delivered a healthy baby.

'What is it, Doctor?'

Taking his coat and wrapping it round the baby as he cut the cord, Doctor Murphy beamed; a warm, genuine smile.

'Fergus, welcome your granddaughter to the world.'

18

Fergus and Helen O'Flanagan sat staring at their granddaughter. It'd been less than a week and the shock of the events of the last few days still had them reeling; the only solace they found was in the chestnut-haired little girl with the startling blue eyes.

Neither Helen nor Fergus had really spoken to

each other, both blaming the other but both secretly knowing the blame rested on themselves as much as anyone else.

Deep in their thoughts, the banging on the door seemed a distant sound. The noise continued and in the end Fergus spoke, grief and anger in his voice.

'Are you not going to get that, woman?'

Without a word, Helen got up. She slowly walked to the front door and was surprised to see Father Ryan at such a late hour, but even more surprised and horrified to see Tommy Doyle with him.

Father Ryan's face was solemn. 'I'm sorry, Helen,' was all the priest said before walking into the front room.

Not understanding what was going on, Helen scurried behind the two men. As she followed them into the parlour, Tommy was holding court and what she heard sent her reeling.

'I've come for me baby.'

Helen's eyes darted from Fergus to Father Ryan. Neither of the O'Flanagans said anything, but looked on in horror as Tommy scooped the sleeping baby out of her cot. Immediately the child let out a scream of discontent. Helen rushed over but was stopped by Father Ryan's firm hand.

'I'm sorry, Helen, but it's true. Thomas Doyle, sinner that he is, is the father of Mary's baby and therefore has parental rights. I am sorry.'

Helen let out a scream and collapsed onto the floor as Fergus stayed frozen in his chair. He stared at Tommy, who walked out of the house without saying anything.

Fergus then looked at Father Ryan who answered the unasked question. 'No, Fergus, there is nothing you can do. Apart from pray. Pray for the sins of the weak.'

'The Gardaí; we could go to the Gardaí. He took her without her will.'

Father Ryan shook his head. 'I've told you before, Fergus; Thomas Doyle will say he had a relationship with Mary. He'll tell lies and spread stories.'

'He needs to be punished.'

'Leave the punishment to God. All that will happen if you go to the Gardaí is that her name will be sullied; there'll be talk, rumours. You don't want that for Mary, do you? Leave her name to rest in peace.'

'But...'

'Trust me, Fergus, I know what I'm doing. It's for the best.'

Outside the O'Flanagans', Thomas Doyle was standing at the gate, baby in arms, watching the car come towards him. It slowed down, then stopped a few metres in front of where he was standing. The tall figure of Donal O'Sheyenne stepped out of the car.

'I hear you have something for me, Thomas.'

'Aye I do... Here.' Thomas shoved the now settled baby into Donal's arms. He stared at him. 'I hope she'll go to a good home.'

Donal sneered at Tommy. 'She was already in a good home, we both know that. What you mean is you hope she goes for a good price. You'll get your cut, Thomas Doyle, and you'll also get your day of judgement.'

Tommy laughed. 'That's a fine thing coming from you.'

Donal walked to the car, placing the sleeping baby into the nun's arms, who sat stony-faced in the back of the car.

'Unlike most men, Thomas, I know who I am. *What* I am. But do you – do you know what you are?'

19

Patrick Doyle sat with his head in his hands listening as Donal O'Sheyenne recounted the story of Mary. Anger was welling up in him, rising like a wave before the sorrow of what had happened crashed back down.

'Patrick, I'm so sorry.' Cab spoke as he stood by Patrick's side, feeling his friend's pain as if it were his own. He looked out of the window, watching the bustle of the Soho streets.

They'd been in England just over a month and, although they were still answerable to Donal O'Sheyenne, the sense of freedom and accept- ance and the hope of building a new life filled Cab with joy each and every day.

The industrial school was only now a memory – except for in his dreams – but the recollection of what his friend Patrick had done and how he'd saved him would stay with him forever.

The night of the escape he'd made a promise

that he'd never leave Patrick's side and whatever he wanted he would deliver. But as Cab stood listening to the saxophone and musicians below he knew he couldn't give Patrick the one thing he wanted: Mary.

Through gulps of pain, Patrick spoke to Donal as they sat in the tiny flat he'd put them up in when they'd arrived in Soho.

'And the baby?'

'Alive.'

Patrick, although only almost seventeen, had grown up in the last few months and the youth he'd once been had disappeared in the basement of Our Lady's, along with his innocence. He slammed his fist on the table, making Donal roar with laughter.

'Where's the baby, Donal?'

'And what concern would that be of yours?'

Patrick's eyes flashed. 'Don't play with me.'

'Why, you're growing up to be a fighter, are you not? The baby's safe.'

'I want her.'

This last comment surprised both Donal and Cab. Neither of them said anything.

'I said, I want her. It's what Mary would've wanted.'

Donal looked puzzled. 'And how is a lad like you supposed to pay and look after a baby? You of all people know how all this works.'

Patrick's eyes were cold. 'I shall be in your debt, Donal. However long it takes. I shall be in your debt.'

Donal mulled this over then nodded. 'If that's what you want, Patrick, but be warned, make a deal with the devil and there's always a price to pay.'

Neither Patrick nor Cab heard anything further from Donal until a few weeks later when, at past the stroke of midnight on Christmas Day, the door hammered. It was Cab who got up and opened the door, letting Donal into the flat in the dead of the night.

'Where is he?'

Cab, always nervous of Donal, quickly answered. 'He's sleeping. I'll go and get him.'

Cab opened Patrick's door. 'Paddy? Paddy? There's someone here to see you.'

Slowly stirring, Patrick sat up and without thought or question followed Cab into the tiny sitting room.

'This is what you asked for.' Abruptly, Donal O'Sheyenne pushed the sleeping baby into Patrick's arms.

Patrick looked at Donal and then at Cab, his eyes brimming with tears. He nuzzled his head into the baby, whispering so the others couldn't hear, 'I'll look after her for you, Mary. I promise I will. I promise.'

Cab, feeling emotional, couldn't help but talk. 'She's beautiful, Paddy.'

Patrick looked up proudly. 'Aye, she is.'

'What are you going to call her?'

A beaming grin spread across Patrick's face as he remembered the conversation he'd once had with Mary.

'I'm going to call her Franny. Franny Mary Doyle.'

20

SOHO – 2013

Franny Doyle opened her eyes and smiled. There on the bed next to her, holding a cup of tea, was Patrick.

After the last few months it felt a relief to be waking up in her old room. She'd wanted to come before, especially when the arguments with her ex-boyfriend, Jack, had got nasty, but she'd resisted the temptation, not wanting to run back; thinking it was somehow the easy option, especially as Patrick tended to treat her more like a child than a grown woman.

'How are you feeling?' He spoke warmly to her.

'It's nice to be back. Gives me a bit of time to be able to think.'

'You know you can stay as long as you like. It seems right you being here.'

'I didn't think you'd be here actually; I thought you were supposed to be going away on business.'

'And miss your birthday, Fran? When have I ever done that?'

Franny didn't say anything. Taking a sip of tea she studied Patrick's face, giving him a sad smile. She hadn't asked him how he was last night and she worried so much about him. She could see the deep lines around his dazzling blue eyes, the frown mark in the middle of his forehead. Although he was as strikingly handsome as ever and looked younger than his fifty-one years, Franny could see an evident fatigue in his features which hadn't been there before.

It was the same every year. As far back as she could remember in fact. Patrick would disappear just before her *real* birthday in October, unable to be around her. Too much of a reminder for him that it'd been the same day her mother, Mary, had died. But then a few weeks later he'd reappear, looking tired and drawn but eager to celebrate what he classed as her birthday; the day she'd been brought to him: December 25th; Christmas Day.

As a teenager, when Patrick had done his vanishing act near her October birthday, she'd always been hurt and angry with him, until one day he'd sat her down, holding his head in his hands as he'd cried, explaining the guilt and pain he'd felt for not being there on the day her mother had died. And it was then that Franny had seen it. Seen the sadness and grief, but most of all the love in Patrick's eyes when he'd talked about her mother, and after that, she'd stopped being angry with him and had only ever looked forward to his return when they'd celebrate the day she had come to him.

She didn't know much about how her mother had died and in truth she didn't want to know. Patrick had told her it'd been in a road traffic accident, but she hadn't pushed it; knowing that was enough. And anyway, why make herself feel sad? She knew how lucky she was. Patrick had

153

explained how her mother had been an orphan and had had no other close relatives. Patrick had been the nearest relative; a distant cousin on her mother's side.

Apparently her mother hadn't really known her biological father. Patrick had told her she'd been conceived after a brief encounter with a boy from Dublin and there'd been no contact ever since, so there wasn't any question of her being looked after by relatives on her father's side; no-one knew who they were.

It'd always surprised her that the authorities had allowed Patrick to adopt her, him being so young, but as he had said, things had been different in those days – and she certainly didn't have a problem with it. Her childhood had been filled with joy and love, and as she had grown older Patrick had taught her everything he knew, bringing her into his business and letting her work alongside him.

There were a few things she didn't know still, such as what her mother had looked like. She had no photo, but when she'd spoken about this to Patrick, he had simply smiled at her warmly, taking her by the hand to the bathroom mirror.

'What do you see, Franny?'

'Myself.'

'Aye, but there, too, is the face of the woman who had the gentlest soul and the kindest heart. You are her, Franny, and I know she would've been as proud of you as I am.'

The other thing she didn't know was anything about Patrick's younger life, but any time she ever mentioned it, Patrick had clammed up, changing the subject.

Sitting on the bed, Patrick gently put his fingers under Franny's chin, breaking her from her thoughts. He lifted her face up slightly so that her green eyes were at the same level as his.

'Hey! No long faces. Look what I've got you.'

Franny grinned, flicking back her long mane of chestnut hair as Patrick produced a diamond bracelet from his pocket.

'It's beautiful, Patrick. Thank you.'

'Anything for my baby.'

Franny laughed. She was thirty-four and Patrick still treated her like a little girl; spoiling her and lavishing her with gifts. The week in the run-up to her birthday in December, Patrick would give her a gift for each day of the week before throwing a huge party for all who knew them; but as wonderful as they were, it wouldn't have mattered to Franny if there had been no presents or parties. All that mattered was the love Patrick bestowed on her and that he was home safely.

'Any problems with the business while I've been away?'

Franny shook her head as Patrick carefully placed the delicate bracelet on her wrist. On her eighteenth birthday, Patrick had put her in charge of the numerous nightclubs and casinos he owned. At first she'd panicked, daunted by the huge responsibility, but Patrick Doyle wasn't a man to take no for an answer; not even from her.

Spurred on by the faith and trust he showed in her and being almost as stubborn as Patrick was, Franny had put her fears to one side, determined

155

to make him proud. She'd spent hundreds of late nights trying to understand the workings and dealings of the businesses; on many occasions falling to sleep in the office as she went through the paperwork, figuring out how to make and not to lose money for the man she adored, in the stiff competition of the nightclub world.

It'd been hard to get the respect from the faces of London at first. They hadn't taken her seriously and saw her as she'd seen herself – just a kid. But each time she'd aired her concerns to Patrick, he'd laughed warmly before adding, 'You'll get there, Franny; do you really think I'd hand over me businesses, no matter how much I love you, if I didn't believe you could do it? Franny, listen to me, I believe in you; always have done, so now all you need to do is just believe in yourself.'

And so that's what she'd done. She'd begun to believe in herself. Begun to believe she could take charge of all the men who worked for Patrick. Believe she could eventually be untroubled by the hard-edged scene of the nightclubs and casinos.

Whenever there'd been any trouble in the clubs she'd known who to call on, but knowing how to fight wasn't a part of it; what she'd needed to know was how to use her brains. How to be shrewd. How to make deals; knowing that she always had to be one step ahead whilst looking over her shoulder at the same time. She hadn't trusted anyone apart from those close to her. And gradually, over time, her approach had begun to work. She earned the respect of the men. Earned the respect of the biggest faces around but, more importantly, she'd earned the respect and pride in Patrick's eyes. She'd been in charge ever since.

'So it's all looking good then, Fran?'

Franny nodded reassuringly, but even as she did so, she knew it wasn't the case. Business was down – quite considerably – and she needed to think of a way to turn it around. Some of the clubs, especially the casinos, were beginning to drain money and over the past few weeks she'd had to let a few men go. It had kept her awake at night, but then, she wasn't about to start troubling Patrick with her worries. He had trusted her to be in charge and she prided herself on not having to ask for his help. She hadn't needed to yet and she certainly wasn't going to start now.

Besides, the clubs weren't the only businesses they had. The other side of Patrick's empire, the darker side – the girls, the money-laundering and to a certain extent the cocaine which Patrick had a small monopoly on, the side she knew all about but took no part in – would keep him busy until she figured out what to do. By the time he realised business had been down, she would've sorted it. So for now, she'd stick to the first rule of business and keep her mouth shut, both to Patrick and his best friend, her beloved uncle.

As if able to see his name in her mind, Patrick spoke. 'Have you seen your Uncle Cabhan lately?' He stretched wearily as he flopped back his muscular body at the end of Franny's bed.

Franny winked, speaking with mock indignity. 'I have and you know I have. You don't fool me, Patrick Doyle. It's always been the worst-kept secret that he's under strict instructions to come and check on me when you're away. When will it sink into that head of yours, I don't need looking after?'

Patrick grinned, playing on his Irish accent. 'Why, to be to be sure, child, we all need looking after.'

Franny threw one of her pillows at him as they both got up from the bed.

'I don't. I can look after myself. You taught me how to do that.'

Patrick crossed his arms, his muscles straining the shirt he was wearing. 'You *think* you can.'

Frahny grinned, emphasising her words. 'Oh, I *know* I can.'

Patrick chuckled. 'Right. I've got to go ... where's my wallet?' He patted his trousers down feeling for it, then looked puzzled. 'Shit, I could have sworn it was in my pocket. I must be losing my memory in my old age.'

'Or been picked. What was that about not being able to look after myself?' Franny held up the wallet and grinned. 'Nice to know I haven't lost my touch! Maybe I should take it up as a full-time career.'

Patrick roared with laughter at his wallet; skil-fully pickpocketed by Franny. His eyes twinkled. 'I'm impressed, Fran; I didn't feel a thing. I didn't think you could still do it.'

'You taught me well. Do you remember when you and Cab first showed me how to do it?'

Patrick shook his head warmly. 'I can't believe we actually taught you. Somehow me and Cab got it into our heads it'd be a good idea if you could pickpocket. Were you eleven at the time?'

'Seven.'

'Seven! Are you sure?'

'Perfectly. It was just after my birthday and I'd been practising on you two, but I wanted to go out to do the real thing ... so you took me out into Old Compton Street and you pointed out that guy who you said looked an "easy touch" and you waited around the corner. Turned out your "easy touch" was an undercover copper!'

Patrick roared again, delighting in the story he'd forgotten. 'That's right! That's right! He grabbed you straight away, didn't he? He was ready to march you off, so to distract him me and Cab had to cause a diversion and pretended to have a fight in the middle of the street.'

'Pretended! If I remember, you both came away with black eyes!'

'Well, it had to look authentic. It worked, didn't it? You managed to run and hide in Lola's café.'

'Whilst you and Cab were taken to the police station for causing an affray.'

Patrick's laughter began to subside. He nodded, reflecting quietly. 'Good times, Franny. They were happy times. Everything seemed so much less complicated.'

Patrick sighed. It would be good to have her around. More than good, in fact. Refreshing. He always missed her, especially when he was under pressure. Lately his 'business trips' hadn't been as successful as he'd have liked them to be. In truth, they hadn't been successful for the past twelve months or more. But he certainly wasn't going to worry Franny with it. He was a grown man and there was no way he was going to

159

trouble Franny, who couldn't feel or be more like his daughter if she tried. His money worries would stay his, and anyway, she was so busy with the businesses she ran, by the time she realised something was wrong, he would've found a solution to sort it out.

With his mind still on business, Patrick spoke firmly. 'I need to go and see Cab. I can't get through to him on his phones; they're switched off. Any idea where he is?'

Franny raised her eyebrows and smiled. 'I'll give you one guess. Though I'm surprised you even need to ask.'

21

Cabhan Morton opened his eyes and grinned. Surrounding him on his circular bed were the sleeping bodies of six naked women. All beautiful. All fuckable. But all very disposable. They all worked in one or other of the various clubs that Franny ran, serving up drinks and extras to the high-rolling punters. They were nice enough girls, pleasing to the eye and especially pleasing to the cock, but he knew he wouldn't see any of them again. He wasn't interested. He'd never been interested. The idea of getting to know any woman for longer than one night had never and would never appeal to him.

But why should it? He had all he needed already. And loved who he needed already. Franny and

Patrick. The two people he'd give his life to and for. They were his family and he was theirs.

There wasn't room for anyone else. Anyone else would get in the way. He didn't need to know what it was like to have children. He knew he could never have loved any child more than he loved Franny.

The early days of him and Patrick looking after her had been farcical. Neither of them knew what it was to bring up a child, let alone a baby. They'd taken it in turns to struggle with the nappies. Struggle with what seemed like endless night-time feeds. Staggering around, trying to keep awake as they gave too little or too much milk to baby Franny, but what they hadn't struggled with was how much they'd loved her. And although it'd been gruelling trying to work and to get money as inexperienced teenagers, the pressure hadn't made them argue and turn on each other; instead they'd laughed and talked, already bonded together by their experiences at the industrial school, bonded by the hope for the future; trusting one another with each other's lives as they fell exhausted to sleep on the kitchen floor, often waking to find Franny staring at them in wonder as she chewed on her dummy.

But then, one day, they'd got it right. The nappies became easier. The milk they'd got right, the sleepless nights were something they became used to and, not only did they watch Franny bloom from a baby into a toddler, then into a wonderful little girl, so too did they watch their business ventures grow from selling knock-off gear in the saunas, working on doors and looking out for a few girls on the street corners, to a booming venture in the nightclub and casino trade. Shortly followed by the high-class hookers and drugs, along with the property deals and money-laundering.

They had come to Soho at the right time and they'd worked hard, but now things were different. Trade had started slowing down. At first it'd been a niggle, and then a concern, but now it was a worry: business wasn't good. The internet had made girls accessible without the need for pimps, the go-betweens. The girls had got wise to the fact they could earn more money with less stress without men like him, and the Russians had started to gain a monopoly on the drugs. But he certainly wasn't going to worry Franny or Patrick with his concerns.

He was Patrick's best friend and protector, as well as uncle to Franny, and he'd made a vow all those years ago to do anything he could to keep Patrick safe and not leave his side, and if that included dealing with these money problems on his own, then so be it.

'Cab, well, this is a surprise. You surrounded by countless women in one of our flats above the club. Who'd have thought it, hey?' Grinning, Patrick winked, genuinely pleased as he always was to see Cab who, with the large gold chains and heavy bracelets he wore set against his velvet black skin, looked more and more like a caricature of a pimp with every passing moment.

Cab jumped up, just as pleased to see Patrick as his friend was to see him. He hadn't been around for a couple of weeks and he'd missed him, and although they'd spoken daily on the phone and

162

he'd had dinner with Franny most nights, not having Patrick about always made him feel uneasy.

Cab grabbed hold of his friend who roared with laughter before pushing him away. 'Can we leave the embraces until you get some clothes on, Cab?'

'Ah! What's a naked hug between friends? Come here and give me a squeeze.' As Cab said the words, he immediately regretted them as he saw the flicker of painful locked-away memories pass through Patrick's eyes. They never spoke of the dark, tortuous days in the industrial school with Father Marley, but Cab would never forget how night after night he'd tried to nurse Patrick's abused and battered body.

Quickly putting his robe on without saying another word, Cab followed Patrick into the next room, slightly disappointed he wouldn't have time to fit in another blow job. Still there was always tonight, and no-one came before Patrick, not even a tight-assed Puerto Rican beauty.

'You look tired, Patrick. Is everything okay? You know if there's anything I can do...' Heavy with concern, Cab's voice trailed off.

Pouring a large glass of brandy, Patrick glanced at Cab. It never ceased to amaze him that after all these years Cab was as true to his promise as the day he'd spoken it as a grateful, terrified young boy.

The pledge of Cab devoting his life to him as they'd escaped the walls of the industrial school had been to Patrick just words, uttered with the naivety of childhood. But as the years passed and Cab's loyalty towards him and Franny had grown

163

ever stronger, so too had Patrick's. And now, as the heat of the brandy hit the back of his throat, Patrick realised he didn't know what he'd do without Cab.

Even though he had been the one who'd helped Cab to escape all those years ago, Patrick often felt it was actually *him* who was indebted to his friend. Cab had sacrificed his whole existence to be at his beck and call. Day or night, Cab had been there whenever he was needed.

In the early days whilst he'd been doing the deals and living a life, it'd been Cab who'd been at home looking after Franny, making it possible for him to build a reputation and make a name for himself. If ever there'd been trouble at the clubs or on the streets, it had been Cab, who'd taught himself to fight in the back streets of Soho, who'd be standing by his side ready to take the blows alongside him. And it was Cab, with his savvy head for figures, who'd taken his business ventures from small-time joints to what they were today. And all without complaints or greedy demands.

For all these things and more, Patrick knew he'd be forever grateful. The likelihood he could ever pay his friend back was slim. Cab had done so much for him and Franny, asking nothing in return, and it was for this reason that Patrick chose to answer his friend's question with a lie.

'Everything's fine, Cab. Just fine.' But as Patrick looked at the flashing caller ID on his phone, *just fine* couldn't be further from the truth.

22

Donal O'Sheyenne laughed, but as he stood in the tiny flat above the bustling streets of Soho listening to the noise of his laughter echo around the room, he came to the conclusion that it sounded less like a laugh than a roar, which in turn only made him laugh louder.

The source of his amusement had always been of choice concern for a lot of people. He remembered how his father had looked at him in shocked disbelief as he'd wiped away tears of hilarity on his sleeve at his mother's funeral. And the day he'd watched an old woman being knocked over and killed by a speeding tram in the heart of Dublin he'd had to hang onto the nearby railings to stop himself from losing his balance, such was the strength of his laughter. And now as he stood face to face with Patrick Doyle, Donal O'Sheyenne once more could see his sense of humour wasn't shared by all.

'Oh for God's sake, Paddy, after all these years are you still telling me you don't see the funny side of it?'

Patrick stared at him coldly. He could feel the twitch of anger on the side of his temple pulsating as he spoke. 'By Christ, you never change do you? How long has it been, hey? How long have I known ye to be the scum that you are? Difference now though is I'm not a kid any longer. Your days

165

of bringing fear are over.'

Donal wiped the last of his tears then sniffed louder before yawning with derision.

Getting out a large black flick-knife – a sentimental keepsake from his teenage years in Tralee – from his pocket, Donal set about picking the dirt out of his nails as he spoke with exaggerated boredom to Patrick.

'There was a time when I thought you were a laugh, but this little speech you do each year has got very boring. It always goes the same way. You say, *you haven't got it.* I say, *I want it.* And then inevitably, I get me way. So why not just cut to the chase, Paddy boy, and give me my money – save us both time and energy?'

Patrick leapt at Donal, grabbing hold of his coat collar. He leant in; his handsome face inches away from the scarred, heavily lined one of Donal's.

'I'm not your boy, Donal. And you can quit speaking to me like I am. You'll get your money all right; as you point out, you have done every year, and you'll keep on getting it till you rot in hell.'

Donal stared contemptuously down at Patrick's grip before looking straight back up with a threatening glare. His eyes flashed with danger but Patrick ignored it, as he listened to the warning words.

'You're making a big mistake, Paddy. I think you need to start showing me some respect, don't you? After all, it's you that owes *me* money. And we both know what will happen if you don't pay.' Donal cocked his head to one side before singing quietly, 'And *Down will fall baby, cradle and all.*'

Patrick's temper took over. He saw only blind rage as he shook O'Sheyenne, jolting his head back and forth, the frustration and anger of the last few weeks showing as he slammed Donal hard into the wall.

With his large hand easily managing to wrap round O'Sheyenne's throat, Patrick squeezed the breath out of him; watching Donal's eyes bulge as he hissed angry words. 'Keep well away, O'Sheyenne. I'm warning ye.'

Without warning, and taking Patrick by surprise, Donal drove the blade of the flick-knife he still held in his hand into Patrick's side.

Immediately, Patrick dropped his grip, stumbling backwards as he pressed down on the wound, aware and grateful that his heavy winter coat had taken the brunt of the blade. But before he could reach out to steady himself, he felt the steel power of Donal's fist batter down on his face, sending him reeling across the cold concrete floor.

As he struggled to push himself up, Donal knocked him back down, pressing his foot into his chest.

'Now there's a sorry sight, Paddy. A man with a reputation such as yourself, brought to his knees by a senior citizen. You'd be a laughing stock.'

The bloody injury to Patrick's side didn't dampen his fight; with lightning speed, he grabbed Donal's foot, pulling hard and twisting it around, causing O'Sheyenne to topple forward and giving Patrick the opportunity to leap up. He gritted his teeth as the pain of his wound shot through his body, but his hatred for O'Sheyenne drove him on.

Once on his feet, Patrick didn't hesitate to rain down vicious blows on O'Sheyenne, stopping only to catch his breath. He stared at Donal's blood-covered face and spoke to him in a whisper:

'You'll get your money, O'Sheyenne, you just have to give me another week. But you stay away from Franny. You hear me? We had a deal and I'm warning you.'

Donal gave a wide grin, exposing a mouthful of bloodied teeth. 'Ah Franny how is she? A spit of her mother no doubt.'

'Don't play games with me, Donal.'

Donal wiped his mouth, observing the trail of blood and saliva on his sleeve.

'But you know me well enough, Paddy; I've always liked a good game, sure I have. And as this is my game, it's *my* rules; and so I've decided to change them. I'll give you your other week to pay the one million, but then I want another five million on the day you celebrate Franny's birthday. Like one of the wise men bearing gifts of gold, Paddy boy.'

Patrick snarled. 'You're a dead man, O'Sheyenne.'

Donal shook his head slowly and smiled nastily. 'Then that'll make two of us, won't it? You know very well if you kill me there are plans in place for the same thing to happen to Franny. And we wouldn't want that, would we? Not after all this time of you and your little nig-nog friend looking after her. What a waste.' Donal burst into laughter, pointing at Patrick. 'Why, you should see your face, Paddy. What a picture. What a picture.'

168

Patrick could feel his body physically shaking partly through pain and partly through the rage he felt towards the man standing in front of him. The man who, from the time he'd first brought Franny to him, had made him pay, each and every year for the *lease* of her. And with each birthday of Franny's which had passed by, Donal had increased the price.

At first the money he'd given to Donal had been to ensure O'Sheyenne wouldn't take Franny back, but then one night Donal had come to him as Franny had slept peacefully in her bed and once more changed the rules, telling him: 'It's a game of life now, Paddy. More fun that way. I've always been partial to high-stake games. So here's how it works; miss the payment and you can kiss your sleeping beauty her final good night.'

Of course Franny knew nothing about any of it – not where she really came from and not about the money. When business had been booming, making the payments just before her birthday hadn't been a problem. He'd either have the money already sorted from his lucrative night-club ventures or he'd go on an extra business trip, making deals with big-name faces like Del Williams, a well-known drug baron. Then things had changed. As the businesses began to lose money and the faces began to deal directly with the Russians for drugs, the pressure to find the money had grown. And this year, it'd become impossible. The money had all but dried up, the drug deals he'd once made had been franchised out to the foreigners who undercut everyone, and the clubs, with their escorts and toms, were now

169

ten a penny.

So as Patrick stared at Donal, listening to the ringing words *five million,* he felt helpless and scared for the first time since his days at the industrial school.

'Don't look like that, Paddy boy; you knew the rules when you took her. She was never yours. Not really; only loaned to you. And besides, I need the money, so I do. Times are hard, what with not being able to ply me trade any more back in Ireland. I'm relying on you to keep me in the life I've become accustomed to.'

Patrick's face was twisted in anger. 'You'll pay for this, O'Sheyenne.'

Donal shrugged. 'That I may, that I may, but for the time being, 'tis you who needs to be paying me.'

About to go on, Donal stopped for a moment, reflecting quietly as he watched out of the window as the first flakes of winter begin to fall on the Soho streets a few feet below.

A few minutes passed before he began to speak again. 'Though, there is one way out of it. Another way. Perhaps you've forgotten me mentioning it all those years ago. On your death, Paddy boy, the payments for Franny will stop; nothing will happen to your sleeping beauty. You have my word. She'll be safe.'

'What ... what are you saying?'

Donal smiled, a large beaming grin. 'Your life for hers, Paddy boy. Your life for hers... And there's you thinking I'm an unreasonable man.'

Franny Doyle looked on in horror as she opened

the door to the large marble bathroom. She gasped to see Patrick lying on the bathroom floor and groaning in pain as Cab attended to his wound.

Running to kneel by Patrick's side, she turned to Cab, her eyes wide with concern and fear.

'What the hell's happened, Uncle Cab? Is he ... is he going to be all right?'

Hearing the anguish in her voice, Patrick opened his eyes and reached up for Franny's hand. He gave her a tiny smile and spoke quietly. 'It's fine, Franny, don't you go troubling yourself, girl. Just a little run-in at one of the clubs.'

Patrick shot a glance at Cab, which didn't go unnoticed by Franny. She turned her attention to Cab.

'Tell me the truth, Uncle Cab, what happened? For God's sake, I'm sick of you treating me like a child; it's ridiculous. You don't have to protect me from the truth.'

Patrick winced as he gave a tiny chuckle. 'I think from the state of me, it's me who needs protecting, don't you think?'

Franny's eyes filled with tears. 'It's not funny, Patrick.'

Seeing the fear in Franny's face, Patrick squeezed her hand.

'I know it's not.' His voice was full of empathy. 'I'm sorry if it's given you a fright, Fran, especially after all you've been through lately, but it really is nothing. Usual story – one of the punters in the casino didn't like the fact he'd lost his money. He started getting loud, and me being the arrogant Irish man that I am I thought I could sort it. And

171

this is what I get for my troubles.'

'Don't you think you should go to a hospital?'

Patrick smiled again. 'Nah, hospitals are for girls. Besides, your Uncle Cab here is a dab hand at the first aid. It's not as bad as it looks... Now, if you want to make yourself useful, go and pour me a large glass of whiskey.'

Watching Franny walk out of the room and making sure the door was firmly closed, Cab turned to Patrick. 'Right then, you're going nowhere until you tell me what really happened.'

23

Franny Doyle sat at her large oak desk. Her view from the bay window looked across the middle of Soho Square. It was one of her favourite views of London. She wasn't entirely sure why. It wasn't particularly beautiful and it certainly wasn't breathtaking, yet it was here she felt the happiest.

Some days she'd just sit and people-watch; seeing the milling tourists and hurrying locals go about their business. Some days, in her office, she'd make hard-fought deals with the biggest faces around, barely having enough, time to look out; and some days she'd look out whilst she listened to Patrick on the phone, telling her as he did each day that he loved her. But today she was doing none of these things. Today, she was worried and she had no idea what she was going to do.

A mound of paperwork was piled up on the

desk in front of her. A few letters, a few receipts, but mainly what was staring at her right in the face and growing ever bigger every day was the mountain of bills. Small ones, large ones, unopened ones; all with one thing in common. They were all unpaid.

Franny sighed, pulling a face as she swilled down the remaining cold drop of coffee from the beaker with the words, 'Lady Boss' written on it – a present from Patrick when he'd put her in charge of the clubs all those years ago.

She wasn't doing any good sitting here. She needed to think, and staring at the depressing pile of paperwork in front of her certainly wasn't helping.

Getting up, Franny grabbed her chocolate-brown Moncler jacket. It'd started to get cold recently and a thin layer of snow lay on the ground.

Walking through the newly decorated foyer, Franny waved at the concierge, suddenly remembering she needed to put him on her staff Christmas present list, although he wasn't strictly *her* staff. Last year she'd forgotten to give him anything and had felt so awful about it, she'd spent the next couple of months trying to avoid him. But then, what difference would it make to put his name down on a list? She hadn't any money to buy anything. Business had really had got that bad.

She'd gone through the accounts, over and over again, but it hadn't made any difference at all. Nothing would. Nothing except for money, that is; and where the hell she was going to get that

173

from? Though there was one idea. Just one.

As Franny walked across the square, lighting up a Benson & Hedges Silver, her mind wandered to the only idea she'd come up with, which just might get everyone out of this mess – though Patrick and Cab didn't know anything about it.

The problem was, she wasn't sure if she should actually do it. It would mean going behind Patrick's back. But only for now. And only to save the business.

When business had been bad in the past and things had got tricky, she'd thought about it before, but then something had always turned up: a last-minute deal had gone through; a property had been sold off; a bad debtor had paid. But this time? This time there were no deals to go through. Most of the properties had gone and, rather than people owing them, they had begun to owe people.

Stubbing out her half-smoked cigarette on the wall as the snow began to fall heavily, she walked into church, deciding she was going to go ahead and just do what she had to do. After all, that was what Patrick had advised her on many an occasion as he'd sat by the fireplace silently contemplating his life. She could hear his words now; picturing him as he broke his silence just to say quietly, 'Franny, sometimes in life, you just have to do what you have to do.' And so she decided. She was going to do just that.

Tomorrow, she would go to the bank and remortgage one of the few properties they still owned: their house in Dean Street. Patrick had put it in her name a long time ago, just as he had put the other properties in Cabhan's name; he always insisted on having a low profile when it came to the banks and the taxman.

She could get enough money to pay off the debts and keep the clubs floating. And, although she'd worked out there'd be no money left, it would give her breathing space and time to turn everything around without the pressure of sinking debts.

And once she'd paid back the bank, perhaps she'd tell Patrick all about it, though she guessed it didn't really matter if she never told him because, as he said, 'Sometimes in life, you just have to do what you have to do.'

Standing in the foyer of the church, hearing the sounds of the busy Soho Square outside, Franny set about lighting a candle for her mother; remembering as she did each year the woman she'd never known.

After a few minutes Franny broke away from the mesmerising flicker of the candle and turned to leave, but then stopped, swivelling quickly back round to the rows of lights. She lit another one, only this time it wasn't for her mother – it was for herself. Somehow Franny Doyle had the feeling she'd need all the help she could get.

24

'I don't understand.'

Patrick repeated the words for the fifth time. He stared at the tiny woman behind the desk who was dressed up to the nines and wearing enough make-up to provide four women with cosmetics.

On another occasion, Patrick might have tried to chat her up, turning on his Irish charm, but today being charming was the last thing he felt like doing.

'Look a-fucking-gain!'

The woman pursed her lips. 'Can you please keep your voice down? I don't take kindly to someone shouting at me. I've told you all I can and even that much I shouldn't really have told you. If you want to know any more, you'll have to ask the named parties.'

Patrick banged his fist on the table, making the woman hover her hand over the alarm bell.

'I made them the named parties. It's *my* money and they're *my* properties.'

'Not according to these bank accounts,' the woman answered haughtily. 'You're only named as being allowed access. As I've just told you, I can't tell you any more.'

Patrick closed his eyes and breathed out heavily, trying to hold onto his temper. It just didn't make sense. None of it did. There must be a mistake.

'Let me look at that computer.' Patrick leant across the desk, ignoring the woman's active threat of calling security. All that stared back at him were numbers and codes.

'What the hell is all that?'

The woman spoke as she pressed the alarm bell on her desk. 'As I've said, all the properties have been recently remortgaged by the two named parties – Cabhan Morton and Franny Doyle – on different dates, and the only money available at the moment is the business accounts' overdrafts.'

Before Patrick could utter another word, two large burly security officers barged into the tiny overheated room. The guards hurried towards Patrick, who was now standing up, his face twisted in anger.

'Put your hands on me and by Christ I'll break your fecking necks.'

Used to dealing with non-confrontational members of the public, the guards shrank back into the wall without saying a word as Patrick steamed out of the room.

Outside in Brewer Street the snow began to fall again, greying the Soho skies. Patrick pulled his phone out of his pocket. His heart raced as Cab's then Franny's mobile went straight to answering machine.

Patrick wasn't sure if his hands were shaking because of the cold or because of anger, but what he was sure about was both of them had a lot of explaining to do and he wasn't going to take bull-shit for an answer.

Putting his phone away, Patrick pulled up his collar on his fawn cashmere coat, feeling the freezing wet flakes from his collar drip down his neck as he did so, magnifying his already foul mood. He stomped down the Soho streets, pushing into Christmas shoppers, followed up with warning looks to silence their complaints.

Turning into Dean Street, Patrick hurried towards the house, cursing as he slipped on the slushy ground. He skidded forward and toppled into his newly painted black front door, smashing his head against the large brass letter box.

Getting up and shaking off the dirty sludge from his coat, he felt a rage of injustice he hadn't experienced since his escape from the industrial school. With fury, he opened the door, almost kicking it off its hinges as it flew open and crashed against the ivory-coloured walls.

Taking the stairs two at a time, Patrick yelled, 'Franny! Franny! Where the feck are ye? Cab? Cabhan? I want a fecking word.'

Nothing.

Charging into Franny's bedroom, he saw it was as neat and pristine as ever but with no sign of Franny. With every minute that passed, his fury rose as he imagined what might have happened to *his* money. *His* properties. *His* only way of saving Franny. With that thought in his mind, he ran through each room, knowing they weren't there but needing to check nonetheless.

An hour later, Patrick found himself walking down Old Compton Street with the sleet being whipped into his face by the biting wind. Still not any nearer to finding Franny or Cab's whereabouts. *Still* letting his imagination run wildly –

envisaging everything from Franny and Cab running away together to them going into league with the likes of Frankie Taylor, a known face and club rival.

He'd checked Franny's office as well as Cab's apartment, then finally he'd checked the clubs, finding only an array of semi-clad girls and work-shy staff, infuriating him to the point of pinning one of the door staff against the wall.

It hadn't made him feel any better; in fact it had made him feel worse. The only person he really wanted to pin against the wall was Cab and, if he were to be truthful with himself, Franny wasn't ruled out of that equation either.

The full flow of his dark thoughts was broken by the sound of his phone ringing. Scrambling in his pocket at the same time as shouting abuse at a speeding cyclist, Patrick, desperate for the with-held number to be one of the people he wanted to talk to, answered. 'Hello? Fran? Cab?'

'Now that's very careless of you to lose not one but two of them.' It was the familiar voice of Donal O'Sheyenne.

'O'Sheyenne, what have you done with them?' Patrick's voice was laced with urgency.

'Now then, Paddy, I only called for a little chat and straight away I'm being accused of doing something to them.'

'Don't play games with me.'

'Calm down. Age has certainly come to dent your sense of humour, so it has. I don't know anything about Fran or that friend of yours. I was just going along with the way you answered the phone. I don't know what's going on but you know what they say ... *a trouble shared is a trouble–'*

Patrick pressed his thumb hard on the red button on his phone, cutting off Donal's words and the call.

Even though the night was closing in and temperature was dropping below freezing, Patrick could feel the heat from his body cranking up and making him sweat. What he needed was a drink. Answers. Money. The latter two he hadn't a clue how to sort out, and especially now, after everything. But the former. The drink – he certainly knew how to sort that and he knew exactly where he was going to do it.

Whispers Comedy Club in Old Compton Street was owned by Alfie Jennings, a London face who'd been at the top of his game a few years ago. Patrick knew him to have been a player both in the business sense and with the women, but that was before he'd got involved with Oscar Harding, a sadistic piece of work, similar to Donal O'Sheyenne.

Rumour had had it that Alfie had turned over his best friend, Vaughn Sadler, a retired and successful face. Alfie had got involved with sex trafficking, and in consequence had lost everything, including his daughter Emmie, who'd apparently been kidnapped by Oscar, though how much of that was true, Patrick didn't know. The gossip mill in Soho was worse than a ladies' nail bar.

All that Patrick knew for sure was that Emmie had left home along with Alfie's wife, Janine – though remembering the loud, foul-mouthed woman, Patrick was sure that *that* loss wouldn't

180

have been so great as the others. But as Patrick walked into Whispers, with its tired-looking chairs and outdated decoration, he realised the greatest loss to Alfie had been money.

From out of the darkness came a voice which was loud and brash; a cockney accent slicing through the words. 'Stone the bleedin' crows, if it ain't the man from the Emerald Isle. How's tricks, Paddy mate? Ain't seen you for some time. More importantly, how's that gorgeous girl of yours?'

'Off limits.'

A spotlight came on followed by warm laughter. It was Alfie. With a sweep back of his thick black hair from his forehead, he hurried forward, taking Patrick's hand firmly and shaking it vigorously.

'That's where we go wrong, mate. Thinking we can protect them from the likes of you and me. I can't be worse than her ex – from what I can gather, he was a tosser of the highest order. We do all we can for them and what do they go and bleedin' do, hey? Rip out your heart, that's what. Look at my Emmie – hardly see her now, though I'm sure Janine's behind it; always was a conniving cow. God knows what I saw in her, let alone how I was able to sleep with the woman. Gives me frigging nightmares when I think that I stuck me dick in her. Fuck knows how it didn't shrivel up in horror. You remember Janine, don't you? Fat, loud and face like a smacked bleedin' arse.'

Patrick, although burdened with worry, couldn't help smiling at Alfie. He was exactly as Patrick

181

remembered him to be and that's what he liked about him. And even though it looked to Patrick like life was a bit tough for Alfie at the moment, he still had a cheeky twinkle in his eye.

'I take it from that polite silence you do remember her. Don't hold back on my account, Paddy. I hope the bitch's ears burn. No, actually, strike that, mate, I hope they set on bleedin' fire.'

Alfie laughed along with Patrick but suddenly stopped, realising himself. 'I'm forgetting me manners. Let me get you a drink. Still on the whiskey?'

Patrick winked at Alfie, surprised he'd remembered. 'Make it a large one.'

Alfie tilted his head to one side. His handsome strong face wearing a look of concern. 'What's going on?'

Patrick didn't answer, just pulled a face.

'Listen, if there's anything I can do. You know what they say, a trouble shared...'

Patrick put his hand up, interrupting Alfie mid-sentence.

'Whatever else you say, *don't* say that.'

Without question, Alfie obliged. 'All I'm saying is, I know from experience how keeping stuff to yourself can fuck you up. Most of what I have has gone. Up to me neck in fucking debt, Paddy. Looks like I may have to sell the club.'

'You're not the only one,' Patrick answered ruefully.

Continuing to talk, Alfie poured Patrick a drink; filling the glass up to the top with whiskey.

'Flipping guts me. It's the only thing I've got to remind me of dear old Mum. Long story, I'll tell you about it some other time, but the point is, if I could just get me hands on some money, everything would be as sweet as.'

Gulping down the whiskey as if it were a glass of Coke, Patrick began to feel slightly better as the heat of the alcohol hit his insides and started to bring a slur to his Irish lilt.

'I don't want to go into it, Alfie, but you could say money was the root of me problems, too. Perhaps we've got more in common than I thought.'

Alfie looked surprised. 'That's a bit of a bubble popper, mate. I thought you were minted.'

'Things change.'

'You can fucking say that again.'

Both of them nodded before they fell into a reflective silence. However, the quiet was soon broken by Alfie letting out an almighty fart.

He grinned at Patrick. 'Sorry, mate, hold yer nose. Me belly's been playing up a bit. Had lunch at Lola's café; didn't realise I'd ordered salmonella with it.'

Staggering to get up, Patrick finished off the remaining whiskey, slamming the glass down slightly too hard. 'Thanks for the drink, Alfie, and for the chat... I needed that.'

As Patrick turned to leave, Alfie spoke. His tone serious and clear. 'Stay and have another drink, Paddy. I've got a proposition for you. Something which might help you *and* me. Might even sort out those roots of yours. It might be risky though, but sometimes in life you just have do what you have to do.'

25

Cabhan Morton was worried. And it wasn't an emotion he was particularly comfortable with. Since the days of the industrial school, he'd always done everything he possibly could to avoid the gnawing, twisting, sinking feeling of worry he got in the pit of his stomach.

It didn't take a psychiatrist to tell him why it was there and where it came from. The industrial school had taken its toll, both physically and mentally.

He'd managed to overcome a lot of the triggers associated with his past, but this was the one which always beat him. The one which always had tiny beads of cold sweat breaking out on his forehead, accompanied by a nauseous sick sensation that hit the back of his throat. Worry. And now, as he sat at the breakfast table of the Doyles' luxury flat, with Franny sitting uncharacteristically quietly next to him, and Patrick leaning dangerously close to his face, smelling of alcohol, worry was once more sabotaging his whole being.

'Well?' Patrick stared at him, his face flushed with the colour of anger and whiskey. He'd been up all night, drinking with Alfie Jennings and listening to his proposition. At first it had seemed absurd but the more he'd thought about it, the more he realized he might have no choice. And as he questioned both Cab and Franny about the

184

whereabouts of his money, he suddenly knew it was no longer a question of *might* have no choice but *didn't*.

Cab, almost afraid to swallow in case it made his obvious discomfort at Patrick's questioning even more apparent, gestured his hands vaguely.

Infuriated by the seemingly casual attitude of his closest and most trusted friend, Patrick bellowed, sweeping the dishes from the table and sending eggs Benedict, sausage and grilled bacon flying across the room to land in a delicious heap for the Doyles' white terrier dog.

Patrick's voice was slurred. 'What the fuck is that supposed to mean, hey, Cab? What the fuck gesture is that? Where did my money go?'

'Patrick. Please.' It was Franny who spoke, softly and quietly with her hands in her lap, unable to look at Patrick. She'd never seen him like this. So angry. So scared. It didn't help that he'd been drinking, but then she didn't blame him. She blamed herself and he blamed her. Her and Cabhan.

Patrick's eyes flashed at Franny. Hurt and disappointment in them. He spat his words, overwhelmed by the desire to smash up everything in his sight. Patrick pointed at her; like Franny, he was unable to look her in the eye.

'Don't, Franny. Don't. I'm not able to hear anything you have to say at the moment. Just do yourself a favour and keep quiet in case I say something I might regret and can't take back. I don't want any excuses. I don't want to hear it was because of your screwed-up love life that you forgot to tell me you spent me money. I don't want

185

to hear fucking anything from you.'

'Paddy, there's no need to speak to her like that.' Before Franny could stop her uncle from defending her, Patrick had leapt at him, pain from his wound cranking up his anger and fine Irish whiskey driving him on.

'Who the fuck are you to tell me not to do something? Who the hell are you apart from some pimped-up leech who wouldn't be anywhere if it wasn't for me? *Me!*' Patrick shouted the last word loudly, causing the dog to scurry under the table.

Regardless of his age and his lifestyle, Cab's eyes filled up with tears as Patrick held the scruff of his shirt in one hand.

'Please, Patrick.'

Intoxicated, Patrick mimicked Cab's voice. *'Please, Patrick. Please. I'm sorry...* You're a joke, Cab. Always have been, always will be. I should've let Killer get his hands on you that first day I arrived at the school.'

Passing hurt went through Cab's eyes. Seeing this and desperate not to feel any guilt, Patrick raised his fist, ready to bring it down into Cab's face.

As it began to descend, Patrick felt Franny grab him, pulling his arm towards her.

'Stop it, Patrick! Stop it!'

Patrick dropped the hold on Cab and turned to face Franny directly. His anger shone through but it wasn't enough to quell the love he felt for her. Because this was what it was all about. He loved her. Loved them both with all his heart. But it was this love which turned his anger stronger and bitterer. By taking the money, they had robbed

186

him of something more important than any wealth he'd incurred: they'd robbed him of being able to protect Franny from Donal O'Sheyenne.

As he spoke to Franny, it was Mary who he saw looking back at him. Her warm eyes. Her soft face. The way she'd cocked her head to one side when she was trying to understand something. He missed her. Loved her. Still, after all these years. His Mary. Taken away from him before they'd even had the chance to live out their lives together.

Perhaps that's why he'd never been able to commit to anybody. Of course, there were and had been plenty of women; but not one of them had ever come close to Mary. Sometimes he resented it. Resented loving her so deeply. It got lonely loving a ghost. A memory, yet here he was unable to stare at Franny because it was Mary who was staring back at him, and he couldn't bear the idea of being angry with Mary.

He turned his back to Franny and banged his fist on the marble counter as he stared out at the now grey and dirty snow lying thickly on the Soho street below.

Seeing an unopened bottle of whiskey on the side, he cracked it open; not bothering to pour it into a glass, he swilled back a large mouthful.

'I won't stop it, Franny. I trusted you. I trusted both of you, and now after all these years you go and turn me over. What for, hey? What for? Didn't I give you and Cab all that I have? Me money, but more importantly me love, and you do this to me.'

Franny ran up to Patrick, placing her hand on his back, but he shrugged it off, not wanting to be

187

touched by her.

It was now Franny's turn to cry.

She'd been trying to save the business without worrying him. What she didn't understand was why he'd gone into the bank to enquire about the money or the properties in the first place; she'd never known him take much interest in them before and had trusted her to run things. It was one of the reasons she'd felt so confident of being able to sort out the mess of the clubs' and casinos' finances without him finding out. At the moment though, she knew better than to ask him.

The other thing she didn't understand was that, from what Patrick was saying, it sounded as if he didn't have any money either – but surely that couldn't be possible? It couldn't be. Patrick was forever going away on business trips; hell, he'd only just got back from the last one. And what had happened with Cab and the money from the businesses he was in charge of was another mystery. But one thing she was sure of was that, like her, Cab loved Patrick and would never do anything to hurt him. The only problem was getting Patrick not only to believe her but to listen to her.

'Patrick, it's not like you think.'

Turning to look at her, Patrick glowered. 'What is it like, hey? Oh, let me see, you're going to tell me the bank accounts aren't really cleared out and the properties haven't all been remortgaged.'

Franny's large big beautiful eyes implored him. 'No Patrick, I...'

'No, I thought not, but until you do, Franny, until you can say that, I don't want to talk to you or Cab. I don't even want to see you.'

Outside in the street, Patrick wrapped his coat tightly round him as he trudged through the snow, feeling it creep over the tops of his expensive shoes, reminding him of the days of his childhood when every pair of shoes he'd owned had holes in them, allowing Kerry's seemingly endless rain to soak his young feet.

Thinking back to Ireland jolted him. He rarely did. There were so many unanswered questions. About Mary and of course about his father, whom he wondered was still alive. He'd desperately wanted to seek out the person who'd attacked Mary; wanting to hurt whoever it was the way he'd no doubt hurt Mary in the woods all those years ago. But Cab had talked him out of it, worried and warning him not to go back to Ireland. So instead Patrick had closed the door on that chapter of his life. For his own sanity.

He tried to pull himself back from these thoughts, hating to remember all that had gone on. He could feel the pain in his chest, just as he always could when thoughts of the industrial school and the related events came into his mind.

A long time ago he'd accepted the fact that he would never know what really happened and why. The only person who had any sort of information was Donal O'Sheyenne, and although at times he'd been tempted to ask, the twisted game-playing and the distorted story he would be sure to get certainly would challenge the truth.

'Are you coming in or out, love? Come on, Paddy, even for an Irish man that decision ain't too hard.'

Lola Harding stood in the doorway of her cafe, grinning an almost toothless grin. Patrick stared at her.

'Er ... er...'

'Bleedin' hell, it's a good job you're a looker, Patrick, 'cos no-one could accuse you of having the gift of the gab. Now are you coming in for a cup of tea or what? You'll have me freezing me tits off, magnificent as they are.'

Absent-mindedly, Patrick answered. 'No, I'll leave it. Take care of yourself, Lola, and I'll see you soon.'

Not hearing Lola's cheery reply, Patrick hurried down the street pulling out his phone to dial a number.

'Alfie, it's me, Patrick. I'm in.'

26

'What are you doing?' Franny Doyle stood in the doorway of the tastefully decorated master bedroom. She waited a minute, but, getting no reply, tried again.

'Patrick! Please...' Her voice betrayed her despair.

Not bothering to stop what he was doing, Patrick answered with quick hostility. 'What does it look like I'm doing?'

Franny stepped into the bedroom. She was tired and had spent the last couple of nights staring up at the ceiling unable to sleep; listening as Patrick paced around the lounge below her room making and receiving late-night phone calls. She hadn't even had chance to think about her ex and what had gone on, but she supposed that was a good thing; what wasn't was the way Patrick was shutting her out.

'It looks like you're packing... Where are you going?'

Throwing a brown cashmere jumper into the Louis Vuitton suitcase lying on the bed, Patrick turned to look at Franny.

'What is it you *actually* want from me, Fran? Because as you can see I'm rather busy here. So if you don't mind...'

Turning his back on her again, Patrick gestured towards the door for Franny to leave.

Hurt and unable to contain her emotions any longer, Franny ran to Patrick, grabbing hold of the pink Ralph Lauren shirt he was about to place in the case and childishly putting it behind her back.

'Don't, Patrick! Don't!' Patrick heard the panic in her voice as tears ran down her face. 'Just stay and talk. We can sort this out. You taught me not to run away from my problems and you're doing just that.'

Patrick, hating himself for it but unable to stop, stared at Franny coldly.

'Give me back my shirt.'

Franny shook her head. 'Not until you tell me where you're going.'

Continuing to stare at Franny, Patrick held out his hand for his shirt. Losing patience and seeing

191

he wasn't going to get anywhere, he mumbled a 'Fine' before walking across to the large custom-built closet which held an array of bespoke shirts and tailor-made suits.

Watching him grab another designer shirt from one of the wooden hangers, Franny implored him. 'Patrick... I don't know what to say.'

'Then try saying nothing, Franny. Leave me alone and just let me do what I have to do.'

'How can I let you go if I don't know where you're going?'

Patrick pushed the last of his clothes into the suitcase then zipped it up with excessive force as he cursed under his breath. Red-faced and irritated, he looked back up at Franny.

'You're not my keeper, Fran, and this is just how it is; you've got no choice. In the same way I've been left with no choice thanks to you and Cab. So I suggest you get out of my way and let me go.'

Franny didn't budge. She stood in front of Patrick, not letting him pass as her long chestnut hair tumbled across her face. Attempting to get past, Patrick tried to move to the side, but was blocked by Franny again.

'*Move,* Franny.'

'No.'

Patrick sighed, 'Fran, get out of my way. Otherwise I'll have to move you and neither of us want that.'

'What's going on?' Cabhan Morton walked into the room; like Franny, he looked tired. His eyes were bloodshot and he was still wearing the same Burberry black shirt and Gucci jeans from the day before.

Patrick's face turned into a sneer. He hadn't had a conversation with Cab since he'd found about the money and he certainly had no intention to, either. 'Get out!'

Franny, relieved to see Cab, blurted out her misery to him.

'Cab! He's going. He won't tell me where. Do something, Cab. Please...'

'Is it true?' Cab stared; eyes almost as wide as Franny's were. 'Paddy man, you can't do this.'

Patrick clenched his jaw, trying to resist the urge to punch Cab in his face.

'I'll tell you what I told Fran. Get out of me way, otherwise I'll move you myself. And, Cab? The way I'm feeling, it'd be my pleasure to put you through the wall.'

Before Cab had a chance to answer, the doorbell rang and a second later a booming voice was heard, followed by a grinning Alfie Jennings appearing in the doorway looking extremely handsome with a cheeky smile plastered on his face.

'All right, mate, you ready? That housekeeper of yours let me in; fuck me, she's a bit of a looker, ain't she? Do me a favour, when you've finished with her, send her my way, will ya? I ain't fussy about second-hand goods.'

Almost without taking a breath and clocking Patrick's suitcase Alfie continued, 'Fuck me, Paddy, you got enough stuff there or what? We ain't going on bleedin' holiday, you know. You're as bad as me ex-bleedin'-wife – she never went anywhere without a fucking truckload of suitcases. It was like going away with the travelling circus.'

Alfie broke off into peals of warm laughter as

the others looked on.

'What's he doing here?' Franny's voice was frosty as she spoke to Patrick

Alfie winked, turning his attention to Franny. He raised his eyebrows and whistled. He'd forgotten how beautiful she was. Porcelain skin, a mane of thick glossy chestnut hair, and although there wasn't any warmth in her eyes as she stared coldly at him, they were wide and mesmerising; almost emerald green in colour.

And then of course there was the body. Just the thought of her body could keep a man content on many a lonely night. Not that it got much action; he knew she didn't put it around like some of the other women in Soho and through Paddy and local gossip he'd also heard she'd split up with her boyfriend.

The way she'd always rebuffed his charms, it had crossed his mind she might be gay, but that didn't put him off, quite the opposite, in fact; it got him hot under the collar. The sight of Franny Doyle rolling around with another naked woman was something he'd pay good money to see.

The only thing he wasn't so keen on was that she reminded him slightly of Vaughn Sadler's missus. Casey Edwards. She was a looker, but a fucked-up one, as well as being a cock tease.

How he ever let her get away he didn't know. He should've fucked her when he'd had the chance but, like a fool, he'd been loyal to Vaughn – for all the good it'd done him.

Vaughn, a retired face, was someone he'd known for a long time and now he hardly saw him. Even when he did bump into him, Vaughn

194

could hardly bring himself to speak to him.

In his opinion, Vaughn had been blinded by his cock when it'd come to Casey, and he, Alfie Jennings, a man once on top of his game, had ended up broke because of it. The man had become weak, and instead of jumping at every money-making opportunity Vaughn had begun to look at the moral rights and wrongs of things. And all because of a woman. It was a joke.

Women were a pain in the ass and he'd rather put his balls in a deep-fat fryer than have a relationship again, though it didn't mean he wasn't going to see if he could have a crack at Franny and get her into bed. And once he had? He'd have her singing like a lark, lesbian or not.

'Franny. May I say, darlin', you're looking the business. You could send a man blind with that form.'

Franny stayed frozen. She'd known Alfie Jennings for as long as she could remember but had also avoided him like the proverbial plague. No-one could accuse him of not being good-looking – he was an extraordinarily handsome man, giving even Patrick a run for his money in the looks stakes – but, unlike Patrick, Alfie was a creep.

Her friend, Casey Edwards, had told her all about his antics with her and his involvement in the sex trafficking business a while back; one of the reasons he'd fallen out with his best friend, Vaughn Sadler.

Alfie was an arrogant harbour shark who thought he was God's gift, and there was no way she was going to let him near enough to even get a bite.

Franny ignored Alfie. Patrick's departure was clearly something to do with him – quite what, she didn't know, but anything to do with Alfie Jennings was bound to cause trouble. She knew Alfie was desperate for money, and desperate men did desperate things; the last thing she wanted was Patrick getting involved in any of his schemes.

'Patrick, *please.*'

Alfie's eyes twinkled. 'I like to hear a woman begging.'

'Shut it, Alf.' Patrick growled out his words. As much as it aggrieved him to let Franny see him come to her defence, there was no way he was going to stand and listen to Alfie's cheap chat-up lines. In that sense, Franny was totally off limits, especially as she was no doubt vulnerable after splitting up with her ex.

Alfie patted Patrick on the back. 'Oh come on, mate, she knows I'm only playing, don't you sweetheart? And she's hardly a little girl; not with those curves.'

Franny's eyes flashed with anger. 'What I do know is you're a creep, but what I don't know, and I want to, is what exactly you want with Patrick.'

Alfie roared with laughter. 'Feisty bird you've brought up there, Patrick. Must be the Irish blood in her. Give me a night with her and she'll come back as meek as a lamb.'

Enraged now and making a mental note to have a word with Alfie later, Patrick shoved Alfie hard towards the door. He gritted his teeth, hissing to Alfie under his breath, *'Just move it. Now!'*

Alfie shrugged, making his way out of the room. He liked Patrick, but he needed to lighten

196

up when it came to Franny; he protected her as if she were a china doll. Christ, the woman didn't need his protection. She was a ball-breaker when it came to business – looking after all those clubs and keeping the men and faces in line certainly wasn't an easy feat, even for a bloke.

As Patrick and Alfie descended the highly polished wooden stairs towards the large front door, Franny followed, pleading as she went. 'Patrick, I've always tried to be independent and I've never asked you for anything, but now I am. *Don't* go – or at least tell me *where* you're going.'

Patrick stopped abruptly on the bottom stair. He turned round to look at Franny, speaking ruefully. 'And you know why that is, don't ye? Why you've never asked me for anything. It's because I've always given it to you. *Everything.* I gave you my whole life, Franny, in more ways than you'll ever know. So let's have it straight; it's actually *me* who didn't ask *you* for anything and doesn't that just make me the biggest fool.'

Patrick marched past Alfie, barging him out of the way with his large suitcase to get to the front door. He flung it open, letting the swirling snow blow into the high-ceilinged hallway.

He heard Franny shout out, 'Do something, Cab. Stop him!'

Patrick didn't wait; he couldn't. His heart was being torn apart and he had the same tight feeling in his chest he always had when things were overwhelming him. He stomped off down the road, feeling the mixture of wet and powered snow under his shoes, hoping Franny wouldn't follow.

Shooting a warning look at the carol singers who were about to shake a large yellow collecting bucket in his face, Patrick crossed over the road to his gun-metal grey Range Rover. Opening the boot electronically, he threw his suitcase in. Patrick felt his arm being grabbed again, but this time it wasn't Franny as he thought it would be; it was Cab.

Cab Morton stood facing his dearest friend as the snowflakes formed a pattern on his well-cared-for Afro. Cab knew he'd let his friend down and had no idea how to fix it. The last couple of nights he'd gone round to all the faces he knew, trying to borrow money and salvage what was left of the businesses.

But to his bitter disappointment, he learnt that the saying, 'You've got no friends in business, only correspondents' was true. No-one had wanted to lend him anything, though perhaps if he had been in their position he'd have felt the same. And now he was helpless to help Patrick; the promise he'd made to him to always be there, no matter what, seemed shallow and empty.

'Paddy, I know you probably don't want to listen to anything I've got to say. But please, don't do this. Whatever it is as Franny says – we can sort it. Both of us. You're not on your own.'

'That's right, he's not, he's got me.' Alfie came up from behind; patronisingly putting an arm round Cab.

Patrick cut his eye at Alfie. He didn't know why he felt so protective after everything Franny and Cab had done, but there it was, he did. He could be angry and have a go at them, but nobody else could. Because no matter what, Franny and Cab were family. *His* family.

'Get in the car, Alfie, and for once try to keep it shut.'

Obligingly, Alfie did as he was asked, blowing a kiss goodbye to Franny who was standing shivering on the pavement without a jacket.

'Get her in, Cab. She'll catch her death.'

Touched but at the same time taking umbrage at the remark, Franny retorted haughtily. 'For God's sake, I'm old enough not to be told what to do.'

Patrick sliced a remark: 'Then act like it.'

Franny's face reddened, tears welling up in her eyes again. She'd cried more times in the last seventy-two hours than she ever had in her life. 'Me grow up? You're the one rushing off and going God knows where without telling us.'

'She's right, Paddy,' said Cab. 'Clearly we can't stop you going, but at least tell us where. Or even why.'

Patrick looked down, shaking his head in despair and absentmindedly kicking some snow to reveal the grey Tarmac of the paving stones underneath. He spoke quietly to Cab as he leant on the door of his car. 'Two words: *Donal O'Sheyenne.*'

Cab's face unveiled his surprise. 'Donal? I thought that was sorted. I ... I don't understand. I thought he'd stopped the payments. You told me he had.'

'Well, I lied. What was the point in worrying you as well? I thought somehow I could cover it.'

'Why didn't you tell me, Paddy? You could've

199

told me; we share everything.'

'Like you shared the fact you took my money without asking?'

'No... I ... no, of course not.'

'No, I didn't think so.'

Cab looked over his shoulder at Franny, making sure she couldn't hear them. 'But what are you going to do now? I mean, what are we going to do?'

Patrick stared with hatred at Cab, his heart aching as he did so. Sarcasm dripped through his words. 'Oh Cab, you've done enough, so you have. The money you fucked away was going to go in part to paying Donal – it might not have been enough but it was something. Something to keep him off my back until I worked out what I was going to do. And now thanks to your stunt, I've got nothing to pay him with. Nothing to offer him.' Then remembering Donal's words about a life for a life, Patrick reflected. 'Well, nothing I want to give him anyway.'

'How much does he want, Paddy?'

'Five million.'

'*What?*'

'Keep your voice down. I don't want Franny getting wind of any of this, you hear me?'

Cab's eyes and voice were filled with concern. 'Of course; you have my word. I think we should blow him away. Get rid of Donal once and for all. Come on, Paddy, what do you say?'

Patrick's voice hardened even further. 'I said, you stay well away from him. Have you forgotten the rules, Cab? If anything happens to him, there are orders for his men to take Franny out.'

'But how will they know it's us? If we're careful we could get away with it.'

Patrick grabbed hold of Cab's arm, shaking him slightly. 'You listen to me. That's not a risk I'm willing to take, because as much as they may never find out, they're just as likely to find out.'

Cab nodded, feeling ill. He'd always known Donal had made Patrick pay every year for what Donal saw as a sale or return on Franny. Foolishly, he'd expected over the years Donal would give up his sick deal and let them all live in peace, but with ruthless persistence, the man had kept coming back, until this year, or so he had thought. He really had thought it was over.

'So, what now?'

Patrick scoffed. 'Now? We hope what I've got lined up works out; failing that? We pray for a miracle, because it seems it's just about all we've got left. Let's hope the god we were forced to pray to, who didn't hear our cries all those years ago, realises he now owes us one.'

With that, and without saying goodbye to either Cab or Franny, Patrick jumped into the Range Rover.

Seeing Patrick leave, Franny ran to the driver's window, banging on it for him to stop.

'Patrick! Patrick!'

From behind her, Cab spoke sadly and gently. 'Let him go, Franny. Trust me; you need to let him go.'

27

'Fuck me, if it ain't the pensioners' outing.' The blond-haired man in the far corner of the empty warehouse jeered as Alfie walked in, followed by Patrick.

Ignoring Patrick's menacing look, the man, no more than twenty-five himself, continued with his derogatory remarks, building a large spliff as he did so.

'Alf, mate, you didn't tell me we'd need to get the Zimmer frames out. Are you sure you've got the right place? The Saga holiday entrance is just next door.' Inhaling the spliff deeply, the man cackled, yellowing bloodshot eyes staring out in amusement from underneath his long floppy fringe.

'That's enough. If I want a comedian I know where to look; until then, shut it.'

'A bit sensitive, ain't we, Alf? Hit a nerve in yer old age, have I?'

Alfie didn't reply; instead he listened to Patrick who had grabbed onto the upper part of his arm.

'What's the craic? Have you lost your mind? You never told me we were going to be with a bunch of fecking amateurs, so you didn't.'

Alfie, pulling his arm away, seethed inwardly at the public dressing down by Patrick. Okay, so he'd been read the riot act in the car about winding Franny up, and he could take that. Accept it.

Because that had been done in private. But this. This? Patrick was taking the fucking piss. After all it was *him*, Alfie Jennings, who'd brought Patrick on board, not the other way round. Yet here he was being reprimanded like a kid in front of a bunch of ladder climbers. Well, it wasn't happening. Not here. Not now. Not fucking ever.

Turning his back on the men in the corner who were clearly taking great delight at what was unfolding, Alfie, hissed back. Just as loud. Just as seething. Just as put out as Patrick.

'Listen, I don't fucking appreciate you showing me up like this. Remember who it was who sorted this out in the first place.'

'By the looks of it, Alf, you shouldn't have bothered.'

'I didn't have to bring you on board. You should be thanking me; not treating me like a fucking muppet.'

Patrick sneered. 'Thanking you? Look around, Alf; what do you see? It's pathetic. Jaysus.'

Alfie had had enough. His voice becoming louder he poked Patrick hard in the chest. 'What I see, mate, is a way out for both of us – but if you've got any better ideas, then be my guest because from where I'm standing this is our only option.'

'Trouble, gentlemen?'

The blond-haired man sauntered across to where Alfie and Patrick were standing. He grinned at them.

'Nothing we can't handle, Trev. Give us a minute, will you, pal?' Alfie spoke with authority to the man, trying desperately to salvage back what he saw as losing front.

Trevor opened his arms wide. A cheeky glint in his eye.

'Well, when you two have decided what to do and finished your grannies' meeting, let me know. I'll be over there with the real men.'

Just as Trevor was about to turn away, Patrick grabbed his wrist. 'Don't push your luck, son; you don't know me and you certainly don't know what I'm capable of.'

Trevor looked at him with amusement. 'You have some grip for an old man. Now if you don't mind I'd be pleased for my hand back.'

Alfie, pre-empting Patrick's reaction, held him back as he lunged towards Trevor, who hopped backwards out of reach, enjoying the wind-up.

'Temper, temper, Paddy boy!'

Patrick's eyes sparked with anger. 'You'll do well to stay out of me way. I swear on the holy Mary, if I get me hands on you...' He stopped, pushing Alfie off and began to head for the door. 'I'm out, mate; whatever you want to do is your call but count me out.'

The click of the safety trigger behind him surprised and enraged Patrick to the same degree. Although he didn't turn round, he stood motionless, listening to Trevor laying down his demands.

'You ain't going nowhere.'

Defiantly, Patrick answered. 'That's where you're wrong.'

'Sadly for both of us we're stuck with each other.'

Still with his back facing Trevor and aware of the gun pointing at his head, Patrick spoke slowly. 'I don't think so. I haven't signed up for anything.'

Trevor walked round in front of Patrick. But the smirk of amusement had gone and in its place was a threatening glare.

'It's not me who's wrong ... pal; it's you. You ain't backing out now and screwing the whole job up. There's a lot riding on this. Everything is in place to go ahead. The security guards at the diamond merchants have had the heads-up. Those that needed paying have been sorted. The others, well, let's just say they've been paid a visit by a very persuasive man. A lot of time and planning have gone into sorting out this robbery. When Alfie told me the rep you had, I didn't think to look for anyone else. And now it's too late. So right there is where we have our problem, *Patrick*. You walk, I'm a man down, which means the job ain't happening.'

Mirroring Trevor's scathing look, Patrick answered. His eyes full of cold hostility. 'Then unless you don't want the job to happen, *Trevor*, you better find someone else. I only came for a meeting so I did. There were no promises and from what I can see you're just a bunch of monkeys trying to play in the big boys' league.'

Choosing his words carefully and not wanting to show his anger, Trevor kicked the roach of his spliff away. He inhaled deeply, studying the man in front of him.

'But you see, when I talked to Alfie, he assured me you were in. If you've got a grievance, take it up with him, but I ain't having some old timer screwing it all up for me. I ain't going to let a few million slip through my fingers because of anyone, least of all you.'

Patrick looked across at Alfie, who lowered his head.

'You set me up. You told me we were just going to have a chat. See how everything lies.'

Shrugging uncomfortably, Alfie muttered. 'Come on, Paddy; it hasn't been that long since you've been in this game. You know how it works. No-one's just going to let you come over and have a cosy chat.' Alfie paused and sighed. He wasn't sure if he was getting through to Patrick but he knew Trevor well enough to know there was no way he was going to let either of them back out.

Alfie continued, this time looking directly into Patrick's face; appealing to him. 'Let's just get this job over and done with, hey? Okay, I should've said what the deal really was, but you won't regret it.'

Patrick shook his head wryly. 'I already am.'

Not enjoying being on the defensive, Alfie changed tack; attacking back. 'Look, for fuck's sake, what was I supposed to do? There was the opportunity. It was either take it or leave it, so I took it ... for both of us. We both need the money. It'll be a straight in and out and then we'll be laughing. So, what do you say?'

Patrick looked around. First at the other men in the corner, then at Trevor, who was still holding the gun in his hand, and then lastly at Alfie, who stood by the side wall where a pane of broken glass let the evening snow drift in.

Sadly, Patrick shook his head before speaking quietly to Alfie. 'I say, it looks like I've got no choice; it seems it's becoming a bit of a habit these days. But, Alfie, I've got a bad feeling about this. A very bad feeling.'

'He could be anywhere. Why did you let him go?'

Cab paced around in the Doyles' kitchen as Franny berated him down the phone. However, he found himself only half-listening when yet another call buzzed in on the other line. It was the twelfth that day. All unanswered. All from Donal O'Sheyenne.

He had no idea what he was supposed to do. He'd tried Patrick but his phone was turned off, so now the decision whether to answer or not was down to him.

But before Cab could begin to think what the best thing to do was, the choice was no longer his. There, standing larger than life – almost a caricature of himself – was Donal O'Sheyenne, dressed in his usual attire of a black floppy hat and a long waxed trench mac.

'Fran, I'll call you back, baby. I have to go.'

'Why if it isn't the little black boy.' Donal laughed as he walked into the room, throwing himself down on one of the white leather kitchen chairs.

Cab stared in horror at Donal. He could feel cold sweat dripping down his back Even after all this time the man made him feel uneasy. 'What are you doing here? How did you get in?'

Donal sniffed as he looked around the expensively decorated kitchen. 'Well, it doesn't take a genius to break into a house and, as no-one was answering me calls, I thought I best come and pay you a visit. Let meself in... So where is he then?'

'How did you get in?'

Donal kicked off his shoes and started to rub his feet energetically. He sniffed loudly. 'I thought the winters back in Ireland were bad, but by Christ, this one seems like it's going to take a lot of beating.'

Cab pushed again. 'I *said* ... how did you get in?'

A derisory expression appeared on Donal's face. 'I've never understood you. Never. You had the opportunity to go and make a life on your own. Go anywhere. Do anything. Yet here you are sniffing around Patrick's tail feather still. Doesn't make sense.'

Cab walked over to Donal, contemplating what approach to take with him. Over the years it'd mostly been Patrick who'd had dealings with Donal, but that didn't stop Cab knowing how wary of him he had to be. He wasn't quite sure how old Donal was but age certainly hadn't slowed him down; he was still as dangerous as he'd always been.

Cab rubbed his chin, feeling the three-day shadow. He walked over to Donal, who'd now pulled off his sock completely and was rubbing his foot in earnest.

Leaning in closely, Cab could smell his sickly sweet breath. He stared, taking in the man's rugged face. Deep lines circled Donal's eyes. His sallow skin hung loosely over his prominent bone structure and his mouth, open slightly, allowed Cab to see his blackened, decaying teeth.

Both Cab and Donal locked eyes at the same time. Neither moved. The moments ticked by as the silence of the room was exaggerated by the harmonious voices of the distant carol singers.

'Get out of this house!' Cab's anger broke through as he grabbed hold of Donal.

Donal pushing Cab off, leant back and grinned. 'Not unless you tell me where he's gone.'

'Who?'

Donal sneered. 'You can do better than that. We both know who I'm talking about. Where is Patrick? Because he and I were in the middle of a conversation which went something like this: I want my money and if I don't get it... Franny will.'

'Did someone mention my name?' Franny walked into the kitchen, hair wet from the snow shower and her cheeks rosy red from the cold.

Noticing the man sitting on the chair with his socks off, and already annoyed with her uncle, Franny looked at Cab quizzically, not bothering with pleasantries. 'Who's this?'

Cab shuffled uncomfortably. 'Er ... this ... this is...'

Donal stood up, and put out his hand. 'I'm Donal O'Sheyenne. Pleased to meet you, Franny. I like to see myself as your fairy godfather.' Donal stopped talking and studied Franny before shaking his head and bursting out into laughter. 'For all that is holy, you certainly look like your mother.'

Franny's face drained of colour. She stared at Cab, searching for answers in his tense expression.

With Cab not in any way forthcoming, Franny turned back to Donal. 'You knew my mother?'

Donal answered proudly. 'That I did.'

'How?... I...'

Donal's eyes twinkled with amusement. 'All in good time. But perhaps I should leave Patrick to tell you. You don't know where he is, do you? He and I have some unfinished business.'

Franny, sensing there was more to this enquiry than innocent curiosity, began to clam up. She answered matter-of-factly. 'No I don't.'

'Really? Now I find that hard to believe. I can't imagine he'd want to let you out of his sight, not with the way things stand.'

Franny spoke firmly, her tone reflecting years of dealing with some of the hardest faces in London. 'Perhaps you'd better leave.'

'Again ... all in good time.'

Donal went over to where Franny was standing. He smiled, reaching up to touch her cheek. 'You really do look like her; to be sure, it's uncanny. Such a waste.'

Franny brushed away Donal's hand. 'Get out!'

'So I will, Franny, so I will. But be sure to tell Patrick I want what's owed; otherwise, I'll have to take back what's mine and I'm not sure I'll enjoy having to do that, Franny, I'm not sure I will.'

28

'Is everybody ready? I'm talking to you, old man.'

Trevor's voice was loud and aggressive as Patrick's fingers hovered over the car door handle. There was still time to leave. If he made it quick.

Real quick. What were they going to do? Gun him down in broad daylight? Try to grapple him back into the car?

But then what? This wasn't about him or what he wanted. It was about Franny. He had to do this for her.

He could feel his heart beating faster as the adrenalin began to pump round his body and a film of perspiration formed on his eyelashes. Blinking away the sweat, Patrick exhaled loudly, trying to steady his breathing.

Looking round to the back of the car, Patrick saw Trevor; his eyes were wide and Patrick could tell he was wired; he'd been banging back the charlie most of the day. Another of the men sat smoking a large spliff, his balaclava perched on the top of his head.

Trevor shouted again; a manic look on his face. 'I *said*, are you ready, old man? Don't fuck this up.'

Patrick hadn't time to speak before the cold butt of the gun Trevor held in his hand was pushed under his chin.

Patrick's mouth slammed shut but he refused to react to the pain which shot through his body as his teeth bit down on his tongue. He tasted the salty blood and grimaced, but he held Trevor's gaze before pulling down his balaclava.

'Don't mess this up, Paddy. There's a lot riding on it.'

Patrick didn't answer. He turned to look at Alfie, who was sitting nervously next to him in the blacked-out Mercedes.

'You okay, Alf?' he asked, his voice muffled

211

under the black balaclava.

Alfie nodded. But he wasn't okay. Far from it. He turned away from Patrick and watched the heavy snow settling on the car window. Christ, what the fuck had he been thinking? Money had once more clouded his judgement and now he was sitting in a car, surrounded by a bunch of gun-toting muppets. Suddenly this didn't seem like such a good idea. Although Alfie hated to admit it, he knew what Trevor had said was true. Both he and Patrick were too old for this game.

'I'm still waiting, old man. I want to hear you tell me you're ready... *Tell me.*'

Trevor hit the butt of the gun into Patrick's chest, who grabbed it, twisting it away as he locked eyes. He looked at Trevor scornfully. 'Oh, I'm ready, Trevor. More than. But the real question is; are you? Are *you* ready?'

Unnerved by Patrick's response and feeling paranoid under his glare, Trevor turned away, barking his orders to the others.

'I don't want any fuck-ups. Everyone knows what they're doing, so there ain't no excuses. We head across to the second warehouse; that's where the diamonds are kept. As you know, the other warehouse is the admin office, so we need to keep schtum a bit. We don't want to be bumping into anybody. If you do see anyone though ... don't hesitate.' As if to prove his point, Trevor released the safety trigger on his gun, prompting the others to do the same.

'No-one said anything about shooting. That wasn't part of it.'

Trevor looked at Patrick contemptuously. 'What

did you think these were for? Playing fucking soldiers?'

'There's a difference between putting the frighteners on someone and pulling the trigger.'

'Then let's hope we don't see anyone.'

Patrick fell silent whilst the other men hung onto Trevor's every word; waiting for his final orders. Trevor smiled, enjoying the sense of power. He bent over the middle armrest to take the last line of the Peruvian cocaine he'd been snorting. It was good shit.

The sensation of the coke hit the back of his nose and throat. He closed his eyes for a moment as he felt it work its way into his bloodstream.

A second later, pulling down his balaclava, Trevor grinned and shouted. 'Come on then, what are we waiting for? Let's go and get those rocks.'

The doors of the car flew open and Patrick jumped out along with the others, clicking down the safety lock on the Colt 9mm sub-machine gun. There was more shouting of orders as the gang ran towards the back of the diamond merchants, adrenalin surging through their bodies.

'Round the back! Round the back! Fucking move it! Move it! Get across to the second warehouse!'

Alfie, the last out of the car, ran forward, panting, pushing his body to the limit as he raced across the lot and towards the warehouse.

Dusk was beginning to set in and the snow was falling even more heavily now. Alfie could see Patrick charging across the lot and occasionally slipping on the wet earth as he made his way to the steel doors.

213

Out of breath and catching up with the other men, Alfie saw Trevor begin to crank open the doors; they'd deliberately been left unlocked by one of the security guards.

Within a few seconds all the men had run through to the warehouse which housed the diamonds, waving their guns in the air as their momentum built up.

There were more doors to go through and, just like the first set, all had been left unlocked by the bribable staff.

Patrick ran along the dark maze of corridors with large heavy doors lining them. The passageways of the warehouse reminded him of those of the industrial school and, aware of his own breathing, he desperately tried to shake off the images spilling into his mind.

'Open the door! Open the fucking doors!' Up in front, one of the other gang members screamed as he saw the double bolt was still locked on the last door.

Trevor raged. 'It's supposed to be open! Fuck! Fuck!' He looked around to speak. 'Shoot it! Shoot the fucking bolt off!' The words were directed at Patrick, who didn't move. 'I said, shoot the fucking door!'

Patrick stared at Trevor through the slits of his balaclava. His warning words were urgent and racing. 'Are you out of yer mind? Look around you. Look out there. We're feet away from where everyone's working.'

'I'm telling you to shoot!'

'No!'

Trevor squared up to Patrick, screaming in his

214

face. *'I said shoot the fucking door ... now!'*

'It's not going to work. We *can't.* You shoot, the Old Bill will be here before you can say bunch of muppets. Face it; it was never going to work. The whole thing was a screw-up from the start.'

High from the coke, Trevor smashed his gun into the side of Patrick's skull. A dark red patch appeared on Patrick's balaclava as he staggered backwards, trying to keep his balance and fight off the swirl of unconsciousness which began to creep over him.

As he fell to the ground on his side, Patrick watched the snow outside turn from white to a crimson-red mass as the blood from his head wound spilled across his eyes, blurring his vision. His thoughts began to spin as he listened to the sound of a machine gun firing.

'Take my hand, Paddy! Come on! You've got to get up!'

Patrick tried to talk but the skin on his lips stuck together. He murmured almost inaudibly to the voice in his darkness. 'Cab... Cab...'

A moment later, Patrick Doyle blacked out as Trevor screamed out the words, *'Leave him, Alf! Fucking leave him!'*

Inside the diamond storage area of the warehouse, Alfie could hear Trevor calling out orders from another area. Spotting some security guards, Alfie hollered, unsure whether they were on Trevor's payroll or not and unwilling to take the chance.

'Get down! Get down! Nobody move!'

The guards immediately dropped down to the

cold concrete floor. Out of the corner of his eye, Alfie saw one of the guards start to move. He spoke aggressively though his balaclava as his eyes darted around the large warehouse.

'No heroics, mate.'

The guard put his hands up and froze as he became aware of the gun pointing directly at him. Alfie's attentions were drawn to Trevor and the other men racing back across the warehouse towards him.

Alfie growled at Trevor. He could see his glassy-eyed stare; he was becoming edgier by the second and the sinking feeling in Alfie's stomach worsened.

'What's happening, Trev? What about Patrick? We can't leave him out there.'

Trevor was animated with anger as he pointed his gun at Alfie. 'You fucking leave him. You hear me? You're fucking lucky it ain't you lying face down as well.'

'We're in this together, Trev. You never leave one of yer own. We need to go and get him.'

'No, what we *need* to do is...' Wild eyed, Trevor stopped mid-sentence as he noticed the guards on the floor. He screamed out his words.

'What did I say, hey? What did I fucking say? Didn't I make myself clear? No hesitation, I said. No fucking hesitation!' With the words ringing in everybody's ears, Trevor pointed his gun at the guard's head. In a crazed frenzy he pulled the trigger and fired off a round of ammunition.

Blood sprayed everywhere. Alfie let out a cry as a bullet ricocheted into his leg. He dropped to the floor, holding it in agony.

216

'Now is that clear enough for you?'

From under Alfie's balaclava his jaw clenched and nausea rose, but he knew better than to say anything. All he wanted to do was get the fuck out. Through his pain he replied. 'Crystal, Trev. Crystal.'

Trevor pulled up his balaclava to wipe the coke-induced sweat from his face. 'Okay, so now we've got that sorted, can we fucking get on with this? Alf, it don't look like you're going anywhere fast, so you stay here; keep an eye on the north side. Me and Steve will go and get the ice.'

'Let's go! Let's go! We've got them!' Trevor and two other men ran through the warehouse holding the gym bag full of diamonds. They shouted at the top of their voices as Alfie, hobbled, trying to keep up.

Before they even managed to get to the first set of doors, Alfie could see the night sky through the window lit up with blue flashing lights. Fuck! Fuck! Fuck!

Alfie grabbed hold of Trevor's arm as he spat out angry words. 'This ain't so crystal clear now, is it, Trev? What the fuck are we going to do? I ain't doing bird.'

'This is the police. The warehouse is surrounded. Give yourself up. If you have firearms—'

The rest of the words were drowned out by Trevor spraying bullets into the warehouse windows.

'Come and fucking get us then, you cunts!' he shrieked at the top of his voice as shards of glass splintered everywhere.

Alfie tried to stop him but he could see Trevor was beyond care. 'Trev! What the fuck are you doing?'

Charged, Trevor bounced around on the spot. 'I'm getting out of here even if I have to shoot all the motherfuckers myself. You can fucking stay, but I ain't. Every man for his fucking self.'

Alfie opened his mouth to speak but the air suddenly became thick with smoke. As his eyes began to burn, he looked up to the shot-out windows, realising the police had fired in tear gas.

Limping out of the room, Alfie looked up and down the maze of corridors. He could hear shots in the background and a cacophony of loud voices, though he couldn't decipher if it they belonged to their own men or the police.

Shit. He hadn't paid any attention to which way they'd come in. He could feel the sweat drenching his body. It was in a warehouse like this one that his brother, Connor, had died during a job with Vaughn Sadler.

Paralysed with panic at the thought of ending up like his brother or facing a twenty-stretch, Alfie leant on the wall, frantically trying to pull himself together and ignore the pain in his leg.

A shout from one of the men in the distance jolted Alfie into action. It was just the distraction he needed. Without another thought, he made his way down the corridor directly in front of him, going as fast as the pain would allow. At the far end of one of the passageways he scrambled up the stairs, making his way along the first landing he came to.

218

He could hear the commotion below him; police and dogs charging into the building. Smoke and lights discolouring the air. Deafening cracks of noise sounded as gunshots blasted out. Raised voices. Dogs barking; all just below. He had to keep on going.

Looking around, Alfie decided to drop his gun. If he did get caught, there was no way he was going to be nabbed holding a firearm. He had enough form to know if they collared him tooled up, they'd throw the proverbial at him.

Finding a dark corner, Alfie threw down the gun. The best bet was to get back on the ground floor and try to head for the exit rather than hiding out; problem was he could see through the glass partition that a couple of the gang members had already been nicked – he suspected that, any moment now, the Old Bill would be heading his way.

Trying to get his bearings, Alfie thought he'd try to head through to the back of the warehouse via the first floor and make his way to the ground floor from there. The pain in his leg was getting worse and he wasn't sure how much longer he'd be able to walk on it.

The next corridor Alfie found himself in was pitch black. It was impossible to see anything and he found himself having to feel along the walls.

Coming round the corner, Alfie heard a noise; someone was coming. Fuck. He turned away from the noise, darting back the way he came. Whoever it was, it sounded like they were right behind him. He could feel the tightness in his chest as the sound came nearer.

'*Motherfucker!*' The manic screech echoed around the corridor. With blood dripping down his leg Alfie began to run. He crossed over to another passageway. There was slightly more light than in the one he'd just come out of, but he still couldn't see well enough to make out the figure behind him. He didn't need to though; he knew the voice. It was Trevor.

'Trev! Trev!'

'*Motherfucker!*'

'Trev, no, it's me, Alfie! Stop! Stop!'

'*I'll fucking kill all you pig motherfuckers.*'

Alfie Jennings had no time to react to the sound of the trigger being drawn back and he certainly didn't have time to react to the hail of bullets being fired in his direction.

29

Patrick Doyle touched his head and winced. He wasn't certain but he thought he'd just heard gunshots. For a moment he wasn't sure where he was. But only for a moment.

He tried to push himself up but immediately fell back down on the ground. The pain from his bead was excruciating and the walls of the warehouse looked like they were swimming around him.

A cold chill of realisation began to creep over Patrick. He could hear a jumble of raised voices, sirens and car engines as well as dogs barking in the distance. And while he couldn't be certain, he had a good idea what had gone down.

He needed to hurry. He had to get up and out of the warehouse if he was going to stand any chance of getting away, though there was no doubt in his mind the whole area was surrounded.

Making a concerted effort, Patrick scrambled up, this time determined to ignore the pain. What he found harder to ignore was his blurred vision; a consequence of his head injury.

Attempting to make his way down the maze of corridors, Patrick staggered along, holding onto the walls. A wave of nausea hit him. Violently retching he stopped to vomit. His whole body felt heavy. The temptation just to sit down was overwhelming but he knew he had to keep on going, whatever it took.

A clatter from the side of him made him halt. Pressing his body into the shadows, Patrick froze as the sound became louder; nearer.

His heart began to race faster. Sweat prickled his forehead as he hid motionless, desperate for the person to pass by without seeing him.

The sound stopped. Whoever it was had moved almost alongside him now and suddenly Patrick wished he hadn't left his gun behind. He wasn't sure if he was strong enough to take anyone on right now. His breathing became shallow as he tried to hold his breath. One... Two... Preparing himself, ready to make his move.

Patrick leapt out; wanting to take whoever it was by surprise. With darkness on his side, he flung himself at the person and dragged them down to the floor with a muffled cry.

He rolled on the floor, knowing he couldn't let the other man get the better of him. The element of surprise had been to his advantage, but now he could feel them fighting back. Heavy weight pushing into his pain spurred Patrick on; digging deeper; fighting harder in the black of the night.

He was on top now. All he needed to do was smash his fist down. Knock them out and get the fuck away. Bringing down his fist, Patrick felt the hard crunch of cartilage and the wetness of blood on his hand. Then a cry.

'Ah! Fuck! You cunt; you've broken me fucking nose!'

Just about to bring his fist down for the second time, Patrick stopped. But it was tempting not to. The realisation of who it was almost made Patrick want to finish what he'd started.

'Trevor?'

'Paddy?... What the fuck!... You've broken my nose!'

'Keep your voice down.'

'My nose!'

Leaning down to Trevor's ear, Patrick whispered. 'I didn't hear you complaining when you smashed a gun in my head. And, to be sure, the only reason I'm not finishing you off right here is because I want to know what the hell is happening.'

Patrick allowed Trevor to scramble up as he talked. His voice distorted from his broken nose. 'Fucking Old Bill are everywhere. Though I did manage to pick one of them off a few minutes ago; he didn't stand a chance.'

Patrick was stunned. 'Have you lost your fecking

senses? Killing a copper? You'll be running for the rest of your life, let me tell you.'

'And who's going to tell, eh?' Trevor sneered. 'Even if the others are caught, they ain't going to grass me up.'

'You're a fool to think they won't.'

'I know my men; if anyone is going to talk, I reckon it'll be you. And I can't have that...'

Patrick heard the safety catch of Trevor's gun being released but he refused to be threatened by it. 'This is getting boring now; if you're going to shoot me, just do it.'

Sounding more like a petulant teenager than a gang leader, Trevor whined. 'I've killed people, you know. Lots of them and I can do the same to you.'

'Well, while you decide whether you're going to kill me or not, I'm going to find a way out of here and I suggest you do the same.'

Not waiting or caring what Trevor had to say, Patrick stood up, using the wall to help him. He blew out the air from his lungs as the throbbing in his head persisted.

The corridor he made his way down began to get brighter as the warehouse roof changed from aluminium to glass, allowing the light from the night sky to illuminate the passageway.

Behind him, he heard a cry. *'Wait!'*

Bemused, he turned around. 'What?'

'I'm coming with you.'

Patrick suspected that Trevor was coming down from the drugs he'd taken; he sounded paranoid and vulnerable.

'I thought you said every man for himself.'

'Yeah, but I'm the one who knows where the other car's waiting. So if you want a ride out of here you better wait for me.'

The last thing Patrick wanted to do was wait around for Trevor. The man was a liability.

'Police... Put your hands up in the air.'

Patrick broke out into a run. He charged down the corridor, closely followed by Trevor. If he remembered rightly there was only one more turning before they got to the back entrance.

A few more metres ahead, Patrick saw the steel doors; pushing them open, he froze in horror as he clocked eyes on a dozen or more policemen. Shit. Shit.

'Get back!' Stumbling backwards, Patrick yelled at Trevor, signalling him to turn around, but he found himself being pushed to one side as Trevor, having managed to flee from the initial crowd of police, bounded past firing off a round of bullets.

Sparks and smoke blistered through the air. Flashing blue lights and sirens sounded amongst the cries and shouts of all those present.

Patrick edged forward, watching Trevor indiscriminately discharge rounds of machine-gun fire.

'Go! Go! Go!' Trevor screamed out to Patrick, who was already racing along the side wall of the warehouse lot.

The snow shower from earlier had now turned into a heavy blizzard, making it impossible to see more than a couple of feet in front. From behind him, Patrick could hear the snow-padded footsteps of Trevor.

'Which way now?' he called out to Trevor, getting a rushed response in return:

'To the fence. The last section. There's an opening.'

Patrick picked up his pace, knowing this might be their one chance. The police wouldn't shoot if they couldn't see the target clearly and they certainly wouldn't follow them with Trevor's barrage of bullets. No doubt they'd be radioing for more back-up, but the blizzard would make it impossible for the helicopters to fly over, giving them a further advantage to get away.

Arriving at the fence, Patrick squeezed through the opening. Once through he turned round, coming face to face with Trevor, who was still holding the gym bag full of diamonds in his hand.

'Where's the car?'

'Down the hill, but this is where you and me say goodbye.'

'What?'

Trevor laughed scornfully. 'You didn't *really* think you were going to come with me, did you? The only reason I wanted you with me was in case I needed to use you as my shield.'

He gave Patrick a nasty stare then started to head off down the hill, but was brought to a sudden stop by Patrick grabbing hold of his arm.

The snow whipped into Patrick's mouth as he began to talk. 'What about the diamonds?'

Trevor clutched the bag under his arm and patted them.

'They stay with me.'

Patrick lurched at Trevor, who immediately aimed his gun.

'Don't do it to yourself, Paddy. I'm happy to take you out.'

Patrick's face drained of colour. 'We made a deal, Trevor... You don't understand. I *need* my cut.'

'My heart breaks for you, Paddy,' Trevor answered sarcastically. 'But save it. Go cry on Alf's shoulder.'

Patrick, triggered into remembering Alfie, spoke, concern in his voice. 'Where is he? Where's Alf?'

'How the fuck should I know?'

'What do you mean, you don't know?' Patrick shouted over the whirl of the blizzard. 'We can't just leave him.'

Trevor shrugged, unconcerned.

'Where did you last see him?'

Trevor scowled. With his face veiled in snow he answered, calling back as he set off down the hill. 'He fucked his leg, okay? Last time I saw him his leg was mashed out. Word of advice, Paddy; forget him.'

As Patrick watched Trevor disappear into the storm every part of him was telling him to follow, to forget Alfie and get the hell out, but instead Patrick Doyle found himself making his way back through the blizzard to find his friend.

30

Patrick groaned. He blew on the top of his fingertips in a bid to warm them up. Even though he'd only been crouching by the side of the stone wall for the last twenty minutes or so, waiting for an opportunity to make his way into the warehouse, the discomfort of being hunched up in the freezing cold made it feel more like twenty hours. Patrick felt sure that if he didn't move now, hypothermia would get him before the police did.

The blizzard began to pick up momentum again, giving Patrick the chance he'd been waiting for. With the air thick with snow, he ran towards the side entrance. He could hear the voices of the police officers and the occasional dog barking, but he couldn't see anyone through the blizzard. More importantly, it meant they couldn't see him either.

Hurtling round the back, Patrick skidded to a halt. Shit. There was the back entrance only a few feet ahead – but standing in front of it were two policemen.

Backing away, he looked around and then upwards. He could see that the glass of the window had been shot out. It was certainly a way in, but the problem was it was too high for him to get to.

Thinking hard, he remembered passing a crate of boxes by the fence. He'd need at least three to stand a chance of being able to reach and climb through the window. It was risky and it'd take time, time he wasn't certain he had – but then what other option was there? All Patrick could do was pray the weather would continue to stay on his side.

Having taken over half an hour to collect the boxes, Patrick climbed up them slowly. Almost to the top, he reached for the first-floor ledge, but the crates, unable to take his weight, began to wobble and then suddenly gave way, tumbling to the ground. He clung to the stone ledge, legs dangling precariously in the air as he frantically scrambled to get some sort of foothold.

Agonising pain drove into Patrick's hands as the broken edges of the glass cut through them; tearing flesh from the tips of his fingers. He gritted his teeth as he pulled himself up.

Directly below him Patrick could hear voices. If they looked up now they'd see him. He had to stay still. How long were they going to be there? He didn't know if he could hold on any longer. He wanted to cry out. His whole body began to shake. Spasms in his arms began to grow and below him the people still didn't move away.

Any minute now he was going to lose his grip. His hands began to slip but as they did so he heard the words which gave him the will to hang on.

'Daniels! Hey! Danny's found some footprints. They look fresh. Over-near the fence, come on.'

The officers left and then there was silence. Patrick chanced his strength to hang on for a few seconds more making sure they'd really gone before he made a move.

The pain still threatened to force Patrick to let go but, with a final effort, he pulled himself up; shards of glass slicing deeper into his fingers; the snow on the ledge turning red from his blood.

Balancing on the edge, Patrick checked the height of the drop, as well as making sure that he wasn't going to jump directly onto a group of waiting policemen. To his relief, there was nobody about and the drop to the first-floor landing couldn't have been any more than six foot.

He quickly jumped down. It was dark but not so dark that he couldn't make out the lines and shapes of the corridors. Wrapping one of his hands in his coat to try to stop the blood from pouring, Patrick began to make his way along the passageways.

It was a maze and he wasn't sure where to start looking. There was of course the chance Alfie was tucked up at home with a hot blanket and a stiff drink. But he doubted it. Maybe the police had collared him, but again, Patrick doubted it. He knew how savvy Alfie was. If there was somewhere to hide out in the warehouse where he wouldn't be caught, Alfie would find it. What Patrick had to do now was find him.

Walking along the corridors, Patrick kept vigilant. Any sound or noise sent him hiding in the shadows of the night. So far he hadn't seen any police officers, only heard distant voices as he crept along.

As he turned the next corner, Patrick had the sinking feeling he'd already been along it only five minutes earlier. He did a sharp right and found himself in a pitch dark corridor. He couldn't see even a centimetre in front of him.

Edging slowly on, Patrick felt his foot hit something. He couldn't decipher what it was and found himself bending down to feel his way.

His hands touched something wet and then something hard. He still didn't know what it was until he heard a moan. Scrambling to unwrap his hand from his coat to get his phone out of his pocket, Patrick hoped it wasn't who he thought it might be.

He shaded the light on the phone with his hand, not wanting it to be bright enough to draw attention. Through the dimness, he could make out the lines of the person's body they were soaked in blood and barely breathing.

Shining the light further upwards, Patrick immediately knew his worst suspicions had been realised.

'Alfie! Fuck! Alfie!' Patrick hoped there'd be some response. Anything. But there was nothing.

From the moan he had made earlier, he knew Alfie was alive, but for how much longer, Patrick didn't know. Alfie was badly injured. He wasn't sure where the bullets had entered but it was clear he was bleeding profusely and he needed help urgently.

Patrick's mind raced. He had to think quickly. He wasn't sure what to do. The most rational thing to do was to call an ambulance, but that wasn't an option. Not for him. Not for men like Alfie.

Patrick knew he had to keep sight of the reason he was doing this. For Franny. Which meant he had to do everything he could not to get caught, including not dialling for an ambulance.

Patrick also knew if Alfie *could* talk, he wouldn't want to be taken to hospital either. He was aware of the unwritten rules of the streets. Men like him and Alfie saw going to hospital as pointless. If they did pull through, they'd be looking at spending the rest of their lives behind bars, which in itself was a death sentence. They'd rather take their chances with whatever help there was on the outside

With this in mind, Patrick grabbed Alfie under his arms. Closing his eyes, he took a deep breath, mustering all the strength he could and, with one almighty heave, he slung Alfie over his shoulder.

With lots of stops and starts, his knees almost giving way with the weight of Alfie and the pain from his hands and head, Patrick finally made it to the window.

There'd been some sounds from Alfie, but only some. Patrick could feel the blood pouring from him down his own neck, which he knew wasn't a good sign.

Placing Alfie carefully on the ground, Patrick looked at the window. There was no way he could get him out on his own. The drop was too big to even attempt to throw Alfie out without injuring him further, and he certainly couldn't lower him down by himself.

Taking out his phone, Patrick pressed speed dial. The call clicked straight through to Cab's voice-mail. *Shit.* He called again. Again, Patrick heard Cab's voice apologising for not answering the phone.

He rubbed his head; the stress of the situation beginning to overwhelm him. He looked down at

231

Alfie: motionless and bleeding, desperately needing help.

If there was any chance of saving Alfie's life, he had to do something now. Looking at his phone once more, Patrick knew there was only one other person he could call. With a weary sigh, he dialled the number and waited for the call to be picked up.

After what seemed like hours, Patrick heard a noise outside. Cautiously he climbed up to look out of the warehouse window, relieved to see help had finally arrived. There with his hat brimming with snow, standing laughing with two of his men by his side, was Donal O'Sheyenne.

31

'Oh my God! Cab! Cab!' Franny shouted to her uncle as she stared in horror. Part of her shock was seeing the bloody state of an unconscious Alfie Jennings being carried through to the master bedroom by two men she hadn't ever seen before and the other part was the sight of Donal O'Sheyenne following closely behind.

Franny's green eyes flamed with anger and her voice rose in panic. 'Where's Patrick? Where is he? What have you done with him?' Her question was fired at Donal, who roared with laughter.

'To be sure, Franny Doyle, you're like Lig-na-Baste himself – the ancient fire-breathing dragon of Ireland, rising up before me very eyes.'

Franny stepped closer to Donal, unafraid of him, only afraid of what might have happened to Patrick.

'I *said*, where is he?'

Donal waved her away, still chuckling as he headed towards where his men had taken Alfie. 'Oh, stop your worrying, Franny. Your mother was the same and look what worry did for her...'

Franny's face hardened as Donal grinned. 'What do you mean? What are you talking about?'

Before Donal could answer, Cab ran into the hall where they were both standing. He was dripping wet and wrapped only in a towel, having jumped out of the bath on hearing Franny's cries.

'What's going on, Fran? What's the matter?' He stopped abruptly at the sight of Donal. Turning his head to Franny, he looked puzzled, but almost immediately he, too, let out a cry.

'Jesus Christ!' From behind Donal came Patrick. His clothes were covered in blood and his hands were swollen and torn.

Franny ran up to him, opening her arms for Patrick to collapse into them.

'Patrick! Patrick!' Her screams were painful, fearful, as she held his ravaged body. Tears rolled down her face as she cradled him. Her head shot up and she stared at her uncle through her long flowing chestnut hair. 'Cab! Cab! Do something!'

Cab bent down to Patrick and tore open Patrick's shirt.

'It's okay, Fran. He's alive. And look, baby, the blood on his top isn't his. He'll be okay.'

'But look at his hands... What's happened?' The

last sentence was to Donal. Placing Patrick in Cab's arms, she got up and once again stood facing Donal. Her distress was replaced by anger. 'What have you done to him?'

'Me? What an accusation. You should watch that tongue of yours. Who knows, you might get it chopped off.'

Franny stood firm. 'You don't frighten me.'

'Then, to be sure, you're as stupid as your mother.'

Only Cab knew that the twitch appearing on Franny's cheek betrayed her hurt and bewilderment, but to an outsider, Franny Doyle held her own; tough, unwavering and taking on a man others wouldn't dare to. She raised her hand and slapped Donal O'Sheyenne hard across the cheek, then staunchly and without as much as a flinch took the slap returned to her.

'I've always believed in equality,' Donal sneered.

'I'll kill you for that, O'Sheyenne.' It was Patrick who spoke as he began to come round. Croaking out his words as he staggered to stand up, helped by Cab.

Donal, amused again, chuckled. 'Now we've talked about that before, Paddy; you know that wouldn't be such a good idea, not if...' Donal stopped talking and indicated to Franny using his head.

'Get out!' Franny moved in front of Donal, blocking his sight of Patrick.

'Now, that's no way to talk to me; after all, it was me who went and rescued Patrick from what can only be called a desperate situation. Isn't that right, Paddy?' Donal craned his neck round

Franny to take a look at Patrick, who was up on his feet now but still needed Cab to lean on for support.

Franny, resisting the temptation to ask Patrick a dozen questions, spoke again, her temper well and truly roused. 'I said, get out! I don't care who you are and what you've done. All I know is, I want you out of this house.'

Donal leant in. 'Don't take me on, Franny; you don't know who you're dealing with.'

Defiant, Franny retorted. 'No, O'Sheyenne, don't take *me* on. It's *you* who doesn't know who you're dealing with.'

'Franny! Stop!' Patrick sounded worried.

'Whatever deal you and Patrick made, we'll sort it. You'll get your money. I'll make sure you do.'

'I doubt that very much.' Donal's tone was patronising.

Patrick implored Franny. 'Just leave it, Fran. *Please.*'

'You should listen to him, Franny.'

Franny's beautiful face was full of contempt. She stared at Donal, not knowing why this man seemed to have so much power over Patrick, who usually answered to no-one. She glanced over at Cab and saw the same look of apprehension in his eyes as there was in Patrick's.

There was something very wrong. And it worried her. Whatever it was, she needed to get to the bottom of it. But not now. She would wait.

She addressed Donal again. 'Like I say, Mr O'Sheyenne, you really don't know who you're dealing with. Now, I won't ask you again. Get out.'

Donal stared back at Franny, studying her. Yes,

235

he'd been right; there was no fear in her eyes when she looked at him. Of course he knew she wasn't Patrick's real daughter, but there was the same look of defiance in her green eyes as there'd been in Patrick's the night he'd escaped from the industrial school and insisted on being driven to see Mary O'Flanagan. The difference, however, was that he'd been amused by Patrick's naive boldness; but there was nothing naive about Franny. Furthermore, he certainly wasn't amused.

'I don't much care for you, Franny. It's a shame, really, because you were such a sweet baby, but for some reason Patrick and the boy wonder here think the world of you.' Donal stopped to button up his coat. He sniffed loudly, looking across at Patrick and Cab. 'I hope she's worth it, Paddy boy. I hope she is.'

'What's he talking about?' Franny looked at Patrick as well but he ignored her and continued to listen to Donal instead.

'Time's up, Patrick. I'll be back; shall we say the 25th? You can tell me what you've decided to do.'

Patrick looked distraught. 'For God's sake, O'Sheyenne, that's Christmas Day, as well as Franny's birthday.'

Donal cocked his head to one side, his dark eyes twinkling with spite. 'And there's me thinking she was born in October. I could have sworn I brought her—'

'That's enough!' Patrick bellowed, interrupting O'Sheyenne and startling both Cab and Franny.

Donal nodded in agreement. 'Aye, it is; you're right. It is enough ... until the next time.' Tipping his hat, he added with a grin, '"Merry Christmas to one and all!" ... Dickens. Wouldn't know the chapter if me life depended on it.'

With raucous laughter Donal turned and headed for the front door, just as the doctor – who'd been called by Patrick from the car – was shown in by the housekeeper.

'Thanks for coming. He was shot. I don't know how many times. He's in the bedroom.' Patrick spoke with urgency to the doctor, who was used by all the faces in Soho for his skill and silence.

Franny followed them through, speaking as they went. 'Patrick, what the hell is going on? First you disappear with Alfie and then you come back like this and with *him*. With Donal O'Sheyenne. Who is he? What's he got over you?'

Patrick's voice was warm as he replied. 'Not now, Franny, hey? Later I'll talk to you later, but for now let's just concentrate on Alfie.'

'But...'

'Sshh, Franny.' Patrick placed his wounded fingers on her lips to stop her saying anything more. She nodded and smiled at him, trying to read what was going on in his head. But even if he didn't tell her, she was going to find out. Find out exactly what Donal O'Sheyenne had over Patrick and – more intriguingly – how he knew her mother.

32

Patrick stood in the doorway, watching Alfie sleep. The doctor had worked on him for a few hours, cleaning and stitching him up. Piling antibiotics into him as well as blood. The place looked more like a sanatorium than a bedroom.

He felt a hand on his back. It was Franny. His face lit up and the love he'd felt for her before she was even born exuded from him. 'Hey, baby. It's late. You should be sleeping.'

'How can I sleep?'

'Birthday excitement getting to you?'

Franny laughed quietly. 'Are you being serious?'

'Oh yes, you never know what treats you may have in store.'

'You mean like the time you decided to buy me three ostriches?'

'You said you liked them.'

'I was eight and I said I wanted an emu, as in the Rod Hull puppet.'

'Well ... emu, ostrich, they're all the same.'

'Not if you're expecting a ventriloquist puppet for your birthday and you wake up to three huge birds almost as tall Cab walking down Greek Street.'

'I'll never forget the look on your face.'

'And I'll never forget the look on Lola's face when one of them pecked at her head. I've never

238

heard and am still to hear as loud a scream.' Franny paused, adding, 'I'm worried about you. How are your hands and your head?'

Patrick absent-mindedly looked down at his bandaged fingers. The doc had done well. He'd had an injection, which had taken away most of the pain in his hands, and his head had been left with a dull throbbing. 'I'm fine. It's Alf you should be worried about.'

Franny looked concerned. 'Is he going to be all right?'

'I think so. Doc says he was lucky; none of the bullets hit any main arteries. But he can't be moved at the moment. So it looks like you'll be playing nursemaid. Lots of TLC and bed baths, apparently.'

Patrick laughed as Franny pulled a face.

'I'll leave those pleasures to Cab.'

He winked, enjoying teasing her. 'You're not tempted? Do I need to keep me eye on you, Fran?'

Franny grinned, enjoying having the old Patrick back. 'Oh, I think you can rest easy. I reckon I'll be able to resist the irresistible allure that is Alfie Jennings.'

They fell silent for a moment then quietly, Patrick asked, 'Are you looking forward to your party, Fran?'

Franny glanced at him. 'How can you even think of a party after everything that's happened? Besides, shouldn't we be saving the money?'

'Money or not, I'm going to celebrate your birthday like we always do. There's no way you're not going to have a night to remember. No expense spared.' Patrick paused then grinned, adding, 'It also helps that Alfie's letting us use his club for free and Lola's agreed to do the food.'

They both chuckled, leaving Alfie to sleep and moved into the lounge arm in arm.

The lounge was a large room, expensively decorated in golds and creams. Huge leather chairs full of oversized fox-fur cushions were dotted around. Pictures encased in gold frames hung from the walls, and family photos of Cab, Franny and Patrick sat on top of the cream baby grand piano in the corner. But it was by the heavy sash curtains bordering the large windows overlooking Dean Street that Franny dreamily stood, watching the snow continue to fall.

'I can't remember the last time we had a white Christmas. It makes everything look beautiful; like a magical kingdom.'

Patrick walked across to where Franny stood. Putting his arm round her shoulders, he brought her into him.

'I'd hardly call Soho a magical kingdom, but aye, Franny, you're right, the snow makes everything look lovely; makes you forget what darkness lies beneath.'

Franny turned, looking up at Patrick's handsome face. Troubled, she studied the lines and the dark circles under his eyes, which she'd noticed the day of his return.

'What do you mean?'

Patrick shook his head. 'Oh, ignore me, Franny Doyle, I'm just a grumpy old man. Today is about you.'

Franny went to sit down, hoping he would join her. But instead, he stayed by the window. 'Tell me what happened with you and Alfie.'

'It was stupid. Nothing really.'

Franny's voice raised. 'Nothing! You're nearly killed and you call it nothing?'

Patrick sighed. 'Don't exaggerate. I just did what I had to do.'

His words infuriated Franny and she jumped back out of the cream leather sofa she'd just sat down on. 'Look at you! Look at your hands! I want to know what happened and then you can explain what Donal O'Sheyenne has over you, as well as tell me how the hell he knows my mother.'

Patrick bristled. Franny was the sweetest woman he knew, just like her mother, and just like her mother she had a fiery temper. Normally it'd make him laugh, as Mary had made him laugh when she'd got cross with him, but this time he wasn't smiling. This time, he needed Franny to back off and let it be.

'We robbed a warehouse; I needed the money, Fran.'

Franny shook her head. 'How can you be so stupid?'

This time it was Patrick's turn to feel infuriated.

'Stupid? Don't push it. Both you and Cab set me afloat with what you did moneywise. How else was I supposed to get money?'

A flicker of shame crossed Franny's face, and although she felt sick with guilt at how she'd handled Patrick's money affairs, she was still furious with him for putting himself at risk like this.

Money could be sorted out. What couldn't be sorted was if anything happened to Patrick. To be honest she'd never really cared about money. As long as all three of them were together she'd be just as happy living in a tiny flat somewhere as a luxurious house in Soho.

So taking chances like Patrick had done last night frightened her and made her angry in equal measure. Her voice was laced with hostility. 'So, how much did you come away with?'

Patrick spoke flatly. 'I didn't.'

'What?'

'I said, I didn't. The guy in charge screwed us over. It's a long story, Fran, and I'm tired. Let's leave it till another day.'

'And O'Sheyenne? I...'

Patrick interrupted. 'Another day.'

'But...'

'Fran!'

Franny fell silent. She knew Patrick and she knew when he wasn't going to be pushed on anything. There were so many questions running through her mind. None of it made sense. For Patrick to go to the extremes of taking part in a robbery well, that was crazy. Alfie, yes. But Patrick? Surely they weren't *that* desperate; they couldn't be. Christ, what was going on?

Her thoughts were interrupted by Patrick's phone beeping. Curious, Franny asked, 'Who's that?'

Patrick didn't need to look to know. 'Nobody.'

Franny wasn't to be put off. She looked at him sceptically. 'It must be *somebody*. Have a look.'

'It's nobody.'

'Patrick? What's happening?'

'Fine.' Sighing, Patrick pulled out his phone. It

242

was who he suspected; Donal O'Sheyenne. The text message simply read: *Time's run out... Merry Christmas.*

'Well?'

Matter-of-factly, Patrick answered. 'Like I say, it was nobody.'

Going to sit on the couch, Patrick patted the large leather sofa, encouraging her to come and sit down next to him. He needed to talk to her. Now more than ever.

'Franny, will you do something for me?'

Eagerly, Franny answered. 'Anything, Patrick. You know I will.'

'I want you to go to New York.'

Franny looked puzzled. 'New York?'

'Yes.'

'When?'

'Tomorrow.'

Puzzlement turned to shock 'Tomorrow? I ... I don't understand. Is it to do with business?'

Patrick smiled sadly. 'I've got a good friend who lives there. I want you to go over and see him. You'll like it there, Franny. He's got a lovely wife and three children. I've spoken to him and it's all sorted.'

'For how long? When will I come back?'

It was a while before Patrick spoke. He listened to the distant sounds of cars and late-night revellers; reflecting on Christmases past; remembering when he and Cab had watched in delight as Franny opened her presents; eager to share everything from her Barbie dolls to her pink-flowered tea sets with him and Cab. Remembering how they'd played for hours until eventually, along with

243

Cab, Franny would fall into an exhausted and contented sleep, surrounded by a mountain of gifts. And he would watch her. Watch her as he thought about Mary, about Ireland and about the life he'd once had which had been stolen away.

'You won't be, Franny. You won't be coming back.'

Franny looked stunned. 'What ... what are you talking about?'

Patrick avoided looking at her directly. 'I've never asked you for anything before. *Please*, just do this for me.'

Confusion cut through Franny's words. 'How can you possibly ask me something like that? Drop it on me like you're asking me to pop out to the shops?'

'I wouldn't ask you if it wasn't important.'

'Important? Is that what you call it? I call it madness. Have you any idea what you're asking me? You're asking me to give up my whole life and go to a place where I don't know anybody. And would you and Cab be coming, too?'

'No, Franny. Only you.'

Franny threw her arms up. 'It's crazy. How could I just go like that? Without you? Without Cab?'

Patrick's voice became hard. 'I'm not asking you, Fran. I'm telling you. You're *going*.'

Franny's eyes flashed. 'No... No. I don't know how many times I've said this but I'm not a child and I won't be treated like one. This is one of the reasons why I had to move out – because you think you can go round telling me what to do.'

Patrick's voice pitched louder. 'Save the speech,

244

Franny, because you'll do as I say.'

'I love you, Patrick, and you know I'd do anything for you, but this? I can't... I just can't.'

'What if I told you it would help me? Knowing that you're safe.'

Anxiety shrouded Franny's face. 'Safe? What's going on, Patrick? I'm safe here with you and Cab, aren't I?'

'*Franny.* My sweet, beautiful Franny.'

'You're scaring me now, Patrick. Does Uncle Cab know about this?'

'He does, and he thinks it's a good idea as well.'

Franny's eyes filled with tears; hysteria in her voice. 'It's almost as if you want to get rid of me!'

Patrick's voice was sad and soft. 'No, Franny. No. Don't say that. If there was any other way...' He trailed off, desperate to tell Franny everything, but knowing he couldn't.

'At least tell me why, Patrick. Why do you want me to go?'

'I can't tell you.'

'Then I can't go.'

'Is that your final answer?'

Franny nodded. 'Yes, it is.'

Patrick stood up solemnly. He walked to the door. His eyes glazed over with tears as he turned to look at Franny.

'I want you to listen to me, Fran; a lot of things are going to change soon. Things neither one of us would want if we had a choice. But you coming into my life, to be sure, it was nothing short of a miracle. Before you came along I'd lost all hope. My heart and my spirit was broken for reasons you don't need to know, but from the moment I saw and held you in my arms, I knew I'd love you forever. The day you came to me was and always will be the best day of my life. Mary had sent me an angel.'

Franny burst into tears. 'Patrick, *please*. Tell me what's going on. *Help* me understand.'

Again, Patrick shook his head. His eyes reflecting the warmth of his words. 'You've given me so much pleasure, Franny Doyle; no-one could feel luckier than I do to have you in my life. *No-one*. And whatever happens, Fran – and I mean *whatever* happens – always know that you were worth it. I have no regrets.'

With that, Patrick turned and left, leaving Franny alone in the room listening to the ticking clock, feeling more confused than ever.

33

'Are you coming, then?'

Franny stood in the doorway wearing a thick grey cashmere coat. Next to her stood Cab, who was also dressed to brave the weather.

'I don't think so.' Patrick spoke as he sat by the large bespoke walled fire, mesmerised by the flames as they danced and weaved.

'For me. *Please.*' Franny's voice pleaded with Patrick. She hadn't seen him since the conversation they'd had in the early hours of the morning. She'd thought he'd gone to bed to have a rest, but when she'd gone in his room he wasn't there.

She'd been desperately disappointed as well as worried. It was the first time she'd ever known Patrick to miss taking her out the day before her birthday. Even when he'd managed to twist both ankles after taking up Cab's challenge of participating in the local fun run, he had taken her for lunch; getting Cab to push him round to the Ivy in a wheelchair where they'd surprised her with a three-foot-high cake. A pre-birthday cake Patrick called it.

Each year had been more extravagant than the last; she'd often joked with both Cab and Patrick that one birthday she genuinely expected to see a giraffe dressed in a gold lamé outfit waiting for her in the elite Soho restaurant.

But this year? This year, he'd disappeared. His phone had been turned off and no-one had seen him all day. And though Cab had tried to dissuade her, she'd found herself hanging around outside the Ivy. Waiting and hoping that she'd see Patrick rushing across the snow-covered Shaftesbury Avenue, flustered and breaking out his Irish charm because he was late. But there'd been nothing. No lunch. No call. No childhood memories, no reminiscing over a glass of Patrick's favourite tipple. Nothing. And that had broken her heart.

Not able to stop herself, Franny, hurt and upset, blurted out her words. 'Where did you vanish to today? I was expecting lunch.'

Patrick, still staring into the fire, answered wryly. 'I would've thought you'd got to the age where you could buy your own lunch. Or have you run out of money like the rest of us?'

Distressed, Franny ran round to Patrick's side.

'You know I didn't mean it like that. I don't care about any lunch. I care about you. Please, Patrick, please. Just tell me what's going on.'

Silhouetted in the doorway, Cab spoke to Franny. 'Leave it, baby. He was probably just busy.'

Taking exception, Patrick retorted. 'What? I can't speak for meself any more, Cabhan? I have to get you to do me talking and make excuses for me now?'

Cab didn't say anything. He knew what pressure Patrick was under, yet he felt helpless in what he was able to do.

He'd made a promise to give his life, to give his loyalty to Patrick, but more than that, more than just honouring his word, he wanted to help because he loved him, as Franny loved him; they were family, but Patrick had closed off to both of them and he didn't know how to reach him.

Franny pushed further. 'Then where were you? I was waiting.'

'You shouldn't have bothered; just like you're not going to bother going to New York.'

Franny flinched. 'That's not fair, Patrick. It's not the same. You're asking me to just get up and go, no questions asked.'

For the first time since Franny had come into the room, Patrick looked at her. He knew she didn't deserve him treating her this way. And she was right – it wasn't fair. But none of it was and he'd run out of options. All except one, that was.

'Cab's right; I was busy. But I'll be there tonight at your party. I wouldn't miss that for anything.' He rested his hand on her head as she sat at his feet.

'Come with me. Come with me to midnight mass.'

'No, Franny.'

'Why not? You've never been before. I'd like you to come; for me.'

'Franny...'

'You know what he's like when it comes to churches, Fran.' Cab laughed nervously, trying to lighten the mood. 'Anyone would think he had something against them.' He could feel the tension in the air and the last thing he wanted was for Patrick to disappear again. Not tonight. Not on Christmas Eve. Not when Franny needed him the most.

Cab walked over to Franny and took her hand, pulling her up gently. 'Come on, Franny, we'll be late. I want to get myself a good seat.'

Allowing herself to be pulled up by her uncle, Franny implored Patrick again. 'I'd like you there. All three of us together.'

'Don't ask me, Fran ... please. You go with Cab and I'll see you later at the party... Go on.'

Without another word, Franny walked out of the room, not wanting to show Patrick how much she was hurting.

Cab hovered, waiting for Franny to be out of earshot. Once he was sure she was, Cab spoke earnestly to Patrick

'Paddy, she doesn't understand what's happening. It's tough for her. She's worried about you... *I'm* worried about you. Talk to me.'

Staring forward, Patrick reached to the side of him, finding Cab to place his hand on him.

'You've been a good friend, Cab. The best. The *very* best. Don't think for a moment I didn't need you as much as you needed me. I did, perhaps more. Your friendship has meant everything to me. So thank you, Cab. Thank you for all that you've done.'

'Paddy...'

'No. No more talking; not now anyway. Go on; don't keep Franny waiting... Oh and, Cab – you will look after her, won't you? Whatever happens, and I mean – *whatever happens.*'

After Cab and Franny had left, Patrick checked on Alfie. He stirred, slightly opened his eyes, then fell back into a deep sleep.

Returning to the lounge, Patrick's thoughts and memories began to take him far away from the snow-filled streets of Soho and back to the lush green fields of Kerry. He could see it all. The village. The church. His house. The river which ran through. Clear vivid colours taking him back to his childhood.

His thoughts were suddenly broken as a noise came from behind him. 'Cab, did you forget something; to be sure, you've a head like a sieve.'

'I always warned you about that friend of yours.'

Patrick sprang up from his chair.

Donal's face carried a large grin. 'You really should get a better lock on that door; it's easy to pick and you never know who could get in. Now, before you ask what I'm doing here, I've come for a mince pie. It is Christmas after all. Goodwill to all men.'

'Get out!'

'Now don't be telling me you haven't got any mince pies. A house without mince pies is like a church without wine.' Donal winked. He sat down on the cream stool next to the grand piano and began to plunk at the keys.

Patrick marched across to the piano and slammed the lid down, narrowly missing Donal's fingers.

'What do you want, Donal?'

Picking up one of the framed photographs from the top of the piano, Donal traced his finger around Franny's face.

'Pretty as ... well, a picture. Now if I wasn't a man of God...'

Patrick snatched the photo back. 'You've never been a man of God.'

Donal smiled. 'Oh, that's where you're wrong, Paddy boy. Didn't I ever tell you I was a priest for a time? I thought you knew. Father Ryan – you do remember him, don't you? – and me. What a pair we were. Mind, Father Ryan lost his way, so he did; got himself into a bit of bother. I managed to sort it, though. Me? I wanted more, Paddy, so I left. But that doesn't mean I'm not a man of God. I carry him everywhere in me heart, so I do.'

Donal broke out into peals of laughter, jarring Patrick's senses. He grabbed hold of O'Sheyenne by his lapels.

'Is it not enough you've won? You have to mock me as well? You've beaten me. Finally, you win. Checkmate. I'm yours. You can take it. You can take me life... Me for Franny. It's over. It's finished.'

251

Donal pulled away from Patrick; he stood up, brushed himself down and walked towards the door. 'Not quite, Paddy boy, not quite. The game's not over yet; there's one more move.'

34

What was he thinking? What the hell was he thinking? How could he have said no to Franny knowing it'd be the last Christmas he'd be around? The last birthday. It was ridiculous. Crazy. He should be spending every last minute with her and Cab, not languishing in the house alone waiting for O'Sheyenne to tell him when and where. For all he knew this might be one of the last nights of his life. If it was, he wanted to be by Franny and Cab's side.

He looked at the clock. It was five to midnight. He had time. If he hurried.

Grabbing his coat from the side, Patrick ran out of the lounge, but abruptly came back, going into the drawer of his private desk. He pulled something out and placed it in his trouser pocket before he rushed down the stairs to the front door and out into the freezing night.

He ran along Dean Street, sliding along in the icy snow. He skidded round the corner of Bateman Street and past Lola's café, along Frith Street then finally into Soho Square, where he hurried across the green.

And as Patrick Shamus Doyle fell into the

heavy wooden church doors, flinging them open, seeing a sea of heads turning towards him, he heard a voice he couldn't mistake. It was Father Ryan.

'And let us also pray for all who have to celebrate Christmas in poverty, in suffering, that a ray of God's kindness may shine upon them, that they – and we – may be touched by the kindness...'

Standing in the aisle, Father Ryan froze when he saw Patrick. His face paled as he visibly shook.

The congregation, who were kneeling in prayer, unsure of the reason for the silence, turned to take a curious glance at the priest who stood stony-faced staring at the tall handsome man covered in snow.

Patrick was speechless; helpless to move as Father Ryan walked up to him. The priest whispered low and harsh, his shock mirroring Patrick's. 'Patrick!'

'Patrick?... Patrick? Is everything all right?'

Franny, surprised and glad to see Patrick but at the same time concerned, stood up from her pew where she and Cab had been kneeling. She looked from the priest to Patrick, who looked mesmerised. About to go to him, she heard someone else coming down the aisle. It was Donal O'Sheyenne.

O'Sheyenne whispered, 'Like a home from home, is it not? A reunion of souls. See what happens when you make a wish to Santa, Paddy boy.' Donal chuckled as he spoke, slapping Patrick on his back.

Father Ryan rushed to the back of the church – the rest of the congregation assumed he'd been taken suddenly ill. Once in the foyer, he hurled his words at Donal. 'You! It was you who had something to do with me having to move from my last parish to this sprawling city of sin.'

Donal tut-tutted at Father Ryan. 'Something? I'd say everything to do with it. It's amazing what having connections in high places does for you. I'm still good friends with the bishop. He owed me a favour for keeping one of his more ... unsavoury of secrets.'

'How dare you! You'll pay for this, O'Sheyenne. I'll see to it.'

Donal clapped his hands together in delight. 'Oh, how I've missed this, Matthew. How I've missed your empty threats. We're going to have fun, so we are. So we are.'

Donal, about to go back into the main church, stopped unexpectedly. He dipped and bowed, making the sign of the cross, before winking at Father Ryan. 'Wouldn't do not to pay my respects, me being a man of God and all... Carry on, Matthew, carry on; get back in there; none of us have got all night.'

Father Ryan shot a glance at the congregation, suddenly becoming aware of the spectacle he was generating. He stared at Patrick, who, without saying anything, turned and ran out of the church.

Seeing that Patrick wasn't coming back into the main church, Franny spoke to Cab in a hushed whisper. 'We need to go after him!'

She began to push past the other people, who were sitting looking baffled in the pew, but was stopped by Cab, who pulled her back by her arm. 'Leave him, Franny, he'll be fine.'

'How can we leave him, Cab? You saw how he looked.' Franny's voice was loud as she remained standing; unconcerned at the stares she was receiving from the other midnight mass worshippers.

'You'll see him soon. He'll be at the party; I know he will.'

Franny's eyes were full of sadness as she held Cab's affectionate gaze. 'How do you know that?'

'Because he will ... because he loves you.'

Patrick ran along the streets of Soho. Past the crowded clubs making Christmas merriment. Past the carol singers; off key and on. Past the pubs of St Martin's Lane where he and Cab had spent many a drunken night. On and on he went running, not knowing where he was going but needing to rid his mind of the memories.

Exhausted, Patrick found himself leaning on the frozen walls of Westminster Abbey. His mind raced violently. *Father Ryan. Father Ryan.* He was here. Close to Franny. Father Ryan, the man he blamed for so many things. The man he blamed for Mary.

'Mary! Mary! Mary! Forgive me, Mary! Forgive me! I've let you down.' Patrick's cries of anguish poured out along with his tears. He dropped to the ground, heedless of the chill of the icy ground through his clothes as his body was racked with grief-stricken tears.

'Are you okay, mister?' A boy, no more than sixteen and shabbily dressed, stood by Patrick's side as he huddled on the ground.

Getting no response from Patrick, the boy

reached into his pocket and brought out a two-pound coin. His hands were red from the cold as he placed the money next to Patrick.

'I ain't got no more than this, but you can have it. There's a late-night cafe around the corner. She's all right the bird that runs it; she'll let you just sit there for hours. Sometimes I sit there all night meself. Her name's Queenie; tell her Harry sent you. Anyway, Merry Christmas.'

The boy started to walk off but Patrick's call stopped him. 'Hey! Harry! Wait up a minute.'

The boy, curious, waited for Patrick to get up and wipe his face from tears. 'Where are you staying tonight, Harry?'

'In the shelter off Leicester Square. I think they're full but I could show you where it is if you like.'

'No, it's fine. Here...' Patrick reached into his coat pocket and took out the five fifty-pound notes in there. He stuffed them in the boy's hand, then as an afterthought he took off his designer cashmere coat and handed that to him as well.

'Take it. Merry Christmas ... and thank you. Thank you, Harry.'

Before the boy could say anything, Patrick set off at speed, knowing where he was heading. To Franny. To Cab. To celebrate the life they had together.

35

The party was in full swing by the time Patrick arrived at Whispers nightclub. In the far corner he saw Cab talking to Franny. Heading over, he made his way through the noisy crowd of friends and acquaintances.

'You said he'd be here,' Franny was saying. 'You promised. Where is he?'

Cab answered; desperate to give some kind of reassurance to Franny. 'He will be, baby. I know it. Just hold on a bit longer.'

'What if he doesn't come?'

About to try to placate Franny further, Cab's eyes lit up as he saw Patrick approaching them. Relief in his voice. 'Look who's here, Fran!'

Franny turned and shrieked with happiness seeing Patrick behind her. She threw her arms round his neck. 'I thought you weren't coming.'

'And miss this? I promised I'd be here, didn't I? Cab knew I was coming, didn't you, Cab?'

Cab grinned, noticing Patrick's bloodshot eyes. He spoke as he knocked back the double gin he held in his hand. 'For a moment I had me doubts there, Paddy.'

Franny tiptoed up to talk into Patrick's ear. 'What was that all about in the church?' she said, raising her voice to be heard over the music.

Patrick smiled. 'Not now, Fran,' he answered simply. 'Tonight we're here to have fun; to

257

celebrate you. Now come on, I've got a surprise for ye.'

Five minutes later, with the help of Cab, Lola and Vaughn Sadler, Patrick had the music turned off and there was hush in the large clubroom.

Everyone was seated, and Patrick, Cab and Franny sat side by side with a large pink and white birthday cake on the table in front of them.

Patrick stood, raising his glass of champagne as he addressed everybody.

'Thank you all for coming. I know we do this every year but this year, for my own personal reasons, is extra special for me. As you all know, Franny is and always has been the light of all I do, and I think I speak for Cab as well when I say that.' Patrick paused for a second and waited as Cab gave a small nod. 'No-one will ever know how much joy and love she has brought into my life, but I know you'll all raise your glasses in wishing the birthday girl a happy birthday.'

The whole room went up in a chorus of birthday cries. Over the roar, Patrick looked at Franny. 'I wanted to give you this. The time was never right before.' Patrick reached into his trouser pocket and pulled out a silver chain and cross. 'Your mother gave it to me a very long time ago. I know she would've wanted you to have it.'

Placing the chain round Franny's neck, Patrick kissed her on her cheek, hiding his tears in her long flowing chestnut hair.

'Happy birthday, baby, and of course, Happy Christmas.'

Franny touched the chain and tears fell from her eyes, mirroring Patrick's. 'Thank you. It's beautiful. I had no idea you had–'

'Happy birthday!'

The raucous birthday greeting cut through the noise, interrupting Franny's sentence and bringing the clubroom to silence. There, holding a sparkling candle, was Donal O'Sheyenne.

All heads turned to look. Lola Harding nudged Casey Edwards, who then nudged Vaughn Sadler, who in turn nudged Frankie Taylor; all faces and friends of Patrick. All curious to see who this tall dark-clad man was, who'd made Patrick, Franny and Cab's faces drop into a blanket of despair.

Patrick stood up and stared at O'Sheyenne with as much hatred as Father Ryan had shown him back at the church. 'I want you out.'

'And there's me thinking I had an invitation.'

'You're not welcome here, O'Sheyenne.'

'Now that's not a nice thing to say; especially as I've brought Franny a card. Happy birthday, Fran.'

Donal threw the card on the table in front of her. She said nothing, glancing quickly at Cab who had a look of fear on his face.

'Aren't you going to open it?'

Franny shook her head. 'I don't think so.'

Patrick held Donal's gaze but spoke quietly to Franny. 'Do as he says.'

'But–'

'Just *do* it, Fran,' Patrick snapped. 'And then we can get on with the party.'

Slowly Franny reached out for the card, which lay in a gold envelope on the table. She looked up at Patrick who smiled and nodded reassuringly.

With her eyes darting between both Patrick and

Donal, Franny ripped open the envelope to pull out the card. Her face drained of colour as she stared at it. Her breathing was laboured as she spoke to Donal. 'What the hell is this?'

Donal gave a grin. 'It's your birthday card. Your birth certificate. I thought you'd like it.'

Franny retaliated. Her voice crisp and cold. 'What sort of sick joke is this? Why have you got my birth certificate?'

'Oh, it's not a sick joke. Is it, Patrick? There's nothing funny about it at all. You were mine before you were Patrick's.'

Patrick grabbed the card from Franny, looking at the birth certificate.

'What's he talking about? Cab? Patrick?'

Patrick spoke. 'It's nothing ... nothing.'

Franny glared. 'I want to know what's going on. Why has O'Sheyenne got my birth certificate?'

Loudly, Donal interrupted. His eyes twinkling. 'Oh, there's more, Franny. I mean, this is your birthday ... well sort of. Who here isn't disappointed when there's nothing inside a card? Go on, Fran, have another look. The anticipation's killing me.'

Trembling and without saying anything, Franny opened her card. A piece of paper dropped out of it. She picked it up and began to read. Puzzlement all over her face. She looked up.

'What is this?'

Donal smiled. 'Your mother's death certificate. Things always come better in twos.'

Patrick, now recovering slightly from the shock, began to rush forward at O'Sheyenne.

'No! Stop! Don't touch him...' Franny shouted

at Patrick as she held up her hand. 'No, Patrick, I want to know exactly what this means. Why does it say *suicide?* On the death certificate?'

Patrick had never felt so much fear in his life. Not when he had been growing up, and not even when he had been in the basement with Father Marley. This fear. This cold fortified fear struck at his heart. And it meant only one thing. His worst nightmare was about to come to fruition.

Patrick's voice quivered as he talked. 'Franny, please. Don't listen to him. Let me tell you; I promise I'll tell you everything.'

Franny ignored Patrick and concentrated on what Donal was saying.

'To answer your question, Franny, it means your wonderful Patrick and Cab here have been lying to you. Your mother was never killed in a road traffic accident; she killed herself. Jumped into an icy river. I never knew why she didn't choose somewhere warmer – but I digress so I do.'

'Fran!...' Desperate and scared, Patrick cried out to Franny.

'Shut up, Patrick! Go on...' Franny cut him down, needing to hear the rest.

Donal's pupils dilated as sheer delight rushed through his veins. 'I've never been one for a long story, so let me keep this simple for you so we can all get on with the party and eat some of that delicious birthday cake of yours.' He stopped and looked around, enjoying everybody's full attention. 'Patrick was no distant relative of your mother, and there was certainly no adoption. The only thing there was, were lies. The truth is...'

Patrick called out. 'No, Donal; don't!... Please! I beg you.'

Donal cut his eye at Patrick. 'The *truth*, Fran, is that Patrick bought you.' O'Sheyenne looked at Patrick and shrugged his shoulders and winked.

Franny was stunned. She shook her head, trying to take in what O'Sheyenne was saying. '*Bought* me?'

Donal did an exaggerated nod. 'Yep! Sick, huh?'

Tears ran down Franny's face. 'You're lying! It's not true.'

Donal put up his hand. Feigned concern laced with ridicule rolled off his tongue. 'Ah, now then, I can safely say it is true, because he bought you from me... With the help of course of Father Ryan and Tommy Doyle.'

O'Sheyenne saw Patrick look up in astonishment. 'Oh, you didn't know the part about your dad and the local priest, Paddy. There's so much to tell you, with so little... Oh look, silly me, what was I thinking, with *no* time at all, Paddy boy. Time's up.'

'Patrick?... Cab?... Tell me this isn't true.'

As Patrick looked into Franny's eyes he could see her heart was breaking, like his and no doubt like Cab's. He wanted to tell her it was lies. He wanted to tell her what Donal was saying wasn't true. He wanted to, but he couldn't.

'I said, *tell me!*'

'Yes. Yes, it's true ... I'm sorry.'

Franny didn't know where to look. She didn't know what to feel. She saw the tears of Cab and Patrick. She saw the invited guests looking on with pity in their eyes, and lastly she saw a reflection of herself in the large mirror at the back of the room. But as she looked and stared, she no longer knew who she was looking at. Everything she'd been told was a lie. Everything she'd been taught wasn't true. And the two people she'd loved with all her heart, the two people who were her soul, her mind, her everything, weren't who they said they were.

'And my father? What about my father, O'Sheyenne? Was he really just a boy from Dublin who my mother didn't know?'

O'Sheyenne shook his head. 'They really have been lying to you, haven't they? But the rest can wait for another time. No good telling you everything at once – some things are worth waiting for.'

'Franny, please let me explain.' Patrick reached out to her.

Anger surged up in Franny. She screamed at Patrick. Hurt and lost. 'Explain? What is there to explain?'

'It's not like it sounds, Fran. Just give me a minute.'

'A minute, Patrick,' Franny scoffed, her face wet with tears. 'You've had the whole of my life to tell me. You're sick. Both of you.' She pointed at Cab, who stood with his hand across his mouth.

'Franny—'

'No, Patrick, no. I loved you. Don't you understand that? I loved you and would've done anything for you.'

Patrick's sobs clouded his words. 'I'm still me, Franny.'

'But that's the point, Patrick, you're not. You're not you.'

'Don't say that. *Please.*'

Franny walked towards Patrick, wiping her tears on the back of her sleeve. 'I never want to see you again. *Never!* And you can keep this...' Franny tore the chain Patrick had just given her from her neck and threw it at him.

'I hate you!... I hate both of you!'

Patrick tried to grab Franny as she ran off out of the club, but his path was blocked by a smirking Donal O'Sheyenne.

'I wouldn't bother going after her.'

36

Franny didn't know where she was going but it didn't matter. She didn't care. All that mattered was getting away. From Soho. From Patrick. From Cab.

She ran through the almost deserted streets; empty of people save a spattering of the last of the tinsel-clad revellers who exuberantly wished her a Happy Christmas as she ran by.

She didn't feel the cold through her thin dress, nor care she'd left her coat back at Whispers. She didn't feel the snow hit her face as it whirled in the air. All Franny Doyle felt was hurt confusion and loss. Loss of the happiness she'd once believed in. Loss of the love she'd once had. And loss of the family who were no longer hers.

Panting, Franny slowed down. She looked around at the city lights. She hadn't realised how far she'd run. At any other given moment she would've thought it was a beautiful sight. Chelsea Bridge in the dark; a row of floodlights shining up from beneath the bridge, light-emitting diodes covering and illuminating the towers and cables to create a twinkling gem arching across the water.

Franny walked up to the side of the bridge, looking at the dark waters below. She felt a shiver run through her body.

The river was frozen with a blanket of snow covering it and Franny remembered the words of Patrick. *'What darkeness lies beneath.'*

Dazed, Franny leant further over the snow-covered side. She closed her eyes, wanting all the pain to come to an end.

'Have you found her?' Patrick spoke into the phone to Cab. His voice was urgent. On the other end of the line he heard the words he didn't want to hear and which made his heart drop.

'Don't tell me you don't know where she is. Don't tell me! Well, where the fuck is she, Cab?' Patrick stood in the middle of the street under a streetlight, watching the snow fall in the spotlight of the beam.

'Find her! For fuck's sake, I need you to find her. I'll go back to the house to see if she's there. I've got Vaughn and Casey and some of the others looking as well, but Cab ... *please find her.*'

Patrick put his phone back in his pocket and hurried along the street, looking down every alleyway as he went. He had no idea where Franny might be. She didn't have any secret places. She was always open; always told him everything. But then, he supposed, she had thought the same of him. Now her trust and faith in him had gone, and perhaps her love, too.

He had to see her. He had to. Even if it was just the once. One more time was all he wanted. To look into her eyes and tell her he loved her. Tell her he was sorry. But he knew if he didn't find her soon, it'd be too late. His time had finally come to an end.

Hurrying into the house on Dean Street, Patrick was surprised to see all the lights turned on. He knew it wouldn't be the nurse they'd recruited for Alfie; it was too late for her to be up and Cab was still out looking for Franny.

He ran up the stairs, not wanting to build up his hopes. He ran through all the rooms, each time praying he would find Franny there. Sitting angrily with folded arms waiting to give him a piece of her mind. But she wasn't. There was nobody there. Perhaps it had been him who'd left the lights on.

His phone buzzed and Patrick dragged it out of his trouser pocket, almost tearing the material, so desperate was he for it to be Franny. But it wasn't. It was the manager from one of the clubs. Holding his head in his hands, Patrick cried out and as he did so, he caught the glint of the top of his revolver, which he kept on the bookshelf.

Without hesitation, he grabbed the gun and ran out of the house. He was going to sort this out once and for all.

37

Donal O'Sheyenne had never liked fuss when it came to home decor. He'd never liked lots of ornamentation and he certainly didn't like the idea of lots of cushions and soft furnishings. So it felt only right for him to be sitting in an almost bare room, perched on a hard wooden chair without so much as a cushion.

His feet rested on the window ledge as he smoked the last drag of his cigar, watching the rooftops of Charlotte Street becoming covered with more snow.

The door behind him creaked open. He didn't move but for the large grin which spread across his face; lit up by the moonlight.

'I was expecting you.'

'And how could that be? Because I didn't know I was coming here myself; I only managed to find out your address less than an hour ago.'

'Well, as you saw, I left the door open for ye; it wouldn't be right to make an awful holler at this time of night, would it ... Matthew? I wouldn't want to disturb anyone. "Thou shalt love thy neighbour as thyself." Mark twelve, verse twenty-nine.'

'I think you'll find that's verse thirty-one.'

Matthew Ryan was furious. He'd had about as much as he could take. The move to London had been difficult enough, but he'd seen it as God

267

testing him. Taking him on a journey of the unknown; like the one the good Lord had undertaken himself. But tonight when he'd come face to face with Patrick Doyle he knew that, rather than it being the work of God which had brought him to Soho, it'd been the work of the devil – who now sat before him. Donal O'Sheyenne.

'I want you to arrange for me to go back to my last parish; I shall not be part of your games, Donal O'Sheyenne. Return me back there and nothing more will be said. I give you my word.'

Donal broke out into laughter; incensing Matthew even further. 'And why would I do that? I'm having too much fun with you here. You should've seen the look on your face when you saw Patrick tonight.'

'That man is a thorn in my side.'

'Really? Is that what he is? Did you recognise the woman he was with?'

Father Ryan's eyes flickered. With the events of the night and coming to see O'Sheyenne he'd forgotten about her, but when he'd seen her standing up defiantly, asking Patrick if he was all right, he'd felt sure he knew her from somewhere. She looked so familiar.

'No, I do not, Donal, and guessing games are not a part of what I do.'

'That's a shame, so it is. But seeing as you won't guess, I'll tell you... Franny Doyle. You'd probably know her better as Franny O'Flanagan.'

'What are you talking about, Donal?'

'Franny Doyle is the daughter of Mary O'Flanagan.'

Father Ryan's face blanched. 'That's impossible.

268

Mary's baby was adopted by the Richards family of Donegal. It was all arranged.'

'No, Matthew, she wasn't. Everybody and everything has their price. And don't think for a minute it was sentiment that led me to take her to Patrick rather than the Richards. It wasn't. Patrick was just willing to pay more.'

Father Ryan stared in astonishment. 'That ... that woman who was in the house of God tonight is the bastard child of Mary O'Flanagan, and you bring me to her to be a part of your games? I will not be a pawn in Satan's pastime.'

'Matthew, you know how I detest melodrama. Hasn't it got into your head by now? We made a deal.'

'A deal we made over thirty years ago. A deal which has seen my faith in God and man tested. Let me out; free me or I warn you, Donal, you shall reap what you sow.'

Donal stood up and went to where Matthew Ryan stood. He towered above him.

'Oh don't worry, Matthew, I'm not going to hit you; age has mellowed me somewhat, and it never was much fun anyway. And as for letting you out of the deal ... *never*. You had a wasted journey, but to be sure, it was good to see you. Close the door behind you on your way out.'

Fifteen minutes after Matthew Ryan had left, Donal was sleeping soundly in his chair. He'd never suffered from sleepless nights, so for him to wake up before the usual chime of his alarm was a surprise. However, it came as *more* of a surprise to find the cold, hard steel of a loaded gun pressing

269

against his temple.

'Get up.'

'To be sure, give a man a chance to wake.'

'You've had your chance... Now *move* it!'

Donal didn't. Instead, he let out a yawn before sniffing loudly in a bored fashion. 'Do you mind if I get meself a cigar, Paddy? I can see it's going to be a long night.'

The gun was pressed harder to his head. 'I *said*, get up. Otherwise I'll be pressing the trigger faster than you can blink.'

Donal reached his arm up and patted the gun and spoke in a condescending manner.

'Ah, you see, that's what you and I both know isn't going to happen. What is it about Christmas Day that makes people think they can come and waste me time?'

Patrick's voice was emotional. 'Why did you have to say that stuff to Franny? Why did you have to do it? *Why?*'

Donal sounded offended. 'Me, Paddy? Oh no, no. I haven't done anything to her. Nobody told you that you had to lie. You did that all by yourself. All of it. The only person to blame here is you.'

Patrick, still pointing the gun at Donal, walked round to face him. 'But it's you who won't let me out of the deal, so it is. You who's made me pay, year after year. Higher and higher, until it became impossible. Playing with Franny's life as if she were a toy. So I'd say it's you, *Donal.*'

'I never forced ye to take Mary's daughter. You and your sentimentality did that. I warned ye, Paddy; don't make a deal with the devil.'

'But I didn't, Donal; I made a deal with you. You're flesh and blood like the rest of us.'

Donal shook his head. 'Paddy boy, you've got a lot to learn; the devil lies within us; he's not some red-horned fiend. He's people like you and me.'

'Not me. For sure, I'm nothing like you.'

'I wouldn't be so certain of that. All I did was tell the truth. I've been honest from the start, and for all that is holy, I get a gun pointed at me face?'

Patrick's hands were trembling as he pulled back the trigger; clicking off the safety lock.

Donal still didn't flinch. 'Pull it ... *pull it.*'

The gun trembled in Patrick's hand so much it was as if it had a life of its own. One tiny movement. Just one. And then it'd all be over.

The sweat dripped into Patrick's eyes as he stared at Donal, deciding what to do. Deciding if he could take the chance.

'What's the matter, Paddy boy? Having second thoughts? Not sure if you should take the risk... Your call.'

Donal, a man who normally didn't go in for melodrama, ripped open his shirt in a dramatic fashion, exposing his chest. 'Shoot.'

Patrick stood, hearing the ticking clock and the sound of the boiler clicking on and off. He heard the light whirl of the wind outside and he heard his own staggered breathing whilst all the time he kept the gun aimed directly at O'Sheyenne.

'Take the gamble, Paddy – you never know, Franny may be okay; my men may take pity on her... So go on, what do ye say? Bang, bang, I'm dead.'

Still the sweat dripped off Patrick. Still he

couldn't decide what to do, when earlier he'd been so sure. He'd come here to finish it all off. To blow Donal away. But he knew in his heart, as he supposed he'd always known, that the risk to Franny's life was too great; and suddenly he understood the real reason he'd come here, desperate, hoping somehow he'd find a way to get out of his deal. It was for one reason and one reason only. He didn't want to die.

But as Patrick stood there, beaten, dropping his arm and passing the loaded gun to Donal, he knew his love for Franny was greater than his fear.

'I'm ready, O'Sheyenne. Do it now.'

Donal smirked. 'Oh no, Paddy boy. Oh no. Like I told you, I haven't taken my last move. But when I have, then it'll be my pleasure. I've waited a long time for this.'

Donal laid the gun on the side. He crossed his legs and rocked back in his chair.

Patrick's voice was strained. 'What *now*, O'Sheyenne?'

O'Sheyenne leant over and pulled the other wooden chair closer to him; signalling Patrick to come and sit down. He grinned widely.

'Patience, Paddy. You never did have patience... I want to tell you a story. A story about a boy who was lied to all his life. Are you sitting comfortably? Then I'll begin. Once upon a time...'

272

38

Franny Doyle sat in the police station feeling many things. Hurt. Anguish. Despair. But the overriding feeling she had as the female police officer handed her a cup of tea was embarrassment.

What had she been doing? If she was truthful she didn't know; everything seemed such a blur. The party. Running down to Chelsea Bridge, and then of course the kindly stranger who'd spoken comforting words before calling the police.

Through her tears she'd told them she had no intention of jumping but they hadn't believed her; and as they'd asked her to stop leaning over the edge so far, reaching out their hands for support, she could see their point.

She felt such a fool. It wasn't like her. It wasn't. Causing all this fuss. There was no way she was *actually* going to jump, but they'd still insisted on her coming back to the station for a cup of tea.

Normally she would never have dreamt of going to a police station of her own accord, but the idea of a sweet cup of tea – even if it was with the police – had attracted her.

'Hello, you all right, sweetheart? Bleedin' hell, girl, you gave me a right fright. You can imagine how I felt when the Old Bill phoned. Thought they'd got wind of me knocking off stolen gear. Well, when they told me what it was about, you should've seen me. I got dressed that quick I think I've even got me knickers on inside out.'

Franny looked up at Lola gratefully. 'Thanks for coming, Loll. I couldn't think of anyone else to call. I hope you don't mind.'

'Mind? Don't talk soft, love. I heard what that fella said; you've had a right shock, babe. But I'll tell you something, you sure know how to throw a party.'

Franny smiled, grateful for Lola's manner. She'd known her all her life and, like her friend, Casey Edwards – who she'd met when Casey had been working in Lola's café – she'd always found Lola to be a person she could turn to when she needed to talk.

'Come on, let's get you back home, doll. Patrick will be going off his head with worry.'

Franny shook her head. 'No... No. I don't want to go home. I don't want to see Patrick or Cab.'

Lola sat down next to Franny. Concern on her face.

'Listen, love, I've known you since you were a baby and I knew Patrick before that. Right back to when I was a hard-faced cow working the streets. Unlike the others he showed me respect; treated me like a human being. The other thing he showed me was how much he loved you. I remember often seeing him and Cab with you. Sometimes struggling for money. Sometimes not knowing which way on your nappy was supposed to be. Oh, they did make me giggle. Oh Christ, they were sometimes all over the place. A few times I watched you for them, remember? But you know, Franny, the one thing which wasn't all

274

over the place was their love for you. That was rock solid. Couldn't fault it. Even though I tried, it put me to shame how I treated me own kids.' Lola paused, reflecting on times gone by, before she'd had her own children taken away by the authorities. Even after all this time the memories of it all still hurt. Pulling herself together, Lola smiled at Franny, then carried on.

'A lot of people in Soho thought they were a couple of poofs the way they fussed and preened you. An odd sight they were; especially in them days. There was big boy Paddy – strong, tall and handsome, as protective as I've ever seen. And always by his side was little man Cab, dark as the night's sky with a kind word for everyone. And of course there was you. The beautiful green-eyed baby.' Again Lola stopped, but this time it was to take hold of Franny's hand; squeezing it in hers before going on. 'I can't imagine what you're feeling right now, girl, but what I do know is, whatever shit that fella spouted – and I know it's rocked your world – don't lose sight of the fact that Paddy and Cabhan loved and adored you from the moment they set eyes on you. Always have done, always will do.'

'Yes, but–'

Lola interrupted. 'They've never wronged you, have they?'

Franny shook her head, even though she had a feeling it was a rhetorical question.

'Well, there you go then. You've been one of the lucky ones. There's a lot of folk round here who haven't had a sniff of the kind of love that Paddy and Cab have given you. So I think you at least owe it to them to let them know you're safe, as well as listen to what they have to say.'

Franny smiled, happy she'd asked the police to call Lola.

'Okay, Lola, but not tonight. Maybe in the morning.'

'Well then, young lady, you are going to come home with me. Chez Lola. And tomorrow it might all look better ... not that it ever did for me, always looked bleedin' worse if I'm honest.' Lola cackled and helped Franny up out of her chair, disgusted at the watery cup of tea the officer had handed her.

Once up, Lola spoke to Franny cheerfully. 'Hold on a minute, love, I need to take a piss. Me bladder isn't what it used to be.'

Inside the ladies' toilets, Lola pulled out her phone and dialled a number.

'Cab; it's me, love. She's safe... She's with me.'

Patrick ran along the road, looking behind him as he went, hoping to see a taxi so as to get there quicker. His mind rushed with incoherent thoughts as he slid along in the unsuitable shoes he wore on the snowy paths and alleyways of the West End; taking shortcuts, jumping down stairwells, leaping over railings like a man twenty years his junior.

He could see the landmarks of Soho rising up in front of him. He was nearly there.

The roads were empty and Patrick found himself racing down the middle of them, finding the snow-cleared streets easier to run on than the thickly covered pathways.

Almost there. Almost there. He heard the church clock strike eight. He was almost there.

The gate was closed. Patrick cursed it. And even though it was only took a minute longer to go the other way, it was a minute more Patrick Doyle didn't have.

Charging round the railings, Patrick slammed open the wooden church doors. The place was empty save one person who was kneeling in front of the altar.

In the flicker of candlelight he marched up the aisle, smelling the heady aroma of laurel and cinnamon, used in the Christmas decorations of the church.

Patrick sat down on the front pew and looked up to the stained glass window. It was a couple of moments before he spoke, his voice echoing round the eighteenth-century church. 'Forgive me, Father, for I have sinned.'

Slowly, Father Ryan turned round and scowled in puzzlement.

'Or should I be the one forgiving you... *Father?*'

Father Ryan, using the corner of the altar to help him get up, snapped, 'You're not welcome here, Doyle.'

'Is that right... *Father?*'

Matthew Ryan bristled. 'It certainly is. You were always trouble, Doyle; always.'

Patrick gave a tight smile. 'Doyle?... Surely that should be Ryan? Isn't that my real surname?... Is it true? Is it true what O'Sheyenne has just told me? Am I your son?'

Father Ryan stumbled over his words. 'I ... I don't know what you're talking about.'

'Don't lie to me.'

Father Ryan raised his voice. 'Get out! Get out, man!'

'Son; call me *son*. After all, isn't that what I am to you? Tell me; are you my father?'

Father Ryan sneered without answering, causing Patrick to raise his voice further. 'I said, *tell me!*' Again the priest didn't answer.

Furious, Patrick towered over Father Ryan. He raised his fist.

'Yes! Yes! For all my sins I am your father.'

Enraged, Patrick shook the priest. 'What did you do to her, hey? What did you do to my mother? Did you take her by force? Rape her when no-one was looking?' Patrick paused a moment. Then a hideous thought came to him. He stared at Father Ryan. 'Was it you who did it to Mary? *Was it?*'

'How dare you, Doyle? How dare you come into a house of God and speak such poison? Be very careful with what you say.'

Patrick looked at Father Ryan. He wanted to kill him. He'd never felt so much hatred in his entire life. It was all beginning to make sense. This was why. Why Father Ryan had hated him with a vengeance. Why he'd helped to put him in an industrial school. Why his life had been ruined. Why *Mary's* life had been ruined. It was all to keep Father Ryan's dirty secret.

'Why? Just tell me why.'

'I don't have to answer to you, Patrick Doyle.'

Patrick shook him. Flipping his head backwards and forwards.

Father Ryan took a look at Patrick's expression. His face was twisted and contorted into a picture of hatred.

'Well, that's where you're wrong. I want answers and I want them now. So help me, God, or I'll kill you.'

Father Ryan had been tested many times over the past few years. In fact he felt he'd been tested ever since the day he'd decided to give his life to God. But this, he felt, of all the tests, was his greatest.

Pushing Patrick off him, Father Ryan moved away slightly. He turned, and with a sigh sat down on the nearest pew full of Christmas carol sheets from last night's service. He rested his head in his hands.

'I loved her.' Father Ryan spoke flatly to Patrick who stared in bemusement at what the priest had just said. He moved from the aisle to sit down behind Father Ryan, who kept his head in his hands as he talked.

'I did. I loved her. I know you'll find it hard to believe, but I did. I even wanted to marry her. Evelyn was everything I wanted in life, and though the call of God's voice had always beckoned me, I was prepared to give it up for her. Then one night, the sins of the flesh took over my body. Satan had won. I'd given in to temptation. Though there was nothing forced. Nothing unspeakable in fact. Quite the opposite; it was the most beautiful moment of my life...'

Father Ryan trailed off, reflecting on a memory he'd hidden away since the day it happened. The minutes ticked by and, just as Patrick thought he'd said his final word on the subject, he began to talk again. This time, though, Patrick could hear the emotion in Matthew Ryan's voice.

'We were both young. Both sixteen and there was really no way I could've married her. Or so I told myself. I was ashamed of what I'd done, yet Evelyn wasn't. She was more in love with me than ever before. I rejected her after that, and then she found out she was pregnant. Of course I denied all knowledge of it and by this time I'd signed up to the priesthood; to get away from Evelyn and my shame. Anyhow, Evelyn was taken to St Joseph's, to have the baby there. I thought it would be the last I heard of it. I assumed it would all go away.'

'You mean you hoped, *I* would go away.'

'As I said, I thought it'd all go away. But one day, Evelyn came to see me. She'd run away from St Joseph's. She begged me to marry her. Begged me not to let the nuns take her baby. And for all I had turned my back on her, I still loved her. So I asked Donal to help me; I'd known him since we were boys and even though I'd no time for his errant ways, the familiarity of him and knowing the way he himself lived his life made it easier for me to turn to him for help. He assured me he could find someone to marry her. Take her far away from Kerry. But as we both know, Donal O'Sheyenne plays cards with the devil. He tricked me and got Tommy to marry her, which he did I understand for fifty pounds and a bottle of whiskey.'

Patrick put his head in his hands.

'Now, of course my secret couldn't go any further and as I made my way in the church I committed myself more and more to God, but

Donal had other ideas. He wanted to destroy me, by telling the world about my sins. Evelyn was no longer my life, God was, so you can understand, this couldn't possibly get out. So I made a deal with Donal. I would help him and he would keep my wickedness a secret. When she died I was devastated. The light had gone out of my life, and a part of me died with her. Sometimes I feel that since her death my outlook on life has been bleaker.'

'And the baby-selling, what about that?'

Father Ryan shrugged. 'What harm would it be, to fill families' lives with children who weren't wanted? I couldn't see the harm ... well, not at first.'

Patrick looked at Father Ryan scornfully. 'No harm?'

'If you're talking about Donal's *unique* way of doing things, I had no idea he was going to lease the children.'

'Yet, you're still a part of it.'

Father Ryan stood up from the pew and began to collect up the hymn books. 'I am like you, held under Lucifer's deal.'

Patrick slammed his hand down on the hymn book next to him, preventing Father Ryan from picking it up.

'Is that all you have to say? Tell me one thing. What do you see when you look at me?'

Even though Patrick had always hated Father Ryan, the derision on the priest's face inexplicably cut deep; wounded a part of him he didn't think could be hurt by this man.

'I see nothing. When you were growing up on

281

occasion I saw Evelyn, but most of the time I just saw my sins. For I was taken by the devil the night I gave into temptation. And you are nothing but a reminder of my weakness.'

'What happened to it being beautiful?'

'It was indeed, Patrick Doyle, and beauty is what the devil bequeaths us; he makes our sins pleasurable so we're once more persuaded to walk under his banner.'

Patrick shook his head. 'How do you live with yourself?'

'I live with God's forgiveness in seeking the way of the light and of the truth. I was a weak man – I'm not proud of it, Patrick.'

Patrick shook his head. 'You have many a person's blood on your hands from your dealings with O'Sheyenne. And now you can add me to the list.'

About to launch into a verbal attack, Father Ryan stopped, mulling over Patrick's words. He closed his eyes for a moment, clasping his hands together then rested them under his chin.

With his eyes still shut Father Ryan began to talk. 'And what *exactly* do you mean by that?'

Patrick looked at his watch. 'In the next hour, Donal O'Sheyenne is going to kill me.'

Father Ryan's eyes flicked open. His voice remained steady. 'May I ask, for what?'

'Does it really make a difference as to why? But since you ask, I can no longer pay what I owe to Donal, like others who have been killed before me.'

'I shall pray for you.'

Patrick exploded. *'Pray for me!* I would rather

burn in hell than have your hypocritical words.'

'You may find solace in prayer, Patrick.'

Patrick continued to rage. He tore off the Christmas wreaths placed on the end of each pew, he dragged down the holly wrapped around the large candles on the edge of the altar, then turned to face Father Ryan, his face wet with tears.

'If you have to pray ... *Father,* pray for revenge.'

And with that, Patrick slammed out of the church.

As Patrick rushed across Soho Square, he heard a voice calling him. 'Patrick!'

He turned and saw Father Ryan chasing behind him, his cassock billowing in the wind.

Breathless, the priest stopped, waving his hands for Patrick to come over to him.

'If this is about purging my sins before my day of judgement; forget it. I'd rather take me chances.'

'No, it's not, but I think you'll be very interested in what I have to say.'

39

'She won't speak to you... I'm sorry, Paddy... Truly.' Cabhan Morton stared at Patrick as he stood next to him in Lola's flat.

'Try again. I need to see her.'

Lola glanced at Patrick, sympathy all over her face.

'Come on, darlin', you know what us women are like; we like to make our point. Give her a day or so, babe.'

Patrick ignored Lola's words. 'Kick the door down if you have to; I need to see her.'

'Bleedin' hell, Paddy, hang on,' Lola animatedly called. 'You know how much I love you and Cab, but you ain't kicking no doors in, otherwise you'll be falling out with me an' all.' She took hold of Patrick's hand and smiled, bringing her voice down to almost a whisper. 'Anyhow, it won't do any good. Franny won't thank you for it. Give the girl some space; she'll come round.'

Cab spoke to Patrick. 'Lola's right. Nothing will be gained.'

'Nothing apart from a smashed bleedin' door.'

Patrick walked over to the grey bedroom door that led off the tiny sitting room. He banged it hard with his fist.

'Franny... Franny, it's me.'

Silence.

'Franny, *please* just talk to me.'

Silence.

Patrick rested his head on the solid wooden frame, his voice breaking as he spoke through the door. 'Fran?... Franny? My darling, you don't have to talk to me, just listen. I love you, Franny, and I always have and sometimes I don't think you'll ever know how much, especially when I mess up like I have done. I never meant to hurt you ... *never*. Forgive me... Forgive me.'

Patrick turned round to see Lola crying her heart out.

'Oh my Christ, Paddy; turn it in. Look at me,

284

I'm a right old wreck. Anyone would think you're never going to see her again.'

Patrick smiled sadly at Lola. He went to her and gently placed a kiss on top of her head, which smelt of hairspray and cigarettes. 'Thank you, Lola... Thank you for everything.'

With Lola promptly bursting into tears again, Patrick walked out of the flat, followed by Cab.

Outside, Patrick hesitated before speaking; searching carefully for his words. 'Don't let her forget me. Look after her, won't you?'

The tears ran down Cab's face. He didn't bother to wipe them away. 'I will ... I promise; as if she were my own.'

'And Cab ... look after yourself, too.'

Cab grabbed hold of Patrick. 'Are you sure there's no other way?'

Patrick nodded; warmth and love in his eyes for Cab.

'We've been through a lot, you and me. Do you remember the time Killer glued our shoes to the floor and we ended up having to cut them free, leaving the soles of the shoes stuck on the floor?'

Cab laughed through his tears. 'Aye, I do. We went round pretending all was well when really our feet were cut to shreds.'

'To be sure, I swear the priests knew about it and just enjoyed seeing us suffer.'

They both laughed; remembering the fun and also the pain they'd shared together.

Patrick held Cabin a strong embrace then whispered the words: 'Let me go, Cab; it's time to let me go.'

'Patrick! ... Patrick!'

Hearing the painful cries of his friend, Patrick Shamus Doyle walked away into the winter sunshine without looking back

40

The candles flickered in the draughty aisles of the eighteenth-century church. And although it was light outside, the stained glass windows set back in the large cold grey stone cast long dark shadows, giving the place an ambiance of gloom and melancholy.

The wooden church door opening furthered the draught; sending the candles into a fervour of dancing yellow flames.

The padded footsteps of the person coming up the aisle echoed all around.

'A strange place for you to choose, Paddy boy. I didn't know you were the religious type.' Donal O'Sheyenne spoke to Patrick as he made his way up the aisle.

'I'm not, but here's as good a place as any.'

Donal chuckled. 'I suppose it'll be handy for them.'

Patrick didn't reply but he did stand up, moving from the pew he'd been sitting in to join Donal by the step of the brass communion rail.

With his eyes locked on Patrick, Donal pulled out a small hand pistol. 'I would say I wish I didn't have to do this but – unlike your *fathers* – I'm no liar.'

Patrick tried to talk but his mouth stuck together; saliva drying up; nerves taking hold of his whole being.

With the gun out, Donal stepped back. 'Aren't you going to turn around?'

'No, I'll face you.'

Donal smirked. 'Any last requests, Paddy?'

Patrick glared. 'I want nothing from you apart from your word that Franny now has her freedom.'

Donal bowed his head reverently. He placed his hand across his chest. 'You have my word.'

'I'm ready.'

Donal grinned. 'Pardon?'

'I said, I'm ready.'

Donal, cupped his hand on his ear. 'Nope, I still can't hear you. Maybe you need to talk louder.'

Patrick flicked his head up, once again staring at Donal O'Sheyenne's dark mocking eyes. Swallowing not only the bile which rose up but also his pride, Patrick spoke, his tone disengaged from his racing heart.

'I said, I'm ready. Where will you find your fun after I've gone, O'Sheyenne?'

'Oh, there's plenty more around. I could always try Cab; he's so easy to wind up.'

Patrick raised his voice. 'You leave him alone. You hear me!'

'Or what?... You'll come back and haunt me?' Donal roared with laughter.

Patrick stared, but instead of allowing himself to be goaded any further, he nodded, then spoke quietly, both resolved and dignified.

'Okay ... okay. You're right. You win. There's

nothing I can do.'

'Oh Paddy, don't be such a bad sport; you know how much I like playing me games. I'm only winding you up. Both Cab *and* Franny will be safe. I'll leave them alone. I can't say fairer than that... Friends?'

Although Patrick had vowed that whatever happened he wouldn't let O'Sheyenne goad him, he felt himself rising to the bait. He dug his fingernails into the palm of his hand; squeezing down hard and aware of the blood he'd drawn.

'As I say, I'm ready.'

Donal looked at Patrick in slight puzzlement. 'You're really not going to turn round?'

'No, I want to face you. Look in your eyes when you pull the trigger.'

Donal smiled. 'Be my guest, Paddy, but if you're looking for a hint of contrition, I'm afraid I won't be able to help you. Okay ... here we go.'

Donal stretched out his arm and pointed the gun directly at Patrick's head. His hand was completely steady.

'What? Not in the heart, O'Sheyenne?'

'Sentimental to the end, Paddy boy. I suppose it's only fitting; after all, it was your heart which got you into this trouble in the first place.'

Bringing his gun down slightly, Donal aimed, his eyes open wide with anticipation.

Not flinching for even a second, he pulled the trigger, firing it directly into Patrick's heart.

The shot echoed out, reverberating around the cavernous church. Patrick dropped to the floor; lying motionless in front of the altar. Before O'Sheyenne had a chance to move, a voice sounded from the side aisle.

'What in God's name is...' – Father Ryan came to an abrupt halt as he came face to face with Donal O'Sheyenne who was now pointing the gun right at him.

Donal winked. 'You need to be careful not to give a man a fright like that, Mattie; I could've clear blown yer head off, so I could.'

'Put it down!'

In the shadow of Donal's amusement, Father Ryan rushed over to Patrick. Bending down, he placed his finger on his neck. He looked up at Donal.

'I can feel no pulse!... He's dead!'

As the blood appeared on Patrick's shirt, trickling down on the sandstone floor, Father Ryan stood up. With his face red, he pointed at Donal, screaming out his words.

'Murderer! Slayer! Executioner! May God forgive you, O'Sheyenne... May God forgive you.'

Without another word, Donal O'Sheyenne turned and walked away.

Outside, the weather had broken. The winter sun had now disappeared, making room for the heavy grey clouds bursting open to begin the first snow flurry of the day.

Donal pulled up his collar; a moment later he brought out his phone. The number he dialled clicked onto voicemail. He smiled pitilessly, talking into the answer machine.

'A life for a life. A deal is a deal and I'm a man of me word, so Cab, rest easy: your precious Franny will be safe now.'

41

Cabhan Morton held the phone in his hand. He closed his eyes with the voice message ringing in his head. His hand shook and it was only Lola's intervention that prevented him dropping the mug of tea he was holding in his other hand.

'Are you all right, babe? You look like you've seen a ghost. Either that or you've got a bit of Delhi belly from the sandwich I got you from the Turkish shop. They've changed and it ain't as good as it was. Proper gone downhill. The last time I went...'

'Patrick's dead.'

Lola blinked, standing upright. 'What?'

'Patrick's dead.'

She shook her head, slumping down on the chair next to Cab. 'No, he can't be. He was only in here a few hours ago threatening to break down my bleedin' door. You must have got it wrong, love.'

Cab looked up at Lola. He could see the bewilderment in her eyes. 'No, Lola. I haven't got it wrong. It's true.'

Lola's voice was a whisper. 'How? How did it happen, babe? It wasn't a heart attack, was it? Mind, he did look a touch peaky. Christ, I should've made him sit down. Now I come to think of it he didn't look very clever.' Lola stopped suddenly, her face draining. 'Oh by Christ, what are we going to tell Fran? She'll be devastated. It

290

ain't right to have to tell her something like this. Bleedin' hell, Cab, are you sure it ain't a mistake? Call the hospital again and ask them. You hear it all the time on the news people being mixed up.'

Cab answered flatly. 'It wasn't the hospital who called.'

Lola looked puzzled, but before she had the chance to say anything, the bedroom door opened. It was Franny.

Thrown by Franny's sudden appearance, Lola found herself grabbing onto Cab's hand and squeezing it tightly. She opened her mouth to say something but nothing came out.

'What's going on? You look like somebody's died.' Franny spoke the words light-heartedly. She looked from Lola to Cab, then back again.

'Cab?... Lola?'

There was no answer, so instead Franny pushed on with what she had come out of the room to say.

'Look, Cab, I've been thinking. Lola's right; I should listen to what you have to say. But that doesn't mean everything is going to be all right and we can just pick up from where we were, pretending this never happened. But I could at least hear what you have to say. What *Patrick* has to say. Can you call him and let him know I want to speak to him?'

Both Cab and Lola stared blankly at Franny. Sensing something was wrong, Franny frowned, walking over to where they were sitting.

'Come on, what's going on? I know there's something because there's no way you'd just sit there without saying anything, Lola. I've never known you not have an opinion on anything.'

'He's dead.' The words tumbled out of Lola's mouth almost before she realised she was saying them. They hung in the air, crashing through the sound of the silence in the tiny front room.

'Who? ... who's dead?'

Lola slammed her hands over her mouth. Franny could see her visibly shaking. She knelt down at her feet, gently pulling down Lola's hands.

'Who, Lola? Tell me. Who's died? Is it a friend of yours?'

Lola nodded, unable to talk through her tears.

'I'm so sorry. That's terrible. If there's anything I can do; let me know.' Franny squeezed Lola's hand and smiled, adding, 'Was it someone I knew?'

With Lola not saying another word, Franny turned to Cab. 'Did you know them?'

Cab's voice was a whisper. 'She's talking about Patrick.'

Franny turned her head to one side quizzically. 'Patrick? I don't think I know any other Patricks, do I?'

Cab put his head down barely able to look at Franny.

'I don't know, baby, but she's not talking about any other Patricks, she's talking about ours. I am so, so sorry, Fran.'

Franny stared at Cab and then at Lola. She began to shake her head furiously and instead of squeezing Lola's hands gently she began to shake them hard.

'Look at me, Lola! Look at me!'

Lola couldn't; she turned her head away, covering her face with her hands. Franny bolted up from her knees, shouting at both of them.

'Tell me this is a joke! Tell me!' Her words screamed with pain.

'Baby, it's true.'

'No! You're lying. Lola, tell me he's lying.'

Lola took her hands away from her face. 'Sweetheart, I wish I could.'

Through her tears, Franny spoke, wrapping her arms round her waist. The agony unbearable. 'What happened?... I want to know what happened.'

'It was a heart attack.'

Lola turned to look at Cab, surprised at the answer he'd given Franny.

'Was it me? Was it because of me, Cab? The stress of the money? I was so horrible to him earlier. I told him I hated him... Oh my God!'

Franny dropped to her knees, curling up tightly as if the pain was crushing down on her.

Cab rushed over and knelt alongside Franny, putting his arms protectively around her. Whispering words into her ear; hoping somehow they might comfort her.

'Franny. Fran. It wasn't anything to do with you. I swear. He knew you didn't hate him. You were just hurt. He knew that and he knew how much you loved him.'

Franny's face was awash with tears and pain, breaking Cab's heart as she looked at him with her huge green eyes. Her words sounded child-like with a torment only loss of a loved one could bring to them.

'How, Cab? How am I going to live without him? I can't do it. I can't.'

'You will, baby. You will.'

Franny shook her head. 'No... No, I won't.'

The tears ran down Cab's face as well. 'Oh Franny...'

'Help me, Cab... Help me. Take away the pain. Please take away the pain...'

With Franny fast asleep in her bed thanks to an injection of Diazepam from the doctor, Cab came back to sit down in the front room having finished making his phone calls.

Lola got up silently to draw the curtains, pausing a moment at the window to watch the snow drift past, lit up in its purity by the street lamp. She spoke, still facing the outside world. 'Why did you say that?'

'Say what?'

'Say to Franny – that Patrick had had a heart attack.'

Cab bristled, not appreciating Lola's questioning. 'Leave it.'

The harsh tone in Cab's voice made Lola scuttle round to where Cab sat. She spoke defiantly. 'No, I won't leave it. What the hell's going on?'

Cab, never usually one to be short with Lola, snapped at her. 'What's going on is none of yer business.'

Lola looked hurt but didn't back down. 'You see that's where you're wrong, sweetheart. I care about you and I certainly care about Franny. She'll need all the help she can get and part of that help will be knowing the truth.'

'She's got the truth.'

Lola scoffed. 'Don't give me that. You told me yourself he didn't have a heart attack.' She stopped, taking hold of Cab's hand. Her voice becoming warmer. 'I know you must be hurting as well, but darlin', don't you see? It's wrong. Hasn't there been enough untruths already? Hasn't that poor girl got enough to deal with, without any more bullshit? Patrick wouldn't want that.'

Cab pulled his hand away verging on aggressive. 'You don't know what Patrick would want. He left me in charge of her; not you.'

Lola frowned. 'What do you mean he left you in charge? Did he know he was ill?'

'He wasn't ill, Lola. He was *shot*, okay – and he knew he was going to be.'

Lola looked stunned. 'But...'

'But *nothing*. I'm going to send Franny to New York, so she can start afresh. Patrick had some friends there; it'll be better for her. No memories. I'll join her when everything's sorted out this end.'

Lola looked incredulous. 'No memories? Cab, you're being a fool. You think sending her to America will make her forget? It's what she'll be carrying in her heart and, darlin', that's a whole load of excess luggage.'

'I know what's best for her, Lola, and it's best she never finds out Patrick was shot. I'll put her on the plane after the funeral.'

Lola raised her voice in frustration rather than anger.

'More lies, Cab! More lies! Haven't you learnt anything?'

'I've learnt not to have people in me business; to be sure, I learnt that a long time ago.'

'There'll be an inquest. The Old Bill will be sniffing everywhere. It's madness, babe.'

Cab raised his voice along with Lola. 'The Old Bill won't be sniffing around. I've sorted it so the coroner will accept a mint and then sign it off as a heart attack; he's someone who used to be on Patrick's payroll. So you see, there's no need to panic. No-one will be asking any questions. And as for her going to the funeral; I'll make sure she won't and afterwards I'll put her on a plane so she'll be none the wiser.'

For a moment, Lola didn't know what to say. But only for a moment. 'It's bleedin' madness. I don't know what yer caught up in, love, but the last person I know who did something like that is now serving a ten-year in Parkhurst.'

'Yeah, well, I won't be.'

'And what if you do, hey, babe? What will happen to Franny if you're put away? She'll have lost both of you then. She's bound to find out eventually; mark my words.'

'Enough, Lola.'

But Lola was on a roll. 'And how do you know she'll even go to America, hey?'

Cab looked at Lola accusingly. 'Not from me, she won't.'

'No, but you know as well as I do that Soho is like a bleedin' ladies' hairdressers when it comes to gossip. She'll find out, Cab; I just know she will.'

Cab rubbed his head. It was all too much. 'Stop, Lola! I'll sort it. I'll work it out somehow, but I don't need you chewing off me ear and adding to me problems, so I don't. Now leave well alone. I've told you too much already. I'll deal with Franny and you deal with keeping your nose out of me business.'

Ten minutes after Cab had left, Lola sat at the end of the bed watching Franny sleep. It wasn't right. Wasn't right the poor girl was going to spend the next part of her life living under the shadow of a lie. She knew Cab meant well and loved Franny with all his worth. And she certainly wasn't a grass, but this was different. If she was in Franny's shoes, she knew she would definitely want to know the truth. Well, if Cab wasn't going to tell her, perhaps she would.

42

The day of the funeral came and the weather had blown in an icy gale along with an icy-faced Lola, who stood in the kitchen of the Doyles' flat, all in black, listening to her close friend and one-time co-worker, Casey Edwards, talk.

'It's terrible, Lola, what a thing to happen. He always looked so fit. I know it sounds silly, but I sent Vaughn off to get his heart checked as soon as I heard.'

Although there was nothing really to smile about, Lola found herself smiling at hearing Casey talk about Vaughn. Casey had worked for her as a waitress and she'd seen her struggle with her own demons as well as seeing her falling in love with Vaughn Sadler, who was a friend of hers as well as a retired face of the area. For a while back then, Lola had thought Casey and Vaughn would never get it together; both were stubborn and they hadn't been helped by Alfie trying to sabotage the situation.

'I know this might be the wrong time to tell you, but me and Vaughn are getting married next year. Things like this make you think about the usual clichés of life being too short.'

Lola grinned, delighted, and proceeded to give Casey a huge hug. 'Oh sweetheart; I'm made up for you. It couldn't happen to a better couple. And don't you worry, I'll do the catering for you. I know how much you like me Scotch eggs.'

Casey's smile stayed frozen, knowing, as everybody did around Soho, that love and friendship were Lola's forte, not her cooking – and certainly *not* her Scotch eggs.

Seeing Cab walk into the room, Lola made her excuses to Casey and went across to talk to him. She whispered, 'Have you told her yet?'

Cab stared hard at Lola. 'Drop it.'

'No, I won't.'

'Look, she's packing for New York; she'll be on the plane tonight. I told you it'll be fine. So quit your meddling.'

It was all Lola could do not to give Cab a dig in the ribs as she smiled out at the other faces and friends of Patrick who had congregated in the designer kitchen.

'Fine? You're having a bubble, ain't you, Cab?

298

You'll lose her forever if she finds out. Are you sure it's worth the risk?'

Making sure no-one was watching them, Cab grabbed Lola underneath the arm, pulling her back into the hallway.

'Lola, I know you mean well. I really do, but you've got to keep out of it; there are some things you don't understand.'

'Try me.'

Cab sighed in exasperation. 'Don't you ever give up?'

'Not when I know you're doing the wrong thing.'

'She knows it's best for her to go to New York. It's what Patrick wanted.'

Lola shook her head. 'Tell me you didn't use that line to get her to go. You did, didn't you?'

Cab looked slightly ashamed. 'She wouldn't have gone otherwise. Please, I'm begging you to leave it.'

'Where is she now?'

'In her room, but stay away, Lola. Stay away.'

That was like a red flaming rag to a bull, because one thing Lola Harding had always struggled to do was to be warned off, *especially* if she thought she was right; and as she stood watching Franny weep away as she packed up all her belongings, Lola knew she was right to tell Franny the truth.

'Hello, darlin', I won't ask how you're doing because I can see it on your boat race. Come and sit down for a minute; I want to talk to you.'

Franny wiped her face on the sleeve of her black Dolce & Gabbana top. 'I can't, Lola; if I stop, I don't think I'll be able to start again and my plane leaves at nine tonight.'

'Would it be so terrible if you missed it, babe? Ain't you rushing this trip to New York? Why don't you stay a while and decide in a few months when you're thinking straighter?'

Franny sounded offended. 'I'm thinking straight now, Lola. I know what I'm doing.'

Lola looked down at the satin bedcover she was now sitting on, absent-mindedly picking at invisible bits.

'Whose idea was it for you to go to New York?'

Franny stopped what she was doing and stared at Lola puzzled. 'What's that supposed. to mean? It was mine.'

'I heard it was Cab's.'

'Lola, if you've got something to say, say it.'

Lola shrugged, trying to sound and look casual, though it didn't help that the knock-off Chanel dress she'd bought from one of the crack-heads down Sonya's sauna was a size too small, and was now unmercifully cutting in underneath her armpits.

'It's just that you never mentioned going there before, sweetheart; in fact, the night I came to pick you up from the police station I remember distinctly you saying that you didn't want to go, and now all of a sudden you're rushing off there like you're Yankee Doodle Dandy.'

Grabbing a tissue from the side, Franny snapped. 'Things change, Lola. Has it crossed your mind I might not want to stay in the flat with all the memories?'

'Is that what Cab told you?'

'He may have helped me see I'd be better off there than here. Yes.'

'Is that why you're not going to the funeral? Did he say you'd be better off here than there?'

Franny's large green eyes flashed with hurt. 'I love you, Lola, but I don't know why you're being like this. Why are you picking at Cab?'

'I don't know either. Why are you, Lola?' Cab's voice boomed out from behind Lola, making her literally jump with fright.

'Bleedin' roll on. Have a word with yourself, Cab; you nearly had me fillin' me pants.'

Cab's tone was sardonic. 'Well, we wouldn't want that, would we now? I think it's probably best all round if we get you to the church. Everyone's heading off there.'

Lola didn't argue. There was still time to change Franny's mind before she went to the airport. 'Are you sure you don't want to come, Fran?'

Feigning a friendly gesture, Cab once more grabbed hold of Lola's arm. 'Oh, she's sure. Like Fran and I discussed, I'll be back straight after the funeral and there's really no need to put herself through it. Patrick wouldn't have wanted that.'

Lola cut Cab a stare but said nothing; instead she stormed out, leaving Cab to kiss Franny good-bye.

Once everybody had gone, Franny Doyle stood by her walk-in-closet deciding but not really caring what else she was going to take. As she went to bring down another suitcase from the shelf, her eye caught a glimpse of the framed photo of her, Cab and Patrick, taken on the day they'd gone strawberry-picking in Somerset over

301

thirty years ago.

Her hands began to tremble as she picked it up and the constant tears she'd been crying over the last few days began to flow again. She missed him. She missed him so much and wasn't sure how she was going to get through the next moments let alone the next few days.

She traced his face with her manicured finger, teardrops splashing down onto the glass of the photo frame. She could almost hear his warm Irish voice telling her what he always had on the rare occasions she'd cried as a child: *'To be sure, Franny Doyle, wipe away those tears from yer eyes, life's for laughing not for crying.'*

Through her tears, Franny began to smile. The smile spread across her face turning into laughter before it slowly turned back into tears. She gazed lovingly at the photo. Patrick had been right, as he so often was. Life *was* for living, and her sitting here crying wasn't what he would've wanted. She was going to make him proud. She *would* go to the funeral. She would celebrate his life with his friends and the people who loved him. Swap stories. Swap memories. Laugh and cry, in the name of the man who'd been her everything.

Looking at the clock, she saw there was still time. She could get there if she hurried. Grabbing her coat, Franny ran out into the storm.

43

'*Requiem aeternam dona eis, Domine. Et lux perpetua luceat ei. Requiescat in pace*. Amen. Eternal rest grant unto him, O Lord, and let perpetual light shine upon him. May he...'

Father Ryan stopped in the middle of the requiem mass as the doors of the Soho church were thrown open. He scowled as he stared at Franny Doyle standing in the middle of the aisle at the back of the church with her long chestnut hair stuck to her forehead, wet from the snow shower.

Franny looked past Father Ryan. Her legs began to give way as she caught sight of the coffin, which was covered in the most beautiful loose-petalled pink roses – the '*Mary Rose*'. Patrick's favourite flower simply because it had the same name as her mother.

She knew Alfie would be sad to miss the funeral, but he was still trying to recuperate from his injuries. There were lots of people she knew from around Soho, paying their last respects to Patrick.

Franny could see Cab and Lola sitting at the front, though they hadn't seen her come in. Her whole body began to shake as the church was filled with choral music.

The flickering candles along with the faces of the gathered congregation started to become blurry as light-headedness hit her. Just as she thought she was about to collapse, she felt a strong arm wrap round her to prevent her from falling.

'Come and sit down, you're wet through; you look fit to fall.'

Grateful, Franny was led to the pew which sat in the shadows of the back of the church. Turning to thank the person, Franny's smile of gratitude froze as she came face to face with Donal O'Sheyenne.

He grinned, leaning in closer, his putrid breath smelling of cigars. 'My sincerest condolences to ye, Franny.'

'What the hell are you doing here?'

Donal raised his eyebrows, looking genuinely surprised.

'To pay me last respects, of course; me and Patrick went back a long way. Perhaps you'd like to come round one evening and I'll tell you all about it? Oh, the stories I could tell ye, Franny.'

'You make me sick. If you've got any decency about you, you'll leave.'

Donal grinned, winking. 'Well, it looks like I'll be staying where I am then.' He roared with laughter, causing everybody to swivel round.

Franny caught a glimpse of Cab at the front of the church, who had now seen her. Without hesitation, he scrambled out of his pew and rushed down the aisle to the curiosity of the congregation.

Following directly was Lola. She caught up with Cab as he began to direct his conversation to Donal. His voice brimmed with anger.

'I want you out of here. And mark me words, Donal, if you don't go of your own accord – you see all them people? Not one of them will have any qualms about helping me drag you out.'

Donal stretched his arms up, then rested them on his head as he leant back. 'I don't think that would be a wise thing to do. Our agreement was one thing but that's very different from you starting something else with me. Don't take me on.'

Before Cab could reply, Lola shunted him out of the way. She pointed at Donal. 'Listen, darlin', I don't know what your bleedin' game is, but folk around here ain't partial to strangers; we stick to our own and we certainly don't like people who come along and think they're the big fucking I am – pardon me French – but since you've come into play you've been reeking of trouble and no-one likes a troublemaker, so whatever grievance you've got with Cab, this ain't the time to air it.'

'Everything all right, Lola?' Del Williams and Vaughn Sadler, two well-known faces of London, stood protectively behind her, their expressions rigid with aggression.

'Well, that all depends on what this fella decides to do. If he does as I suggested and leaves without bother, then everything is all right; otherwise I'd say things ain't looking too rosy.'

'So which one is it going to be, mate?' Vaughn sneered at Donal.

'What in all that is holy is going on here? Have you forgotten you're in the house of God?' A red-faced Father Ryan addressed Vaughn and Lola.

Vaughn snapped back. 'Do one, mate.'

'How dare you...' About to go on, Father Ryan was taken aback to the point of silence at the sight of Donal O'Sheyenne sitting relaxed in the nearby pew.

Donal chuckled. 'You heard them, Mattie; do one.'

Lola interjected. 'You think this is funny, pal?'

Getting up, Donal draped his coat around his shoulders. He looked at Lola in disgust. 'What I think is you're all out of your league. Now excuse me, gentlemen, I know when I've over-stayed me welcome.'

Donal left to go but stopped and turned back to where Franny was sitting. He tipped his hat, adding a simple farewell greeting: 'Franny.'

As he began to make his way out of the church, Donal felt his arms being grabbed on either side by Vaughn and Del. A wide grin spread across Donal's face.

'Oh, I wouldn't do that, fellas. To be sure, I don't think that's a good idea, do you, Cabhan?'

Cab's face tensed; he could feel his temples pulsating. Maybe it was stupid of him to have thought Donal would stay away, but there was no way he wanted this to go any further. All he needed was to get to the end of the day and get Franny safely on that plane to New York.

'Leave him.'

'What?' Vaughn's voice showed his surprise.

'I appreciate it, guys, but I'd be grateful if you'd leave it to me.'

Donal chipped in, enjoying the moment. 'You heard the man.'

Without further ado, Donal's arms were released and he walked out into the square.

'Oi! Sunshine, not so fast; I want a word.' It was Lola.

Donal stopped and waited for Lola, amused by

this woman who reminded him of the hard-drinking hags back in Dublin.

'I want to know what's going on with you and Cab. He's me mate and I won't let people take the piss out of him.'

'I think perhaps you'd better ask Cabhan there.' Donal nodded over to where he saw Cab escorting Franny quickly out of the church and towards the other side of the square.

'Cabhan, your woman here wants to know what's going on with you and your million-dollar girl – or should I say five-million-dollar girl.'

Hearing what Donal was saying, Franny, who was now in tears, turned to Cab. 'What's he saying?'

Holding her hand to encourage her to continue walking, Cab, full of anxiety, shrugged, desperate to remain calm. 'I don't know, baby, don't worry about him; concentrate on staying strong and before you know it you'll be flying across the Atlantic.'

As Cab tried to hurry along the street with Franny he found himself cursing the snow in his head; it was preventing him from moving faster and getting away from Donal. He *had* to get Franny out of Soho and onto the plane.

'Hey Fran, what's it like to be the five-million-dollar girl?'

Franny resisted Cab's tug as she stood facing Donal. She wrapped her coat around her, feeling an extra icy chill from the weather.

'What are you talking about?'

Donal flicked a stare at Cab. 'Shame on ye, Cabhan, how's the girl supposed to live a happy

307

life if she doesn't know the truth… Oh look, we've got an audience.' Donal gestured to Lola, who panted up behind them with a cigarette hanging out of her mouth.

Lola spoke firmly. 'Take her home, Cab; now!'

'I'm not a child; I want to hear what he has say. Go on, O'Sheyenne.'

'Stop, Donal; we had a deal!' Cab's voice was urgent, which only fuelled Franny's desire to know what O'Sheyenne was talking about.

'Cab! *Please.*' The pain was clear to hear in her voice. 'Please don't tell me you've been lying to me; not again.' She covered her face with her hands for a moment whilst listening to Donal speak to Cab.

'We did have a deal. We *do* have a deal and like I say, I'm a man of me word, but that never included not being able to tell Franny the truth.' He turned to face Franny. 'I heard Patrick had a heart attack and I'm sorry, or I would be if that was what really happened.'

All those present saw Franny's face blanch and they were aware her shaking wasn't entirely to do with the winter weather.

'Paddy boy was shot. Isn't that right, Cab?'

Franny was stunned, she could hardly breathe. The word kept spinning round in her head; finding it hard to concentrate on the rest of what Donal was saying.

'He gave his life for you.'

'What?'

'It was either him or *you*, Franny.'

It was Lola's turn now to be stunned. The shocked gasp was palpable.

'We had a deal, me and Patrick... Five million or a life. And he chose his. So you see, Franny you really are the five-million-dollar baby. Now, if you'll excuse me, I need to go and have a word with Father Ryan. If the man's going to speak Latin, he really needs to get it right.'

44

'What are you doing?' Cab stood in Franny's bedroom as she tore the things out of her packed suitcases. She didn't bother to stop throwing her clothes out of it as she half talked and half cried to Cab.

'What does it look like?'

He ran over to her, picking up the clothes from the floor and throwing them back into her suitcase.

'What it looks like is you're throwing away an opportunity to start again. Franny, you need to catch that plane.'

'Are you crazy? How am I supposed to go now?'

'You'll be safer there. I don't trust O'Sheyenne, no matter what he says.'

In her upset, Franny threw the clutch bag she was holding across the room. It landed on the Venetian dresser, sending all her perfumes flying everywhere.

She sat down on the bed, sweeping everything off it. Immediately she began to cry, making it difficult for Cab to hear what she was saying. 'So Patrick gave his life for nothing? Did I kill him, Cab? Did I? If I'd gone to New York when he'd asked me, would he still be alive?'

Cab sat on the bed next to Franny, talking and rocking her in his arms whilst being tortured by her pain; remembering the times he'd rocked Patrick when they were boys and the agony of the abuse he'd suffered had become too much for him.

Cab kissed the top of Franny's head, smelling the scent of sweet honeysuckle from her freshly washed hair. 'Please don't cry, Franny; please. O'Sheyenne wouldn't have stopped if you'd gone to New York; he still would've wanted his money and then come after you.'

It was a few moments before Franny spoke. She sat up and stared intently at Cab, noticing the worry lines etched onto his dark skin. 'What are you going to do?'

Cab looked puzzled. 'What do you mean?'

'I mean *what* are you going to *do?* He can't get away with it.'

Cab rubbed his face. He could feel the pressure beginning to build up and the throbbing headache begin again. He grabbed hold of Franny's shoulders, staring intently at her.

'Listen, Franny. Listen to me. I'm not going to do anything. Not now. Not ever. It's over with, and that's the way it's going to stay. It wouldn't take much of anything for O'Sheyenne to have an excuse to start something.'

'But...'

Cab shook Franny. 'No, Fran. I'm leaving well

310

alone; it's what Patrick wanted.'

Her voice strengthened. 'Then if you won't, I will.'

'No... No. You'll leave well alone, too. If you loved Patrick at all, you'll do as I say.'

Franny's face crumpled. 'How can you say that to me? You know I did.'

Cab refused to back down. 'Then if you did, you'll listen. He wanted you to be safe. If you start something with Donal, it'll all have been for nothing.'

Franny looked exasperated. 'We can't just let him get away with it.'

'We *can* and we will.'

As Cab held eyes with Franny, his phone rang out. Pulling it from his pocket he looked down at the screen to see who was calling. 'I ... I have to take this call.'

'Who is it?'

Cab hesitated before getting up off the bed. As he rushed out of the room, Franny called after him.

'Cab? *Who* is it?'

Looking awkward, Cab hesitated then replied. 'No-one... It's no-one.'

Five minutes later, Cab still hadn't come back, leaving Franny alone to reflect. She stared at the framed photograph of the three of them together as a variety of thoughts and memories rushed through her mind.

The doorbell rang, and hearing no-one else answer it and knowing the housekeeper – who'd insisted on staying on in her post although they

311

couldn't afford to pay her – had a day off, Franny made her way slowly down the stairs.

The hallway was dark and Franny could feel the drop in temperature as the evening air whistled through the gaps around the large Georgian door. Before she was able to get to it, the ringing changed into a knock and the knock changed into a loud hammering.

Surprised by the urgency of the caller, Franny hurried to unbolt the door. Her surprise was further increased by the identity of the visitor. Standing covered head to toe in snow and shivering on the doorstep was the cheerless figure of Father Matthew Ryan.

His words were clipped. 'Franny, I need to speak to you. We've met briefly but as you're not a churchgoer, aside from on high days and funerals, allow me to introduce myself officially... Father Matthew Ryan; I was known to your mother.'

Franny, too taken aback to speak, watched as the priest barged into the hall and proceeded to shake down his black cloak, leaving a small pool of water on the marble floor, before pompously handing her his wooden-handled umbrella.

Father Ryan radiated disapproval and Franny, still bemused by his presence, watched in astonishment as he marched uninvited up the stairs.

'I presume the lounge is this way?'

'Yes ... yes it is.'

Franny shook her head in bemusement. She stood at the bottom of the stairs then, realising Father Ryan had disappeared out of sight, she hurried up after him, fascinated to know what the priest had come for.

312

Arriving at the doorway of the lounge, Franny watched as Father Ryan picked up one of the photographs from the top of the cream baby grand piano. He sniffed disapprovingly at the photo of Patrick looking tanned and standing bare-chested holding a large fish on-board a luxury boat. Sensing Franny watching him, Father Ryan turned and cleared his throat.

'Now, Franny, I want to know what you're thinking about this sorry business.'

'Pardon?'

'Child, it's no good trying to hide it. The Lord sees and hears everything we do.'

He paused, waiting for Franny to speak. It soon became clear, she wasn't going to be forthcoming in her response, however.

'Saints and heaven preserve us. Come on, child, come on. Speak up. What are you thinking?'

Franny blinked several times, then opened her mouth to say something before closing it straight away, realising she didn't actually *have* anything to say.

Infuriated by what he saw as insolence, Father Ryan tutted loudly.

'The apple, Francesca, clearly does not fall very far from the tree.'

Not liking Father Ryan's comment, Franny spoke very firmly to the priest. 'It's not *Francesca*, it's Franny and I'd appreciate it if you could tell me *exactly* why you're here.'

Father Ryan found himself praying for forbearance, as he did so often these days. How very similar her daughter was to her mother. Obstinate and opinionated, which he acknowledged caused

313

the same sense of frustration and irritation within him as Mary had when he'd spoken to her.

Walking towards the window, his hands behind his back, Father Ryan noted by the ornate silver carriage clock sitting on the bureau that he'd been in the house for the past ten minutes but had yet to be offered a cup of tea.

Pondering on this fact, Father Ryan came to the conclusion that English hospitality and their reverence for a man such as himself was certainly scant compared to that his fellow countrymen showed him. The sooner he was back in Ireland the better; there at least he would be shown his true worth by the people of Kerry.

'Franny. Do you know much about the teachings of the bible?'

Franny said nothing and wondered if she should ask Father Ryan to leave, but the oddity of the priest turning up to speak to her made her curious to see where the conversation was going to lead.

'I take it from your silence that, like Patrick, you're a heathen who rejects God, and now have the emptiness of a life without Christ.'

'Don't you dare speak about Patrick like that!'

Father Ryan's expression didn't change. 'I'm not here to enter into a discussion with you, Franny.'

'Then why are you here?'

Father Ryan's face was tight and drawn. 'I imagine it would be easier to talk after a cup of tea.'

Franny had had enough. 'I want you to leave.'

'Not until you hear what I have to say to you.'

'Father Ryan, perhaps you don't approve of my way of life or the way of life Patrick had, but what

314

I do is to try to live a life where I respect others, something which Patrick taught me. But at this moment, I am finding it *very* difficult to be civil to you.'

Ignoring her words, Father Ryan looked contemptuous. 'You must be mourning your loss, Franny.'

Unexpectedly, Franny's eyes filled with tears. She nodded, not trusting herself to say anything.

Father Ryan sighed again. 'Perhaps we *really* should do this over a cup of tea.'

Five minutes later Father Ryan found himself sitting at the kitchen table mulling over the complex matter of genetics. The fact that a person may or may not have been brought up within their blood family didn't seem to make a difference, as was clearly proved by the tepid cup of over-milked tea Franny had given him. How disappointingly alike Franny was to her birth family. He really couldn't recall a time Helen O'Flanagan, his housekeeper and Franny's grandmother, had brought him a decent cup of tea.

Irritated by the memory, Father Ryan spoke sharply. 'Franny, for different reasons you and I have something in common.'

Franny, not wanting to, but unable to help herself, raised her eyebrows in surprise.

'We do?'

'Yes.'

'And what would that be?'

Looking annoyed, as if she should already know the answer, Father Ryan stretched for the open packet of custard creams lying on the table.

'Satan.'

'Excuse me?'

'The name of Satan befits he that is evil. I am talking about Donal O'Sheyenne, Franny.'

It was the first time Franny had taken Father Ryan seriously since he'd arrived. At first, she'd presumed that for all intents and purposes the priest, no matter how cantankerous, had just been carrying out his official duties. But on hearing Donal's name, a chill came over her and she could feel her pulse beginning to race.

She joined Father Ryan at the table, her face noticeably drained of colour.

'Father Ryan, how has Donal got anything to do with you?'

A sudden thought occurred to Father Ryan. 'Did Patrick say anything about me?'

Franny shook her head. 'No, not really.'

Matthew Ryan nodded his head, satisfied. It was good to know that Patrick hadn't told her anything of the nature of their relationship. If necessary he'd tell her later, but for the time being, he'd keep it to himself and use it further down the line if he had to. The less people who knew the better.

Father Ryan dipped his custard cream into his tea and absent-mindedly watched tiny bits break off it. He spoke quietly, and Franny could have been forgiven for thinking he was talking to himself.

'I have spent my life, Franny, trying to be a servant of God and at times it has been fraught; but I have always found my strength and been guided by the words of the bible. When I was moved here, I was ashamed to say I was angry with God,

316

not understanding why he had forsaken me, but then it all became clear. The good Lord knew my tormentor and, instead of me being brought here and being forced into his lair as I had first thought, he is in fact setting me free; ridding me of this man once and for all. My prayers were answered, Franny. In the words of Saint John, the apostle, "I shall ask the Father and he shall give you a helper." God indeed moves in mysterious ways. 'Tis wonder to me, and although it would not be my choice to choose a Doyle, neither is it my place to question it.'

Franny frowned, perplexed. 'I'm sorry but I *really* have no idea what you're talking about.'

Still not entirely sure why, but presuming the choice of Franny was another test for him to earn his rightful place in heaven, Father Ryan answered matter-of-factly. 'You, Franny Doyle, have been sent to be my avenging angel.'

Franny was amazed at the audacity of this man. For a while she stayed both silent and motionless, before saying, 'Why would you think I would help you?'

Father Ryan leant in, speaking in a hushed tone. 'Because, Franny, you and I both know *you* want Donal O'Sheyenne dead.'

45

Franny sat at her kitchen table a long time after Father Ryan had gone, staring at the small bible he'd left her. With a decisive movement, Franny snatched hold of it.

Noticing a page marker sticking out, Franny opened the bible, reading the highlighted passage.

And he that stealeth anyone and selleth them, shall surely be put to death... And if mischief follow then thou shalt give lift for lift. **Eye for eye, tooth for tooth, hand for hand, foot for foot, burn for burn, wound for wound, stripe for stripe.**

Franny stared at the page, reading then re-reading the passage. She thought of what Father Ryan had said to her. She thought of Donal O'Sheyenne and then she thought of Patrick. His face. His love. His absence.

Scraping back the chair, Franny quickly grabbed her coat and ran out of the house, ignoring Cab calling her back.

It was dark, not to mention freezing cold. Franny sat shivering on the hard seat. She jumped as the tiny wooden screen opened.

'May the Lord be in our heart to help you make a good confession.'

A lattice wooden screen separated them and

the darkness didn't allow Franny to see anything, but she knew it was Father Ryan.

'It's me.'

There was silence but for the sound of the staggered breathing of the priest.

'And what is it you want, my child?'

'I'll help you. Now tell me what I have to do.'

46

'Can you talk to her?' Cabhan Morton stood in the kitchen of the Doyles' house, his voice sounding as desperate as his expression.

Lola Harding gave a warm sigh. 'I'll do me best, Cab, but she's as stubborn as Patrick was. And I hardly helped with matters, did I? Telling her to stay when that nutter's about.'

Cab winked. 'I know your heart was in the right place, Lola.'

Lola laughed. 'That's code for, you nearly messed everything up, you interfering old cow!'

Cab grinned. 'Your words, Lola; not mine.'

'So what time is this plane leaving then?'

'She's missed check-in, but I spoke to British Airways; they can get her on the next flight... That is, if she'll go, of course.'

Lola's eyes were full of sympathy. 'Listen, Franny's a tough cookie when she needs to be. She'll be all right, you know.'

'I hope so, Lola. I really do.'

'You know it's for the best, Franny. We both do.' Lola stood with pleading eyes at the doorway of Franny's bedroom.

Sitting cross-legged on the satin bed cover of her queen-size bed, Franny answered Lola, trying not to sound too hostile. 'I appreciate your concern, Lola, but wasn't it you who was telling me I should stay?'

Lola waved her hand, trying to look nonchalant. 'Oh don't listen to me, love; I mean, what do I know, hey? I'm a gobby mare. I've always got an opinion on one thing or another. I didn't know all the facts.'

Franny flicked her hair away from her eyes. 'And neither did I, and now I do; I'm staying.'

Throwing off her cool demeanour, Lola rushed over to the bed. Kneeling on the edge, she implored Franny. 'Oh Christ, Fran. Don't you see, Cab's beside himself with worry. He thinks you could still be in danger.'

Franny didn't reply. She got up and pulled on her boots.

'Where you going, love?'

Franny smiled warmly, illuminating her natural beauty. There was a sadness in her eyes.

'Lola, I've made my decision and nothing you or Uncle Cab can say will make me change my mind.' Franny paused, looking up as Cab walked into the room. 'I'm sorry, Cab; I know you asked Lola to talk to me, but like I told her, it won't make a difference. I'm staying.'

Cab shook his head, watching her as she put on her cashmere coat and Burberry scarf. 'Why, Fran? Just tell me why.'

Franny blinked, noticing a change in how she felt. She was ready to show Donal O'Sheyenne just what she was made of. She was ready to take her revenge. She slipped on her black leather gloves, pushing down in between her fingers so the soft leather sat comfortably round them. 'Because I'm not letting him get away with it.'

Cab stood in Franny's way as she began to walk out of the room. His eyes filled with tears. 'No! Franny. No. Don't even think of it. I can't let you do it.'

'Cab, you don't have any choice. You're either with me or you're not, but either way, I'm doing it.'

Cab's voice was urgent. He held her arm tightly. 'I can't let you go.'

Franny studied Cab's face before she said anything. The lines. The smile. The eyes. She loved him so much. He and Patrick had been her everything and Cab was all she had left. She was devoted to him as he was her and the last thing she wanted to do was hurt him. But no matter how much she loved him, no matter how much she wished she could say the words he wanted to hear, she had to avenge Patrick's death and she wouldn't rest until she did.

Franny leant forward, kissing Cab gently on his cheek.

'You'll have to, Cab. You'll have to let me go. Sometimes in life, you just have to do what you have to do.'

She didn't know what time it was and she didn't care. The temperature had dropped to well below freezing, so instead of using her hands to knock as she had been doing, Franny Doyle continued to kick at the door, waiting for the person inside to answer.

Finally, Franny saw the lights flick on. Even though she was wearing her Salvatore Ferragamo shearling knee-high boots, her feet were frozen and she found herself having to jog on the spot to try to keep them resembling anything near warm.

Another few minutes passed and then the blue front door opened. Standing in a flimsy mini see-through nightdress, and clearly wearing no knickers, was a woman no older than twenty. A cigarette hung from her red bee-stung mouth and Franny could see she was stoned. She stared at Franny coldly, eyeing her up and down suspiciously.

'Yeah? What do you want?'

Franny smiled wryly but didn't bother saying anything as she pushed past the woman.

'Oi! Where the fuck do you think you're going?... Hello! Oi! I'm talking to you. Listen, sweetheart, if you...'

Franny didn't bother listening to the rest of the woman's ranting as she marched up the stairs. She knew exactly where she was going.

Standing in the doorway, Franny's voice was loud and clear. 'I want a word with you.'

'I'm sorry, Alfie, she just barged in!'

Alfie Jennings looked up and grinned. 'Come to give me my Night Nurse, have you, babe?'

Franny didn't smile. She kicked Alfie's legs off the coffee table they were resting on. He groaned, feeling the pain from his healing gunshot wounds.

'Do you want me to throw her out, Alfie?' The woman folded her arms and stared at Franny haughtily.

Franny walked up to the woman. She spoke quietly, keeping eye contact with her at all times. 'If anyone is going to do any throwing out it'll be me; but be my guest and try it.'

The woman, about to say something else, saw the steely look in Franny's eye and quickly thought better of it; instead she looked at Alfie and whined. 'Alfie *baby*, you ain't going to let her talk to me like that, are you?'

Alfie shuddered. The only thing that whining women did for him was remind him of his ex-wife Janine. He snarled, feeling slightly embarrassed at Franny turning up to find him with a two-bit piece of ass.

'I'm not only going to let her talk to you like that but *I'm* going to talk to you like that. Now shut the fuck up or, bad leg or not, I'll throw you out meself ... and go and get some fucking clothes on.'

Throwing back her hair, the woman stormed off, slamming the door behind her.

Franny glanced at Alfie, sprawled out on his cream leather couch dressed in a pair of Ralph Lauren black silk pyjamas. She shivered, remembering the stories her friend Casey Edwards had told her about him.

'As charming as ever I see. Even a body full of bullet holes seems to change nothing.'

Alfie winked and rubbed his muscular chest suggestively. 'You could have some of it, you know, Fran.'

Franny pulled a face. 'Not to put too fine a point on it, but I'd rather...'

Smiling, Alfie put his hand up in the air. 'Don't say it, Fran, we both know you won't mean it. I mean, how could you resist a body like this?' He paused then added, 'I'm sorry about Patrick, Fran. I owe him my life.'

Franny stayed standing. 'You do, Alfie, and that's exactly why I'm here, because now you owe *me*.'

47

Trevor Foxwell sat back and smiled. He'd been smiling since the day of the heist. The other thing he'd been doing was counting. Counting diamonds.

It was dark outside and the day had long since drawn in, taking with it the beam of sunshine which had bounced off the tiny cut stones, pouring out a spectrum of colours which projected and bounced off the walls.

He knew he was supposed to hand them over to the Russians; it was part of the deal he'd made last year with them – a payment for providing him with an arsenal of guns. But he couldn't. He just couldn't. They were his and there was no way he was about to share them with anybody else.

The other men on the heist had either been arrested or hurt; like that fool Alfie Jennings and the old man he'd had as his sidekick. Trevor snorted to himself at the thought. Those two muppets had been mugs to think he'd had *any* intention of giving them their cut. Not only had they been desperate, they'd also been past it. Going on a heist was a young man's game, *not* a game for men who probably had the combined age of a hundred and twenty-two.

Trev cackled out loud; partly influenced by the crack pipe he was smoking. The world was his oyster now. He could go anywhere. Slip out from underneath the Russians' noses before they even noticed he'd gone. And by the time the others got out of prison? Well, they'd be too old to spend the money anyway. Trevor smiled again. It was almost as if he could taste the pina coladas already.

About to take another hit from his crack pipe, Trevor heard a noise coming from the back. He frowned, wondering if it was the effects of the gear kicking in.

After a moment, Trevor put the pipe to his lips again and decided it was just his imagination. He inhaled deeply, then jumped at what sounded like breaking glass.

Getting up from the couch, Trevor froze as the lights went out.

'Fuck!' He cursed loudly. He hated the dark and the crack cocaine circulating in his body wasn't helping either. It was making him feel paranoid and edgy.

Feeling his way in the dark, Trevor's blood ran cold as he heard another noise. Christ, there *was* somebody there. He crouched down at the base of the sofa. Where was his gun? He couldn't focus his mind. The drugs were making his thoughts

325

fuzzy. He rubbed his head, feeling the sweat dripping off his face; a side-effect of the crack. He had to try to think. *Think.*

The bathroom! He'd left the gun in the bathroom. If he could only make his way across the front room without being heard, he'd be home dry. Whoever it was would regret thinking it was okay to come and play hard man with him: Trevor *Fucking* Foxwell. He would show them what he was made of but, more to the point, he'd enjoy every second of blowing them away. He giggled manically, unable to control the heightened sense of crack-induced excitement.

Getting down on all fours, Trevor began to crawl across the room. His head immediately banged into the coffee table. 'Jesus, fuck!' He yelped out, then banged his hand over his mouth. He'd forgotten the poxy thing was there.

Beginning to crawl again in the direction of the bathroom, Trevor came to another abrupt halt as the sound of loud music filled the air. He closed his eyes, shaking his head as his heart began to race. What the fuck was going on? It must be the gear. Fuck. He hated it when he got some bad shit; making him trip out.

He had to keep telling himself it wasn't real. The music wasn't real. Fuck. He rubbed his head. He needed another hit.

Trevor stood up and instantly heard a noise coming from behind him. He began to whimper. This wasn't funny. Tomorrow, he'd be fucking pulling the muggy cunt up who'd given him this crack.

He felt, or he thought he felt, a tap on his shoulder. He was beginning to lose all sense of reality. Now he didn't know if he was *actually* having a bad trip or if somebody really *was* in the flat.

He span round. 'Who's there? Because you're fucking with the wrong person. You know that? Do you hear me?'

He was sure he felt the tap again. Fuck; he didn't know. If he could only get to the bathroom and to his gun, he'd feel safer.

There it was again. He span round the other way, feeling the sweat flick off him. 'I *said* who's there? But I tell you this: I wouldn't want to be in your shoes when I catch you.'

Trevor pushed himself back against the lounge wall. His whole body was trembling. *It was all in his head. It was all in his head.* He wiped his mouth; it was dry and sticky, and even in the darkness Trevor's terror showed in the white of his wide eyes.

Panic began to overwhelm him; pushing down on him, crushing his chest and making it difficult for him to breathe. He scuttled along the wall, stumbling over the various unseen items in the dark.

Making it to the large bathroom, Trevor scrabbled for the light, but found that wasn't working either. Before he had time to try to think about what happened to the electrics, Trevor heard a noise again, but this time it was directly behind him.

With his eyes adjusting to the darkness, Trevor threw himself down, desperately grasping hold of the gun from underneath the sink. His hand shook with fear.

There. Over by the wash basket. He thought he could see someone, but he wasn't sure. Maybe it was a shadow. He rubbed his eyes hard, then harder; hoping whatever he was seeing – *if* he really was seeing it – would disappear.

'Who ... who's there?' Trevor's voice quivered as he pointed the gun around the room and then towards the doorway. Nobody answered; the only noise was the loud music that continued to sound, though Trevor still didn't know if it was only in his head or not.

'I'll shoot; don't think I fucking won't.' Trevor's hands trembled so unsteadily he found it almost impossible to hold the gun properly.

A crash coming from the lounge prompted Trevor to begin shooting. He fired aimlessly, flashes of bright white light sparking everywhere. Four shots. Five shots. Six shots. Then ... *shit*.

Trevor frantically clicked hard on the trigger. He was out of bullets. Then he felt something brushing up against his legs. Still sitting on the floor he scampered away, using his hands to help him. 'Hello?... Hello?'

A moment later, Trevor froze, feeling the unmistakable cold steel of a gun against his forehead. 'Hello, Trevor. I think you've got something I want.'

48

The car was covered in snow and, although the heat in the blacked-out Range Rover was at full blast, Franny felt cold. It'd been over a week since she'd talked to Alfie and gleaned the information out of him. Then, with each and every day that had gone by, Franny had been determined to do it, but then each and every *night*, Franny had made an excuse not to. Until tonight that was.

Taking off the black balaclavas covering their faces, Franny smiled at Alfie. She let out a huge sigh of relief and exhaustion as she stared at the bag of diamonds he handed her as she placed the gun in her bag.

'Now that wasn't too hard, was it?'

Alfie shook his head in amusement, feeling the pain in his leg from his injuries take a hold. 'For you or for me, Fran?' Franny didn't say anything. It was starting.

'Fran; where've you been? I've been worried about you.' Cab sat by the front door in the hallway looking frozen as Franny walked in.

She smiled at him, then frowned as she noticed his shoes and the bottom of his trousers were wet with snow and ice. Her voice was warm.

'Hey mister. What's going on? Why aren't you upstairs?'

'I've been out looking for you. You weren't

answering your phone. I thought...'

'What?'

He shrugged. 'I thought something had happened to you. Perhaps Donal had...' Cab trailed off again, not wanting to look Franny in the eye.

Taking Cab by the hand and leading him up the stairs to the heat of the upstairs rooms, Franny talked kindly. 'There's nothing to worry about, Cabhan. I'll be fine.'

Without thinking, Franny threw her bag on the table. Immediately she regretted her action. The bag flew open, spilling out several dozen large diamonds along with a Colt semi-automatic pistol.

Cab stared at her, anger welling up inside him. He grabbed the pistol, waving it around in his hands.

'What the fuck do you think you're doing with this?' He stopped, noticing the scattered diamonds on the oak table. He scooped them up in his hands and shook his head in horrified amazement. His voice was flat. 'What the hell have you done, Franny?'

With hurried movements Franny grabbed the bag, gathering up the stones. Her face was lined with sternness as she glanced at Cab.

'I told you. I'm not going to let him get away with it. Maybe you don't have a problem with someone killing Patrick, but I do.'

Cab grabbed Franny. He shouted his words. 'I've listened to you saying what you want to say on this matter, Franny, but now you're going to listen to what I have to say. Patrick left me in charge. *Me.* He thought long and hard about what he was going to do and *how* he was going to do it. All that mattered to him was that you'd be able to live a life free from harm. And, more importantly, free from that man. And I'm not going to stand here and let you mess that up.'

Franny pulled her hand away angrily. 'Give me back my gun, Uncle Cabhan.'

Cab stepped back, shaking his head. 'No. I don't think so.'

'I said, *give it to me.*'

Again, Cab shook his head. 'No way, Franny, that would be like me agreeing to what you're doing.'

Franny's voice was hostile. It was probably the first time in her life she'd ever spoken to her uncle in this way.

'I'm not asking you to agree with me; all I want is for you to give me my gun back ... now!' – Franny reached out her hand, waiting for Cab to give it to her.

'Franny, why are you being like this? Can't you see?'

'I can see that you and Patrick brought me up to stand up for what I believe in and not worry about the consequences. And that's exactly what I'm doing. Now *give* me the gun.'

Franny stepped forward and made a grab for the gun. Cab pushed her away, stumbling under her strength. She caught his arm as he tried to put it behind his back.

'Cab! Stop! Just give it me!' Her voice wasn't menacing, just desperate as she tackled Cab for the gun. He pushed her hard, sending Franny forward, tumbling towards the ground. She reached up to try to stop herself, but as she did so, she grabbed Cab's hand, who was caught off guard, causing the gun to go off.

The bang was loud and immediate and Franny fell to the ground.

To his horror, Cab saw that Franny was bleeding. He bent down, his face full of anguish. Distraught, he lifted Franny's head up, not noticing the tears running down his own face.

'Oh my God, Fran, I'm sorry... Fran, talk to me. *Please.*'

Franny moaned, holding her leg. She sat up, using the back of one of the chairs for support. Grimacing, she rolled up her trousers to expose her bloody leg.

Frantically, Cab grabbed a cloth from the side and pushed down on the wound, trying to stop the flow of blood. The burning pain made Franny shout out.

'Fran, I know it hurts, but you have to let me do this. It looks like it's only a graze; the bullet must have skimmed past your leg. You were lucky.' Cab looked up and saw a hole in one of the kitchen cupboards at the far end of the room, where the bullet had entered, confirming his suspicions.

Franny pushed Cab's hand away. She held onto the kitchen top and hobbled up to her feet. With the blood trickling down her leg, she scorned Cab. 'Lucky? You think *this* was lucky? I told you to give me the gun.'

Cab looked down. 'Franny, I'm sorry. I just want...'

'To keep out of my business. From now on, Cabhan, that's *exactly* what you're going to do. Or I'm telling you; you'll never see me again.'

The throbbing in her leg didn't disappear, even after Franny had dressed it and taken a couple of painkillers. But that didn't matter now. What mattered was finishing what she had started.

'Father Ryan?' Franny spoke to the priest as she stood in the gloom of the church. His back was turned to her as he knelt at the altar.

His voice was harsh. 'Can't you see I'm praying?'

Franny stood waiting for the priest but after a couple of moments she sat down, wanting to rest her leg.

It was at least two more minutes before Father Ryan got up from his knees.

'What is it?'

Franny tried to hide her dislike. 'I did it. I got the diamonds.'

'Then you'll know what you have to do now.'

Putting her head down, Franny took a deep sigh as a wave of despair came over her. She felt so lost, and the hollowness of life without Patrick hurt. She'd never thought this much pain was possible. And that was the other reason why she had to do this, why she had to play along with Father Ryan; no matter how much Cab's face came into her mind, hurt and begging her to let it go. Because if she stopped and did nothing, the pain of a nothing without Patrick would be too much to bear.

'I don't.'

Father Ryan looked at Franny and wondered once more if he indeed would have followed his chosen path of life if he'd known how very testing it would be.

'I don't understand what you want me to do.'

Father Ryan feigned incomprehension. He narrowed his eyes with a sneer painted on his lips. 'Me, Francesca? Oh no, your will is your own. What you choose to do is entirely of your own making. Now, if you're not here to pray, I think we have no more business.'

Without another word, Franny got up and walked out of the church.

A few minutes later, Father Ryan heard the church doors bang open. He scurried through from the vestry into the main part of the church. His voice was loud and rebuking.

'Franny, didn't I...' He stopped, seeing Franny was no longer there. Almost straight away, he heard another noise sounding from the wings.

Annoyed by the disturbance, he snapped out his words. 'Hello? Who's there?' No-one answered and, full of exasperation, Father Ryan made a hasty dash towards the direction of the noise.

Unlike the main body of the church, the wings were dimly lit and no candles were burning to bring light or warmth to the night-time chill.

The rows of chairs, complete with red bibles tucked into their back wooden compartments, stood in regimented precision, all the way down to the back of the church, and it was there that Father Ryan came to a sudden halt, seeing the hunched figure sitting in the shadows at the back

'I'm surprised to see you here.'

'I doubt that.'

Matthew Ryan walked further forward, resting his hand on the notch of his belt, which sat tightly round the black cassock he wore. His voice was severe.

'You'll kindly leave my church. The likes of you aren't welcome here.'

Cabhan Morton stood up, meeting the priest in the aisle, matching his contempt.

'Leave her alone, Ryan. This isn't what we agreed. You and I both know that.'

Father Ryan feigned ignorance. 'Leave who alone?'

'You know exactly who I'm talking about.'

Father Ryan turned and walked away. It was late and the comings and goings of Soho were beginning to tire him. How he longed for the simplicity of Ireland. Nobody bothered him or questioned his authority there. And soon, if all went well, he would be back in his homeland. Celebrated and revered for who and what he stood for. How cruelly he'd been snatched from the bosom of his parish by the influence and games of Donal O'Sheyenne. But what did give him hope was the fact that his prayers would be answered. Finally, after all these years, these long tortuous years, O'Sheyenne would get his retribution.

'I haven't finished talking to you.'

Cab spoke, interrupting Father Ryan's thoughts. Without turning around the priest replied. 'Cabhan, you and I both know Franny is free to do as she will. If she feels she needs to do something, the only thing I can do as her priest and a man of God is guide her to look at her conscience.'

Cab grasped hold of Father Ryan's hand. His face was taut with anger. 'Why, Ryan? Why her? What's this really about?'

Father Ryan wasn't sure whether he should answer or not, but his arrogance drove him on. '*This*, Cabhan, is about my rightful place.'

Cab scoffed, still holding the priest tightly. 'Your rightful place? You're more deluded than any of the priests back in the industrial school.'

Losing all self-control, Father Ryan yelled, his face almost purple with fury. 'I have devoted myself to the church my whole life. Sacrificed things most mortal men could not go without. I sacrificed being with the only woman I have ever loved. I have been a servant to both man and God, whilst all the time being tormented by my persecutor, and finally I will be rewarded with the demise of O'Sheyenne.'

'Rewarded? By who?'

Father Ryan looked at Cab, clearly mystified at his apparent lack of understanding. 'By God.'

'There's no reward, Ryan. Only Franny. Lost, hurt, confused Franny.'

'This was Patrick's choice. Not mine.'

Cab answered ruefully. 'Oh, and doesn't it just suit you? Play right into your hands. Does it mean nothing to you that Franny is risking everything and is set on finishing what you and Donal started?'

'How dare you suggest that I started this ungodly set-up? I am just as much a victim as Franny.'

It was all Cab could do not to grab Matthew Ryan by the throat. He closed his eyes in frustration.

'And Patrick; your son. What about what he wanted?'

Father Ryan's demeanour changed. The anger turned into cold hatred and his eyes seemed to cloud over, seething with venom. He hissed through his teeth, 'You will *never* repeat that. Not as long as you live.'

49

'Now I really know you're off your fucking head. Looney tune.' Alfie Jennings stared at the mobile phone Franny was trying to give him.

'Just do it, Alfie.'

Alfie scratched his head. As birds went, he'd always thought Franny Doyle was a top one. But that was before he got to know her properly. And now he did, he was finding it hard going. He'd almost prefer to have his ear chewed off by his ex-missus. Almost.

The problem with Franny – as with a lot of women he knew who thought they had a pair of bollocks between their legs – was that she had some of the worst traits a woman could have: assertiveness, opinionated to the point of making him want to drive his fist into something hard, and superiority, as well self-worth, which he always found was the most frustrating trait of them all; it made it almost impossible for him to get them into bed. Almost.

With Franny still staring at him and waiting for an answer, Alfie found he'd no other alternative but to answer her.

'You're having a bubble, ain't you? It ain't ever going to work. Why don't you just leave it, darlin'? You've got the ice, so take yourself away for a bit or buy yourself a nice bag. My daughter Emmie used to love shopping when she was feeling a bit down. Always made things better.'

Franny had to take a very deep breath to prevent her from saying anything which might sound mean. She knew perfectly well from her friend Casey Edwards that, far from things being well between Alfie and his daughter Emmie, he was to all intents and purposes estranged from her.

'Alfie, no amount of shopping or going on holiday is ever going to change what happened or make things better. The only thing that will make a difference is what I'm doing now.'

'I dunno, Fran...'

'Well I do, and if you won't help me, I'll have to do it myself.'

Alfie Jennings was many things, but one thing he wasn't was a man who could step aside and let a woman deal with what he saw as *man's* business. He was old school. Men were men, and women? Well, women should be just that.

He didn't even believe in women going to work once they became someone's missus. It'd always bemused him how Patrick had put Franny in charge of his clubs – what the fuck he was thinking of, Alfie had no idea.

When Franny had told him what really happened to Patrick he'd been shocked, but then maybe Patrick hadn't been keeping house properly. He didn't know all the ins and outs of it – Franny had refused to go into details – but any geezer who'd been shot by a disgruntled business associate, well, it was clear someone had done some fucking up, big time.

Patrick'd taken his eye off things and left it to Fran. But Alfie supposed that's where it all went wrong. A woman in charge of business was like a woman in charge of a football match. So wrong. If it hadn't been for that bird refereeing the Chelsea game at the weekend, there was no doubt in his mind they would've won two-nil. How she could've said it was offside, he didn't know, and it *still* pissed him off.

Alfie sighed. Well, no bird he was with would *ever* work, and there'd certainly be no discussion about it; something he could imagine a woman like Franny would want to do all the time – discuss. A sure way to destroy any healthy relationship.

He thought about his own mother, who had taken her own life when he'd been a kid. She'd worked all the hours God sent whilst his waste of space dad drank himself into violent oblivion. It was one of his few great regrets that his mother wasn't around today. He could've looked after her and spoilt her rotten like the princess she was.

He heaved another sigh, knowing there was no other option.

'Fine. Fine. You win, Fran, but don't say I didn't warn you.'

Franny shoved the phone into Alfie's hand. 'Well, you didn't, did you... Now call.'

Snatching the phone and giving Franny a hostile glare, Alfie dialled a number, mentally preparing himself as he did so. It rang. 'Yeah?' The person on the other end answered.

'Trev, it's me. Alfie.'

'What the fuck do you want?'

Alfie turned his whole head away from the phone. He chewed on his lip trying to hold his anger down. He'd been too busy recovering to *really* think about Trevor and what had happened that night. And even afterwards, when he'd broken into Trevor's place, he hadn't *really* thought much about the heist. But now, as Alfie listened to Trevor's voice on the other end of the line, what had happened in the warehouse was *all* he could think of. And the more he thought about it the more he warmed to Franny's idea. There was no way *he,* Alfie Jennings, was going to let a cunt like that get away with what he did, let alone turning over Patrick.

Duly wound up, Alfie played along nicely. 'I heard something you might be interested in.'

There was silence on the phone then a suspicious-sounding Trevor replied. 'Yeah, like what?'

'I heard talk.'

Trevor's voice was scornful. 'Big fucking deal. I hear talk every day, but I ain't phoning people up and wasting their time to tell them. And what I'm hearing now is less like talk and more like bullshit. Get off me fucking phone, Alf, if you ain't got nothing to say.'

Alfie clenched his fist as he looked at Franny watching him. Never in his adult days had Alfie Jennings allowed people to speak to him like that without putting his fist down their throat. But then, that could wait. Trevor would be getting his and then some.

Feigning cordiality, Alfie gritted his teeth. 'Maybe I'm not explaining myself properly, Trev, but I was offered some diamonds. Tasty ones. Anyhow, me and this guy go back a way so he didn't feel in any way worried about talking to me. So when I heard the story how he came across them, it got me thinking. Maybe I'm barking up the wrong tree, mate, but I ain't been around this long without being able to put two and two together. Sounds like someone turned you over.'

There was a long pause. A very long one during which Franny spent her time mouthing to Alfie, *'What's he saying?'*, whilst Alfie ignored her. Then Trevor spoke. Sounding more suspicious and more distrustful than ever before, he said, 'And why would you want to give me the heads up, Alf?'

'I don't. I want a cut. You owe me.'

Trevor laughed nastily. 'Not a chance.'

'Then I ain't got anything to say.' With that Alfie put the phone down. He looked at Franny whose face had paled.

'Don't worry, Fran. I know what I'm doing. He'll call back.'

After five minutes of Franny pacing up and down, looking frantic and making unhelpful comments like, 'Why the hell did you have to say that to him?' 'You think you know it all; but you don't. Now look.' 'So tell me again why you thought it was a smart idea?' Alfie was beginning to wonder if he really *had* done the right thing telling Trevor to do one. But he knew Trevor. He knew his greed. His disloyalty. His ego and because of that...

341

'Quick!' Franny hollered at Alfie as the phone rang, waving frantically at him to pick up. She paced around his luxury flat above Old Compton Street, listening to his side of the conversation.

'Yeah, Trevor? What can I do for you, mate?'

'Don't play fucking games with me, Alf. Seems to me I'm doing you a favour deciding to let you come in on it and have a slice of the pie. But of course, I can change my mind if that's what you want.'

'You know it's not.'

'One thing I don't understand is why you don't go and get them yourself. You could have the whole lot then.'

'It's like you said, Trev; I'm a bit past it.'

Trevor paused before saying, 'Yeah, that's what I thought the reason was.'

Alfie didn't say anything to Trevor. He just smiled ruefully to himself and let him talk.

'So you tell me where and who has them, then we have a deal; you can help me on the job. What shall we say ... seventy/thirty? What do you reckon?'

'I reckon you're taking the piss.'

Trevor cackled down the phone. 'That's the best offer I'll give you. You're lucky I'm giving you anything.'

Alfie answered sardonically. 'Yeah, I'm a lucky man.'

'Okay, then give us the squeal. I'm all ears.'

When Trevor put down the phone he roared with laughter. He picked up his crack pipe off the coffee table. He was right, Alfie Jennings was a fucking muppet. The man really thought he was going to give him something. Poor deluded cunt. Fuck him. He'd go in and get them himself now he knew where they were; after all, he had a date to keep with a beach. Satisfied and with a big grin on his face, Trevor took a hit from his pipe.

'Do you think he fell for it?' Franny looked nervously at Alfie from across the other side of the table. He winked at her as he lit a cigarette. 'Hook, line and fucking sinker.'

50

Cab sat opposite Franny in the front lounge. It was good to see her, but he hadn't a clue what to say. Apart from a passing greeting, they hadn't spoken to each other since the other night.

He massaged his temples; tired from another night of broken sleep. Attempting to strike up a neutral conversation, Cab smiled, slightly wary of the reception he'd get.

'How have you been, Fran?'

Franny glanced up from the paper she was reading. Large beautiful green eyes looked up at Cab with graceful coolness, her tone matching her demeanour.

'You mean, apart from my leg? Oh, I've been just fine.'

Having wanted to avoid this kind of conversation, Cab found himself becoming animated and being drawn in.

'Franny, you know I'm sorry, and Jesus does it frighten me to think it could've been so much worse, but you had a gun. What was I supposed to do?'

'Not shoot me.'

'Fran, that's not fair.'

'I told you to leave well alone.'

'Why won't you listen?'

Franny threw her paper down on the side, startling her dog who'd been sleeping peacefully at her feet.

'This is getting boring now, Cab. I warned you to stay out of my business.'

Cab's sadness shone through, appealing to her as much as he could. 'Franny, what's happened to you? I know you can't be happy being like this...'

Standing up and grabbing her bag, Franny interrupted Cab; 'You just don't get it, do you?'

'No, Franny, *you* don't get it. You don't have a clue what Father Ryan is really like.'

Looking very uncomfortable, Franny stared at Cab. 'Father Ryan? I don't know what you're talking about.'

'Come off it, I *saw* you. I followed you.'

'How dare you! Who do you think you are, hey?'

'I think I'm someone looking out for a person I love; trying to save her from herself. I may not have known Father Ryan like Patrick did, but he and I still go way back. Can't you see he's not doing this for anybody but himself? In fact I'd say he's not doing anything at all; you are. He's got his own agenda and he's sitting pretty in his ivory tower, and when it all goes wrong – which it will, Franny – it'll be you who'll get hurt.'

Franny looked at him scornfully. 'Don't you think I know that? I'm not stupid, Cab. I know Father Ryan wants something out of this. He's had enough of O'Sheyenne torturing him. I know that. It's quite straightforward when you think about it.'

Cab shook his head. 'No, Fran, it's not as simple as that. Nowhere near.' He paused, looking hesitant. He couldn't let her destroy herself. 'Listen, Fran, I need to tell you something about Father–'

His phone rang. He quickly looked at it then spoke to Franny as he hurried out of the room. 'Stay there. I have to take this call. But we need to talk.'

Ten minutes later Cab walked back into the room. His heart sank. There was no point in looking round the rest of the house. He knew she'd gone.

'Maybe I should just do this on my own, Franny? You go home.' Alfie sat in the driver's seat of her Range Rover outside Donal O'Sheyenne's flat.

She shook her head. 'No, Alf. I want to see him.'

'Look, it's covered. Once it's done. I'll call you.'

Franny turned her head, wiping the window to look out onto the deserted street. 'Do you think he'll come tonight?'

'I don't know. Maybe. I've got my men watching his flat and if he makes any moves they'll follow him. If he comes this way they'll call me straight away. I arranged to do the job with Trevor on Thursday night. So by my reckoning, he'll try something either tonight or tomorrow. But he'll come all right and, knowing Trev, he'll be here sooner rather than later; snapping after that bait.'

Franny nodded her head as she mulled over what Alfie was saying. 'I hope so, Alfie. I really do.' She hesitated for a moment and a small nervous smile showed on her face. 'I appreciate you having my back.'

Alfie grinned. 'It wasn't like you gave me much choice.'

Impassively, Franny spoke. 'You can have the diamonds.'

He raised his eyebrows. What was it about Franny? Just when he thought she knew her, she'd go and say something which threw him. She drove him mad with her demands and she thought differently to him, as well as categorically rejecting the Alfie Jennings' charm offensive which usually worked on most women. By rights he should dislike her; yet there was something about Franny Doyle which had him thinking about her at most hours of the day. Fuck, being around Franny was starting to make him soft and that was the last thing he wanted to happen. Love, marriage and headaches.

'You don't have to pay me.'

Franny looked at him. 'I know and that's why I'm going to.'

He studied her face as he thought. He'd been happy, albeit slightly reluctant, to help out at first, but not for one moment did he ever presume he was going to have a cut of anything, much less the whole lot. Granted, he could get himself straightened out. Get his business back to how it was. And then he could get himself back to *who* he was. The person he had once liked.

'I'll take half. That's all though, the rest are yours.'

'I don't want them.'

'Franny, you might not want them now and I understand why, but one day you will. If you won't take them, then I'll keep them safe for you and when you want them, they'll be there.'

Franny didn't give an answer. Instead she watched the light snow fall on the ground. The weather reports had said it was getting warmer, but each day that passed she felt colder.

'I saw Emmie the other day; she looked well.'

Alfie flinched. 'Did she ask about me?'

Franny turned to Alfie, looking into his eyes. She could see the sadness there. She wanted to lie to him, but through bitter experience she knew how much lies destroyed the world around you. The truth might be hard, but it was better than waking up one day and realising everything around you wasn't what you thought it was. She took his hand and squeezed it gently.

'No, but I'm sure she will, Alfie. I'm sure of it. Just give her time.'

The phone rang, saving Alfie from having to open the Emmie box in his head. He listened to the caller, nodding and humming in agreement. Clicking off the phone, Alfie turned to Franny. 'He's coming. He should be here in about fifteen minutes. Trevor's on his way. Now all we have to do is wait and watch.'

Trevor Foxwell was high. He liked to be high. He liked to be high for the sake of it, but he especially liked to be high when he was about to go on a job. Getting the diamonds from the heist was one thing, but getting them back from whoever had stolen them from him – well, that was entirely something else and ever more the sweeter.

Hurrying down the street and checking no-one was about, Trevor resisted the urge to slip down an alley and take a hit from his crack pipe. Soho was crawling with drugs police and the last thing he wanted to do was risk Alfie getting his hands on the diamonds while he was banged up for using and – more to the point – for carrying a loaded pistol. He grinned as he felt for the Colt .380 Mustang in his pocket.

The outside of Donal's flats was nondescript. Thinking he'd have to take time out to get through the main security doors, it came as a pleasant surprise to Trevor to find the main entrance open. The flats weren't even equipped with CCTV cameras either; whoever this man was, it was obvious he was an amateur and deserved everything he was about to get.

Walking up the stairs, Trevor hoped the person was in. He wanted to get a look at this geezer. Anyone who had the front to break into his flat; well, he wanted to look him right in the eye. Christ, he was charged. It wasn't just the crack, it was the fact he was about to do someone some serious damage.

He pulled out his gun and, with a quick look up and down the corridor, Trevor walked towards Donal's door. The getting in was easy; it always was. Trevor had never bothered with anything as sophisticated as lock-picking. He did it old school. A crowbar and a bit of elbow grease.

With the crowbar in one hand and his gun in the other, Trevor crept into Donal's flat. He found himself in the front room, which was empty but for a single chair. His finger rested on the trigger.

Cautiously Trevor checked the bathroom and then the kitchen. He wanted to see if there was anybody in before he began to look for the diamonds.

Disappointed at not finding anybody, Trevor saw there was one more room to check. Licking his lips, he made his way to what he presumed was the bedroom door.

Placing the crowbar down on the floor, Trevor slowly began to turn the handle.

51

'What do you think's happening in there?' Franny stared through the windscreen towards O'Sheyenne's block of flats. Alfie shrugged.

'I dunno, babe.'

'Is that all you've got to say?'

Alfie rubbed his head again. He was trying to be understanding, but he was tired, not to mention hungry. Two of the worst combinations, especially as he knew there was a big piece of steak and a superking-size bed waiting for him just around the corner in his flat.

'I'm going in.'

'For fuck's sake, Fran. This ain't *Thelma and Louise* and you ain't Bonnie Parker 'cos that would make me Clyde and we all know what happened to him.'

'I'll go round the back. I know there's an emergency stairwell there. I saw it when I came here before.'

Alfie's voice was a mix of worry and surprise. 'You've been here before?'

'I had to see where he lived. Don't you get it?'

Alfie shook his head. 'Fran...'

'I won't go right in, but I can't just sit here.'

'That's exactly what you're going to do, darlin'. Last thing I need is something happening to you.'

Stressed, Franny's eyes filled up with tears, causing Alfie to look away embarrassed. He'd never been good with emotions and sitting in the car in such close proximity to them made him feel very uncomfortable.

'I'm doing this for Patrick. Don't you get it, Alfie? I really don't care what happens to me, as long as they get payback.'

'They? I thought this was about Trev?'

Franny's voice was urgent. 'No, it's about all of *them*. Everyone who ever hurt him.'

Alfie whistled. He wasn't quite sure what to say. Well, he hoped she wasn't expecting him to get involved in that as well. He wasn't looking for an all-out war with anyone and besides, he wasn't exactly up to it physically. Far from it. By rights he should still be resting; his wounds still needed to heal and were often painful.

'Fran, don't you think this is getting out of

hand now?'

Franny bristled. 'Patrick's dead. How much more out of hand do you think it can get?'

Alfie's eyes were full of warning concern. 'A lot more, Franny.'

Franny exploded in frustration. 'You're such a hypocrite. What? Because I'm a woman it's different for me? I should let the people who hurt Patrick get away with it? I'm sick of everyone telling me that. Am I the only one cares?'

Alfie spoke gently to her. 'No, of course not.'

'And you know what makes it worse is that I don't see any of you living your lives like that. You, Cab; none of you. If anyone dares try anything you don't like, you're there guns blazing, so don't tell me to do something you wouldn't do.'

Franny opened the car door, getting out and walking towards the back entrance of O'Sheyenne's flats.

'Franny!... Franny!' Alfie called after her but she didn't bother turning round. 'Fine, but if you're not back in ten minutes, I'm coming in.'

The pain to Trevor's face shot up and down his body. He staggered to the side, trying to hold onto the walls as blood poured down his face. 'Fuck! Fuck!' he screamed in agony.

'Can I pass you a tissue for that? It looks nasty.' The man stood in a pair of striped pyjamas with a cricket bat in his hand. 'To be sure, son, I can't hear what you're saying.'

There was only another groan followed by a heavy thud as the bat came down, this time on the side of Trevor's head, perforating and ex-

351

ploding his eardrum and causing blood and pus to seep everywhere.

Trevor's screech was blood-curdling. He dropped to the floor, holding his ear as his body jerked in pain.

Donal bent down, grabbing Trevor by the hair.

'I don't think I've had the pleasure. I'm Donal; Donal O'Sheyenne. But the big question is: who are you?'

'Fuck off.'

This time Donal didn't bother using the bat. Instead, still holding Trevor's hair, Donal took his other hand and used his thumb to drive deep into Trevor's eye, twisting and gouging it out.

Donal let go and immediately Trevor fell backwards, writhing about on the floor in a pool of blood. Seeing the gun dropped by his side, Donal picked it up. He nodded his approval as he studied it before crouching down and forcing Trevor's mouth open by smashing his teeth.

'Now, how about we start again...'

The emergency stairwell at the back of the flats was dark and Franny slowly crept up the stairs, feeling her way as she went. No lights were on, only windows, and she could see the rooftops of the West End as she made her way up. Only once did she pause when the landmark of Gatsby's café in Tottenham Street came into sight; a place where she and Patrick had often gone for an early morning coffee when they'd wanted to get away from the world of Soho.

Reaching the top landing of the stairwell, Franny tried the door and discovered it was locked. Out of the small black bag she was carrying she took out a torsion wrench as well as a set of pin tumbler lockpicks followed by a shook and snake pick. Tools of the trade, given to her by Cab and Patrick when she was a girl. A present she'd asked for instead of the usual set of dolls after she'd seen it on a film. They'd laughed at her, but had still presented her with the box of tools wrapped up in pink paper and a pink bow.

As a child she'd practised for days, for months, until picking a lock became her party trick, and then she'd insist on performing it at the parties Patrick held for the other faces of London, who'd slap Cab and Patrick on their backs, telling them she was a chip off the old block. And now here she was, without Patrick. Somewhere she thought she would never be.

Quickly and expertly, Franny used the picks, sliding and turning the lock until she heard a click. She paused, closing her eyes before turning the handle and going in.

Keeping well in the shadows, Franny crept along the corridor. At the end she could see Donal's flat. She could also see the door was open. She stood motionless, listening for any sound. All was silent. Taking a deep breath, Franny walked towards the door.

Pushing the front door open, Franny paused to make sure there was nobody there before walking into the front room. It was empty. Again she paused, before going into the kitchen, then the bathroom. Nobody. Finally she turned to the room to the right and slowly opened the door.

Franny's whole body jerked in shock. Blood was

everywhere. She covered her mouth as she saw the mutilated remains of what could only have been Trevor's body. Beginning to retch, Franny backed out of the room. Once outside in the corridor, she began to run.

Outside, Alfie realised he'd nodded off for a few minutes. He rubbed his eyes then reached for the electric window. The cool air hit him immediately, making him want to take a piss. He looked at his phone; the battery had died, but he didn't think he could've been asleep longer than a few minutes, though he couldn't be entirely sure. *Shit.*

Getting out of the Range Rover, Alfie heard the crisp snow under his feet. It was fucking freezing. Going to the rear of the car, Alfie unzipped his trousers, looking round out of habit rather than caring if anyone saw him, but still keeping his eyes on the front doors of O'Sheyenne's building.

It felt like such a relief. His piss steamed in the air and Alfie, even though his mind was on Franny and her safety, found himself making patterns in the snow; yellow initials followed by the shape of a love heart. Christ, what the fuck was he thinking? He shivered. Right, he had to focus. Franny wasn't out yet which meant only one thing; he was going in. Zipping up his trousers, Alfie froze.

'For sure, this is some night I'm having. It's good to see you again. Why don't ye turn round and let me take a look at ye?'

Feeling the gun in his back, Alfie knew he had no choice. Turning round he came face to face with O'Sheyenne and his two men.

52

'...Come as quickly as you can. Alfie's in trouble. Cabhan, please!' Franny clicked off her mobile, leaving another voice message and directions for Cab.

She glanced through the crack in the wooden panel, looking down as she watched Donal and his men surrounding Alfie who was now sitting blindfolded and tied to a chair in the middle of a large room in a disused warehouse. The roof of the warehouse was broken and a heavy snow shower floated in, soaking the concrete. Pieces of corrugated iron lay discarded on the floor and shards of broken glass sat in neglected frames.

Franny could see Alfie shaking violently. It was freezing, but she was certain it was the torture he was being subjected to rather than the cold.

Sweat and blood ran down Alfie's chest. Right there, Franny knew she had to do something. Picking up the phone again, Franny dialled Cab, listening as O'Sheyenne talked.

'Now, I would have thought you'd had enough trouble of late. Yet there ye are pissing outside me house. To be sure, Alfred, what sort of man does that?'

Alfie's head was bent forward on his bare chest. Although conscious, he was barely able to look up at Donal.

With a large grin on his face, Donal, who'd taken

355

his jacket off to reveal an immaculately ironed shirt, spoke in a mocking manner. 'Has nobody got anything to say for themselves these days?'

He puffed on his cigar, glancing over to Alfie. He winked. 'I can see you're healing nicely.'

He walked across and ran his yellow-stained fingers down Alfie's chest; stopping at one of the gunshot wounds he'd received from the heist. 'Nasty that.'

Without warning, Donal took his cigar from the corner of his mouth and stubbed it into Alfie's healing wound. The skin hissed and smoked, emitting a pungent smell.

Alfie's body spasmed, his head jerked backwards as the whole warehouse filled with his screams.

Franny turned away in horror; she couldn't stand it. By the time Cab eventually got in touch it would be too late.

Quickly, looking around, Franny wondered what she could do. She had nothing of use on her.

When she'd left O'Sheyenne's flat, she'd seen his men bundling Alfie into a car. Quickly, she'd followed, keeping far enough behind not to be seen but close enough not to lose sight of them. She'd seen what Donal had done to Trevor and she was sure he'd do the same to Alfie given the chance.

Donal and his men had pulled up into a builders' merchant, not far from Holloway Road. She hadn't wanted to risk being seen, so she'd parked her car at the entrance, making the rest of her way on foot. It'd taken another five minutes or more to track exactly where they'd taken Alfie, but by then it had already begun.

Crouching down and moving along at the same time, Franny kept her eyes firmly on the ground, desperate to find something which might be of use.

At the end of the landing Franny could see the stairs leading down directly to the room Alfie was in. Finding another gap in the derelict walls, she could see Donal take the chain he held in his hand and begin to take a run up towards Alfie.

He whirled the rusty metal chain in the air, bringing it down as it whistled across Alfie's body, dragging flesh from his muscular torso.

In an instant, Franny raced across to the far end of the landing. A metal barrel sat in the corner. With all her strength she kicked it, hoping to send it flying forwards. It didn't move, but she needed to cause some kind of distraction. With grim determination Franny tried again. This time she threw her whole body against it. The force of her full weight had the metal barrel clanging onto its side.

She scrambled up to her feet as the noise thundered through the warehouse. Another kick sent it tornadoing down the landing. She watched it pick up speed, hitting the corner and taking off the already cracked plasterboard.

'Saints in heaven. What the...' Donal turned at the sound. Seeing the barrel break through the wooden stairs and smash down onto the ground to splinter on the uneven concrete, Donal pulled out his gun, signalling to the two other men.

'That way! You go that way!' he shouted, gesturing to them to head towards the back stairs as he ran towards the main set.

From where Franny was standing, she could see Donal charge to the bottom of the stairs. She ran, desperate not to be seen, tripping and stumbling over the rubble on the landing. Faster and faster she went, hearing the sound of Donal's men speeding somewhere in the darkness towards her, with Donal some way behind.

Just in front of her, Franny saw a fire escape running up to the roof. The rungs were broken, but if she could make it up to the top, they probably wouldn't see her in the pitch black of the high ceiling.

Clambering up, Franny's hands gripped onto the freezing rusty metal, but they were icy and her arms weren't strong enough to pull her up, and the slipping of her feet made it impossible to hold on.

She could hear them coming. Nearer. Nearer. It was no good, she couldn't make it; they'd see her. Dropping back down to the floor, panic began to catch hold of Franny as she realised there was virtually nowhere to hide.

Her eyes rested on a large hatch in the floor by the adjoining corridor. She had no clue how far down it went or where it went. But what choice did she have? She looked at the dark hole then looked up as a shadow began to creep across the ceiling. They were coming.

Knowing she didn't have any more time to think about it, Franny threw herself down into the abyss of the darkness; a split second later, Donal's men rounded the corner.

Down, down she fell. Descending further into

the blackness. She scrabbled, trying desperately to grab hold of something; anything to break her fall.

The air suddenly felt different, colder, and Franny knew her drop was about to come to an end. Bracing herself, she closed her eyes.

The water felt like crashing into a steel wall. It was instantly followed by a sensation of paralysing cold. Franny's body rotated, twisted and winding as she fought against the shock of the fall; disorientated, she couldn't get her bearings in the water as her chest began to tighten; her breath being squeezed out from her.

It was almost impossible to see underwater, but in the distance Franny caught sight of a sparkling fragment of light. Certain it was the surface, she began to swim, feeling her muscles starting to tighten from the cold as she pushed against the water towards what now she knew was upwards.

The cold air hit her. Gulping several times, she opened her mouth, struggling to breathe.

Eventually managing to get her breath, Franny could see she'd come up in a small water-holding by the side of the warehouse. There, only a few metres in front of her, was a low bank. Exhausted, she made her way towards it.

Gasping and reaching for the side, Franny slowly pulled herself up, but abruptly she felt her head being pushed down into the water. Her arms began to flay as she struggled to stay above the surface.

Through violent splashes, Franny could see the feet of one of O'Sheyenne's men. Making a quick decision she dived further under; out of the man's reach.

Knowing she only had so long until her body went into shock from the cold, Franny frantically dragged something out from her pocket.

With the man unable to see where Franny was, she kicked back up in a fluid movement to break through the surface of the water. With one hand pushing down on the wall and with all her strength, Franny flung her arm back, then lunged forward to where the man stood, driving the snake lockpick she'd had in her pocket deep into his foot.

O'Sheyenne's man yelled in agony, bending down and pulling at the embedded metal spike.

Taking her chance, Franny dragged herself out onto dry land, but she wasn't quite quick enough. Her hair was grabbed and the force of it slammed her against the wall.

Struggling, Franny pushed and grappled, bringing her nails across her assailant's face, but she was weak with cold and no match for him.

'O'Sheyenne, I think we've found someone!... O'Sheyenne!'

Slightly distracted, the man gave Franny the opportunity she was looking for. She brought up her knee, slamming him hard in his testicles before driving down her elbow in the side of his temple; a move Patrick had taught her as a teenager.

Stunned with pain, the man doubled over, allowing Franny to dart along the pathway leading back to the warehouse. She was aware of other voices behind her as O'Sheyenne's other man came to assist.

Weighed down in her wet clothes, Franny ran through a narrow door, which took her along a reeking dank corridor through to the heart of the warehouse.

She could still hear them. Not far behind. She dashed ahead, clipping and tearing her ankle flesh on the corner of a sticking-out piece of metal shard. She shrieked, gritting her teeth but refusing to let the tears come.

Through her pain, Franny suddenly had an idea. She grabbed the piece of metal, tugging it hard to release it from the metal sheet it was still threaded to.

With renewed energy, Franny raced along, speeding round the corner into the room where Alfie sat still blindfolded. She splashed through the pools of water towards him. Throwing herself down at his knees. Seeing him shrink backwards Franny tried to reassure him.

'It's okay, Alfie. It's me... It's only me. I'll get you out of here.' She used the piece of steel to cut through the rough ropes. The pressure needed to cut it caused the metal to gouge into her palm, drawing blood, but she ignored the pain and carried on.

As she cut the last part, Alfie groaned and Franny looked up at his swollen and battered body.

'I'm so sorry, Alfie...'

'Well, well, well. Franny Doyle, now this is a pleasure.' From behind her, Donal O'Sheyenne's voice boomed out.

Franny's face hardened. She stood up, spinning round to face Donal. Quickly, she put the piece of metal behind her back, slipping it down into her pants.

Franny said nothing. She stared and stood shivering, watching Donal tap the chain he was carrying against his leg.

Franny stood in front of Alfie. 'Don't come any nearer.'

O'Sheyenne roared with laughter. 'Or what, Franny? You'll stab me with your lipstick? Okay, me against you. How about it?' Donal started to whirl the chain in the air. Again, Franny didn't move.

'Come on then, Franny... Don't you want to play?'

With his legs untied but his hands still bound, Alfie jerked in his chair. Donal nodded in his direction.

'I think he's trying to tell you something... What's that, Alfred; we can't quite hear you.' Donal roughly pulled the gag out of Alfie's mouth.

Through a swollen mouth, Alfie mumbled, 'You leave her alone, O'Sheyenne.'

'Oh no, Alfred; I'll take her with me if you don't mind. Me and her have got a little catching up to do.'

O'Sheyenne cackled, then drew back the chain, but just as he was about to smash it down, Franny screamed out.

'Cab! Look out!' She hollered as she suddenly saw Cab, who hadn't noticed the taller of O'Sheyenne's men poised behind him, about to bring down the steel wrench he had in his hand.

Cabhan Morton moved with lightning speed, years of practise from ducking out of the way from the cane-carrying priests. He dived to one side, turning his gun on the man and firing off a round of bullets.

From over the other side of the warehouse, the second and last of O'Sheyenne's men came hobbling in, only this time waving a gun.

'Get down, Fran! Get down!' Cab's voice was urgent.

Flashes of gunfire shot out, ricocheting against the piles of discarded metal. White light sparked in the darkness as the deafening sound of the bullets being sprayed against the rubble made it impossible for anyone to be heard.

Rolling to the side behind a mound of sand, Cab saw he had a clear aim. He fired at O'Sheyenne's man; shots ringing out. A moment later there was silence.

Cab rushed to where Alfie was sitting. He pulled off his blindfold. 'Alf? Alf? Fuck, are you all right?'

Alfie managed to nod. Cab looked around and spoke hurriedly, almost to himself. 'Where's O'Sheyenne?'

In a whisper, Alfie answered. 'More to the point, where's Franny?'

53

He was only a few hundred yards ahead now. But there was no way Franny Doyle was going to let him out of her sight. In the commotion of the shootout, she'd watched O'Sheyenne try to slip out into the night.

She'd followed him along the quiet streets of North London; pulling back several times in the stolen car she'd taken. It wasn't what she would've chosen to do normally, but her car hadn't started and there was no way she was going to lose sight of Donal, so she'd hotwired another vehicle; something Cab had taught her to do and she'd been particularly good at.

She hadn't hotwired since a teenager when she and her friends had missed the last train back from Brighton. She'd known Patrick would go ballistic with her for being out so late, not to mention for going to Brighton without his permission. Unfortunately they'd been stopped by the police before they'd even got out of the seaside town and consequently Patrick had been called to the station. He'd been beside himself with fury, while Cab had looked on proudly at her ability to hotwire a Mercedes – one of the hardest cars to steal.

Franny hadn't known where Donal was heading but presumed she'd have a long drive ahead of her. So it'd surprised her to follow him right back to where they started. Soho.

The door creaked open and Franny winced at the loud sound it made. She crept slowly into the vestibule, mesmerised for a moment by the rows of flickering candles. In the light, Franny could see wet footprints on the stone floor. O'Sheyenne was here.

Making her way round the back of the church, Franny's heart began to race as adrenalin rushed through her body. Cautiously, she walked through the arch, edging along the gridded lattice floor at the back.

The main part of the church was almost pitch black save for two large candles which burnt majestically, lighting up the altar.

Franny crept further forward but jumped in fright as a quiet yet menacing voice cut through the stillness of the night.

'Do you like them? Seemed a bit cosier. Churches can be very uninviting places, you know.'

Donal O'Sheyenne stood up from the back pew. Stepping into the shimmering glow of the candlelight, his face was twisted with venom.

'Did you really think I didn't know you were following me? Tut-tut, Franny Doyle, you do me a disservice.' Donal grinned but his eyes were cold.

O'Sheyenne began to walk towards Franny, who started to back off. She banged into the pews, stumbling as she felt her way.

'It's a shame your mother didn't have the same spirit as you, Franny, perhaps then things might have been different.'

Franny's eyes cut at O'Sheyenne. Her voice dark and hostile. 'Don't speak about my mother.'

'Blue she was, blue with cold. What a lonely death it must have been.'

'I don't want to hear anything you have to say, O'Sheyenne.'

'They say she screamed in terror as she went under the water.'

'I *said*, I don't want to hear.'

'All of her own doing. A sin against God. Poor wretched soul she was.'

'Stop! I'm not here to listen to this.'

Donal cocked his head to one side. 'No? Then why are you here?'

'Because of what you did to Patrick.'

Still moving towards Franny, Donal laughed. 'Oh yes, Patrick, now I wondered when we'd get to him. He was the only one there for Mary, you know, yet she turned her back on him. And yet, even after all that happened, he still wanted you. Problem is he couldn't finish what he started.'

Franny's voice was raised and loaded with anger. 'But you thought you would. You thought you'd finish it for him.'

'And that's why you're here, isn't it, Franny? "The righteous will be glad when they are avenged; when they dip their feet in the blood of the wicked." Psalm fifty-eight, verse ten.' Donal paused, studying Franny, whose eyes darted about nervously. 'Well, perhaps instead of looking to avenge him, it would be better for you to join him instead.'

Without warning, Donal pulled out his gun, aiming at Franny. She dived to the side, scampering along the stone floor; heading for the door over the other side of the church.

Franny ran as fast as she could. Past the choir stalls and the large pipe organ, accidentally banging her hand on the keyboard and sending a cacophony of discord soaring through the church.

Arriving at the door, Franny crashed through it, taking the stone spiral stairs two at a time. She pushed onwards; blinded by the darkness of the narrow twisting staircase. She let her hands guide her; sliding them along the sides of the rough ancient stones.

'Franny; to be sure, there's nowhere to run, because simply, there's nowhere to hide.' Donal's voice and laughter rose up to where she was. As she went higher, light emitted through the tiny glass windows.

As it became lighter, Franny could see a door on the left of her but decided to press on ever upwards.

The stairwell became narrower as the stone ceiling dipped so low Franny had to bend down.

Moving round the next corner, Franny baulked. The top door she'd presumed would be there had been concreted over. Frantically, she ran back down, hurtling round the twist of the stairs, desperate to arrive at the door she'd seen before O'Sheyenne did.

'Franny!' Donal was already standing by the door, pre-empting her movements. She skidded to a halt. Quickly weighing up the situation, Franny put her hand behind her back and pulled out the metal shard she'd tucked in her pants at the warehouse.

Lunging forward, she slashed at Donal. The angle he stood at made it awkward for Franny to get a proper aim. Although the sharp metal didn't make full contact, Franny still felt it catch O'Sheyenne across his chest. Donal took a step backwards, holding his chest as the blood seeped out over his arm.

Unable to get past him, Franny dashed forward, pulling open the door with its heavy iron latch. She found herself in the gallery on the upper floor of the church overlooking the left wing.

The sudden noise behind her had her spinning

round. The injury hadn't impeded Donal. He was staggering along the gallery with blood soaking through his crisp white shirt. Pointing his gun at Franny, he grinned. 'Don't look so worried; it looks worse than it is; sadly, that can't be said for your situation.'

Franny could hear herself breathing hard as she pushed her whole body against the wall, keeping her eyes constantly on Donal.

'You shouldn't have taken me on, Franny. You could've walked away. Stay away was all you had to do. Even tonight. For sure, I don't understand. But tell me, was it worth it? All this. For what? For revenge? For hatred?' Donal stopped, then drew his head backwards, roaring with laughter. 'For love. It was for love, wasn't it, Franny?'

Franny's eyes flashed with anger and pain. She spiked her words. 'I'd take just a moment of love with Patrick over a whole lifetime without it.'

'Then 'tis a pity that he's gone.'

Franny shook her head. 'No. Not if he had to live a life where he owed you. Where you made him pay for loving me. My love doesn't cost anything.' Franny's voice broke off, understanding something for the first time since Patrick's death. 'And therefore I'm happy, O'Sheyenne. I'm happy he's finally free.'

Donal scoffed. 'Franny, as much as I'd like to hear the rest of this...' He shrugged adding, 'It's boring. Head or heart, Franny?'

Even in her fear Franny looked puzzled.

'Head or heart? Apparently you can choose.'

Franny paled as the gun pointed at her only feet away. Tears poured down her face as her body

368

began to violently shake, watching as O'Sheyenne drew back the trigger.

The gunshot echoed around the church, but it was Franny Doyle who stood in a daze unhurt. Still alive, watching in horror and amazement as her clothes were splattered in blood and tiny flecks of flesh. But not with her blood or with her flesh. It was Donal's.

She stared at the sight unfolding in front of her. Donal O'Sheyenne sloping backwards over the balcony with a gaping hole in his forehead caused by a single bullet fired to the back of his head. A moment later, he tumbled to the ground below.

The thud of his body hitting the ground jerked Franny out of her trance-like state. She charged down the stairs and into the main church, seeing the broken lifeless body of O'Sheyenne.

'Hello?' Franny called out, expecting to see someone, but nobody answered. She looked round the dark church. 'Hello?' Nothing.

The wooden doors of the church banged shut. Wanting to see who it was, Franny ran down the aisle, through the candle-lit vestibule and out into the snow-filled night. In the distance she could make out a dark figure but she couldn't see clearly who it was.

Running to the railings of Soho Square Gardens, she leant on them, holding her head against the cool. And as the snow began to fall, Franny Doyle began to cry for everything that was and everything that had ever been.

54

Franny stared in the mirror, looking at her swollen eyes. They stung from all her crying and she was struggling to put eye drops in. The last few days she'd been in a daze. Cab had recruited some of the other faces from Soho to help dispose of O'Sheyenne's body, somewhere no-one would ever find him.

Cab had told her the shooting was nothing to do with him. He'd *also* told her it shouldn't matter who had done it; all that mattered was it was over. But it did. It mattered to her.

Leaning closer, the tip of her nose touching the glass, Franny caught sight of someone standing behind her. It was Father Ryan.

His smile was tight and his overgrown grey eyebrows shielded his small deep-set eyes. 'I've come to say goodbye, Franny. My prayers have been answered; the righteous are always rewarded. Yet with answers, only then can we justify our existence. Only then will we know if we are *really* at the end of our journey. God is not unjust; he will not forget your work and the love you have shown him as you have helped his people and continue to help them.'

Franny spoke quietly. 'Father Ryan; I wish you well, but I don't want to hear any more.'

Father Ryan sniffed disapprovingly. There were some people in this life you just couldn't help, and he had learnt through bitter experience that the Doyle family were front in line.

'Now then...'

Franny interrupted Father Ryan. 'Was it you?'

One of the many things Father Ryan disliked was being interrupted, *especially* with nonsense talk, and asking half a question fell into that category.

'Was what me?'

'The person who killed O'Sheyenne; was it you?'

Father Ryan bristled. He didn't want to hear that name again. 'Let the dead rest along with their secrets, even if their resting place is in the fire of hell... Now then, why don't you make me a cup of tea, Francesca?' Father Ryan paused, remembering the last time, then added, 'On second thoughts, why don't I make it myself?'

'Father Ryan, I'd appreciate it if you went. Cab wouldn't like to find you here.'

Matthew Ryan pulled a face, not interested in what the likes of Cabhan Morton would or wouldn't like. 'Indeed. Sit down, Franny, I think what I have to say will be of interest. It's about your father.'

'Patrick?'

'No, your real father. I think you deserve to know who it is, and then I shall leave it for you to decide what ... what action to take.'

Franny looked shocked. 'You know who he is?'

'I do.'

'O'Sheyenne said something about him at my party but I thought he was playing more of his games. Did Patrick know who he was?'

'No, he did not. But he *knew* him.'

Relief showed in Franny's face for a moment; she hadn't wanted there to be another lie. She looked at the priest.

'What do you mean? How did Patrick know him?'

'This I'm sure will be very difficult for you, but your mother was raped by a man called Tommy. Thomas Doyle... Patrick's father.'

Franny threw the last of her things in the bag. Checking her laptop, she wrote down the information which had just popped up on her email.

'Hello Franny.'

Slamming down the lid, Franny turned to see Alfie Jennings standing at her bedroom door.

'Going somewhere?'

'Not really.'

Alfie looked at her suspiciously then glanced across to her laptop. 'It's good to see you, Fran.'

Franny answered distractedly. 'Yeah, you too, Alf.' Suddenly sensing she was being cold, Franny stopped what she was doing. 'I'm sorry. That was rude... How have you been?'

'Okay, getting back on top. Think I should stay out of trouble for a while though, so if you've got any more ideas, maybe we could put them on hold for another couple of months, hey...' The room fell silent but for the sound of Franny zipping up her bag. After a few minutes, Alfie, looking uncomfortable, spoke again.

'I thought I might have seen you before now. The last time wasn't exactly ideal.' He gave a nervous smile.

'You've got the diamonds, you should be fine.'

A flicker of hurt flashed through Alfie's eyes. 'Yeah, well, I guess that's that then.'

'I've got to go. Let yourself out.'

Franny went to walk out of the room but was held back by Alfie's grip on her arm. 'Maybe next week I could take you out for dinner?'

Franny looked bemused. 'What? You and me, go out to dinner?'

Alfie let go of her arm. He shrugged, feeling embarrassed. 'I know. Stupid idea. Forget I said anything.'

As Franny got to the door she stopped, looking down at the carpet. She turned to look at Alfie, her big eyes highlighting her striking beauty. 'It's not stupid, Alfie... I'd like that. I'd like that very much.'

Hearing the front door shut, Alfie, who couldn't stop smiling, was left alone in Franny's room. He looked around. His eyes fell on the laptop she'd been using. Partly because of the way he lived his life and partly because of downright curiosity, Alfie, unable to help himself, opened the computer to get a glance of what Franny had been looking at.

His face dropped and the smile on his face fell away immediately as he read what was there.

Rushing through to the lounge, Alfie could see Franny on the other side of the street. He banged hard on the window.

'Franny! Franny! No! Franny!' She didn't turn round.

Getting out his phone, Alfie dialled a number. 'Cab! It's me, Alfie. I have a very bad feeling...'

55

The banging on the front door was loud and frantic.

'Christ, what's all the panic for? Has there been a second sighting?' The door flung open and Thomas Doyle stood facing Franny.

Tommy stared, his head shaking in confusion. However, his bewilderment didn't last long as Franny barged into the neglected cottage.

She stared at Tommy, who over the years had aged badly. Excessive drinking and bad diet had rendered him a shadow of his former self. Loose skin hung round his bloodshot eyes. A flushed red face held spidery veins which ran in purple patterns throughout his skin. And his scraggy frame held a large pot-belly.

'My name's Franny... I'm your daughter. You raped my mother.'

Tommy was shocked, but his expression soon turned into a sneer. Picking up a bottle of whiskey by the side of him, he swilled it back, draining the bottle. He wiped his mouth on his sleeve, glancing at Franny through hazy drunken eyes. 'Who told you?'

It was Franny's turn to be shocked. She hadn't known what to expect, what to feel now she was in front of the man who'd raped her mother. Yet there was no monster before her, no giant – only a pitiful figure of a man.

She looked at him and saw nothing in his eyes. No remorse. No love. This was her father. The man Patrick had trusted; the man who'd betrayed him.

'It was Father Ryan. He told me.'

Tommy smirked, speaking scathingly. 'And how is the good Father? No doubt still doing the Lord's work in only the way Father Ryan does.'

Franny didn't say anything, mainly because she didn't know *what* to say. She watched as he threw himself down on the threadbare chair in the corner, strewn with papers and circled by empty beers cans. Tommy lit a cigarette. He burped loudly, contempt tinged with boredom in his voice. 'I hope you haven't come for anything be- cause I don't owe you anything.'

'I have.'

Tommy growled roughly, needing another drink from the empty bottle of whiskey. 'Well, I haven't got any money if that's what you're after, so piss off, will ye?'

'I'm not after money. I want to finish it. For my mother and for your son, Patrick.'

Tommy looked up in time to see Franny take out a small handgun. Her hands shook as she aimed it. Streams of tears ran down her face.

Tommy paled but a hostile gaze stayed locked on his face.

'He wasn't my son. I was paid to look after him. To take him on as my own.'

It was Franny's turn to pale now. 'What are you talking about?'

'Didn't you know? Father Ryan was his real da; not me. You were all pawns in his and O'Sheyenne's games.'

There was the sound of feet running down the road outside and a moment later the cottage door of the Doyles' house swung open. Standing there, out of breath, were Cab and Alfie.

Cab gently reached out to Franny. 'Give me the gun, baby. It's okay, I'm here now.'

Franny shook her head. 'No, Cab. Is it true, Father Ryan was Patrick's father?'

'Yes, but he didn't know until the end. It wasn't another lie, I swear. I know it's all a mess but we can sort it out, I promise.'

He urged her again, only this time he joined her in her tears. 'Franny, *please.*'

Her voice was weary. 'I'm so tired, Cab.'

'I know, baby. I know... Just give me the gun.'

Franny's whole being trembled. 'I can't. I miss him so much. I want to finish it all.'

Tommy interjected. 'Get the crazy bitch to put the gun down.'

Cab turned on Tommy. 'Tommy Doyle, I'll shoot ye myself if you don't keep quiet.'

'Franny, look at me, sweetheart; *look* at me.' It was Alfie.

Turning her head, she saw Alfie standing by the door with an anxious expression on his face. His eyes were warm as he smiled. Slightly self-conscious about how emotional he was feeling, he talked, his voice continuing to be soft.

'You know, a few years ago, I went out with Patrick for a drink; we got talking about you. You were always his favourite subject. Anyhow, he told me in no uncertain terms that you were off limits. I can hear him now even: *"To be sure, she's too good for the likes of ye, Alfie Jennings, too beautiful, too delicate, too strong ... too loving.*" And he was right about all those things, Franny. And that's why you don't have to do this. You can finish it right now by walking away. You ain't like me; you've got a pure heart, darlin'. If you kill him, believe me, a piece of you will die, too. That ain't what Patrick would have wanted. You're one of the good ones, babe, and that's why so many people love you. Cab, Lola, Casey...' Alfie stopped, struggling to say the name Vaughn, but after a moment's hesitation he was able to rise above it. '...Vaughn; all of us do. Patrick wanted you to live. To be free. To have a life he never had, that Mary never had... So give me the gun and walk away. *Live* for him, Franny. *Live* for you ... and live for me. I'll take care of you; if you'll let me. I ain't ever going to let no-one hurt you.'

Suddenly a realisation hit Franny. 'It was you, wasn't it? You killed O'Sheyenne. Why didn't you tell me? Cab, you *knew*.'

Cab shrugged his shoulders, knowing the answer he was about to give sounded hollow. 'He asked me not to.'

Franny spoke reflectively. 'Secrets? More lies?'

Alfie shook his head. 'No, it wasn't that, Fran. I just didn't want you to think you owed me anything. You don't and you never will.' Alfie stopped to smile at her. 'So, to use the words of a very beautiful woman who ain't standing more than a few feet away from me now: *"My love doesn't cost anything."*'

Through her tears Franny Doyle looked at Alfie then at Cab. And her heart was filled with love as she thought about Patrick. He'd given her so much, when he'd had so little. He'd fought and suffered so much pain, but he'd never stopped loving. Loving her with the kind of love which never died.

Franny looked through the window. She could see the green fields he'd once described to her when he'd had happier times as a boy. She could see the far-away river which ran through them. And if she looked hard enough, she knew she would see him. Hear him. Walking hand in hand across the fields with *his Mary.*

Lowering the gun, Franny knew Alfie was right. She'd come to the end of her journey. In the place it had all began.

Followed closely by Alfie and Cab, Franny walked out of the cottage, leaving Tommy Doyle alone. She never looked back.

With Cab filling Franny in on the story about Patrick's and his, and all he knew about Mary's, days in Ireland, it began to pour with rain. He looked up to the skies, grinning as they walked along before coming to a halt outside a stone cottage.

'Why, Ireland, how I've missed ye. According to the woman in the bakery, this is the one. Are you ready, Franny?'

Franny smiled. A smile which lit up her eyes. 'Ready as I'll ever be.'

They waited a few minutes for the door to be opened. A small grey-haired man stood with stooped shoulders, a look of forlornness about him. He greeted them, his manner warm. 'Yes?

378

Can I help ye?'

'We're just...'

Cab began to speak, but was suddenly pushed aside by the man stepping forward; his eyes full of wonder.

'Mary! Mary!... Is that you, Mary?... You came back to me.' Weeping, Fergus O'Flanagan dropped to his knees at Franny's feet.

She crouched down in the rain, staring and smiling at this man, wiping away his tears. 'No, I'm Franny; her daughter.'

'Her daughter?'

'Yes.'

Fergus, who was almost lost for words, stuttered, 'I'm ... I'm Fergus. Which means...'

Franny grinned, helping him finish his sentence. 'Which means, by my reckoning, that would make you my grandfather.'

The enormity of what Franny had just said hit Fergus. He shook his head, half laughing, half crying. 'Saints in heaven preserve us! Just wait till me wife Helen comes back home from County Limerick tonight, she'll scarce believe her eyes... You are going to stay so she can meet you?'

'Of course.'

Fergus tapped Franny on her hand. 'Grand. That's just grand ... she'll be delighted so she will; delighted, and I'm sure she'll make you a nice cup of tea.'

Franny spoke quietly. 'I'd like that very much.'

Fergus Flanagan beamed. He touched Franny's face; tracing the contours with his frail fingers. 'To be sure, Mary has sent me an angel.'

On the bridge, Franny, Cab, Alfie and Fergus stood under the shield of their umbrellas as the rainclouds continued to burst.

Franny stared into the rushing water. It was strange. Instead of feeling troubled by being at the place where her mother had taken her own life, Franny felt at peace, and closer to her mother than she'd ever felt before.

'Franny, Patrick asked me to give you this when the time was right. I think that's now.'

From his pocket, Cabhan Morton pulled out the chain with the tiny cross that Patrick had tried to give Franny at the party.

'He wanted you to have it.' Franny's eyes filled with tears as Cab put the chain round her neck. She nodded, unable to speak.

'I also brought this. I know he would've wanted it. So he could be with her.'

Franny stared at the silver box. She took it in her hands, caressing the top of it. As she leant over the bridge she kissed the box, then opened it, letting the wind take and soar Patrick's ashes high into the sky.

Holding hands with Franny on the bridge, Fergus O'Flanagan exclaimed. 'Why will you just look at that, Franny; the sun is coming out! To be sure, there are miracles to be had today.'

The publishers hope that this book has given you enjoyable reading. Large Print Books are especially designed to be as easy to see and hold as possible. If you wish a complete list of our books please ask at your local library or write directly to:

Magna Large Print Books
Magna House, Long Preston,
Skipton, North Yorkshire.
BD23 4ND

This Large Print Book for the partially sighted, who cannot read normal print, is published under the auspices of

THE ULVERSCROFT FOUNDATION